ANGELIKA FLEISCHER IS ready to call it a day: after years of looting the battlefields of the Old World, she has decided to retire. However, the prospect of one more job is too tempting. After helping a halfling warband defend their village from a Chaos raid, Angelika, Franziskus and their companions are swept up into the army of Jonas, a charismatic Imperial commander who may not be quite as cunning or brave as he makes out.

As the hordes of Chaos move in for the kill, Angelika and her companions find themselves running out of options. Despite his fine speeches, just how competent is their fearless leader? Will the halflings keep their nerve in the heat of battle? And just who has stolen Angelika's life savings?

The tale of Angelika Fleischer continues in a blend of action and intrigue in the dark and gothic Warhammer world!

The Angelika Fleischer Novels
HONOUR OF THE GRAVE
SACRED FLESH

A WARHAMMER NOVEL

ANGELIKA FLEISCHER

LIAR'S PEAK

ROBIN D LAWS

For Griff and Zab.

A Black Library Publication

First published in Great Britain in 2005 by
BL Publishing,
Games Workshop Ltd.,
Willow Road, Nottingham,
NG7 2WS, UK

10 9 8 7 6 5 4 3 2 1

Cover illustration by David Gallagher
Map by Nuala Kinrade.

A CIP record for this book is available from the British Library.

ISBN 13: 978 1 84416 233 8
ISBN 10: 1 84416 233 8

Distributed in the US by Simon & Schuster
1230 Avenue of the Americas, New York, NY 10020.

Printed and bound in Great Britain by
Bookmarque, Surrey, UK.

See the Black Library on the Internet at
www.blacklibrary.com

Find out more about Games Workshop
and the world of Warhammer at
www.games-workshop.com

THIS IS A DARK age, a bloody age, an age of daemons and of sorcery. It is an age of battle and death, and of the world's ending. Amidst all of the fire, flame and fury it is a time, too, of mighty heroes, of bold deeds and great courage.

AT THE HEART of the Old World sprawls the Empire, the largest and most powerful of the human realms. Known for its engineers, sorcerers, traders and soldiers, it is a land of great mountains, mighty rivers, dark forests and vast cities. And from his throne in Altdorf reigns the Emperor Karl-Franz, sacred descendant of the founder of these lands, Sigmar, and wielder of his magical warhammer.

BUT THESE ARE far from civilised times. Across the length and breadth of the Old World, from the knightly palaces of Bretonnia to ice-bound Kislev in the far north, come rumblings of war. In the towering World's Edge Mountains, the orc tribes are gathering for another assault. Bandits and renegades harry the wild southern lands of the Border Princes. There are rumours of rat-things, the skaven, emerging from the sewers and swamps across the land. And from the northern wildernesses there is the ever-present threat of Chaos, of daemons and beastmen corrupted by the foul powers of the Dark Gods. As the time of battle draws ever nearer, the Empire needs heroes like never before.

CHAPTER ONE

THE RING – ANGELIKA had to see it again. She could feel its presence easily enough, patting the spot above her right hip where she'd sewn its secret pocket to the inside of her tunic. There it was, safe as ever, beneath her fingers: the round band of metal, the tiny claws holding the gem in place, the stone itself. This was not sufficient. She had to look at it, perhaps to be certain it was real, that all of her work – the danger, the exhaustion, the rough living – was almost done with. Though not given to self-indulgence, Angelika was ready to grant herself this one foolish impulse. There was no one around to see her, to take it from her, to observe her in this instant of weakness.

Angelika Fleischer sat against a mossy, rotten log. Her body was slight, but lithe and muscular. Dark eyes glittered above her high cheekbones and knife-point chin. Before she stirred, she completed yet another unobtrusive check of the dark pines all around her, their grey trunks balefully lit by a pregnant moon. At length, when no sign of surveillance had presented itself, she decided it was safe. She leaned against the fallen tree and slid gracefully up to a standing position. Her worn leather coat moved silently with her, hardly daring to crack or squeak. Under it she wore a coal-coloured tunic that extended halfway down her thighs, partially covering tight woollen leggings. A belt with a knife in it encircled her waist; a second dagger waited snugly in the cuff of her boot. She'd recently used it to cut her silky dark hair; her work had made even more of a mess of it than usual.

Angelika was young, but the wary grace of her movements displayed a hard-won competence that was neither youthful nor feminine. She was as beautiful as a razor.

Faint snoring sounds, half murmur, half purr, escaped from a lanky, blanketed bundle at her feet – Franziskus, her self-appointed bodyguard. They'd been on the trail together for more than a year. He still hadn't told her his last name. She still hadn't asked.

His sleeping body eased itself onto its back; a flap of bedroll fell away to expose his face. The lunar light flattered his fine, aristocratic features. Months of outdoor living had done little to weather his skin or dull his cerulean eyes. When lit by the sun, his long, rich hair shone like gold; now, by night, its sheen was more like silver. His rough elk's-hide cloak, which he wore under his blanket, added bulk to a still-boyish frame.

Angelika wondered where the young man would go, and what he would do with himself, after they parted ways. That time would be very soon in coming. It was a subject Franziskus, otherwise talkative to a fault, had punctiliously avoided throughout their long trek out of the frontier regions of the Blackfire Pass and back into the Empire's outlying provinces.

She'd expected more enthusiasm from him when she'd announced the imminence of her retirement. For years, long before meeting Franziskus, she'd made her living as a scourer of battlefields. She rolled the corpses of recently slain soldiers, gleaning their weapons, armour, jewels, and the contents of their purses. At least until recently, Franziskus had never missed an opportunity to express his disapproval of her profession.

Despite his annoying bouts of moralising, Angelika had allowed him to tag along after her. It was her punishment for one of her periodic lapses into foolish altruism: she'd risked her own neck to save him from a mob of blood-mad orcs. In return, he'd vowed to stick by her side and return the favour, whether she liked it or not. She was pretty sure he'd discharged this duty at least once, perhaps even on multiple occasions. Nonetheless, he persisted.

She examined his pale, sleeping face. If he was prone to a certain vexing self-righteousness, it was because his heart was good. He hadn't seen as much of the world as she. Angelika had learned to see through the world's many lies at a tender age. Franziskus had so far blissfully evaded any such disillusionment.

There would be some sadness in their parting, she had to admit, and he would take the brunt of it. If it was his genuine desire to return home, he'd have done so already. She'd grudgingly come to accept his presence, to respect his usefulness and pluck, even perhaps to feel a touch of sisterly affection for him. But in the new life she was headed to, there'd be no place for him.

Certain no one could see her, she reached up past her tunic's frayed lower hem and into the crudely fashioned pocket. From it she withdrew her ruby ring.

She'd bought it from Max, the vendor to whom she sold her gore-grimed merchandise. Over a period of months, she'd taken a final tour of her various crannies, caches and hidey-holes, scattered throughout the dangerous, inhospitable reaches of the Blackfire. With deft fingers she'd retrieved the coins Max had paid her over the years. With girded dagger, awaiting ambush from every cave and cliff-side, she'd hauled her swelling purse of gold and silver out of the pass and to her rendezvous with Max on the Empire's borders, near the town of Grenzstadt. There, she'd converted her money into its present eminently portable and resaleable form.

She held up its slim and filigreed mount of gold, so that its translucent red gem covered the moon, and was illumined by its light. Its clarity, its exquisitely cut facets, stood out to her as never before. This jewel was as valuable as Max had claimed, maybe even more. It would buy her an entire life of modest ease, away from corpses, from battlefields, from nights spent out on the cold ground, from monsters, bandits and madmen. Away from accursed, damnable mountains. Angelika never wanted to go up another mountain for as long as she lived.

Everything else in the world might be a lie, but this ring, this tiny object – it was truth.

CHAPTER TWO

THIS IS THE sound of the world ending, thought Jonas Rassau: the scream of dying horses. All around him the poor beasts writhed, upended, their bellies pierced by the swords and lances of the advancing Chaos army. Dead or wounded riders had fallen beside them. Each was a lord or heir to an estate, laid low by a Chaos axe.

The battlefield stank of mud, manure and gore. A stale wind carried resinous smoke from the north, where a pine forest burned, torched by the Kurgan horde. The smoke blew into Jonas's face, welling his eyes with angry tears. It swathed the battle, so that men who fought only a few yards away, friend and foe alike, were obscured from view, shrouded as if they were already ghosts.

Jonas called out to his men as they braced themselves to charge the enemy's flank. He heard his own hoarse, ruined voice as if it came from someone else. Blood dripped from his face down into his mouth. It was not his, but the enemy's. The experience of battle was exactly as his father had said: time had slowed. Opposed sensations, of calm and of terror, ran through him like strong drink. He gripped the hilt of his sword more tightly. Only this cold, hard weapon, Jonas told himself, was real. Nothing mattered but the trajectory of his blade as he brought it down on the bodies of his foes. He would not die here today: it would be the enemy who would fall. Today, Jonas Rassau assured himself, his father's reputation would pass to him, like a mantle.

He repeated his cry to his men, his words nearly unintelligible. 'Victory,' he howled. The men responded with a chorus of roars. Jonas looked back, showing them a lupine grin. He was a head taller than any man with him. His shoulders were broad; his waist, slim and his legs long. As did his comrades, Jonas wore the yellow and black of the Stirland armies. A new breastplate, polished to a sheen, bulwarked his midsection. The plumed helmet that denoted his junior officer's rank had been knocked from his head, and was lost somewhere on the battlefield. Sweat stuck strands of sandy hair to his neck and brow.

Heredity had blessed Jonas with a magnificent jaw and a sublimely symmetrical face. If it bore an imperfection, it was a slightly prominent brow. In refined company, these features, along with his loping, restless gait, made him seem too much the tiger. Here, with sword unsheathed, he was a man others wished to follow.

He pointed the tip of his weapon toward the dark, smoke-wreathed figures ahead. They fought on the hilly pastures of Stirland, north of the River Aver and south of the Stir, a good threescore leagues to the west of the World's Edge Mountains, over which the Chaos tribes had come. This range comprised the Empire's south-eastern border. Over the centuries its tall and toothy reaches had provided a reliable barrier against the barbarians of the Kurgan steppes. Now, spurred by some harsh new leader, they'd found the unity and purpose to pour across its length, intent on destruction. In the time it had taken Stirland's armies to muster, barbarians had already overrun dozens of border villages, their every conquest a massacre. Advancing as ragged marauders, they'd spread themselves across the plains, forcing the Stirlanders to do the same.

This clash was but one of many. Throughout the borderlands, other similar engagements would be raging. Every time an Imperial regiment failed, a column of pillagers would be loosed into the province's heartland. They would not stop with Stirland. Armies from neighbouring provinces, from Averland, Talabecland and even Wissenland, were on their way to staunch the flow of Kurgan fighters before their own lands were ravaged. Few expected them to arrive in time.

Morale was poor; gloom had fallen on the regiments of the Empire like a dusting of snow. As they huddled at night, when they thought no officers would hear them, the common soldiers whispered the unthinkable, forbidden thought: that the last days might finally be at hand. Because they felt them, too, the officers found it difficult to suppress the foot-men's trepid pangs. Even if they won this nameless battle, the war had barely started.

The Empire, forged in battle against Chaos, had survived for twenty-five hundred years. Even the simplest man knew of its eventual doom. One day the skies would run crimson and Chaos's seething armies would rain down their final victory. The Empire, along with all the lands of men and dwarfs, would be consumed. It was a testament to the grim fortitude of the Empire's heroes, and the power of its rival war gods, that the men of the Old World had for so many centuries staved off this inevitable cataclysm.

When Jonas was a child, in the days when his father rode lustily into battle at the head of a shining regiment, people talked about the doom of the Empire, but as a prophecy of the distant future, not an event they would live to see. It was a campfire ghost tale, a figure of speech. A generation later, it had taken on a terrible credence. From three directions, from north, south and east, the various hordes of cultists, beast-men, mutants, marauders and daemons that made up the hosts of evil overran the Empire's gates.

Jonas knew these things without having to think them. All that mattered now was that his arm was strong, his eye was quick, and that his hunger for glory was no less than his enemy's for murder and destruction.

The engagement was seventeen minutes old. Two regiments of Empire forces, mostly Stirlanders, but with a smattering of free companies from Averheim and the Talabec, marched to meet an unruly column of marauders as they made a fast march through the province's eastern dales. Acting on the orders of regimental commander Henlyn Vogt, a man Jonas loved with a fervour he otherwise restricted to blood relatives, the Gerolsbruch Swordsmen had stood in formation, drawn the foe out, and sent their young highborn bravos around on horseback to encircle them. Then hundreds more of the wild-eyed Kurgan footmen had boiled out from the burning forest to the north of their chosen battlefield. They surrounded and killed the lordly riders.

Jonas had been ordered to come at the enemy from the flank with a third of the Gerolsbruch Swordsmen at his side. There had been empty ground, and smoke, and enemy fighters. These they had slain; the two who sank under Jonas's blade were the first men he'd ever killed. They deserved it, and he was proud. He whooped with heartless joy that he was alive and they were not. After making sure that no fallen foe would again rise to his feet, Jonas and the men had run blindly through the smoke, seeking more fodder for their longswords.

Now they were upon them: a crew of barbarians gathered together in a ragged rank, likewise on the prowl for new opponents. Each had clad himself in partial armour, haphazardly rigged together with straps of blackened leather. In matters of battle gear, the Kurgan allowed themselves no middle ground: either an arm or torso had been plated in steely armour, or it lay entirely bare. Dark lines of tattoo ink trailed across the tight layers of skin covering their hard and fatless flesh.

Some marauders stared madly out through horned helmets; others trailed long top-knots of black, greasy hair from otherwise shaven heads. Some were bearded; others, not. Many were lightly wounded, sporting fresh gashes that would, if they survived the day, join the legions of scars traversing their drawn hides.

Jonas resolved that not a one of them would survive to see another scar form. He screamed and ran at the nearest Kurgan fighter, who happened also to be the largest. Jonas exulted in the shouts and mucky footfalls of his men as they joined him in the charge.

As Jonas reached his chosen foe, his perception of time slowed further. He heard his thundering heart as a distant drum beat, marking out a rhythm for his courage. The Kurgan opened his mouth wide and howled furiously. Blindly, he swung his long-hafted axe. It took him hardly an instant to loose his blow, but Jonas, instinctively calculating its arc, ducked easily under it. The barbarian's thwarted momentum sent him off-balance and Jonas pivoted, stepping beside him to aim a powerful strike at the back of his neck. He felt the blade find and overcome resistance in enemy musculature.

In anticipation of a counter-attack, Jonas moved back to crouch behind his shield. His opponent let his weapon slip from trembling fingers, then clapped a hand to the back of his neck. He did not hesitate; he pushed into the Kurgan with his shield and stabbed him between the ribs. The marauder slumped into him and Jonas slipped back under his slackened weight. He eased out of the way to let the Kurgan plummet onto the ground, face-first. He stole a fraction of a moment to note the depth of the blow on the back of his dead enemy's neck then he readied himself for the oncoming axe of the next man in line.

On his father's parade grounds, from the age of six onwards, Jonas had been schooled in sword and shield. Three different sergeants had taught him their best tricks. Combat was a language of motion, it came to him instantly and without effort, as words appear on a man's tongue when he speaks.

The bald-headed marauder who came at him was strong but clumsy, sweeping his axe about in wide, uncontrolled arcs. His technique was difficultto predict. Jonas watched his eyes; their frenetic jerking reliably betrayed his upcoming actions.

Jonas skittered back, as if pressed hard by the blows, allowing the Kurgan to develop and repeat a cycle of moves: step forward, swing axe down, to the side, swing axe up, step back, swing axe overhead. The axe banged against Jonas's shield, the blow's force rippling up through the bones of his forearms.

Finally, near the end of the cycle, the Kurgan did what Jonas knew he would, and left his throat exposed. Jonas shot his sword up to gash it open; blood fountained from the wound. Jonas kicked the dying man over, into another, tangling him in his comrade's limbs. He ducked low, flanked the astounded marauder, and dug his sword tip-first into his lower back. From the corner of his eye he saw that one of his men had stopped to marvel at his three quick kills.

A Kurgan shield clipped Jonas solidly behind the ear and hurled him to the ground. He shot out his shield-arm to break his fall. The shield did so, but he landed on it with a crunch, bruising the muscle of his upper arm. He rolled, but not in time; he got onto his back before his foe leapt upon him. The barbarian pressed his knees, each protected by a spiked section of plate, onto Jonas's chest. They could not pierce the thick front of his cuirass, but this was not the Kurgan's aim: he meant merely to keep Jonas down as he drew his axe back for a *coup de grâce*.

For the first time, Jonas saw his attacker well: he was a wiry with crazed eyes. Jonas rocked back to free himself, but the old man rode him with daemonic persistence. He madly clanged his axe down on the young officer's breastplate. Jonas's teeth rattled in their sockets. The man lifted the axe to aim a blow at a softer target.

Tiny hands enfolded themselves around the bony wrist of the wrinkled Kurgan's weapon-hand. The barbarian screeched in anger and pivoted to address this affront. Jonas took advantage of his distraction to buck him off with pushing hips. Now the barbarian was pinned, his leg stuck under the back piece of Jonas's cuirass.

Jonas saw his saviour: not one of his own men, but a halfling, a fat-fingered man barely three and a half feet tall. He struggled to wrest the axe from the barbarian's hand, eyes blazing blue, a wild mop of curly hair casting droplets of perspiration into the air. Just to the south lay the Moot, the bumpy lowland these miniature folk called home. They, too, had mustered to fight for hearth and home.

The halfling, who'd had both hands clamped around the barbarian's wrist, detached one of them to reach for the dagger at his belt. The Kurgan caught him in the throat with his elbow. Choking, the halfling reeled back, relinquishing his hold on the barbarian's wrist. Jonas grabbed tight his sword, but could not find the proper leverage for a decent blow without also freeing his target's leg. The Kurgan dug his axe deep into the halfling's shoulder. The brave little fellow whitened and sank to his knees, a crimson stain rapidly spreading across the quilted cotton vest he wore for armour. The barbarian yanked again to get his leg out from under Jonas, who, sword at the ready, let him do it. He shoved his weapon deep into the man's back, cutting through his spine. The Kurgan's body shuddered; his limbs flopped. He jolted up, then dropped to the ground, Jonas's sword still spearing out of him. Even then, his leathery muscles held tenaciously to life.

Jonas stepped forward to seize his blade-hilt, to pull the weapon from his dying victim. He was still struggling to free it when he saw another Kurgan crunching toward him, swinging a gigantic two-handed mace with a studded, globe-like head. Jonas ducked down to pluck the dying Kurgan's axe from his twitching fingers. He had a second to heft it and test its weight before the mace-man bore down on him. He swung, notching it uselessly into the mace's pole-like haft. The barbarian smashed him in the chest, the blow's force hauling him a few inches up into the air. Jonas fell backwards and landed with a bone-jarring thump. He scrambled his legs out and pushed his shield against the ground to quickly right himself. The axe had flown from his grip and his weapon hand was again empty.

His attacker was gone from view. Jonas looked behind him just in time to evade a blow aimed at the back of his head. A swordsman of his company charged at the mace-wielder from the side, winning time for the unarmed Jonas to pull back. The swordsman, a moustachioed carouser whose name was Döring, slashed at the big man's back, drawing him away from Jonas.

Growling deep in his throat, the mace-man switched his homicidal intentions to Döring. Shield held high to protect his face and throat, Jonas skimmed across the muddied ground in search of a usable weapon. All around him, smoke-obscured figures grunted and clashed. Jonas's gut churned: a comrade's face stared up at him, eyes widened by death. It was impossible to tell what had killed him; aside from his stricken posture and expression of frozen panic, he seemed utterly untouched. Jonas muttered a hasty prayer to Sigmar, who would surely clasp the soul of a fallen warrior to his armoured breast, then stooped to take up the soldier's unblooded sword.

He turned to rejoin the skirmish just as the ball of the mace-man's enormous weapon smacked against the side of Döring's head, breaking it open. Döring collapsed, and Jonas darted toward him, prepared to avenge his death or injury, whichever it turned out to be.

At that moment, a collective, despairing sigh arose from the main site of the battle to the north-west of Jonas's position. Men of the Empire groaned. Worshippers of Chaos croaked in bloodthirsty jubilation. Barbarian horns blatted and shrilled. Kurgan drums pounded while those of Stirland were silent.

The Kurgan horde had broken the Imperial ranks. Now they could dash unmolested to the undefended towns and villages to the west, south, or north.

Jonas's target, the mace-man, swivelled his massive neck toward the breach in the Empire line, where his brethren would already be trampling on through. Jonas hurled himself at the man, shield-first, realising even as he did it that he was making a stupid, hot-headed mistake. The first rule of battle was never to let anger rule your actions. Anger leads to error. Errors are for the enemy to make, and for the clever warrior to turn against him.

The mace-man swept out of his way, then tripped him. Jonas hit the mud for the third time in but a few minutes of fighting. It was a bad place to be. He gripped his dead comrade's blade and held it up, preparing as best he could to defend from his inferior position. The Kurgan mace-man, though, looked down at him with a contemptuous curl of the lip, kicked mud Jonas's way, and turned to join his fellows in the rushing column headed for the breach in the ranks. Jonas sprang up from the slippery mud, only to be bowled over by the falling body of a Talabec gunner, whose arm had been shorn off below the elbow. The man threw himself gasping into Jonas's arms.

Even though he knew better, Jonas was still surprised by the utter confusion of the battlefield. What his father's sergeants had told him was true: when you're fighting it, a war is not about great movements of troops, of thrusts and counter-thrusts as played out on a map by generals in training. Instead, it is like the world's largest, most lethal tavern brawl, except that it is unbounded by walls – and afterwards, it's much harder to locate the grog.

The gunner's breathing accelerated, then grew shallower. He expired with his head in Jonas's lap. Relieved, Jonas slid him down on the ground, broke himself from his unworthy reverie, and stood to pursue the barbarians. Yet in the thickening smoke, he could see neither foe to harry, nor friend to call to his side. He ran toward the fading sounds of battle, but got lost in the smoke. He tripped over a gutted halfling and was nearly kicked in the groin by a wounded horse. He dropped into stance to fight a man who came toward him in the smoke. As the man drew nearer he turned out to be not an enemy, but an especially burly Stirland halberdier. The left side of the man's beard was burned away, most likely by a torch thrust into his face.

'Don't slice me, mate,' said the halberdier, 'unless you want to finish me, in which case you'd be doin' me a favour.' Considering that he addressed an officer, he spoke with undue familiarity, but Jonas was not the kind who'd upbraid a soldier for petty reasons. Especially not one from another command. Instead, he subtly straightened his shoulders, so the man could see the braids that marked his rank.

The halberdier changed his attitude straightaway, and the two of them walked through the smoke. It got into Jonas's lungs making him cough and choke.

The involuntary movement awakened the pain from his blow to the head and his fall upon his shield. He tried to ignore these aches, but as the ardour of battle faded, they took a stronger hold on him. Soon they reached a point that was empty of slain and battered bodies. Jonas realised he'd got himself turned around and was undoubtedly moving in the wrong direction, away from whatever regrouping would be underway. He stopped and tried to guess where he ought to head.

A distinctive rapping of sticks on kettle drums started up. Jonas perked to attention; it was his company's muster call. He moved towards the sound. The halberdier tagged along.

'How many did you kill, soldier?' Jonas asked him.

The halberdier spoke in a dull, sleepy tone. 'None, I don't think. I nicked one, maybe.'

'You'll have your chance sooner than you think, my friend.'

The bleary halberdier registered little enthusiasm for this prospect.

'They possessed the upper hand from the start,' said Jonas, not sure which of them he hoped to reassure. 'We had to defend many points; they could choose to attack but one. We'll pursue them to the ends of the Empire if need be. One by one we'll cut them down.'

The man wiped his nose with the back of his hand.

They trudged toward the sound of the drums. Jonas picked up his pace but the halberdier lagged behind and within a minute or so was lost to the billowing smoke, which was increasing in intensity. Jonas wondered how many acres of timber would be lost to the fire. The sky was clear, and only the gods in their celestial perches knew when the next rain would come.

From the smoke stepped others of his company: there was Glauer, who cut his beard in a muttonchop, and Madelung, who was broad-faced and earnest. They were barely recognisable under a dusting of ash. Jonas had to figure his face had been similarly adorned. Companies of swordsmen were more freewheeling than other Empire troops, and Jonas felt a more potent bond of comradeship with his men than would a junior officer in charge of hand gunners or archers. 'What news of the others?' Jonas asked them.

Glauer shrugged. 'We got separated early. Kurgan scouts were hiding in the bushes and drove us down toward the river.'

It did not take them long to find the drummer. Beside him, astride a nervous, cantering steed, waited Jonas's commander, Henlyn Vogt. Vogt was his patron in the regiment, not that he ever showed a hint of kindliness to Jonas's face. Perhaps he'd smoothed Jonas's way because he still remembered the achievements of Jonas's father, who had held this very position over two decades before.

A straight, thin nose bisected Vogt's long, pitted face. Weariness was his standard demeanour, but now he projected a distracted energy. His eyes flitted from right to left as he rode toward Jonas and spoke.

'You live,' he said, as if at a mild, pleasant surprise.

'You should have seen him, sir!' It was Pinkert, the sauciest of the men. His hand was bandaged. 'He killed four of them, just like that. Chop chop chop chop.'

It was three, Jonas thought, but did not correct him.

Vogt waved Pinkert away like he would a beggar. Pinkert's shoulders sank. He slunk away from Vogt's horse, mouthing the words he'd just uttered, sifting for the offence in them.

'Listen carefully, lieutenant,' Vogt said. 'I've already sent most of our units off in pursuit and must make haste to rejoin them.'

Jonas looked up at Vogt. The angle was unfortunate; he had no choice but to gaze straight into his superior's oversized nostrils. 'Yes, sir.'

'There's no guarantee these are the only Kurgan who'll come at us over those peaks,' he said, gesturing to the purple reaches of the World's Edge Mountains, on the eastern horizon. 'In fact, we must assume the contrary. These are barbarians. They lack the organisation to agree on and execute a single rendezvous.'

'Indeed, sir,' Jonas agreed.

'For all we know there's an even bigger force gathering up there in those mountains to strike after we've gone off chasing this lot. But we can't afford not to pursue, can we?'

'Absolutely not, sir.'

'You're in command of the Gerolsbruch Swordsmen. Also I'm giving you the remnants of the Chelborg Archers. In addition, you're to pick up whatever other stragglers you find wandering about this accursed field and attach them to your company. Yes?'

'Yes sir, but what about Lieutenant Oerlenbach?' Jonas referred to his immediate superior, the leader of the Gerolsbruch Swordsmen.

Vogt expressionlessly tilted his head, drawing Jonas's attention to a makeshift pallet laid out on the trampled ground. A body lay there, its head and torso covered by a woollen blanket. Oerlenbach's boots, as polished as ever, still secured his feet. The company standard-bearer stood to attention, the flag of Stirland listlessly wrapped around its pole of oak.

'Congratulations. You've just received a battlefield commission. First Lieutenant Rassau.'

Jonas bit down to suppress a stammer. 'Thank you, sir.' He'd looked up to Oerlenbach. A bit of a taskmaster, but a good, caring leader. It would be hard to match the job he'd done.

'No time for thanks, Rassau. The battle's far from over. This is just a regroup, that's all. We've to chase those stinking Kurgs wherever they run. My other companies are already biting into their backsides and I've to hasten after them. So listen quick; you'll get these orders but once. I don't suppose your father and his sergeants schooled you in the principles of mountain combat.'

Jonas shook his head. 'Neither my father, nor his men, ever had cause to serve in the mountains, sir.'

Vogt stared unhappily into the east. 'You'll need a good scout, then. Preferably one who knows his way around a mountain. Do you have a good scout?'

'Yes sir, there's Baer, sir. A huntsman that Lieutenant Oerlenbach attached to our group. I don't know if he's had mountain experience specifically, sir, but–'

'Pray he does, Rassau. Your mission is this: make your way to those mountains. Go up into the hills and harry any Kurgan you find still straggling their way towards us. Understand?'

Jonas nodded. 'Who do I report to, sir?'

'To yourself, Rassau. This mission is yours alone. We lack forces as it is. If I had huntsmen to spare, I'd send them, but I don't, so it's you.' Vogt seemed to spot the trepidation on his protégé's face, and moderated his expression. 'I see what you're thinking.' He leaned down from the saddle and spoke with greater sympathy. 'You're right, Jonas. If there are Kurgs still coming over in substantial numbers, this could be like trying to empty a bucket by tossing a rag into it.' He paused, phrasing his next thought carefully. 'You're a bright boy, Rassau. Bright on the parade grounds, at any rate. Here's your chance to prove yourself a real leader.' He straightened himself in the saddle, once again adopting the posture of command. 'Be smart. If the hills seethe with the accursed scum, hide, manoeuvre, and take your chances as you get them. You have a company, and then some. Make them seem like a regiment. And waste no time provisioning. Go now. You see another large force massing, send messengers to warn us.'

'Yes sir.' Jonas pulled the muscles of his legs tight, to hide the quivering of his knees. Standing beneath Vogt's coldly assessing gaze, he was frightened, more than he'd been in the heat of combat. Realising that he was not paying full attention to Vogt's words, he forced himself to concentrate.

'Remember,' Vogt was saying, 'the Kurgan aren't mountain people either. They come from a land flatter than this. Make the rocks and hills your handmaiden. If he's got half a lick of sense, your scout can show you how.'

'Now wish me luck. I've Kurg to slay.' Vogt rode abruptly off, and soon was swallowed by the smoke.

Jonas stole a moment to compose himself before striding over to the company drummer, Mattes. Many of the other swordsmen had gathered around him, in varying postures of doubt and dismay. It was right that they should mourn the death of their

lieutenant, but Jonas could not allow their morale
to sink, or to let them see that he shared their trep-
idations. He cleared his ashy throat and called for
his sergeant-at-arms. 'Where is Sergeant Raab?'

'Here, sir,' said Emil Raab. He'd been kneeling
beside the corpse of his dead commander, perhaps
in prayer. Emil had survived nearly two decades of
battle and at the age of forty-two he was the oldest
member of the Gerolsbruch Swordsmen, by far. A
bushy, peppered beard sprouted from his weathered
cheeks to completely hide his jaw and neck. An old
river of a scar meandered across the furrows of his
brow.

Emil left his old commander to approach his new
one, eyes cast respectfully downwards. Jonas tried to
think how many first lieutenants of the Gerolsbruch
Swordsmen Emil had outlived. Some, like Jonas's
father, would have risen to other commissions, but
surely he had buried many others.

'Sir,' said Emil.

Though the word choked Jonas with emotion, he
did his best to suppress an unmanly display. The
men would be depending on him to remain stoic.
'How many?' he asked.

Emil spoke tonelessly; to list a roster of the dead
was scarcely new to him. 'Four dead: Allgau, Hoger,
Vosgerau, Döring.'

Jonas curtly nodded. He had seen Döring die, and
Hoger dead.

'Kuhlmann,' continued the sergeant, 'was run
through by a spear and will soon be joining them, I
reckon. Eichhorn and Becker are too badly hurt to
go anywhere. And six still unaccounted for.'

'Then keep drumming out for muster!' Jonas cried, yelling out to the drumsman. He turned to address his sergeant. 'That leaves us thirty-seven?'

'Thirty-five, sir, but we'll find some of the six, I'm sure of it.'

Arranged in an anxious perimeter around the sword company stood somewhere between one and two dozen men wearing quivers on their backs. They clutched bows in their hands; some allowed them to disconsolately rest in the mud. These would be the Chelborg Archers Vogt had spoken of. Later, Jonas would introduce himself to them, ask after the fate of their commander, and appoint a sergeant from among them, if they lacked one. It surprised him that a company of archers, who should have been far from the fight, had fared so badly in it. He would inquire after the details when time allowed.

'How many are they?' he asked Emil.

'Seventeen, sir.'

Sixty men to stop what might well be an entire second Kurgan army. Jonas wondered if he'd been given the mission based on talent, or expendability.

The prevailing winds changed. Cold air whipped down from the mountainous east, entering into battle with the clouds of smoke from the burning forest to the north. The company flag rose from its torpor to flap noisily from its standard.

Jonas asked his sergeant to fetch him Baer, the huntsman.

'Baer's among the missing, sir.'

Jonas could not hear him above the rapping of the kettle drum and the rising wind. 'Pardon?'

'He hasn't come back, sir.'

The wind sent the smoke pluming high up into the air, dispersing it. Low wisps of it blasted like fog, close to the ground. Otherwise the battlefield stood revealed as if by the raising of a curtain on a stage. Jonas gasped at the sight.

Bodies of the dead and dying stretched out for half a mile in all directions. Many lay half-buried in mud. A gravely wounded man, his legs shorn from his body, pulled himself up onto the carcass of a lifeless horse, then slid down again, motionless. Lost helmets, weapons and armour pieces were strewn throughout. The hafts of spears and axes jutted from the ground like saplings. Crows and ravens, who had been circling overhead, swooped down through the clearing smoke to hunt for morsels of flesh. Jonas was surprised by the numbers of slain Kurgan; though victors, they'd paid a heavy toll for their triumph. For every one of them slain, though, there were two or more Empire fighters, especially near the spot where their line had broken.

Emil pulled his helmet from his head and bowed it down.

'We've got to find Baer,' Jonas said, plunging on into the field of slaughtered men. He stepped over a toothless Kurgan, its visage fixed in a final glare of intermingled joy and hate. Jonas wondered how these men thought, how they were driven to such madness. Supposedly, the Kurgan considered warfare and pillaging to be acts of worship, which would win them the blessings of their corrupt and feral gods.

Jonas waved the drummer, the weather-beaten Mattes, to follow him.

'I'll assemble a party to look for the others, sir,' Emil offered.

'I'll do it,' Jonas replied, impatiently. 'I want to do it.' Without Baer, his first command would be lost before it started.

Emil followed after Jonas as he wove his way between the slain. He stepped on a hand, and its owner hissed. It was a barbarian with blood oozing from his chest and side. Jonas stood back as Emil finished him with a sword-thrust to the throat. This pause gave the drummer time to catch up, and the three swordsmen plunged further into the corpse-field, bringing with them the kettledrum's rap-tap-tap.

To their left, he saw three men approaching. Their gaits and frames were well-known to Jonas: three of the missing men. Behind them, Jonas beheld a series of black mounds. Squinting, he saw that they were dead horses. Jonas pointed. 'That must be where we first hit the enemy's flank,' he said. He leapt over bodies to move quickly to the three men. Indeed, he recognised one of the lifeless cavalrymen. This was the spot.

'Where's Baer?' he asked the men.

In unison they shook their heads.

He pushed past them, then stopped suddenly short. At his feet lay the wracked and torn body of the huntsman, Nathan Baer. An axe-blow had torn him open from hip to shoulder.

Jonas dropped to his haunches beside the poor fellow's remains. He wiped his hand wearily across his face, pushing back loose strands of hair. They smelled of smoke.

Where was he going to find someone who could scout the mountains for him now?

CHAPTER THREE

ANGELIKA FLEISCHER LOOKED overhead to the cloud of converging crows. The black birds were peeling off now, diving down to the earth below, a sure sign that the commotion of the battle was over. She'd never seen so many carrion birds gathered at once; in the Blackfire Mountains to the south, they were neither as numerous nor as fast to gather. She guessed that she and Franziskus were still a league or so away from the main site of the engagement.

'You seem uneasy,' she said to Franziskus.

'We're travelling at speed to a place where a gigantic plume of black smoke fills the air,' replied Franziskus. 'Where carrion crows circle to feast on the flesh of the dead. In what way could these facts possibly breed unease?'

'I liked you better before you discovered sarcasm.'

Strapped to his back was a sabre, a weapon heavier than the rapier he'd favoured when Angelika had first met him.

She grinned puckishly, an expression Franziskus had learned to dread. She would tease him, and he would take her too seriously, and wind up flustered and blushing.

'Franziskus, Franziskus… I'm startled.' She spoke with mock innocence, also never a good sign.

Franziskus wearily humoured her. 'Startled?'

'Ever since my announcement, I've been observing you keenly. But you've yet to leap out of your skin in celebration of your hard-fought victory.'

The young Stirlander's feet hurt, they hadn't stopped to rest or eat for many miles. Their canteens were in need of filling, too. 'If I've won any victories of late, I regret to say they have not greatly impinged themselves upon me.'

'All the time you've had yourself clamped to my side, you've been at me to abandon my livelihood. Now that I'm about to do it, I think you should at least perform a little jig of happiness or what-not.'

'Perhaps I'd feel greater jubilation if we weren't currently speeding to another cadaver-strewn battlefield.'

Franziskus laboured to accept this teasing with good grace. It was, he reminded himself, her only way of showing affection toward him. Any straightforward expression of comradely feelings would be, in her eyes, an admission of weakness. If there was one thing he'd learned during their awkward partnership, it was that she would never allow herself to depend on anyone, even slightly.

Franziskus knew that beneath it all Angelika had a good heart; he had seen her act selflessly, even heroically, on numerous occasions. Mind you, she complained the entire time and then denied that she'd done anything at all, but nonetheless she had time and again demonstrated her potential for redemption. It was his profoundest desire not only to protect her from harm, as she had done for him, but to dissuade her from her loathsome trade.

Now suddenly his tireless exhortations had finally achieved their desired effect, or so she claimed. Franziskus had long awaited this day, and now that it was imminent, he felt none of the satisfaction he'd always imagined. He had to admit that over the course of the journey north, he'd been positively sullen company. Or, rather, he was prepared to admit such a thing to himself. To Angelika he would make no such concession. The ring: Franziskus knew what it looked like; she'd shown it to him, once, in a moment of giddy abandonment. She'd gone so far as to let him hold it, as they sat by the fire on a chill summer night. It seemed pretty, to be sure, but Franziskus had never seen the value that men attach to certain stones and metals. Perhaps his upbringing, amid the trappings of wealth, had dulled him to the allure of mere adornments.

'You don't believe me when I say I'm quitting?'

They'd already had this conversation a hundred times in the weeks of travel up the pass and into Stirland. 'I will judge your actions when they, in fact, occur.' he said.

A note of offence crept into her voice. 'You think I'm lying to you?'

'No, to yourself. I am but a collateral recipient of any unfounded claims.' Franziskus smiled. He rarely scored as well as she in their verbal fencing matches, so any clear hit was a thing to be savoured.

'My goodness,' tut-tutted Angelika, recovering her air of good-natured repartee. 'Were I capable of feelings of guilt, I would in all likelihood be feeling them now.'

'On what grounds?'

'All this time, you've been working to infect me with your idealism, yet I fear the interchange has gone the other way: I've turned you cynical.'

'I'm not a cynic. I'm a sceptic. There's a difference.'

'And what would that be?'

'A sceptic would say that the mere intention to quit means nothing, until virtuous action is in fact taken. A cynic would say it doesn't matter.'

Angelika nodded thoughtfully. 'I will contemplate that distinction, my friend, when I sit at nights in my cosy cottage, a fire blazing by my feet, a cup of brandy sitting at my elbow. Perhaps I'll get me a kitten to play with.'

'Now you're mocking me.'

'Not one bit. That's precisely how I mean to while away the rest of my days. I don't see what's so incredible about it. Aren't you tired of sleeping on hard ground and waking up with cold in your bones? Of tramping through pine forests and up the sides of mountains? I want to be able to go inside when it rains. To light a fire when I'm chilled, without having to worry about attracting a host of enemies. I'm sick of having to fight for my life, and of getting dragged off onto wild crusades and goose chases. Many of which were at least in part engineered by you, I hasten to add.

'You may think me some kind of restless freebooter, but I swear to you, I've counted my days in coins of gold, and now, in this ring' – she patted her pocket – 'I have all that I need to get out, for good and ever. I'm sorry if that interferes with your plans to die alone and unmourned on top of some wintry peak, Franziskus. I've tolerated your judgement of me when I was rifling the purses of slain men, but I scarcely thought you'd be fixing me in your faultfinding glare now that I want to give it up.'

They'd stopped walking and now stared at each other uncomfortably. Franziskus was taken aback by her vehemence; she seemed to be, too. 'I'm sorry,' she said.

These last two words were so shocking to Franziskus that he had to concentrate for a moment, to be sure he'd heard them. Then she turned away and increased her speed towards the crow cloud.

Franziskus felt ashamed. He knew, in truth, why he was unhappy. There were at least two reasons, neither of which he'd dream of admitting to her. One impulse was completely unworthy, the other less so, but at any rate, he had spoken selfishly, and done a disservice to them both. 'Of course it is right that you should want to leave this miserable profession of yours,' said Franziskus. 'I apologise if I offended you.'

'How could you possibly have done that, Franziskus?' she asked.

They walked in leaden silence for twenty minutes through the eerily empty fields of Stirland. On a normal day, these lands would be alive with farmers and livestock. Now the rolling pastures were eerily absent of all activity. Even the bees and butterflies had abandoned the air.

'We're going the wrong way,' Franziskus said.

Angelika pointed unerringly to the distant battlefield. 'We haven't wavered, Franziskus.'

'If you want to quit, quit. Let's turn around. Let's simply go.'

Angelika shrugged and continued on. 'You may, as always, go where you will. As for me, fate has given me one last gift – from what we've heard, a battlefield bigger than any I've ever seen. One last harvest, Franziskus, and then it's over.' She increased her pace to a rapid stride.

'Angelika!' Franziskus sprinted to catch up. 'I remember someone telling me once – or perhaps it was dozens of times – that fate never has our best interests at heart. I don't suppose you recall who it is who always says that?'

She spat dismissively. Though not aimed in his direction, Franziskus nevertheless had to turn to avoid the spray. 'You well know, Franziskus,' she said, into the wind ahead of them, 'that when I speak of fate, I do so metaphorically. There is no such thing as destiny. Life proceeds by accident and mishap. Some suffer, some prosper, nothing really means anything, and no curse awaits us on that battlefield ahead.'

They came upon a silent farmhouse, its stone walls scorched by fire, its thatched roof consumed. Flies buzzed around a bull's severed head. From the state of decay, it had been dispatched no more than a day ago. Angelika crept up a worn pathway to pause before its shattered gate.

Franziskus's premonition of doom redoubled itself. 'You don't mean to go in there?' he asked, under his breath.

She drew her dagger. 'Is a sacked home different than a battlefield?' She stepped over the flattened gate and into the yard. A smallish well stood in a rock garden beside the house. Franziskus reached into his pack for his canteen, then asked Angelika for hers. 'We're running low,' he said.

Angelika stepped up to the farmhouse door, which was half way ajar. As she drew closer to it, strengthening winds seized it and slammed it against its frame. She started. Franziskus, halfway to the well, paused. 'An omen?' he asked.

'No omen tells me what to do,' replied Angelika, grabbing the door and stepping through it. Inside she found a family of half-burnt corpses, a man and a woman old enough to be her parents, and a woman about her age. The marauders who'd killed them had then arranged them in an obscene manner. Angelika was hardened to the aftermath of violence, but this appalled her. Franziskus appeared over her shoulder, and winced.

'Why do they do this?' she asked, her voice quiet.

'To show their hatred of mankind,' Franziskus answered.

They made the wordless decision to disentangle the bodies from their disgraceful positions. Though the raiders had set the place alight, burning off the roofing, the fire had consumed only sections of the farmhouse interior. Chairs and a chest by the far wall were deeply scorched, but other furnishings near the door had been spared by fickle flames. Franziskus found blankets on a bench in the untouched area and placed them reverently over the dead. Outside the distant noise of feasting crows grew louder.

Angelika had yet to search the farmhouse for loot. 'There won't be anything in here,' she announced. 'The warriors of Chaos will have scoured it well.'

It did not seem to Franziskus as if the marauders had done anything but kill and desecrate the occupants, then spark a half-hearted fire. He did not, however, argue with Angelika's decision to leave it uncombed.

'Now that we're nearing civilization, perhaps it would be best if you stopped using that word,' Franziskus said.

'Chaos?' During their time together, they'd grown all too familiar with this awful force.

'Here in the Empire, most folk fear to even call it by its name,' said Franziskus.

'Wisely so, perhaps.'

'These days, *The enemy* is the correct euphemism.'

'I'll try to remember that.'

As they drew closer to the place of battle, bodies began to appear in the pasturelands, like scattered seedlings. A few were dead Chaos troops, pierced by arrows or downed by sword blows. Though normally a marauder could be counted on to possess nothing of value, Angelika paid special heed to these, as some would be carrying sacks of booty taken in previous stages of their invasion.

She rolled each dead marauder over, the especially muscular ones requiring considerable effort on her part. Franziskus, as was his custom, withheld his assistance while she robbed the dead. Instead, he stood watch, the quiet of the scene doing little to calm him. Angelika grunted in disappointment each time she pushed a Kurgan over. She hoped they'd have sacks or purses pinned beneath them, but after half a dozen tries, none did.

Most of the dead were ordinary Stirland folk in farmer's garb. These Angelika hesitated to disturb. Many had been subjected to extraordinary mutilations, as if their attackers despised them for the crime of living. None of these poor wretches could have offered a meaningful defence to the onrushing horde; they were slaughtered for sport. Angelika moved on, in hope of finding soldiers, who were both more likely to have valuable items still on their person, and less troubling to disturb.

They walked along a soft, grassy ridge overlooking a narrow gulley. Improbably, a small herd of sheep still grazed down there, nonchalantly feeding amid a collection of tiny corpses. For an instant Angelika thought they were the remains of armed and armoured children, but then she understood: these were halflings. The area just to the south was crawling with them. Angelika rubbed her hands together in anticipation of profitable labour and searched out an easy path down the hillside. To strip dead halflings of their belongings would cause her no qualms. Many people of the Empire regarded this diminutive race with fondness, at least in principle, but, having met several of them, Angelika harboured no such sentiments. In her experience, the little blighters possessed all of the mendacity and spite of regular people, compressed down to fit inside their freakishly small frames.

She looked back at Franziskus, who'd staked out a high vantage on the ridgeline, to survey the area in four directions. Annoyed, she beckoned him down. He wavered, then obeyed, crashing through a stand of goldenrod. She waited for him.

'If anyone was coming, I wanted to see them,' he said.

'And up there, everyone would have seen you,' she replied. 'For miles.'

'If there's trouble, don't we want to see it coming?'

'Stand out like a beacon and you'll attract it,' she said, making straight for a halfling, who lay on his face under a broken shield. 'We're not in the mountains any more, where there's cover everywhere and always a higher spot.' She knelt over the halfling and yanked a fat-hilted dagger from the fellow's belt. Soft blue gems encrusted its pommel; she squinted at them as they caught the sunlight.

'Of course, you're right,' Franziskus murmured, looking away from her.

'Of all people, you should be the last to want to make himself conspicuous in Stirland,' she said.

The remark stung Franziskus. So she had remembered his situation, after all. Franziskus had been down in the Blackfire as a junior officer in the Stirland army. When Angelika rescued him, his entire regiment had been wiped out in a battle against orcs. Though his comrades were all dead, duty compelled him to return home for reassignment to a new unit. Instead, he'd stayed behind in the wilderness, with her. Franziskus was a deserter. His parents had every reason to believe him dead. Franziskus did not wish to be returned to either his superiors or his family.

If Angelika quit, he had no place to go.

Angelika shoved the dead halfling over, looking for a purse. Human soldiers typically kept chains of gold or other small treasures in their boots. Halflings, annoyingly, had no need of footwear, instead preferring to gambol about the battlefield on nothing but their hirsute, bony-soled feet. She unbuckled the halfling's undersized hauberk, then reached down the front of his tunic, where she found a silvery locket. This she added to her purse. Then, ducking down, she moved to another halfling body, bypassing the mostly naked remains of a Kurgan axe-man. She found no weapon on this next halfling, whose round face looked disconcertingly childlike.

Angelika had his breastplate half unbuckled when she abruptly froze.

She held up a hand of silence, to warn Franziskus.

'We're being watched,' she hissed.

CHAPTER FOUR

ANGELIKA FLATTENED HERSELF on the ground behind a row of tall, dry weeds. She seized Franziskus by the coat collar and pulled him down next to her. With a flick of the head, she directed his eyes to a smoothed knob of grassy rock rising from the lip of the gulley. The spot stood about twenty yards away from them, to their right, there were another seven or so up the gulley slope. It poked up from the ridge line like a boil on a plague sufferer.

Franziskus squinted, unsure he was even looking in the right place. 'I don't see anything,' Franziskus said.

'Just wait,' Angelika whispered.

Franziskus concentrated his attention on the bump's highest point. For a moment a black speck of movement flickered, then ceased. He gave Angelika a questioning look. She pointed him back to the knob. The movement repeated.

'A spear tip,' said Angelika.

Franziskus studied the object, whatever it was, as it poked intermittently up behind the wall. As far as he was concerned, it could have been anything. Perhaps a flitting bird. A darkened leaf or seed pod on a bush, blown back and forth by the wind. An old coat caught on a branch. Franziskus listened. A songbird chirped. Blowflies buzzed.

Now a flash of motion came from the side of the rocky knob. Franziskus thought he saw a hand, perhaps holding the haft of a spear, as Angelika had said. She was right. Someone was back there, thinking he was hiding from them. Under a gaze less keen than Angelika's, he would have been.

Franziskus widened his eyes, cupped his palms out, and held them out to Angelika, asking, *who is it up there?*

Angelika shrugged, a tight twitch of a gesture.

'What do we do?' Franziskus asked, quiet as he could.

Another tight gesture, a shake of the head: *nothing*, it said.

Franziskus hunkered down. The thing to do was wait. Let whoever it was expose himself, come to get them. Then act accordingly.

It occurred to him that the two of them communicated best when words were disallowed.

On top of the outcrop, a hat appeared. Franziskus found it difficult to make out, from so far away. Eventually he identified it as a floppy felt cap, green as the grass around them.

'Halflings!' Angelika growled.

'Halflings?' Franziskus asked.

Angelika's reaction was one of an exasperated tutor. 'That cap's too small for a human head. Or a dwarf's, for that matter.'

Franziskus frowned. He had learned to trust in Angelika's keen senses, but it was a mite unfair of her to expect the same acuity from him. 'They've put the hat up there on purpose,' he said, hoping to prove himself less than a complete dullard.

'Yes, testing us to see if we have missile weapons, and are so dumb as to fire them.' Neither Angelika nor Franziskus were, in fact, equipped with gun or bow.

'If these are halflings, you don't imagine they are friends or relatives of these poor wretches here?' Franziskus indicated the slain half-men she'd just been manhandling.

'I do imagine.'

'And if they meant to dispute with us in a civilised manner, they wouldn't be skulking behind that rock, would they?'

The question was rhetorical, so Angelika let it go unanswered. 'We have the superior position here,' she said.

'When we're sprawled flat on wide-open ground?'

'They can't see us until they charge from out behind that rock. When they do, follow me. Be ready to—'

She stopped short. A flare of reflected sunlight blazed from the gulley's opposite ridgeline. She pushed Franziskus flatter into the ground.

JONAS RASSAU WATCHED the two freebooters through his spyglass. The woman seemed to look directly at him, then freeze. He cursed and slipped back below the ridgeline: she'd seen the sun flash against his lens.

Beside him was Emil, his sergeant. Below were the unit's two remaining horses. The unit was safely encamped a mile or so to the west.

'The halflings spotted you, sir?' Emil asked. There was reproach in his flat tone. Without saying so, he'd already made clear his disapproval of Jonas's side mission. He was one of those sergeants who thought a commanding officer should never go off and do anything for himself, that Jonas should instead sit like a wilting flower inside the perimeter, and let others do for him what glory demanded he do himself. Also he'd taken none too kindly to Jonas's bringing him along. One of the two of them should be with the men at all times, he'd argued. Jonas thought otherwise. If the men couldn't secure a simple encampment on their own, they'd be no good whatsoever in their new role as mountain harriers. He'd given Glauer his old rank, as second lieutenant. To command a camp at rest would be an easy first test of his abilities.

'No, not the halflings. The woman,' he said, answering his sergeant's question.

'With respect, sir. We've better things to do than trail halflings about while they chase looters.'

Shouting from the opposite ridge drowned out Jonas's reply. He popped his head back up to see a trio of halflings boil over the rocky knob to slide with uncontrolled speed down the gulley slope. The two human looters on the floor of the hollow were already in motion. To Jonas's surprise, they did not flee directly away from their short-legged pursuers, toward his ridge. Instead, they ran south for a few yards, then up onto the same slope the halflings hurtled down.

Jonas tapped Emil on the shoulder, tugging on his garment until he crawled up alongside him. 'Watch this,' he said.

The halflings reached the gulley floor, one of them losing his footing and tumbling face first onto the chewed-up sod. His spear flew out at his side. His fellows grabbed an arm apiece and roughly hauled him to his feet. They ran down the gulley floor to the spot where they'd first seen the two looters. For their part, the looters had already scrambled up the slope and were a mere few yards from the far ridgeline. The baffled halflings scoured the tall weeds for them, poking at every bush and bramble with the heads of their spears.

'I don't understand,' Emil muttered. 'Can't the half-men see the looters up on the slope?'

Jonas grinned. 'No, they can't.'

Emil hunched forward, face screwed up in confusion. 'But they're right there. What is it? Magic, of some odd sort?'

Jonas slapped his back and laughed. 'The magic of geometry, sergeant. It took me a moment to see it myself. It's a matter of sightlines. These slopes curve and swerve, and appear wholly different from any given vantage. By running south, these two obscured themselves behind that bend in the gulley wall there.' He pointed to the relevant spot and Emil peered quizzically at it. 'We could see them from over here, but to the halflings it was as if they'd vanished. Most clever, wouldn't you agree?'

The two soldiers watched as Angelika and Franziskus reached the ridgeline and hopped down, disappearing behind its other side.

'Not so clever now that you explain it.'

The halflings had fallen into quarrelling. The largest of the three had seized the smallest by the tunic and was shaking him. The remaining one kept fruitlessly poking the ground with his spear, declining to intervene in the struggle between his mates.

'You're always slow to admire, Emil. If we go down onto that gulley floor, I'll show you how clever it is.' He stood, placing himself in the halflings' plain view. Emil reached up to pull at him, but he ignored his sergeant. Raab stood beside him, the lines on his face contracting as the sun hit them. Jonas turned himself sideways to make his way deftly down the slope toward the halflings. Emil stuck close to his side.

'Besides,' said Jonas, 'they were wily, and did the unexpected. If you were being chased by halflings, what would you do?'

'Halflings? I'd stand my ground and cut them down.'

'Well, granted,' said Jonas. 'But let us say you had reason to fear them should they catch up with you.'

'I'd run away.'

'In the opposite direction, yes?'

'Naturally.'

'Did these two do that? No, they defied these little beggars' expectations.'

Finally the halflings ceased their quarrelling and took notice of them. They wheeled, spears at the ready, even though Jonas and Emil were still many yards away, and were advancing on them at a casual pace, weapons sheathed.

'Not so startling an accomplishment,' said Emil. 'These ragamuffins are dumb as dirt.'

'Who goes there?' called the tallest of the halflings, who wore a beaded ring through the lobe of his right ear and was missing much of his left. He gripped his spear tightly and pointed it toward the approaching humans with as much menace as he could muster.

'I am Lieutenant Jonas Rassau, of the Gerolsbruch Swordsmen,' said Jonas, his voice calm and commanding. 'This is my sergeant. Who are you, and what's the commotion down here?' Neither soldier slowed his stride.

The one-eared halfling widened his stance and jabbed his weapon at them. 'Leader of swordsmen you may be, but you've no right to order us around or question our movements.' The other two gathered themselves behind him, spears in hand and trepidation on their faces.

Jonas became stern as he swept toward them. 'This is a battlefield and I am an officer of the armies of Stirland. I may order and question you as I deem fit. Now stand your weapon down.'

The smallest of the three, whom One-Ear had been wrestling with, placed a hand on his arm, prompting him to lower the spear. Eyes cast down, he pushed himself forward. His hair was dark, his features compressed and somewhat ratlike. 'We're from Hochmoor,' he said, pointing vaguely south-east. 'A little town not far from here. I'm Filch, and these are my brothers, Curran and Deely.'

The one-eared brother, evidently the one called Curran, clouted Filch on the back of the head and stepped forward to bear the burden of Jonas's attention. 'Many of our boys made up a militia and went out from town to fight the enemy. This is what's happened to them.' He gestured to the bodies sprawled in the grass. 'That's my cousin there, and that's our town blacksmith, Elias Two-Beer. So we're good and loyal sons of the Empire, and you've no right bossing us around nor threatening us, neither. We've bled for you, and haven't much to show for it, have we?'

Deely, whose thinning pate and crow's feet made him seem the eldest of the three, interposed himself between Jonas and his brothers. 'Don't be mad at my brother. We're all cut up by grief, seeing our friends all dead like this.'

Curran wheeled on him, jabbing a thumb back toward the humans. 'It's them what let us down, isn't it? They couldn't hold the Kurgan horde, could they? Why should we take orders from them?' He spun around to Jonas, still brandishing his spear. 'This here's what you ought to know. There was grave robbers down here, desecrating our dead. That's what the commotion was. We was chasing them, ready to run them through. I don't suppose you saw hide nor hair of them, did you?'

Jonas scratched idly at his nose. 'No, we didn't. We were out for a forage, heard you shouting, and came down to see what was afoot. I thought you fellows might have run into some Kurgs and could use the help. You know there will still be scattered elements of the barbarian army about.'

Curran dropped his spear to his side. 'Well if we run across them they can fear the same fate as those accursed grave robbers.'

Jonas fixed the halflings in the light of his finest smile. 'You must be mindful, my friends. There may be further fighting, and Stirland needs all its able-bodied sons hale and ready.'

The one-eared halfling studied him intently, then took a similar appraisal of Emil. 'You didn't see nobody leave this gulley?'

'If I had, I would certainly tell you. I'd pursue them myself. The Empire takes a dim view of looting.'

'But they was just here.'

'What way would they logically have gone?'

The three halflings fell into fretful conference, reconstructing their movements and pointing out possible exits from the gulley. At length, they concluded that they must have run to the west. Jonas concurred with their reasoning, then asked for a description of the looters. 'Should we run across them,' he said, 'you can know we'll capture them and take them to your townsmen for just punishment. In the meantime, perhaps you should go back and get pallets to reclaim your dead. You don't want the wolves getting at them. Or more looters, for that matter.'

Curran was unconvinced. 'Maybe I'll send Filch back. Someone's got to pay for what was done here.' Shoulders slumped, he stalked off to the west, remaining on the gulley floor. His brothers tagged after him. Jonas and Emil watched them until they rounded a bend in the ravine and were gone from sight. Then Jonas beckoned his sergeant to the spot where the two looters had lain. He kneeled down, and gestured for Emil to do the same.

'Look here,' he said. 'Lying here, would you have known to run *that way*?' He pointed to the southern slope, where Angelika and Franziskus had fled.

Emil removed his helmet and massaged his scalp. 'I suppose not, but like I said, with just those three halflings why not stand and fight?'

Jonas clapped arms around the big man's shoulders. 'You really don't see it, do you, Emil? The brilliance of it. Think.'

With straightened spine, Emil staunchly withstood his superior's unseemly familiarity. 'I don't understand, sir.'

Jonas gesticulated wildly. 'The bend in the gulley wall is hard to see from here, yes? Much harder than from where we were before.'

'Yes.'

Jonas urged him on, dragging up the slope to the knob of rock where the halflings had hidden. He pointed to the spot they'd just occupied. 'Now, from up here, you can see how obstructed the view is. How they're completely out of sight if they simply run a few yards to our left.'

'Yes I see it sir, but what has this to do with our mission?'

Jonas circled around the gulley's edge, where the two ridgelines met, heading back toward the old fence where they'd tethered their horses. Emil struggled to keep up with his commander.

'That woman, from down on the gulley floor, could look at the terrain and calculate in her head what it would look like from up on the rock. Two completely different views, Emil. In her head.'

Ravens had gathered on the ridgeline, waiting for the soldiers to depart. They scattered into the air, then lazily circled overhead, knowing they would soon return to their meals.

'We're going to catch up to those two,' Jonas said. 'She's what Vogt told me to find – a proper scout. I bet she knows mountains like she knows her own name.'

'A woman, sir?'

'A gift of the battlefield, sergeant. Fate has provided her to us, and we shall take her.'

CHAPTER FIVE

ANGELIKA AND FRANZISKUS ran until they found a place to hide. They dashed across a meadow overgrown with fiery summer wild flowers. Angelika skirted around a mound of piled human bodies, barely pausing to note that most of them still wore expensive armour pieces.

Corpses grew scarcer as they travelled. Occasionally they glanced back; Franziskus thought he might have seen shapes on the horizon behind them. Finally, they spotted a dark tangle of what seemed like gnarled, stunted trees and made for it. Only when they were closer did they identify it as a burned-out vineyard. They charged downhill and vaulted a wall of crumbling stones. They sat up against it, gasping for breath. With jittery hands they rubbed at the cramped muscles of their sides and legs.

'You should go home, Franziskus,' Angelika said, when she had air to speak.

'Home?'

'It's somewhere around here, isn't it? Your family's estate?'

'Did you hear hoofbeats behind us?'

'Hoofbeats?'

'I thought I heard hoofbeats.' Franziskus turned to peer back over the wall. Angelika winced. He caught the message and hunkered down again. 'I admit that I am a merely serviceable swordsman, Angelika, but it is humiliating to have to cower before mere halflings.'

'We likely could have taken them,' said Angelika, tossing her head back against the wall. 'But you never know. You can't get killed in a fight you don't get into.'

She reached into her pack for her canteen and guzzled its contents. 'You can go home now, Franziskus. Your promise to me is done with.'

'I swore to stay by your side in times of danger. If this isn't danger, what is?'

She handed him the canteen. 'As soon as we're sure we're not pursued, we'll part ways. I was an idiot to…' She paused, her words swallowed by the need for air. Finally she composed herself. 'It was stupid to try to work here, where people live. Down in the inhospitable Blackfire, it's different. No angry relatives to catch you in the act as you're stripping a corpse of the family heirlooms. But here…'

He drank her water sparingly as he had his own. 'We'll have to lay low here for a while, I think. We can worry about the future when we're sure we lost them.'

Angelika shook her head. 'No, the future is now. Continuing is out of the question. I owe those halflings a debt of gratitude, Franziskus.'

'Personally I feel poorly disposed toward anyone who tries to stick me with a spear.'

'That time it was only halflings, but next time it could be a whole regiment. This is likely the richest battlefield I've ever stumbled across, but why should that matter? I've already got all the money I need. Isn't that what half the stories in the world are about? Fools destroyed by their own greed?'

'It is a common theme of troubadours and minstrels. Yet they pass the hat around at the end of every show.'

Angelika threw up her hands and let out an incredulous laugh. 'I don't believe what I was about to do.' She tapped her forehead, as if attempting to jolt her brain back into proper balance. 'I was about to fall into the oldest trap in the book.' Then she settled back. 'If I let myself be killed or captured now, over a few more measly coins, I'd never forgive myself.'

Franziskus saw a look on her face he'd never seen before – not only was she smiling, but she seemed to be mocking herself, and in a comradely manner. He should have been glad to see her finally treating him in this way. Instead, her smile made his heart sink, for it meant their time together was over.

Her words confirmed his worries. 'This is it,' she said. 'I'm done. Retired, as of this instant.'

Franziskus saw a small stone building a few dozen yards away, with a root cellar entrance. He chose to seem jolly. 'You think there's wine in there?'

'Yes,' she said, 'let's celebrate. Toast to the end of cold mornings and danger, and clinging to the sides of godforsaken mountains.'

Neither of them moved.

'When we've caught our breath.'

They sat in silence for a few moments.

The sound of beating hooves, distant yet growing steadily closer, assailed them. They made themselves small against the eroded stone wall. Each wrapped fingers around the hilt of a weapon. They locked eyes, ready to bolt at the merest signal. Angelika listened. She held up two fingers: a pair of riders neared.

The hoof beats quieted. Angelika and Franziskus tensed, this meant that the riders had stopped. The horsemen were looking for them. They heard a muffled utterance: an instruction, most likely, from one man to the other.

Angelika studied the rows of charcoaled trunks from which the grapevines grew, gauging distances, hoping they were too close together for a horse to navigate. They were not. With the vines themselves scorched away, the rows between trunks gaped disconcertingly wide.

It would do no good to bolt. There was one horseman to chase each of them and nowhere to run where steeds couldn't follow. They had only the slim hope that the men would give up looking before finding them slouched down against the wall. Angelika cursed herself. It had already happened; she'd been done in by her own stupid greed, after all.

A dozen yards to Angelika's left, the vineyard wall was broken. A chestnut horse stepped across the breach, a handsome young man perched on its saddle. He wore a Stirland officer's uniform, soiled in recent battle. For a moment, it seemed as if he would ride on through without noticing the two fugitives pressed against the wall. Then he turned, betraying no surprise, and held his palms up in a gesture of placation.

If it weren't for the second horseman, his position unknown, Angelika would have thrown her dagger at this one. Instead she relaxed, feigning nonchalance. She stretched her feet out in front of her as if enjoying a casual vineyard picnic. She yawned and stretched. When she was done, her hand had migrated from the knife at her waist to the one in her boot.

Franziskus watched her do this and tried clumsily to play along. The sight of a Stirland officer's uniform suffused him with guilt and dread.

From his horse, Jonas Rassau smiled. 'I thought I might find you here,' he said.

Angelika abruptly straightened herself. Once standing, she saw that the second horseman had ridden up to the other side of the wall. He was directly behind them. The second man, burly, grizzled and bearing shoulder insignia that marked him as a sergeant in a sword company, projected an attitude in sharp and threatening contrast to his superior's show of bonhomie.

Franziskus warily rose to stand by Angelika's side.

She concentrated her attention on the officer, who eased his horse closer to her. Franziskus kept the sergeant in his peripheral vision.

'You speak as if we know each other, lieutenant,' said Angelika. She leaned against the wall, cocking her knee forward, placing her boot dagger again within easy reach.

He mimed the doffing of a non-existent hat. 'Excuse my rudeness, fraulein. I am Jonas Rassau, first lieutenant of the Gerolsbruch Swordsmen. This is my sergeant,' he said, barely nodding in Emil's direction. 'I am forward, I know, but these are times of war and urgency demands it. I happened to observe the two of you back in that hollow, just now.'

It was Angelika's policy, when caught red-handed, never to compound her humiliation with ridiculous denials. So she said nothing.

Jonas dismounted, but refrained from moving any nearer. He glanced at her boot-cuff, to let her know he'd seen the dagger there. She shifted positions, taking her hand away from it. She twitched out an unhappy smile.

'I imagine we're equally acquainted with the penalties the province of Stirland metes out to looters,' he began.

'It is fortunate, then,' Angelika replied, 'that I was interrupted before any such crime could be committed.'

Jonas burst out laughing. 'A fine answer. Though not one that would hold up before a magistrate. I've told you who I am. Perhaps it would be polite to reciprocate.'

Franziskus stepped between them. 'I am Franziskus. This is Angelika.'

Jonas ignored him. 'Angelika, with so many about to die, unless we strike hard and well against the armies of the damned, I cannot bring myself to care for the dignity of those already killed. I have the authority to subject you to summary justice, but not the will. So the two of you may relax and be at ease.'

Angelika did neither. 'What do you want, then?'

Now he edged towards her. 'You're wasting your talents, fraulein. The way you judged the lay of the land, when the halflings chased you. That sort of feel for terrain and tactics is not a skill one acquires by accident.'

'Yet you claim you don't care that I may have looted the odd body, now and then.'

'If you've been in this line of work for a while, you've been down in the Blackfire Pass. Haven't you?'

It occurred to Angelika that she ought to be dissembling, at least a little, until she knew exactly what the officer wanted from her. Overcome by her customary frankness, she went ahead and told the truth anyway: 'It is good to be where opportunities are plentiful, and summary justice is not.'

'You know your way around a mountain, then.'

It all became clear, he meant to recruit her. Angelika's stomach rolled. 'Perhaps.' She judged the odds of escape. If she came at him quickly, caught him in the throat with her knife as she passed him, then kept on going, she could...

...get about a dozen yards, at best, before the sergeant rode her down and hacked her apart.

Damn, she thought. Damn. She would have to talk her way out of this.

'You are accustomed to autonomy,' Jonas said, in a silky voice one might use to calm an injured doe. The sun had begun its journey down to the western horizon and its light played flatteringly on his chiselled features. 'I understand this. You are unwilling to submit to military discipline.'

'I am, after all, a woman,' Angelika said.

She wasn't entirely pleased by the evaluating glance she received from Jonas. It was not that she found him unattractive. She had the opposite problem: often she was drawn to men like him, whom she might be better off stabbing.

Thought, it might have been a trick of the light, Jonas appeared to blush. 'You are, at that, milady.'

'I said woman, not lady.'

'From these few moments together, I can tell already that you're better disciplined than most of my unruly sex,' riposted Jonas.

Though far from amused, Angelika laughed. 'You want me to go with you into the mountains?'

'My company has been assigned a mission there, and I lack a scout.'

'No sane woman would place herself alone in the wilderness with a company of soldiers.'

'I suspect any man who tried any thing with you would soon face your dagger's wrath. My men are good men.'

'Your men are soldiers.'

His eyes shone. 'The world is ending, Angelika, unless we fight to save it. Every man – and every strong woman – must rise to the call.'

'The world is always threatening to end, yet never seems to follow through.'

Jonas's face knotted up. 'You want pay? I'll see to it you get pay in excess of your dreams.'

Angelika shrugged, her indifference withering. 'Pay? As the Empire burns? I bet your men haven't been paid in months.'

Franziskus heard scuttling sounds from deeper in the vineyard. The sergeant was still watching him closely; he did not want to alarm the burly man with any sudden movements. He edged sideways, hoping to see what was making the noise. Other members of Jonas's company, perhaps, lurking in ambush?

'I will see to it, when we've done our job, that you are compensated,' said Jonas, spitting out each syllable of that stark last word.

Angelika remained steadfast in the face of the soldier's rising anger. In fact, it excited her. Now, even though he was undoubtedly the better fighter, she half-hoped he'd go for his sword, and the two of them could have it out.

Franziskus had seen this look before and, leaving the scrabbling out in the vineyard as the lesser of two threats, moved towards her.

She ignored him, instead remaining fixed on the lieutenant. 'Money has abruptly lost its allure for me.'

Jonas took a step back. 'Then what do you say to this: you may loot what enemy bodies we find, under my protection, unfettered by the law.'

'You're fighting Kurgan,' Angelika scoffed. 'The wealth they carry typically extends to a bird's skull and a bag of rocks.'

Franziskus's head turned; there'd been a blur of movement out among the burned vine-trunks.

'Besides,' Angelika continued, 'you happen to have caught me on the day of my retirement.'

Franziskus saw that Jonas was now looking at him, and seemed to have taken notice of his discomfort. Jonas squinted down the vineyard's rows, where Franziskus had been directing his anxious glances. He appeared to come to a decision, and clapped his hands together.

'Very well,' he said. 'As you are a woman, I cannot legally press you into service.' He paused. 'Not as I could with this one here, if he seemed useful. You, Franziskus.'

'Yes?' Franziskus unknowingly placed a hand on his thumping chest.

'You're no particular help as a scout, are you?'

'I have taken a vow to stand by Angelika,' he said.

Jonas seemed puzzled by the indirect response, and by Franziskus in general. Finally he asked, 'You'll not try to persuade her?'

'I would if I thought it possible.'

'Very well,' said Jonas, planting a foot in the stirrup of his saddle. 'That is that, then.' He heaved himself onto the back of his horse. He waved to Emil and the two of them rode off, in the direction they'd come from. They seemed to slow just as the crest of a hill cut off Franziskus's view of the departing riders.

Franziskus sidled up to Angelika and spoke from the side of his mouth. 'Someone or something's lurking just behind those trunks over there. Waiting for them to leave.'

They turned slowly and moved together, as if nothing was wrong, toward the breach in the wall. An angry cry howled through the vineyard.

The three halflings burst out from hiding, spears out-thrust, charging.

Angelika leapt over the wall.

Franziskus hesitated, half reaching for his sword. 'They're only halflings,' he said.

The small one threw a rock. It hit Franziskus in the temple.

Franziskus went down.

CHAPTER SIX

ANGELIKA HEARD FRANZISKUS'S groan and then the smothered thump of his body as it collapsed to the gravelly vineyard pathway. She turned to see a second fist-sized rock hurtling toward her own head. She ducked and it landed uselessly in the grass behind her. It was the rat-faced halfling who'd thrown it. His two slightly bigger compatriots galloped on prodigious hairy feet toward the prone Franziskus, spears out. Angelika soared back over the wall to grab at Franziskus's coat. He moaned and rose up onto his elbows. Angelika expected to see a red rivulet running down from his scalp line, but the stone had left his skin unbroken. She tried to pull him to his feet, but he was too dizzy to make his way up.

The halflings were just a few yards away. Angelika had no choice but to stand her ground and defend Franziskus from their steely spearheads. She growled one of her best obscenities and yanked her knife from its belt.

Curran, the leader, boomed out into the lead, bellowing, displaying his yellow back teeth. Deely sprinted to keep up. Pebbles crunched beneath their feet as they charged.

Angelika faked a knife-throw at Deely. The halfling awkwardly ducked, slowing his momentum. Then he stopped to look for the supposed dagger, hoping to pluck it up. Filch was still searching for another suitable rock to hurl, leaving only Curran for Angelika to deal with.

His spear afforded him a substantial reach advantage, but, as a knife-fighter, Angelika was used to getting in close to better-armed opponents.

He closed the distance and came at her with his spear. She waited until he was fully committed to the thrust then slid aside from the blow. Curran's rushing legs flew into Franziskus's prone body. The halfling tumbled over him and onto his back, landing on the haft of his spear. A dizzy Franziskus rose up to his knees, then threw his dead-weight on top of the halfling leader. Curran protested and struggled beneath him, limbs working like those of an upended beetle.

Deely rushed at Angelika. Over his shoulder, she could see that Filch had acquired another chunk of stone and was winding up to throw it. It sailed across the vineyard at her. She jogged suddenly sideways, putting Deely in its path. It hit him in the back of the knee, then rolled down to the ground, where it got beneath his foot. Deely tripped and as he fell, Angelika wrenched the spear from his grip. Having no particular desire to kill these absurd assailants, Angelika let her dagger drop point-first into the dirt and then whirled Deely's spear around, reversing it so she was fighting with its haft. She brought it down like a club above Deely's ear. He grunted in complaint, then retreated under her blows, protecting his face with his arms.

When it seemed he'd been beaten into submission, she turned to see that Curran had crawled out from under Franziskus. He was reaching down to pick up a heavy object. He lifted it up over his head, and Angelika swore in dismay as she realised that it was a loose chunk of wall masonry about a foot across and four inches thick. Curran raised it up over Franziskus's head. Franziskus tried to crawl away, but the halfling easily matched him. Angelika dashed his way, slamming into his shoulders. She slid in the pebbly dirt and the rock came down painfully on her shoulder.

She got up and surveyed the state of the opposition: Curran was prone and appeared dazed, while Deely had taken up her abandoned dagger and now hopped toward her with it.

Then a heavy weight was on her back, clawing hands digging into her neck and chest. It was Filch, who'd leapt down onto her from the nearest grape trunk. She ducked down to grab her boot-knife, but his weight overbalanced her and the two of them collapsed in a heap. The little man tightened his hold; he choked the air from her windpipe. She tried to jolt him with her elbows, but missed. Blackness rolled in on her and she lost consciousness.

ANGELIKA JARRED AWAKE. She saw blue sky, the ruined vineyard, Franziskus tied up beside her. Curran the halfling had thrown a pail of water onto her, to bring her around. No, it wasn't water. It was wine. He'd tossed wine in her face. Some of it got into her eyes and stung them. She tasted what little of it remained on her tongue. A vintage of indifferent quality.

'You awake?' Curran asked. Rather redundantly, Angelika thought, as she was already angrily staring at him.

'No, I'm having a dream, in which I've been captured by pint-sized idiots,' Angelika replied.

He slapped her with a tiny hand. She smiled. When taken prisoner, her first priority was always the severe annoyance of her captors. Distracted by temper, they would then make blunders, which she could exploit in making an escape. At the very least, they would let useful information slip. Or so the theory went.

Franziskus was already conscious. Like hers, his wrists were bound tightly behind his back with a thin, strong length of silky rope. It was a better quality rope than her adversaries usually bound her with. It was heartening that the legendary halfling love of comfort extended to the imprisonment of their enemies. The beginnings of a bruise mustered itself on Franziskus's temple, otherwise he seemed ruffled, but uninjured.

Curran poked her shoulder with the butt of his spear. 'Stand up!' he ordered. He glanced up; inky clouds invaded the sky from the cold north. 'We must get home before nightfall.'

His younger brothers, Deely and especially Filch, hung back from him, a hint of shame in their bearing. These weren't warriors, they were rustic village folk. Angelika imagined that this was their first taste of fighting, and that it had simultaneously thrilled and frightened them. If so, they were decent men. It was Curran, who'd caught a whiff of exhilaration from it, who might prove dangerous.

Perversely, this insight impelled Angelika to further antagonise him. 'How can I stand when you've got me sitting on the ground with my hands tied behind my back?'

'Get her to her feet,' Curran bellowed. Filch and Deely hurried to comply. An awkward waltz ensued, as the two diminutive men pulled at Angelika's elbows and made themselves her leaning posts. Having learned the technique, they repeated it for Franziskus.

The halflings led their prisoners at spear-point out of the vineyard and through a series of gulleys. The winds whipped up again, their fierce sound mingling with the howling of a distant predator. Curran had his spear at Angelika's back while Deely covered Franziskus. Filch tagged beside Angelika, skipping excitedly through sheep-shorn grass. 'You are an adventurer, aren't you?' he asked.

Angelika did not respond, so Filch repeated the question.

'Adventurer? I don't know what that means.'

'Shut it, Filch,' Curran commanded.

Filch was undeterred. 'You know. A freebooter. What I mean, is, you've been out and done things. Haven't you?'

'Yes, I get waylaid and choked by halflings. It is quite a glamorous life.'

'I tied those knots around your wrists, you know,' Filch piped.

Angelika tested them again, for his benefit. 'And what a splendid job you did.'

Filch beamed. Curran told him to shut it.

The wind gusted, dusting them in ash from the forest fire. The howling seemed closer still.

'It surprises me that we haven't run into any stray barbarians,' said Angelika.

Curran scanned the horizon, as if expecting some Kurgan to abruptly make themselves known.

'Yes, you'd expect some stragglers to hang back from the main force,' Franziskus agreed. Though Angelika was surely saying it to discomfit their capturers, it was also the truth. It was odd that they'd seen no signs of Chaos since the great battle earlier in the day. Unsettlingly so.

'Why?' blurted Filch. 'They've all gone on to attack the interior, haven't they?'

'They'll hit whatever targets arouse their lust for rape and pillage,' said Angelika. 'What about your home village? Has it been razed to the ground, and all its people driven out?'

The three brothers exchanged perturbed glances.

Angelika took this as a 'no'.

'Then you may have bigger worries than a couple of scroungers,' she said.

Curran got close enough to breathe onto the back of her neck. He smelled of chives and butter. 'The man whose body you desecrated was my dearest friend. He led the toasts at my wedding.'

'If we are ambushed by barbarians,' said Angelika, 'I trust you'll cut our bonds and hand us back our weapons.' Angelika's blades were in Filch's belt; Deely bore Franziskus's sabre on his back. 'If it comes to a fight, you'll need our aid.'

'I see no difference,' hissed Curran, 'between them and you.'

THE ENCAMPMENT OF the Gerolsbruch Swordsmen lay a few leagues to the north-east of the vineyard, in a hollow shrouded by ancient willows. The men roused themselves at the sound of pounding hooves; Jonas and Emil rode back in. At Jonas's command, Emil called for Pinkert. Pinkert hopped to it: 'yes sir?'

'You were raised near here, yes?' asked Jonas, still on his horse.

'That's right. Over that way.'

'Any villages which might have halflings in them?'

Pinkert contemplated for a moment and pointed to unmarked spots on a map Emil unrolled for him. 'I forget the names of the other two,' said Pinkert, 'but the likeliest one is called Hochmoor.'

AFTER ANOTHER HOUR'S walk – which Angelika and Franziskus could have made in forty minutes, without short-legged halflings as pacers – they were led along a dirt road up a gentle hillside dotted with low, shambling hovels. These were of two types: stone houses with thatched roofs, in the standard style of Stirland peasants, and also squat wooden structures built right into the hill, as halflings did. The stone houses occupied flat shelves of cemented earth carved out from the hill. Some boasted untamed wildflower gardens, or jostled for space with ramshackle poultry coops. The flat shelves of lawn in front of the halfling dwellings were strewn with the remnants of ale casks, broken down for firewood. Amid their unkempt flowers lay emptied brandy flasks and the odd shattered wine bottle.

Angelika counted a few dozen of each type of house as they were prodded up the roadway. A wooden arch spanned it, staffed by a trio of bored humans, who lolled torpidly on stools. One leaned near a bristly, twine pull-cord connected to a bronze bell dangling from the arch. It was clear to Angelika that the war had not yet touched the place; if it had, its sentries would not be so blasé. They would not last long if the enemy arrived. They stood as the party approached. To Angelika's surprise, it was Deely who told them to be at ease. She'd taken Curran for the leader. Apparently his authority was unofficial.

'Welcome to Hochmoor,' chirped Filch, as if Angelika and Franziskus were their willing guests.

The windows were shuttered, the doors slammed tight. No children played on its emerald slopes. An escaped chicken clucked desolately from the top of its coop, vainly begging for a safe return to its imprisonment.

'Turn and walk backwards,' Curran ordered.

Franziskus complied and Angelika reluctantly did the same. Curran placed the head of his spear at her throat. Deely's spear kept a less menacing distance from Franziskus.

A few hundred yards further up the road, Curran placed his free hand to the side of his mouth and called out to the villagers locked inside their homes. 'We caught some,' Curran cried. 'We caught the looters.'

Windows opened. Heads, human and halfling both, popped out from behind doorframes. Some villagers seemed confused or frightened. Others joined Curran in his righteous exultation.

Angelika searched for a means of escape. Curran's spearhead kept close to her throat. The halfling trio walked her and Franziskus backwards up to the very end of the road, which terminated at the gates of a decrepit stone fort on top of the hill. Angelika was not especially good at judging the age of buildings, but this one had to go back several centuries. In its prime, it would have served as a stout retreat for the entire village in times of war. If invaders came today, they'd have an easy time passing their way through its ruined outer walls.

Several grim-faced human men joined Curran's procession. Angelika and Franziskus were led through the outer gate and into an equally worn-out inner keep. Curran gestured them onwards through a metal doorway into what might once have been an armoury. The men hauled the door shut, locking it with a heavy key. The room was bare; its stones, at least, still held firm to their appointed places.

Deely stood on tiptoes to peer at them through a barred panel in the middle of the door. 'Spend these few moments searching for sincerest contrition,' he said. 'The tribunal will take but an hour or so to convene.'

'Don't waste your sympathy on them,' said Curran. Deely detached his child-like fingers from the bars and disappeared from view.

Angelika got to work searching for loose stones, but found none. 'How's your head?' she asked Franziskus.

'It wishes to remain attached to its body.' Franziskus inspected the door, finding it all too sturdy.

'I agree with it wholeheartedly.' Angelika paced. 'I refuse to be executed by halflings. Maybe we can break out as we're led to the tribunal. Or at the proceedings themselves.'

'Or it's Deely who's right, and we should express contrition and seek their mercy.'

Angelika bleakly laughed.

'It is not us they truly seek vengeance against,' said Franziskus. 'It is the barbarians – the savages who made this war on them. How many men do you think they've lost? We must make them see that, whatever crimes we have committed, we are not the enemy. Beheading us will not return their beloved dead to life.'

Angelika crossed her arms. 'I won't bow and scrape to Curran, or any bully.'

'He's not a villain. He's a decent townsman, scourged by grief.'

'He stuck a spearhead in my face.'

Franziskus attempted to take her hands in his, but she resisted, turning away from him. 'I'm not asking you to prostrate yourself before them, or to beg. Just let me do the talking. Sheathe that cutting tongue of yours.'

She nodded, but he was by no means certain she could bring herself to do it.

THE GEROLSBRUCH SWORDSMEN, now incorporating a third of the Chelborg Archers and nine soldiers separated from other units, marched east, towards the mountains on a route set to take them past the village of Hochmoor. Jonas rode in front of the column whilst Emil paced his steed so that he was sometimes at the rear, other times beside the middle ranks, and, on occasion, at his superior's side. Like most sword companies, the Gerolsbruchers cultivated a reputation as a high-spirited bunch, but now they were silent. Dark clouds clung to the sky like a low ceiling. Sparks of lightning skittered through them, but the threatened thunder never came. Heavy winds flapped at the soldiers' cloaks. The swordsmen, who took a peacock's pride in the splendour of their wide-brimmed hats, had surrendered to the grabbing wind, folding them away in their packs.

They came to a river, and traversed alongside it. The river had ebbed down below the limits of its marshy banks. Cat tails, swamp gorse, and other wetland weeds, dried brown by the high summer sun, spiked up along them. In the far distance, ahead and to the right and left, rounded hillsides sloped.

About half an hour before, Jonas had become aware of a nervous mannerism: he caught himself repeatedly gazing through his spyglass, directing it compulsively toward the horizon. Eventually he sensed that the men grew more quiet each time he did this. He'd accordingly resolved to keep the device in its place, hanging from his saddlebag, until confronted by something genuinely worth looking at. The mere cry of faraway wolves, for example, provided no justification for panic. Now that he was first lieutenant, it was Jonas's duty to present an image of solidity and dash to his men, even when he did not truly feel it. Most especially then.

Jonas tensed. Hunched figures skulked in the reeds ahead. He saw a horned helmet and a barbarian shield. He tore his sword from its scabbard. 'The foe,' he called. His eager horse responded, plunging headlong toward the stand of rushes. His swordsmen followed, blades out, screaming.

Confronted with the oncoming hooves of Jonas's steed, the would-be ambushers turned and fled. One fell under his horse's churning legs. Jonas kept on, pursuing the second of them, leaving the trampled barbarian to be pierced by the points of his soldiers' swords. Desiccated weeds slapped into his legs as he charged through them. Two Kurgan stood in the river's calf-deep waters. One resumed his flight; the other threw back his head and roared in defiance, standing to receive Jonas's charge.

Jonas's steed crashed boldly onward as the Kurgan lofted his axe. Water sprayed the air. The fleeing barbarian slipped below the river's surface to swim for the other shore. Jonas reached his quarry and let his reins drop free to swing at him two-handed. The blow rang off the enemy's ox-horned helm. The helmet fell down over the enraged man's eyes; Jonas wheeled his steed to come in for another pass. Already his men were wading into the shallow river, ready to engage. Jonas rode past the Kurgan as he struggled to see, driving a mortal wound into the flesh of his back.

On the other side of the river, the Kurgan climbed onto the banks. In the rushes there, the Chelborg Archers saw two more barbarians about to aid their comrade. Swiftly, they drew their bows and sent arrows slicing across the river at them. One found its mark between the shoulder blades of the swimming barbarian; he slumped. His fellows abandoned him, darting across a brushy field.

The wading swordsmen made to pursue, but Jonas held up a hand to halt them.

'Our post awaits us in the mountains,' he said. 'This bunch is but poor meat for our hungry blades.'

The men hurrahed him, and they continued on, cheered by their brief and sudden win.

THE ESCAPED KURGAN lay flat in the grass. They had shamed themselves. They should not have run from an enemy, even when they were only a pair of warriors, facing an entire company of black-and-yellows. It was better to die than to flee. The two of them, if any of their tribesmen had seen them, would now be branded as *mutaa* – cowards, less than men. Women would spit in their faces. Men would treat them as dead.

They rose and surveyed the brambly field around them. They stood, then slowly crept back toward the riverbank. The enemy army was disappearing from view ahead. They would follow it and attack.

They opened their throats and bellowed then turned and ran at speed toward the riverbank.

Behind them, a fiendish and familiar tattoo pounded out: the hoof beats of their chieftain's eerie steed. The barbarians stopped in their tracks. As if from nowhere, as shadows pass across the sun, Ortak Nalgar appeared, booming toward them.

He stood six feet and four inches tall. From his towering helmet, a rack of twisted iron antlers grew. Behind it flowed a mane of pitch-dark hair. Plate

armour shielded him from head to toe, covered in a
raised ornament of thorns and serpents. Jagged spikes
sprouted from his knees and elbows. A pair of gargantuan swords crisscrossed his back.

His mount was sized to carry his mammoth frame.
It was not a horse, not exactly. In the sockets of its
eyes, green orbs glowed. When it rode its master to
battle, its cries were those of a roc or eagle. It was
watchful, and malignant.

As their war-chief came at them, the smaller of the
two Kurgan conceived an idea. He turned on his companion and drove the three spikes that protruded
from his wrist-guard deep into his throat. He held on
tight as his battle-brother convulsed and died. The
Kurgan felt no qualm – this man was, after all, a
mutaa. A coward.

The dead man flopped at his feet. The barbarian
steeled himself as his chieftain approached. Ortak
Nalgar slowly dragged a well-notched greatsword
from the rough sheath across his back.

The Kurgan spoke: 'Oh mighty chieftain, this man
was a *mutaa*, so I slew him. I saw him run from black-
and-yellows, across this river.' He pointed.

Ortak Nalgar turned his helmeted head. He saw the
enemy warriors.

He looked at the living man's boots. They were
coated with the same river mud as his slain comrade's.

Ortak Nalgar muttered a low command to his
mount, not in the language of the steppes, but in an
older, inhuman tongue. The horse-thing snaked its
head forward, clamped its jaws around the
marauder's throat, and viced them shut. It shook its

muscled neck; a grinding sound followed. The creature snorted and dropped the *mutaa's* carcass to the ground.

The Kurgan had a word for the weak, lazy, doomed men of the civilised lands: they were merely *turm*. Ortak Nalgar watched the last of the *turm* as they crossed the horizon.

He'd received commands from Vardek Crom, the Chief of Chieftains, who had defeated the leaders of all the tribes, including Ortak Nalgar himself. He had business in the mountains. He had gathered many dislocated tribesmen in the hours since the battle; they would come with him.

But first he would follow those *turm*, and see where they led him.

ANGELIKA AND FRANZISKUS spent several hours in their makeshift cell, tensely resting themselves. Finally, the snap of a key in the door lock brought them to attention. Angelika pressed to the wall by the door frame, in case whoever stepped through it was sufficiently incautious to let her out behind him.

Curran inched prudently in, preceded by his spear. Angelika shifted instantly to a pose of casual boredom, and pretended to have been startled by his entrance. He edged into the room, spearhead trained on Angelika, but alert to Franziskus's position, too. Deely followed, to put his spear at Franziskus's back. Angelika couldn't help but admire their technique. Rustic townsmen they might be, but they put to shame many of the supposed professionals who'd tried to keep her prisoner. They were good because they were unsure, and so remembered to fear her.

The halflings prodded their prisoners out into the old fort and through its broken entryway. Gathered around it were dozens, perhaps as many as a hundred, townsfolk, divided equally between humans and halflings. The human men wore unassuming, colourless tunics over plain leggings while their women dressed in drab and sack-like frocks. Their halfling counterparts preferred more elaborate garb, adding ruffles, fringes, lace and embroidery patterns to the outfits of male and female alike. Every garment, whether humble or showy, exhibited the fraying scars of repeated mending.

Whatever good impression their frugality conveyed was, to Angelika, dispelled by their apparent desire to kill her. Women beheld her with seething rage; some spat as she was pushed out into the courtyard. Clean-faced children stared out with bald curiosity from behind the skirts of their mothers. The men grumbled to one another; Angelika heard the word 'strumpet'. The people pushed so tightly around her that Curran had to shout at them to make room. So much, thought Angelika, for avenues of escape.

Townsmen dragged two long and battered benches from the fort out into the dirt. Children and an elderly woman lunged for them, but Curran shooed them off, declaring the benches as seating for the tribunal. Seven villagers shouldered through the crowd to take their seats. Angelika's hopes sank when she saw women among them. Though esteemed as the more forgiving sex, Angelika was well-acquainted with the vindictiveness of wronged women. If these were new widows, the sentence would be death. Overall, the tribunal consisted of four humans and three halflings – only three of them male.

Rickety chairs were provided; Franziskus and Angelika were shoved down into them. Angelika's was sized for a halfling. Though shaped for an expansive backside, its legs were short, forcing her to sit with raised knees, like a mantis. Filch again showed off his mastery of knots, tying both prisoners' wrists and ankles to their chairs.

Curran led the proceedings, an unfairness that came as no surprise to Angelika. A lengthy preamble laid out the rules, the clauses of the village's ancient charter that granted them the authority to mete out any sentence to defendants of lowly rank, such as themselves. Curran would declare the charges against them; they would be permitted to speak in their own defence, or to admit fault and plead for clemency. Then Curran could, if he so desired, question them to clarify their testimony. Witnesses might then be summoned by Curran to rebut any factual claims she or Franziskus might make. Then the tribunal would decide their fate. They could be acquitted, banned from ever again entering the village, maimed, or put to death.

To refrain from saying that it would be a great favour to be eternally disallowed from again setting foot in Hochmoor required self-control of monumental proportions. Angelika congratulated herself for successfully exercising it.

'Do the defendants have any questions regarding the rules I have just laid down?' intoned Curran. Angelika nodded distractedly, intent on studying the seven jurors, to see how they regarded him. She

hoped for looks of boredom or, better still, of
strained forbearance. Unfortunately, they all seemed
rapt and attentive, and respectful of her prosecutor.
Angelika shifted uncomfortably against the ropes that
bound her to her chair.

Curran told the jurors how he and his brothers
had gone out to recover the remains of the heroically slain, only to discover two grave robbers
desecrating the bodies. The jurors recoiled on their
bench, lips curled. Behind them stood Filch, who
seemed excited, and Deely, on whose face Angelika
read the only mercy in the crowd. She wondered if
Filch still had her daggers, and where Franziskus's
sabre might be. Then she saw the hilts of her knives
sticking up from Deely's belt. Could she maybe con-
trive a demonstration that would get her out of the
chair, where she could seize a hostage?

Finally Curran finished calumnising them, and
called on Angelika: 'how do you defend yourself
against this monstrous charge, witnessed in the light
of day by three of us here?'

'May I be freed of my bonds, to speak and gesture
freely?'

'No you may not.'

A woman juror smirked as Curran made his rul-
ing.

'In that case, I protest the manifest injustice of this
proceeding. What does your charter say as to the dignity in which a prisoner is permitted to plead his
case?'

She could see that Franziskus was displeased by
this line of argument, but it was she that Curran had
called on to speak, not him.

Suddenly she understood why this was: Curran knew her temper. He wanted her to annoy the jurors.

She regarded their prim, disapproving faces. She wanted to slap them.

Angelika swallowed. If she could fight goblins, hold her own against orcs, and survive climbs up icy glaciers, she could summon the willpower to be pleasant to a covey of sour-faced townsfolk.

'The charter makes no specific provisions for a criminal's dignity,' Curran announced.

'But as we have, of yet, not been proven to be criminals, surely you will show me the justice you'd expect yourselves, if you were tried in some other town.'

A rejoinder formed on Curran's lips, but before he could give voice to it, Deely stepped forward to untie her. 'It is only fair, brother,' he said. The crowd murmured its displeasure at the halfling's gesture of decency. Angelika took care to thank him as she stepped from the chair, but pleasantries were not her specialty, and her words seemed forced. She rubbed her wrists and wondered what to say.

'I won't lie to you,' she began. 'Nor will I dispute your friend's account. Yes, I was looting a fallen soldier on the battlefield. And if Curran identifies the dead man as one of your neighbours, then of course, he is right.'

Curran dangled the locket, which he'd confiscated from her during the forced march to the village. 'This is what you took.'

'Yes, I took that locket,' said Angelika.

Unprepared for honesty, the jurors exchanged confused glances.

In an attempt to put herself on eye level with the seated jurors, she perched herself on her chair's unsteady arm. 'I have two things to say to you. The first, and most important, is that my companion here, Franziskus, is not guilty of this theft. Curran told you as much – he described me searching the bodies. Me taking the locket. Franziskus did neither of those things. Though he does not despise me, he does despise the act of looting, as he will tell you, if you ask him. He takes no part in it. He had no part in this.'

'He protects you,' Curran interjected. 'He is therefore your accomplice.'

'How did he protect me? You came at us and we ran. You pursued us and waited in ambush. Your brother hit him with a rock, and he fell to the ground. He neither assisted me, nor impeded you.'

Curran moved close to her, propelled by a jabbing finger. 'He would have, though.'

'If you were to start prosecuting folk for what they might have done, given the chance, I daresay you'll have to string up half the Empire.'

A snort of laughter erupted from the crowd. It was Filch, covering his mouth. Beside him stood two other halflings, both of whom seemed at least partially amused.

Curran glared at his sibling. 'Shut it, you,' he demanded.

Emboldened, Filch stepped forward. 'But she's got you there, hasn't she? We didn't wait and give the fellow a chance to see if he was good or bad.' He addressed Franziskus, who was still yoked to his chair. 'If it turns out you aren't bad, I'm sorry for hitting you with that rock. Normally my aim's not that good.'

A few townsfolk suppressed snickers and grins. More shushed Filch and waved him back into place.

He adopted a hangdog look. 'Can't a fellow be sorry now?'

'Shut it,' Curran hoarsely cried.

Filch sheepishly melted back into the crowd, but soon his friends were lowly conversing with him, adding a distracting buzz to the proceedings.

'The tribunal has heard this first point you wished to make,' said Curran. 'You seek mercy for your accomplice.'

'The point is that he is not an accomplice.'

'Speak to your second point.'

'All right. Everyone here knows one thing. You may dislike the thought of people removing goods from a battlefield–'

Curran interrupted. 'Desecrating the corpses of our loved ones, you mean.'

'It may not please you to think it, but the day the first war was fought, the first looters cleaned up afterwards. I don't pretend it's a reputable undertaking. You've caught me with something that belongs to one of you. Normally this would not embarrass me in the slightest. I have never believed in the existence of good and honest folk, outside the stories and fables we tell each other. Certainly I have never met any – though perhaps you're the ones who'll prove me wrong.'

'A peculiar line of defence,' muttered Curran.

Angelika shrugged. 'You may find many of my beliefs peculiar. Franziskus certainly does. But here is

one thing we can agree on: I did not bring sorrow on
your heads today. It's the war. Blame who you want.
Blame the hordes of Chaos. They're the ones who
want nothing from you but your complete eradica-
tion. Blame the Empire, for not protecting you, so
you had to send farmers out to do the work of soldiers.

'Me, I prefer to direct my rage at fate itself, at this
entire stinking world of death and falseness. As
someone who's seen it, I can tell you – life's all sorrows and betrayals. It rewards and punishes us at
random, whether we are good or bad.

'You grieve, and wish to feel better. You can't
behead Chaos, or the Empire, or fate, so you seek
solace in killing me. I seem to have no way of stopping you, except to warn you that my blood won't
lighten your hearts, not for the tiniest moment.
You'll feel sick and empty, and nothing more. If you
really are the clean, honest, hardworking people
you think you are, I suggest you stay spotless, and
not stain your hands with yet another pointless slaying.'

Curran's spear rested against the fortress wall. He
dashed to grab it and wheeled on Angelika. 'A disgraceful plea. An obscene plea.'

She stood her ground and he stopped just short of
stabbing her. 'Lies are soothing. The truth is not.'

'You call that the truth?' Curran yowled. He turned
to the jurors. 'I say we have heard enough. Now's the
time for our righteous verdict – a verdict of death.'

Angelika decided to grab Curran's spear. Her odds
against an entire angry village were terrible, but she
would not go meekly to her–

Franziskus, she saw, had a dagger against his throat, held by a gaunt human townsman.

Damn, she thought. She would have to find another way.

Then came a shout from the back of the crowd: 'Soldiers! Soldiers are here.'

CHAPTER SEVEN

THE KNOT OF townsfolk turned in rough unison, giving Angelika their backs. Curran, she was annoyed to see, had shifted his gaze from her only slightly – and his spear, not at all. The bony human, however, had enthusiastically abandoned his post at Franziskus's throat, sliding his knife into his belt and pushing into the crowd, craning his neck to see what they saw. Curran grimaced and called him back; he returned grumpily to hover over the prisoner. The knife, Angelika noted, remained on his hip. She feigned a relaxed and casual posture, vowing to find a moment she could exploit. At the same time she rehearsed a new clemency plea for use on whatever new authority was entering the village. If made aware of her crimes, any officer would want to make her an easy example of his stern discipline. Perhaps she could somehow pit townsmen against soldiers...

Wooden sticks beat against the tight skin of a kettledrum and their echoes hit the fortress walls like cracking muskets.

A head bobbed above the crowd. It was Jonas Rassau, on horseback.

The villagers parted, revealing an entire company of mixed Stirland forces, finishing its ride up the dirt road to the old fort. Angelika quickly counted upwards of threescore men. At the rear of the approaching column she spotted Rassau's sergeant. Even though the lieutenant seemed unconcerned by her looting activities, and his sudden appearance could theoretically offer up a useful distraction, instinct told Angelika that her troubles had taken a sharp turn for the worse.

The inky sky lent a sharp backdrop to flatter Rassau's sculpted features. He peered down at the thronging civilians. 'Who speaks for you townsmen?' he called.

Deely approached Rassau, signalling meekly that it was him. 'Our headman went out with a dozen volunteers to join this morning's battle,' he said. 'If the fight had gone well lieutenant, he'd be back by now. I am the village reeve, though.'

Jonas smiled and swung from his horse's saddle. Deely tugged nervously at the collar of his tunic. Angelika wondered why. Curran chewed his lip impatiently throughout these formalities, as if he thought he should take charge of the parley.

'Ah, I was hoping this would be your village up here. Deely, wasn't it?' said Jonas, thrusting out his hand for the halfling to shake. Deely shyly complied.

'Yes, I am Deely.'

Jonas swept his head around. Angelika was sure he could see her, but he gave no sign of it. 'Did you find the looter you were seeking?'

Angelika figured it out: they'd already met. The halflings had asked if they'd seen her. Then, later, in the vineyard, they'd hidden from the lieutenant as he attempted to recruit Angelika. Hence Deely's nervousness. Jonas might be displeased if he realised they'd been skulking around on him.

'Ah,' said Jonas, his gaze landing showily on Angelika and Franziskus. 'Would this be them?'

Feeling suddenly light-hearted, Angelika happily retook her spot in the chair she'd been bound to. A fascinating performance was about to commence. The halflings knew Jonas had already seen and spoken to her, but couldn't accuse him without also admitting to spying on him. Angelika savoured the disconcerted mix of anger and dismay on Curran's one-eared face. Finally he'd grown distracted, and lowered his spear.

Rassau's soldiers coolly ringed themselves around her – she was as trapped as before.

'This would be them,' Curran announced, 'and you have interrupted our tribunal.'

Jonas's expression turned grave. 'They stand accused of battlefield looting?'

Curran puffed out his tiny chest. 'Indeed they do.'

Jonas scratched his stubbly chin as if wrestling with a delicate conundrum. 'Then as a commissioned officer in time of war, it is I who have jurisdiction over crimes committed on the battlefield. We'll take these wrongdoers off your hands, good Deely and Curran, and subject them to military justice.'

He nodded to his men. Two swordsmen moved to clap a hand on each of Angelika's shoulders. Another pair marched to Franziskus. Curran wheeled with his spear to hold them off. 'No you don't,' he growled.

The men stood their ground, hands slowly drifting to sword hilts. The other soldiers reached for their own weapons.

'Curran, don't,' Deely said.

Curran stamped his foot like a bull announcing a charge. 'This is our village and it's our friends they defiled.'

'They are soldiers,' said Deely.

'I uphold the charter of our village.'

Jonas moved between the men Curran held at bay. He held up his hands. 'It is you, and your kind, we soldiers are sworn to protect. Do not make us draw on you.'

Curran flushed with helpless rage. 'It's our friends they defiled.' Other townsmen gathered behind him. The gaunt one pulled his knife.

'Stop this, all of you,' Deely cried.

Curran pointed his spear at Jonas, the motion was half gesture, half threat. 'You know what he'll do if we hand them over? Nothing. He wants her to scout for him.'

Jonas stayed still. 'Why do you say that, Curran?'

Curran looked to his fellow villagers for support. 'Do you deny it?'

'I ask you what makes you say it.'

Curran addressed the townsmen. 'As we waited for an opportune moment to seize these vile desecrators, we heard you make that offer.'

Jonas sternly crossed his arms. 'You hid from us?'

Curran increased his volume, but also trod back a step. 'We heard you with our own ears.'

'Why did you not come forward, to press your claim?'

Curran sputtered. 'We heard you say you did not care.'

'You mean to say you eavesdropped on us? Like vile and furtive sneaks?'

The flustered halfling failed to summon an answer.

Jonas turned to address the other villagers, turning his back to Curran's spear. Angelika followed the ready gazes of the two swordsmen who flanked him; if Curran lunged, they'd cut him down. 'Yes, this is what I said: we are at war, my friends, and today the enemy has dealt us a fearsome blow. This village has been spared the foeman's merciless attack. Your neighbours have not been so lucky. Even now, the Kurgan horde rampages further into the heart of our land. And in those mountains' – he pointed to the looming peaks of the World's Edge range – 'that malefic army will fester and grow. They will come sweeping down again, and soon, you can be sure of that.

'Who is there to staunch their hideous advance? Only we few soldiers. A mere handful of men. To protect this village, here, and all the others around here, and our very nation. Curran is correct to mourn the dead. He makes the gravest error, however, if he blinds himself to the true nature of the threat we face today. Do not spare these criminals. Force them to serve you, by binding them over to me. This woman's skills, honed in a loathsome trade, must now be bent to the most righteous of causes. I assure you, my friends, it is not a fate she relishes.'

He paused to let the crowd confer with itself. He waited till the murmuring had crested. 'And further, my friends, I beg you this: if you truly wish to avenge your fallen, you'll send men with us, to join our fight. We need every able-bodied slinger or spearman your village can spare. Take up the weapons of your forefathers. Fight so that you may have descendants to pass them onto. Fight lest these lands become a blasted plain, a graveyard for your women and children.'

The people of Hochmoor nodded in glum agreement. Angelika had to credit his eloquence. Filch and his friends seemed especially roused by Rassau's words. She checked Curran's attitude, he would be the key.

He stuck his spear into the dirt, his fist tightly balled around its haft. 'Don't listen to him. He doesn't care a fig for us. If there are more of them coming, we need every able man here.'

'Perhaps, brother, it'd be better to stop them from getting this far,' said Filch, his voice meekly trailing.

Curran spat. 'The hope he offers you is nothing but a lie.'

Rassau turned on him. 'I've had all I'm ready to stand from you, little man.'

He stopped himself short, but it was too late. Offended muttering broke out among the village's halflings. Curran sizzled with happy spite.

'Hope is never a lie,' said Jonas. It was a game try, but he'd punctured his own authority.

Curran pressed his case, gesturing to Angelika. 'You wish a decision from our people. Well then, let's have the defendant speak. You do, I suppose, wish to be spared, so that you may be press-ganged by this fiery hobnail?'

'I wish to be spared,' said Angelika.

'And should we send our soldiers with him?'

'That's none of my concern.'

'Would you do it, in our shoes?'

You don't wear shoes was the first answer that came to mind. After discarding that response, Angelika said, 'I don't know what you want to hear, so I'll tell you the truth. You're probably doomed no matter what you do. If you send men with him, they'll likely die. If you hole up here and wait for the enemy to come and get you, I imagine it will. Get you, that is. Maybe your best bet is to abandon your homes and flee – though with that barbarian horde rampaging unchecked through the land, that's not such a safe bet, either.'

She was sitting, so the tightly grinning halfling was able to go nose-to-nose with her. 'But if you had to choose?'

'If it were up to me, I'd do whatever let me feel free, till my moment of reckoning came.'

Curran broke from her to confront Jonas. 'The scout you want so badly has little regard for your chances, lieutenant. I guess you were wrong about her.'

Jonas was unfazed. 'She doesn't know me yet.'

Curran poked his spear at Franziskus. 'What about you?'

'I go where she goes.'

The halfling's air of bloodthirsty amusement returned to him. 'In that case, my friend, I daresay you're accompanying her to hell. Tribunal, what say you? Render your judgement.'

Jonas had withdrawn from the circle and was conferring with his sergeant. Angelika took this as proof that a fight would break out between villagers and soldiers if the tribunal refused to bind her over. That would be her time to bolt. She looked to Franziskus, and saw that he was ready, too.

The sentry bells rang briefly, then fell silent. Kurgan war horns blasted from below. Half a dozen figures pounded up the road, astride dark horses. Angelika looked down the hillside; barbarian fighters swarmed up all sides of the slope.

The village burned.

CHAPTER EIGHT

TOWNSMEN DASHED TO the lip of the hilltop. When they saw their homes afire, they ran down toward them. Humans and halflings spilled down the slope in scattered groups. Curran ran among them, trying to block them, crying out for order. Women and children fled for the doubtful safety of the crumbling fort.

Angelika looked for the hillside escape route most likely to bypass the swarming barbarians. She was still unarmed.

'Stay up here,' Jonas cried. 'Defend in good formation!'

The townsmen, drawn like moths to the flames of their blazing homes, ignored him.

Mounted Chaos marauders threw up clouds of dirt as they thundered up the road. Townsmen scattered as they came, diving into the bushes and saplings that grew alongside it. A rotund halfling tumbled beneath the hooves of a black steed and squeaked as it trampled him.

A halfling girl fell in front of a corpulent human woman who dashed for the fortress entrance. Franziskus swept in to snatch her up.

Angelika searched for Deely, who had her blades. She spotted him dashing for the slope and sprinted furiously after him. Her long legs gave her dominance over a thump-footed halfling. She tackled him, hitting him in the shoulders and bringing him down.

Deely rolled. Angelika, waiting for him, pounced, planting her pointy knee on his sternum. He threw his arms back into the grass, in submission, seeming to know what she wanted from him. She rolled him onto his side, fleeced her twin daggers from him, and leapt off. Returning to the edge of the hilltop, she plotted an avenue of escape that would circuit through the invaders in their various groupings. She looked for Franziskus.

At their sergeant's command, the soldiers formed a semi-circle inside the broken gate, braced to receive the charging Kurgan cavalry. Jonas shouted for the remaining townsmen to join the formation. Curran surged at him like a furious bantam, uselessly waggling his spear, hectoring him unintelligibly. Jonas's elbow shot out, catching the enraged halfling in the forehead. Curran wove, staggered, and folded in two. An unruffled Jonas resumed his barked commands.

Filch and several other halflings, ignoring the indignity dished out to their compatriot, rallied to the Stirland officer. Clamouring for their friends to follow, they joined the half-circle of human soldiers, as other townsmen poured away down the hillside to fight for their hovels and cottages.

Six barbarian riders reached the top of the hill. Their sturdy steeds broke easily through the wide gaps in the ruined stone gate. They crossed through a single volley loosed by the Chelborg Archers. Arrows clunked off helmets and shields. One found purchase in a patchy equine flank, another in the leg of a howling Kurgan. Barbarian horsemen rode into Stirland swordsmen. Axes and maces hammered down; heavy sabres jabbed and pierced in return. A mace smacked squarely into a swordsman's face, pulverising it. Its owner flew backwards into the dirt and lay there, stunned and dying. The Stirlanders groaned in wrath and consternation.

A sole Kurgan horseman, his armour bulkier and more ornate than the rest, had paused in a slight depression in the middle of the road about twenty yards from its summit. He sat confidently upon his huge and snorting horse, surveying his battlefield to see where he was needed. This was the Chaos chieftain, Ortak Nalgar. He waited, holding back from the battle.

Jonas mounted his horse and Emil, who'd done the same, rode after him. Jonas bore down toward the barbarian who'd downed his man. The Kurgan wheeled his mount to better face his charge. Jonas rode past screaming and countered the swing of the Chaos worshipper's mace with a brisk downturn of his sabre. The blade hit the Kurgan's fingers, severing two and ruining the others. He squalled in agony as his weapon fell between his horse's hooves.

Jonas came circling back for a second charge. The barbarian rode off toward the ruins of the fort, where the women and children were. Jonas urged his steed on and overtook the barbarian's. He struck wildly at the enemy's back until he slumped in the saddle, then keeled over. Upended in his stirrup, the barbarian's head bounced from rock to rock as his mistreated horse, freed of its reins, zigzagged aimlessly down the hillside.

A pair of Kurgan footmen reached the hilltop and stampeded over its lip. They saw Franziskus standing alone, blocking the fortress entranceway, and heaved their massive bodies toward him. He hadn't recovered a weapon. He reached down for a rock to throw. Low chortles arose from barbarian throats as they came at him.

One tumbled headlong, his chin smacking the dirt. A knife protruded from the back of his neck. Angelika, perched on a fallen slab of outer wall, had thrown it. Franziskus had no time to thank her; the second Kurg was charging fast. For an instant he saw Angelika advance on the dead barbarian, to retrieve her dagger. Then the big man was on him. He ducked a swiftly-swung axe, and kept his balance to evade a repeat thrust. He jogged back, hoping desperately for aid or respite.

Jonas rode between them, tossing Franziskus a spare sabre. He masked Franziskus's vulnerability with a sweeping feint at the Kurg's head. The Kurg swivelled to protect himself, only to see Jonas's steed gallop back to the main mêlée at the roadway's head.

The marauder turned his attention back to Franziskus. They circled one another, testing sabre against axe. The enemy had fifty pounds on Franziskus, all of it heaving muscle. A filament of drool hung from the side of the Kurgan's mouth. Franziskus wondered if there might be some way to bring his obviously superior intelligence to bear on the situation. He shifted his weight to his left side, winced, and limped backwards, holding his leg to feign an ankle injury. The barbarian smirked. They swayed around each other, Franziskus faking his injury and allowing the Kurgan to back him into the fortress wall. Then, foretelling his blow with his eyes, the Kurg aimed a low strike at Franziskus's supposedly bad leg.

It threw him off-balance, just as Franziskus had reckoned, exposing the steppe fighter's neck. Franziskus slipped out of the way and slammed Jonas's razor-sharp sword down onto the enemy's naked spine. The wound seemed paper-thin at first then it welled with blood. The barbarian belaboured him with a wide and impetuous strike. Then he stopped, seeming to realise that he was dead. He sank to his knees, teetered, and slumped to the dirt.

Franziskus heard a shouting voice – it was Angelika, beckoning him to follow her down the hillside. He wondered why she meant to join the battle down there, when it was best to keep the most dangerous foes, the mounted warriors, up on the hilltop, where Jonas's forces were concentrated. He followed her a short distance to the lip of the hill. There he realised that Angelika, who skittered sideways down the slope, meant simply to flee the town. Franziskus watched her run.

Widening his view, he saw helpless villagers falling beneath the clubs and axes of the Chaos horde. He turned to join Jonas's men. As he ran toward their formation, Chelborg arrows downed a Kurgan steed. Stirland swords flew into the air and then down to slash at the unhorsed foe. Two barbarians clambered up the slope to dash at him, one from the front, one from behind.

Angelika stopped midway down the slope to see Franziskus facing two bigger opponents. She called uselessly after him, hesitated, and reversed course, climbing up to help. All the way up she swore dark thoughts at him: if he wanted to rejoin the army he'd deserted from, that was fine by her, but if he was going to get himself killed, he should show the basic courtesy to wait till he was out of her sight to do it. No, Angelika wasn't having any of that. Franziskus could under no circumstances die in a way that would induce even the slightest shred of guilt. Not with her new life of calm and safety so close at hand.

When she reached the top, one of the barbarians had compassed his arms around Franziskus's, and held him, squirming and kicking, chest exposed. The other Kurgan, pausing to savour the moment of slaughter, swung his axe in a circle on its leather throng. He ululated a war-cry in the glottal Chaos tongue. He had his back to Angelika, and he was both helmeted and cuirassed, offering no tempting targets to her knife. The marauder holding Franziskus, on the other hand, wore no face-plate.

She took a chance and threw her dagger at his face.

It burrowed itself deep in the man's eye socket. He grunted and fell from Franziskus, who stepped deftly away, to avoid being brought down with him. The axe-wielding man erred, turning back to see who'd thrown the dagger. Franziskus took the opportunity, snatching his dropped sabre from the ground. He swung the heavy sword into his enemy's well-protected temple. The barbarian staggered back, stunned, then shook it off.

Angelika ran toward the mêlée, as if ready to join it, though her intent was merely to circle around the barbarian, distracting him. Franziskus now seemed to have little need of her help, pounding his sword repeatedly across the helmet and breastplate of his opponent. She turned to tug her dagger from the skull of the Kurgan she'd killed.

She stalked the battlefield like a crow, looking for safe blows to strike. Franziskus was wearing down his opponent; intervention in that fight did not justify the risk. Amid the clanging of weapons and the crackle of burning thatch, she felt the calm and detachment of being outside herself. Angelika was where she never wanted to be – in the heart of battle.

Ahead of her, at the meeting point between road and hilltop, Jonas Rassau's men appeared to be making headway against the invading barbarians. Only one Kurgan horseman still contended with them; the rest of their foes fought on foot, as they did. The defenders' ranks had burgeoned, increased by townsfolk, including a few halflings, crazed with sudden bravura.

Shelter. That's what she needed. A vantage point. Especially now that the battle was turning, it would be unbearably ironic to be injured by a stray arrow or flying axe-head. She would find a safe spot, wait for

Franziskus to get his alabaster hide out of harm's way, and then quickly decamp, before the lovely folk of Hochmoor remembered their plan to lynch her. She looked to the dark walls of the crumbling fortress.

Keeping a wary watch for enemies and flying objects, she skipped to a crumbled bit of wall and hauled herself up onto it. The missing bits of mortar made for fine handholds. With the facility of a stick insect, Angelika scaled a lone, freestanding section of wall. She perched about fifteen feet above ground level to watch the mêlée below. The wall creaked and shifted, then adjusted to her weight.

A cacophony issued from the Stirland ranks. Suddenly men were falling back, bowled over. A new horseman, larger than the others, had joined the fight. Ortak Nalgar waded into the press of attackers and defenders, moving men aside with axe and elbow. The weapon-sharp hooves of his nightmare steed slashed into the chests of swordsmen and archers. The chieftain's followers took heart and redoubled their attacks against the Stirland formation. Defenders fell or fled. Ortak Nalgar swung his axe and the heads of two archers separated from their bodies and sailed above the crush of men.

Jonas's horse reared back, withdrawing from the battle. Hugging tight to its muscular neck, legs wrapped firmly in the stirrups, he regained control of the panicked beast. He rode it in a circle around the hilltop, readying a charge against the Chaos chieftain.

Spotting an opponent on horseback, and deeming him to be the leader of the enemy tribe, Nalgar trampled his massive steed over both barbarian and Imperial soldier in an effort to get to him.

Angelika calculated the Chaos chieftain's trajectory. He was headed straight for Franziskus and his opponent. Occupied by their exhausted, fruitless exchanges, neither saw the chieftain soar at them. Nalgar raised his axe.

Angelika decided to do something stupid.

Before Franziskus and his opponent, long before he reached his final target, Lieutenant Rassau, the chieftain would pass within a few feet of Angelika's wall.

His horse swung past her.

She leapt.

She fell onto his back. The impact knocked the wind out of her. She bounced off his thickly armoured frame and into the air. Ortak Nalgar flew from his saddle, beside her. He hit the earth first. She landed on him, his body breaking her fall. Feeling him strain beneath her, she scrambled off his back to land, dazed, a few feet away. Pain shooting through her, she got up to a crawling position. She heard a snort behind her. The gigantic chieftain was already on his feet, fixing her in his gaze. His axe lay in the dirt between them. He strained down but she grabbed it first. His boot crunched onto her fingers. White dots of agony pulsed in Angelika's vision.

Pounding hooves approached: Rassau was finally upon him, holding his sword out like a lance, aiming to run the chieftain through. Ortak Nalgar stepped off his axe, freeing Angelika's hand. She rolled out of the way, executing a half-formed backwards somersault.

Ortak Nalgar grabbed Rassau's sword arm as he charged, yanking him from his horse. Rassau leapt onto him, gloved hands punching without effect on the chieftain's helmet. Nalgar wormed his vambraced

arm between them and pushed at Rassau's throat,
heaving him away. By some miracle of agility, Rassau
managed to remain standing, falling back onto his
heels.

Angelika's head spun. She understood that she
should be getting off the battlefield and out of the
way. She blinked and tried to bring the world back
into focus. The fight between Rassau and the chieftain became a struggle between slowed and
lurching cut-outs.

Skirmishes elsewhere on the hilltop and on the
slopes of the village echoed distantly. Angelika
wrenched around. Franziskus and his opponent
had fought to a standstill, and now stood staring
and panting at one another, neither able to take a
step forward or raise his blade for another blow.
Tears of effort streamed down both men's faces.

Angelika spun again. Ortak Nalgar suffered several free blows from Jonas's sabre, then stooped to
recover his axe. Thus equipped, the chieftain
manoeuvred the smaller man easily around the
battleground, pushing him back, draining his
strength with one feint after another. Then
Franziskus lurched into view. His opponent had
somehow fallen, and had now wrapped one leathery hand around his ankle.

Franziskus kicked him in the face, but he would
not let go. He lifted Franziskus's boot off the
ground. Franziskus fell onto his back, ripped off
his helmet, and smashed him a half-dozen times
on the back of the head. The Kurgan kicked,
twisted, bucked and finally slumped. Franziskus
tore free from him and, in a daze, wandered into

the fight between Jonas and the Chaos chieftain. Ortak Nalgar swiped at both men and they stumbled back.

A third Stirlander leapt over to help bring the chieftain down. Though forced into a defensive mode, Ortak Nalgar fended off all three men with apparent ease. Angelika wanted to shout to Franziskus, to urge him away from the battle. To remind him that these people wanted him dead, just minutes ago, and would likely turn on him again, if their anger remained unsated. There would be no use in it, though: it would merely spur him on. Despite all their time together, he was still in thrall to romantic notions of heroism.

On the edges of the fray, she beheld Filch, as he fled from a huge Kurgan warrior. She remembered his facility with a thrown rock. Angelika regarded the wall behind her, and recalled how unstable it had seemed when she'd jumped from it. An idea coalesced. While the three Stirlanders worked to keep Ortak Nalgar encircled, she snatched a large piece of dislodged brick. Too large, in fact; she dropped it in favour of a smaller cousin. She weighed it in her hand. She thought about throwing a knife, and the differences between a dagger and a rectangular chunk of stone. If she erred, this could go very wrong. But the chieftain seemed to be gaining his second wind, so the risk seemed worth taking.

She waited for the fighting men to reach the right point in their orbit. To mark out their pace, she counted in her head. *One gold crown, two gold crown, three gold crown.*

Angelika threw the rock.

It banged into Ortak Nalgar's helmet, striking a few inches above the bridge of his nose. A flanged ornament of cresting spikes detached from the dented headpiece. It swung uselessly, humiliatingly, from a tiny screw. Ortak Nalgar turned to Angelika. Quaking with fury, he ripped the ornament from his helm. He pushed past Franziskus, knocked down Jonas, and charged at her, swinging his axe and shouting out foul Kurgan curses.

As Angelika had guessed, it was a particularly gruesome blow to a steppe barbarian's pride to be assaulted by a combatant of the female persuasion. He would have to act immediately to recover his honour. He hurtled at her.

The next move was more than risky. Possibly fatal, if she got it even a hair wrong. So dangerous that she could not conceive of a solitary rational reason to even attempt it, except that it was already too late to stop.

At the last possible moment, she adjusted her stance. She readied herself to receive the blow, and turn it to her own ends. As he made impact, she drew back and around him, pivoting him into the decrepit wall, letting the force of the slam throw her clear.

Half a ton of ancient brick escaped its bonds of decaying mortar to shower down upon him. Ortak Nalgar wailed in outrage and then fell silent, entombed in a heap of rubble. A cloud of brick dust drifted from it.

Angelika had landed painfully on her tailbone. Jonas came to her side and pulled her up. The pair of them stood dumbly before the debris pile. Jonas held his sabre ready, in case the chieftain suddenly shrugged his way through the crushing stone. Behind them, where the main mass of men battled on at the head of the road, the sounds of combat had dulled.

She promised herself that that trick was the last foolish risk she'd ever take.

Ortak Nalgar's black steed wheeled, stamping the ground in a tight, crazy circle. Through foam-flecked teeth it howled, producing a sound more like a wolf than a horse. It bolted at Angelika and Jonas, intent on trampling them. Angelika turned and leapt into a space between sections of fortress wall. Jonas stood his ground as the beast bore down on him. He drove his sabre deep into the raging animal's underbelly. Its momentum took it headlong into the pile of bricks, where it collided with a terrible impact. Jonas flinched at the sound of its cracking bones. The dying beast writhed and groaned, waggling its broken limbs.

A lone Kurgan marauder, unchallenged by any defender, wandered toward the debris pile, mouth agape. Two halflings charged, flanking him; Angelika recognised one of them as Deely. The Kurgan, his fortitude sapped by his master's demise, turned and ran. He swung his axe wildly out at his side, trying merely to fend off his tormentors and escape. Deely fell back, clutching his throat. The marauder picked up speed, though it did not matter: the second halfling had dropped his spear and rushed to Deely's side, holding him upright.

The Kurgan ran past the ranks of his compatriots at the roadhead, squalling in disbelief. His cries struck confusion into his fellows' hearts. If unengaged, they froze. If stuck in combat, they faltered. A few, torn by grief, fell abruptly beneath Stirland blades, or quivered, impaled, on halfling spears. Most, feverish with unreasoning fear, disengaged deftly from their mêlées.

Jonas moved to his skittish mount, clucking soothingly at it. He hauled himself up onto the stirrup and, caressing the horse's neck, impelled it forward, toward his men. 'Stand down!' he called. 'Do not pursue.' The men regarded him with obvious relief, then watched as the barbarians dispersed. A few, bolting from burning homes, were trapped, brought down and slaughtered by furious townsmen. Dozens more escaped. Within minutes, the surviving Chaos troops were gone, each routing in his own random direction.

Emil led the Gerolsbruch Swordsmen in tending to their dead and wounded. A pair of swordsmen had been killed, along with the two archers whose heads the chieftain had taken.

Worried halflings gathered around Deely, who lay prone near the rubble pile. The right sleeve had been ripped from Curran's shirt and wrapped around his brother's torn throat. It was already stained through with bright arterial blood. Filch was at his brother's side, too. Deely tried to raise himself up on his elbows to speak to him, then sank back down.

Angelika ventured from her hiding place and Franziskus hobbled over to join her.

'Wounded?' she asked him.

He shook his head. 'Tired.'

'Let's go.'

'Shouldn't we at least–'

'I'd prefer to subject my execution to a permanent postponement.'

'That was before you saved their village, Angelika.'

'If you want to count on their forgiveness, you're free to stay. I'm going.' She clenched her fists, Jonas was approaching. An unobtrusive exit would not be possible until she'd shaken him.

He stood beside Angelika. Together they watched as a grey-bearded village healer dribbled a thick brown potion onto Deely's resistant lips. 'You see the dangers now,' said Jonas.

'I was never unacquainted with them.'

'You must help us. We must stop more of these barbarians from crossing the mountains.'

'I'm no soldier.'

'Soldiers I have already. It's your services I require, Angelika.'

'No.'

'You dealt ably with that chieftain.'

'I wouldn't be able to repeat that trick up in the mountains.'

'You've more tricks than that, I'll warrant.'

'My answer remains no.' She indicated the rubble pile. 'Maybe you should move some of those bricks and make sure that chieftain is truly dead.'

'He could not possibly be alive under there.'

Angelika shrugged. 'I wouldn't want to be in this village if you're wrong. He seems likely to bear a grudge.'

'By the by,' she said, raising her voice so that the townsmen gathered around Deely could hear, 'how is it that the barbarians arrived here so quickly after you did? It isn't possible, is it, that you led them here?'

Heads turned their way. Jonas flushed. 'Of course not,' he said.

'So you saw no enemy marauders on your way here?'

Emil, along with others of the Gerolsbruch Swordsmen, came near, attracted by the rising edge in Angelika's voice. The disquiet on their faces was plain: her guess was right. They'd encountered Chaos forces, who'd followed them to Hochsmoor.

'We did not,' said Jonas.

'Then they were able to follow you completely undetected.'

Villagers drifted nearer, among them, the gaunt knife-man. Franziskus attempted to interpose himself between Angelika and Jonas; she moved to prevent him.

Jonas spoke soothingly. 'It is not seemly to argue now. We faced a common foe. Working together, we drove it off. That is what counts.'

'The truth is,' said Angelika, 'that these folk might not have had to drive it off, were it not for your lack of caution.'

'No,' said Jonas, punctuating his exclamation with a snap of his cloak. 'What is true is that we are at war. Against an enemy who hates all that we stand for, and wishes harm to all of us. You of Hochmoor have fought gloriously today, and brought defeat to that common adversary. Again, I say, it is time for loyal sons of Stirland to step forward, to join us as we journey to the mountains, to staunch the flow of barbarian foemen.'

'Join you?' The gaunt man pointed his knife at Jonas. 'Your soldiers have brought us nothing but disaster.' His bloodied friends murmured their assent.

'Our homes are aflame,' an old woman cried.

'Imagine your fate if we hadn't been here to protect you.'

'The grave robber's not right, is she?' asked the gaunt man. 'You couldn't have led them here, to a defenceless village, its best fighters already slain on your godforsaken battleground.' He advanced on Jonas, brandishing his weapon.

Jonas's swordsmen had casually encircled him, and now closed tighter, to defend him. They pushed past Angelika, leaving her outside the stiffening jostle. Angelika inched crabwise, toward a promising route of escape.

'Listen to me!' Jonas called. 'Are you cowards, or are you Stirlanders? You are Stirlanders, are you not? Is that not the important truth?'

His ardour increased. 'You are right to protest the injustice of war. But it's the wretched enemy you must blame for the harm done to you today. Are we such fools that we'll allow him to divide us?'

Angelika's estimation of his oratorical skills, already high, increased by yet another degree. Already he had the distrustful, grief-maddened villagers at least halfway swayed. It was time for Angelika to speed her exit. Franziskus would have to shift for himself. He could find her later, or join Jonas, if he preferred. They were due to part, anyhow.

A halfling voice threw a declamatory obstacle in Jonas's path. 'If you led them here, tell us the truth, and we'll forgive you.' It was Filch, Angelika realised. He seemed to think he was being helpful. Angelika was almost tempted to stay, just to see how it all turned out.

Angelika found herself at the rubble pile. She looked at it uncertainly. The corpse of the chieftain's steed still lay on it. There was no sign of the barbarian leader beneath it – not a leg, not a protruding hand. No way of being sure he was dead. The stones were heavy, but the Kurgan had been well-armoured. Despite Jonas's certitude, he might still be breathing under there.

'It pains me to say it, Filch,' came Jonas's reply. 'But do we know for sure it was not you and your brothers who were followed here?'

The crowd hummed its horror at this unthinkable suggestion. There was no truth to it: if Chaos had been on their trail during the trek to Hochmoor, Angelika would have noticed.

She froze. One of the bricks seemed to shift.

'Deely's dead,' Curran ran toward her, from the side, blinded by tears. He had his spear out.

'Stay back,' Angelika cried. 'The barbarian–'

'If it weren't for you, he'd be alive.' Curran came at her from her right, occupying her chosen path out of the village. Behind her was the rubble pile, which she had no desire to interfere with. If she ran ahead, she'd be right back in the crowd. She ran to the left, toward the treacherous fortress walls.

Curran hurled his spear; it came at her as she wove between gaps in the wall. She skipped left to avoid it, her shoulder grazing the still-extant part of the wall she'd toppled. Stones barraged down onto her head and shoulders. Her chin hit the ground and her vision blurred. Before she lost consciousness, small, angry fists were grabbing her hair, pounding her skull against the stony ground.

CHAPTER NINE

HER BEATING AND rescue swam before her in flashes of dulled, fragmented awareness. The halfling was on her, a tenacious daemon crawling on her back, hurting her, shrieking into her ear. Voices chorused: an audience to watch her downed and brutalised. The daemon was lifted from her back, screeching, demanding blood in the disconcerting voice of a child. There were blows struck, not against her, but against him. His face fell in the dirt before her, a soldier's boot at the back of his neck, holding him in place as he sputtered and jigged. Crimson trickled from his scalp; his cheeks puffed out in impotent fury.

More contending voices: the villagers arguing with the soldiers. Jonas placating. Unfamiliar voices demanding. Swords unsheathed. A hush – the quiet that precedes a fight. The delicate tread of boots on gravel, men shifting positions, preparing to spring.

Lower voices, full of threat. A stand-off. A resolution. A falling-off of tension. Negotiations.

Angelika lifted up into the air. Droplets falling on her lips. Tasting them: blood, presumably her own.

Trying to walk. Unable to do it. A familiar smell nearby: Franziskus's hair. He was carrying her on his shoulders. Someone else holding her up from the right. Jonas?

Lifted up further. Bonds tying her in place. Breathing shallowly. Her vision labouring to unblur. The rhythm of her own breathing, against that of another creature. Lying against the neck of a horse. Tied into the saddle. They had her on a horse. Her pulse, against its. Calmness, blackness.

She was being taken into safety, and also danger.

Jonas had rescued her from the villagers.

Jonas had taken her prisoner.

She was going to the mountains.

JONAS AND FRANZISKUS walked together beside the horse that bore Angelika along. The Gerolsbruch Swordsmen marched toward the World's Edge Mountains, Emil in the lead. Hochmoor was only an hour behind them. Jonas had allowed himself to straggle back from the pack, though not so far that he and Franziskus could not rejoin the column should enemies crash suddenly into view. The soldiers trudged along a wide and treeless plain, far from the threat of ambush.

Franziskus checked Angelika's condition. He'd replaced her head bandage twice already. Unlike the others, this one had remained white and pristine. He wondered whether he should wake her for water, and decided not to.

'Not nearly as bad as she looks,' Jonas said. He was only a few years older than Franziskus, but addressed him with an air of confident seniority. 'She'll be up before we know it. Mostly shock, I think.'

Franziskus walked closer to the horse to check on Angelika's condition. He'd be happier if they found a safe, stationary place for her to rest. 'I was afraid she wouldn't stop bleeding.'

'Scalp injury,' shrugged Jonas. 'They always look worse than they are. Plenty of blood, but the wound's superficial.' Franziskus had stood over while the unit's medic stitched her; it was true that the cut was much smaller than he'd imagined.

'I hope you're right. Head injuries can fool you.'

'Unfurrow your worried brows. That hot-headed halfling may have bashed her around some, but I got to him before he did any real harm.'

Franziskus winced. Jonas had probably broken several of Curran's ribs when he threw him down. Though naturally glad to see him pulled away from Angelika, Franziskus was nonetheless twinged by a residual sympathy for the poor fellow. He'd lost his best friend, and his brother, too. If Franziskus had got to Curran first, he wouldn't have hurt him so badly. But then, Jonas did what needed doing. Any injuries the halfling had suffered were ultimately of his own making.

'Franziskus, I'll be frank with you. The simple truth of it is that your friend will be assisting us in our mission. Make it easy on her. Help her to see the way.'

Franziskus grimaced. 'I don't see how you intend to get her into those mountains if she doesn't want to go.'

Jonas spoke softly. 'That's your job, my friend.'

'Why do you think you need her so badly?'

'I know it, because my commander ordered me to find someone like her, and there she is, right before me. The gods have provided. Surely you have faith, Franziskus?'

'Yes. Sigmar will deliver us. But I suggest you not use that argument on Angelika.'

'The gods may bind the godless to their cause.'

'Especially don't say that.'

Jonas laughed, though Franziskus had not been joking. 'You're a Stirlander,' he said.

Franziskus couldn't deny it, his accent gave him away.

'Like me, you come from a pedigreed family.'

Unwanted emotion choked at him. 'I have lost any claim on a noble name,' he said.

'Maybe we've even met before. When we were children, perhaps?'

Franziskus shrugged.

'Which unit did you desert from, Franziskus?'

He buttoned his coat, as if torn by a chill wind. 'If you wish to bring me up on charges, the articles of military justice of course permit you to do so.'

The lieutenant's hand appeared on his shoulder. 'You're here, aren't you? Fighting when it counts.'

'As a warrior for the Empire, I've proven myself of little use. Instead, lieutenant, I've adopted a narrower goal – the aid of a single person, who protected me when there was no one else to do it.'

'We are peers, Franziskus. Honour me by referring to me as Jonas.'

'You spoke very eloquently to those townsfolk back there, Jonas.'

'You think me a silvertongue? A dissembler?'

'I wouldn't say that. But you look quickly into a man's heart and plumb there for ascendancy.'

Now Jonas chuckled. 'Your meaning eludes me, Franziskus.'

'You can tell I yearn for the respect of a man like you. A leader of soldiers. A hero of the black and yellow. So I'll warn you – the more I argue your cause, the more Angelika will resist. On my clumsy lips, any call to virtue or sacrifice seems absurdly naïve.'

'I suspect you've more influence over her than you know.'

'You haven't seen us together much.'

Jonas's voice dropped down into the conspiratorial registers. 'You aren't the first man to ever doubt himself, Franziskus. I might look to you like a great hero or somesuch, but this is my first command. And I tell you, I will not allow myself to fail. You agree that the enemy force – that which we cannot name – it must be vanquished, yes?'

'Without question.'

'You saw how unprotected that village was, from even a few stray marauders. If there's a second wave of enemies about to swarm down those mountains, and you have the power to stop them, then you must. Yes?'

'If I could, yes, I would.'

'Well, Franziskus, we can, together. With your friend's help. And if what you say is right, that you can't secure that help, well then you must do your bit to advise me. Yes?'

A vague nausea swept through the blond deserter. 'She won't do it. She'd sooner slash her own throat than follow an order. Nothing matters to her more than her freedom.'

'That will mean nothing if the Empire falls.'

'Here's what she'll say to that: that ever since it was founded, twenty-five hundred years ago, the Empire has been falling, and it's nowhere nearer to hitting the ground than it ever was.'

'She's wrong. Never have we been more besieged.'

'If there is a fact she does not wish to hear, she will not hear it. By the end of the argument, she may have you convinced you're wrong. That up is down, and the sun rises in the north each afternoon.'

'It would require a certain contrariness, to live as she does.'

Franziskus nodded vigorously. 'You don't know the half of it.'

'She loots graves for a living?'

'Battlefields only. She lives by a strict credo. Never does she rob from the living. Nor will she kill, except in self-defence.'

'That will pose us no difficulty. The moment you meet him, any Kurgan warrior will give you ample reason to kill him. How long has she plied this trade of hers?'

'I'm not sure. She was quite experienced when I met her, nearly two years ago now.'

'It can't be a lucrative profession.'

'You'd be surprised at the wealth soldiers carry with them.'

'You take a share of this money?'

'She has offered it but I refuse, always. Though I am still a little tainted: sometimes she pays for my lodging and food, with the gold she's earned.'

'She fritters away the rest on drink? On other amusements?'

'She's no wastrel.' Franziskus blurted the words a bit curtly. He took a breath, to tamp down his growing anger.

'I meant no offence. And surely it takes a kind of bravery, to do what she does. Sometimes the dead are less so than they at first appear.'

'Or they have angry relatives,' said Franziskus. 'I've begged and pleaded with her to stop, you know.' He looked to Jonas for a response, but the lieutenant simply waited for him to continue. 'And she's retiring, finally.'

'So you do hold sway over her, after all.'

'It's nothing I said. To that I can attest. But now she's left the Blackfire, and – she's already admitted it, the attempt to loot up here in Stirland was a foolish, greedy error. We were about to part ways. Jonas, you can't drag her off to war. I won't have her put in danger again, now that she's at last decided to live a quiet life.'

'You fear fate's cruelty?'

'The gods are too fond of irony. Now that she seeks safety, that's when they'll strike her down.'

'The gods are on our side, Franziskus.'

'Let her rest up, then go on her way.' Franziskus seized the lieutenant by the sleeve. 'I'll go in her place. I've learned my way around crags and forests. I implore you, Jonas, don't make her go with you.'

Jonas patted Franziskus's hand as he detached it from his arm. 'I'll ask her to come. I won't force her, I give you my word on that. If it's gold she craves, I can offer it.'

'She doesn't need any more–' Franziskus cut himself off.

'She has all the wealth she needs?'

'She has given up this life.' Franziskus's ears burned. He looked over at Angelika. She seemed to be stirring. He dashed to her side, then took a canteen from the horse's saddlebag to wet a cloth. He pressed it gently to her cheeks. Her eyes opened.

'I'm going to kill that halfling,' she said, and fell back into her wounded slumber.

HANDS CLASPED BEHIND his back, Curran hunched over the pile of rubble on Hochmoor's fortress hill, stubborn annoyance tightening his rounded features. Strands of Angelika's dark hair still clung to the cuffs of his shirt and to his perspiring palms. At Curran's side hovered his gaunt human friend.

'But Gundred,' Curran said to him, 'it only took you and Ingwold here half a week to move that garden wall from the old Hide property.' He hiked his thumb at a freckled young man, Gundred's cousin, who lingered nearby, eager to be assigned an important task.

Wind gusts seized smoke from the town's smouldering homes and pulled it like spun sugar into the sky above them.

'I think we should leave it,' Gundred said.

'Leave it? We can't leave it,' said Curran.

Gundred called back to Ingwold. 'How about you? Do you think we should leave it?'

Curran did not wait for Ingwold's opinion. 'Who knows what contagions his corpse will release as it rots? We must get it out of there and burn it. It is a thing of the enemy.'

'He may worship that dread force, but he is a man.'

'A man from the lands of madness. After all we've been through, do you wish a plague on us besides?'

Ingwold wandered closer. He kicked tentatively at a mortar chunk on the pile's edge. 'You don't think he could still be alive under there, do you?'

Curran grunted his exasperation. 'Of course not. If he was, he'd have crawled out from under there already. Wouldn't he?'

'I suppose,' Ingwold allowed.

Curran stalked over to a wheelbarrow some feet away from the pile, seizing a shovel and thrusting it into Ingwold's callused hands. Ingwold took the spade but made no move toward the heap of stones. Curran snorted contemptuously at him. Ingwold gestured feebly and thrust the point of the spade into the pile. He overturned one stone, then another and they tumbled down into the grass.

Ortak Nalgar erupted up through the rocks, mortar dust plastering his face and unfettered, shaggy hair. He snatched the shovel from Ingwold's hands and brained him with it. Terror locked Gundred's feet in place. The chieftain stepped carelessly over Ingwold's twitching body. Bellowing for help, Curran ran to his spear, which leaned against the fortress wall. Gundred collected himself and drew his knife. Ortak Nalgar clamped a hand over the gaunt man's wrist and snapped its bones, releasing the blade. Gundred tripped back as Nalgar stooped to claim it. The barbarian charged him, sweeping the knife before him.

Gundred felt his throat: wet blood gushed from a deep slit opened by Nalgar's wide swipe. The gaunt man fell to his knees. Nalgar left him to bleed and

turned his attention to the halfling. A chortle rattled
in his throat as Curran bolted at him. He rocked back
in his boots, bracing for the charge. The halfling's
spear hit the centre of Nalgar's breastplate, barely
swaying the much larger man.

'Curran,' a voice cried. A townsman peeked up over
the lip of the hill. Nalgar turned to look and without
further utterance, the man reversed himself and fled.

'Help me,' Curran keened.

Nalgar grabbed the spear haft to pull the halfling
toward him. Curran let go, turning to sprint for the
road. Nalgar pursued him, outpacing him without
effort. He tripped the fleeing halfling, bouncing him
like a ball across the grassy hilltop. Curran struggled
to right himself, but then the chieftain was on him.
Nalgar placed one wide hand between his legs and
another on his neck.

Groaning in gleeful exertion, he hoisted the squirming halfling up into the air, then brought his spine
down on the point of his armoured knee. Curran felt
himself instantly paralyzed; the barbarian tossed him
onto the ground to gasp for air. The last thing he saw,
before his fatal impalement, was his own spear in the
chieftain's hand, poised to pierce his throat.

Ortak Nalgar cast his eyes about for his great-axe.
When he did not see it, he strode confidently down
the hillside. It would be somewhere in this town. And
once he had recovered it, he would assemble for himself a new troop of raiders for a second assault on the
Empire. He would go to the mountains.

CHAPTER TEN

THE GEROLSBRUCH SWORDSMEN hiked out of the valley and into hillier terrain. As the high summer dusk filled the sky with pink and orange light, the unit passed a series of stone markers, some recently over-turned. They marked sheep pastures, explained one archer who knew the country. They trudged on. Angelika was still slumped over Jonas's horse; it made a hard ascent up ever-steeper slopes. Franziskus kept by her side, to catch her if she slipped from the saddle. A pulsing, organic sound buzzed up ahead.

Clearing a rise, they beheld clouds of blowflies, shining blue and green, swarming around the corpses of slain sheep. Their meat had rotted and was falling from exposed femurs and ribcages. The animals were two or three days dead. Further ahead lay a large wooden structure, partially burned: a sheep-herder's barn. Beside it stood a set of stone foundations, half-buried by wood ash – the remains of a home. A smaller hayloft, only lightly scorched, sat a few dozen yards away from the main structures. Fire-red sumacs, arrayed like a horseshoe, surrounded the enclosure on three sides.

Jonas conferred with Emil. He ordered his men to take the barn as their base, and to set up a perimeter including the hayloft. He returned to his horse. Angelika was awake and blinking, rubbing the back of her head with the heel of her palm. Franziskus stood by, to help her dismount. She slung herself down into the stirrup. Wavering only slightly, she stepped down onto the grassy ground. Franziskus went to her, to hold her up. Jonas moved to take up position on her other shoulder.

'We'll get you into that hayloft over there,' Jonas grunted. 'Get you some privacy, away from the men.'

'I'm fine,' Angelika muttered. She squirmed, but both the men kept a tight hold on her.

'You need to rest a bit more – then you'll be fine,' Franziskus said.

'What kind of a delicate blossom do you think I am?' Angelika twisted free of them, then pitched forward onto her knees. They came to help her but she waved them off. 'I've been awake for hours,' she said. 'What I need is to walk around for a while. And some food, if you have it.'

Jonas gestured to Emil, who barked out an order to the supply chief. He went ahead into the hayloft, with sausages, cheeses and a smallish cask of brandy. A swordsman laid a fraying blanket out on the straw-covered floor. Jonas, Angelika and Franziskus dug into the provisions in relative silence. Only after repeated invitations did the latter two accept the lieutenant's brandy. Angelika sipped gingerly, then rolled her eyes. 'My head isn't ready for this,' she said.

Emil knocked lightly on the loft's open doorframe and Jonas leapt up to hear him. They spoke softly; evidently, the men had found bodies in the barn. Jonas shook his head. 'Bury them out back, behind that grove of trees.'

He sat on the floor, placing his back against a support beam, eating nothing more. Angelika and Franziskus kept ravenously chewing.

'This is good food,' said Angelika.

'It isn't, but you're hungry. A shock can do that to you.' Jonas closed his eyes; for a moment, it seemed as if he'd nod off to sleep.

Angelika cocked her head charily. 'I suppose I owe you thanks for rescuing me from that tiny lunatic.'

'I suppose you do,' replied Jonas, eyes still shut.

Silence returned.

Angelika was the one to break it. 'Perhaps I was dreaming, but it seemed to me like the two of you were talking the whole way, like long-lost brothers.'

'We spoke for part of the way,' said Franziskus.

Jonas hunched forward. 'Franziskus and I were acquainting ourselves with one another, alone. I'm hoping he'll excuse himself, so that you and I can do the same.'

Franziskus remained in place.

'I owe you the courtesy of a chat,' said Angelika, 'but your rescue party has taken us in the wrong direction. I'm not going with you.'

Jonas smiled. 'Your candour is appreciated. However, you may be the last woman I see for a long time. You can't deny me a few pleasantries, can you?'

Angelika dragged herself over to a beam opposite Jonas's. 'You heard him,' she said to Franziskus. 'He'd like to flirt with me a while.'

Franziskus slowly stood. He stalked gradually out of the loft, taking care to step close to Jonas's feet on the way out.

'He's protective of you,' said Jonas, when he'd gone.

Now Angelika's eyes closed. 'Do you require a bodyguard? He'll soon be at a loose end.'

'It's a scout I need.'

'He might do a passable job of that. There's probably a warrant for desertion out on him. You could help him clear that up, reunite him with his family.'

'Your young friend is a deserter?'

'I'm telling you nothing you haven't already figured out on your own.'

'It is rather plain.'

'Then belay the gamesmanship. He needs your help. You need his. What could be more perfect?'

'I'll do all you ask for him – if you come with us.'

She swatted the air dismissively. 'That would repay his services, not mine.'

He positioned himself next to her. She let him. 'What fee do you desire?'

'I'm not for hire.'

'Franziskus says you don't like taking orders.'

'Who does?'

'Most men, as a matter of fact, but let's not distract ourselves with philosophy.' He held up his brandy cup and made a toasting motion.

Angelika inserted a pause, then mirrored his gesture.

'I feel sorry for him,' he said.

'Who? Franziskus?'

'He loves you.'

'I, too, feel sorry for anyone in love with me.'

'You can't be that horrid, can you?'

'I most certainly can.'

'His chances are nil, then?'

'Did he promise to talk me into going with you, if
you pitched woo for him?'

'He told me I'd never convince you.'

'He's right on that count.'

'He's glad you're giving up your unwomanly ways, to
live in a manner more fitting to your sex.'

Angelika sat up. 'He said that?'

'Ah. I've committed a gaffe. Please consider that I have
paraphrased him liberally.'

'What else did he say?'

'You can't blame him if he's a mite possessive.'

'I suppose you're the same way.'

Jonas laughed. 'No, the opposite.'

'You flee from women?'

'Only afterwards.'

'My policy also. Avoid romantic entanglements.'

'No wedding ring will yoke you?'

'A woman should buy her own ring, that's my theory.'

'Is that so?' Jonas appeared lost in thought for a
moment.

Angelika leaned forward to take more brandy. This
time she filled her cup near to the top, and drank
heartily from it. 'I can't believe Franziskus came out and
said that.'

'Perhaps I'm exaggerating.'

'He didn't say he loved me.'

'No, but it's plain after half a minute, isn't it?'

'I try to ignore it.'

'You prefer a fellow with a bit more meat on him, and a few more years.'

'Not too much more of either.'

'Most of all, you prefer a man who's about to depart for a long journey.' He placed his hand on her knee.

She let it lie there. 'One I'm not going on.'

'Me, I like a sharp-edged woman. You know, a spot of trouble.'

She placed her hand on his. 'Everybody makes a foolish mistake now and then.'

FRANZISKUS SAT AMONG the men of Jonas's unit, in the barn as they drank well-watered grog and chewed on hardtack. The Gerolsbruchers laughed and told bawdy jokes, each one filthier than its predecessor. One of the men suffered an epic bout of flatulence and his fellows guffawed until tears filled the creases of their cheeks. They threw dice and laid copper-penny bets. The archers took seats apart from the swordsmen, muttering amongst themselves. The stragglers from other regiments sat even further away. Emil leaned himself in a distant corner, cataloguing the scene through half-open eyes.

Franziskus thought he perhaps ought to be doing the same, but another matter occupied his mind. He couldn't believe it. All that time Jonas had been prying information from him, and it hadn't been for a noble purpose at all. It wasn't about saving the Empire, or receiving a gift from Sigmar, or requiring a scout for his regiment. His plans for Angelika were of the most selfish, basest kind. And Franziskus had been entirely taken in.

He left the barn. The situation demanded the most delicate circumspection. Though resistant to his advice in general, Angelika would not tolerate even the tiniest intervention in her amatory activities. Yet, if his vow was to protect her, the attentions of this snake – this wolf – were surely as ripe a danger as a pit trap or goblin nest. She'd recently been hit in the head. By definition, then, she was in no shape to make decisions, especially not of a delicate nature.

Franziskus paced outside the barn, hoping to summon the proper argument, or simply a credible diversion to pry the two of them apart.

Watchers posted by Emil followed his movements.

He forced himself to calm down. He was aware that he wore his emotions like an emblazoned tunic, rendering them all too clear to casual observers. If he hoped to be successful, he would have to conceal his feelings behind a hard and neutral mask – the way Angelika did.

He required a pretence. A reason to casually appear. To split them up, or merely to interpose himself. Without giving himself away. Then later he could think of the right thing to say to Angelika, once they were apart. Franziskus thought. And thought, until perspiration soaked his collar.

To blazes with it, he thought. That was his problem – he thought too long, and never acted. He would go to them, and then something appropriate would pop to mind. As would occur for any true man of action.

No, wait. He would pretend to be heading out back, to – well, to attend to bodily needs, of course. And he would simply walk past them, and see.

Franziskus walked past the open doorway and saw Jonas and Angelika locked in an embrace.

Shaking sweat-drenched locks, he stomped away from the buildings.

A rustling arose in the high bushes a few yards away. He glimpsed a spearhead.

Not again! 'Intruders!' he cried. 'Intruders!'

CHAPTER ELEVEN

TWO SMALL FIGURES wriggled from the bushes at Franziskus as he drew his sabre. They hit his legs, giving a clear chance to bring his sword slashing down into either attacker's spine, but instinct told him not to do it. One of the tiny men wormed his way behind Franziskus's right leg; the other pushed, to trip him. Franziskus shifted his weight, to throw them off, but misjudged and the three of them plummeted to the ground in a thicket of battling limbs.

Soldiers ran from the barn, the light of swinging lanterns playing wildly over them. A third figure emerged from the bushes, pulling and tugging at the two who'd positioned themselves on Franziskus's chest and legs. 'No, no,' he shouted. 'That's Franziskus!'

Tired of playing patsy, Franziskus got his fingers around the throat of the halfling sitting on his chest.

Lantern light briefly filled his face but Franziskus did not recognise his gurgling assailant. 'Will you get off me?' he demanded. The halfling, though limited by the choking grip on his windpipe, nodded and rolled away. Franziskus kicked at the other attacker, bringing his boot heel into solid contact with a halfling shoulder. Rassau's swordsmen reached them, pulling the halflings to their feet and holding them fast. They fruitlessly kicked and squirmed.

The unimpeded halfling stepped into the light, palms up in surrender. It was Filch. He grinned, as if in expectation of a hearty welcome. 'We've come to join you.'

Franziskus helped himself to a soldier's lantern and held it to his two captured fellows. 'Who is *we*?' he enquired. He saw Emil joining the crowd from the barn, and both Angelika and Jonas emerging from the hayloft, but, as the aggrieved party, felt he had standing to lead the interrogation.

Filch attempted to sidle his way, but found himself restrained by a pair of Gerolsbruch sabres across his chest. Through his feathery brows a sense of concern belatedly flickered. 'You know we've come to join you, don't you? It was his speech that told us to come. We want to fight for our people. Go the mountains with you.'

'Release them,' Jonas commanded.

The captured halflings brushed daintily at their calf-skin coat-sleeves. One still bore the red imprints of Franziskus's fingers on his throat: at a full four feet, he stood a few inches taller than the average halfling. 'This is Bodo,' Filch announced. Bodo's face was bony and hard, lacking the wreathing of fat typical of his food-fond race. His eyes were wet with bottled fury. 'You said we'd be well-greeted here,' he said to Filch, accusingly.

'You should have approached us openly, then,' Franziskus said, smacking dirt from his trousers.

'And this is my other friend, Merwin,' Filch said. Merwin's gaze shot around the encampment; his thick, shoeless feet jittered anxiously beneath him. Beside the broad-shouldered Bodo and slender Filch, Merwin seemed an altogether average exemplar of his kind: nearly four feet tall, with a rounded face and a roll of fat shelved over the rope-belt that held up his short-legged trousers. Of the three, it was Merwin, with veiny nose and florid cheeks, whose features most clearly relected his people's reputation as a race of prodigious drinkers. An unmistakeable whiff of spirits clouded the air around him.

'As Filch has said, we have come to fight with you,' said Bodo. Implicit in his tone was a demand for an apology. He held himself more like a miniature man than the typical hunched and furtive halfling.

'You're right,' Filch said to Franziskus, 'we should have better announced our coming. But we wasn't sure entirely that you were who you are, so we thought it best to have ourselves a recce first. You understand – in case you was more barbarians.'

Jonas took a moment to unravel this statement, then posed a question to Franziskus: 'Are you satisfied by this explanation?'

'No harm has been done,' said Franziskus.

Jonas approached his new recruits, his demeanour brightening. 'So it was my words that stirred you to follow us?'

Bodo answered: 'One thing we have learned today. The fight will not pass our village by. Let us then take it to our foes.'

'You move me, halfling friends.' Jonas held out his hand for each of the new arrivals to clasp in turn. 'We need every sword, every bow, every spear. I welcome you to our brave and blooded company.'

'I don't suppose,' interjected Angelika, 'that any of you happens to be a seasoned mountaineer?'

They shook their heads in sorry unison.

'We are farmers,' said Bodo. 'Not warriors, nor scavengers.'

Angelika accepted the insult unblinkingly. She took note of Emil's reaction: he crossed his arms, as if unconvinced of the halflings' usefulness.

'Though Bodo's actually a butcher,' said Filch. 'Not to undercut your point, you understand, Bodo.'

Jonas hunched down to speak to him. 'Your brother did not choose to come with you?'

Filch dropped his ratty face downwards. 'Curran's dead. Just like Deely.'

'How so?'

'That barbarian general, chieftain, whoever he was – the one you left under the pile of stones. Well, he weren't dead after all. Hours later he came out from under there and killed three more. Including my brother. At least him and Deely will go together to the world beyond. Protect each other along the way.' Filch sniffled and rubbed at his nose.

Jonas reached into an inside coat pocket to give the tiny man a handkerchief. 'I mourn with you, my friend. And I will see to it you have your chance to avenge them.'

Filch loudly blew his nose. 'Yes. That's what we want. To make those Chaos scum pay for what they did to us. For no reason. We never attacked them. Well, we'll show them, won't we, lieutenant?'

'That we will, Filch.'

Angelika surveyed the soldiers. Though they tried to camouflage it, the little man's grief moved them.

'Tell me, Filch,' asked Jonas, 'which way did the Kurgan chieftain go?'

'He came this way. To the north.'

Jonas turned to his men. 'He's headed the same place we are.' Then back to Filch and his companions: 'You've brought good bedding with you, I hope.'

Filch nodded.

'And food?'

'How could we not?' declared Merwin. The halflings seemed shocked by the suggestion.

Jonas caught himself before patting Merwin's tousled head. 'Tonight that barn shall be our barracks. Emil will get you squared away.'

The halflings gathered around the sergeant, who led them to the barn. The other soldiers drifted after them.

This left Jonas, Angelika and Franziskus.

Franziskus hiked a thumb toward the barn. 'Should I...?'

Angelika's hand snaked to Jonas's shoulder. 'Perhaps you should.'

Franziskus felt a punch to the gut greater than any halfling could deliver. 'Yes well then,' he said, remaining in place.

Angelika turned; Jonas followed. 'Goodnight, Franziskus.'

He watched them stroll back to the hayloft.

'Are you sure...?' he called after them, but his voice did not carry. Shoulders sagging, he shuffled back along the path to the barn. He kicked at a rock. It turned out to be more firmly lodged in the earth than it looked; pain radiated out from his toes and into his foot. The sensation improved matters, somehow.

He reached the doorway of the barn. Emil hovered there. He too, looked unhappily at the hayloft doorway. Franziskus turned back to see Jonas hanging his cloak up over it. The sergeant's glance invited no conversation, so Franziskus scouted for a spot inside the barn. The halflings had installed themselves in a corner, to covertly swig from a pewter flask. For every sip Bodo took, Filch had a gulp and Merwin drank twice that much again. The soldiers ignored them, returning to their dicing and their crude jokes.

Franziskus made it a point not to hear the men's jests. He could tell from their sniggering tone that they concerned their commander's obvious trysting. Surely this was a violation of good discipline, to behave this way in front of one's men. Franziskus would not have done so, in his place. But then, Franziskus would never be in his place, because he had deserted – to be with Angelika.

He sat down near the halflings. Filch, at least, seemed happy to see him.

JONAS FINISHED PINNING up his cloak and turned to Angelika. She paced around him like a fencer alert for an opening. 'This won't be a discipline problem?' she asked.

His laugh was uncertain. 'I don't follow you.'

'With the men. You're taking a bit of license in front of them, aren't you?'

He stopped to lean against a timber support beam. 'The men and I understand one another.'

'They mustn't think I belong to the company, as a prize to be passed around.'

He came toward her, taking her into his embrace. 'Angelika, you are my prize alone.'

She slipped from his arms. 'Oh no. Whatever we do together, it will not make me yours. Understand that, or go no further.' But she said it with a predatory gleam.

He untied the lace that kept closed the collar of his tunic. 'I am accustomed to the opposite. In my circles, a woman demands mutual possession before so much as a kiss is exchanged.'

'I am not the women you know.'

He sat on a hay bale and fought to ease his boot off. 'None of them would be any use, where we're going.'

'You still think I'm going with you.' She sat on the bale, behind him. She kissed his neck. 'You're fetching, not irresistible.'

He turned to reciprocate but before he could return her kiss, she'd resumed her prowl. 'I won't cage you, Angelika.'

'So you understand, then.'

'Yes, I do.'

'What do you understand?'

'Um...'

She straddled him. 'That this means nothing, other than what it is. It is only tonight.'

He bit her ear. 'Yes,' he said. 'This means nothing.'

* * *

JONAS SAT UP on his elbows. The lamp still faintly flickered. He'd convinced her to leave it burning. She looked more lovely in its light, and he wanted to look at her, he'd said. It was not untrue: he paused to again admire her captivating surfaces. The perfect paleness of her skin. The sharp and unyielding curve of her shoulder beneath the blanket. If the woman he married was half as alluring as her, he'd count himself a fortunate man.

It had taken Angelika at least an hour to doze off. To stave off sleep for himself, he'd dug his fingernails into his palms, every time he'd felt himself drifting. He sat and watched her for a good long time. She'd fallen deeply into slumber. He congratulated himself for successfully wearing her out. He, too, was exhausted, but had a mission to complete.

Slowly he shifted himself into a sitting position. That was one good thing about sleeping in a floorless building: there were no boards to creak when you moved. He crept over to her ball of passionately discarded clothing. There was a leather purse on her belt. As he had expected, it contained nothing.

From what Franziskus had told him, she'd been scavenging for years, then had decided to retire. She had to have some way of transporting her years of earnings out of the Blackfire. There would obviously be a valuable object on her, small enough to conceal from casual eyes. She would not be so stupid as to keep it in her purse. It wasn't a jewel she wore on her person; he'd pored over every inch of her. There had to be a secret pocket. He took her leggings in his hands and methodically searched them with his fingers. Nothing. Next, her tunic.

He found it. A round band and a stone: a ring. He took it from its pocket and held it up to the light. A ruby. Quickly he stashed it under a bale of straw. Later he'd transfer it to a better hiding spot.

He laid himself down next to her, but the flush of his success kept sleep away. He huddled in next to her pale, warm body, and breathed as she did.

CHAPTER TWELVE

A FAMILIAR, AWAKENING hand lightly pressed itself against Franziskus's shoulder. Months ago, a touch like this would have jolted him into consciousness. He would have cried out, thrashing his arms and legs. Now Angelika had him well-trained: he snapped silently to alertness, already reaching for his sabre. He saw her looming over him. He remembered where he was, and why: the barn, the Gerolsbruch Swordsmen, the halflings. The capture, the escape, the journey north.

The light of early morning crept diffusely into the barn: soldiers, scattered across its floor, snored and tossed. The halflings snoozed on either side of him. Filch's sleeping face was a picture of forgetful contentment.

Angelika placed a silencing finger across her lips. Franziskus nodded. There would be no goodbyes.

This morning, he was more than ready to forgive her habitual unsociability. He folded and tied his bedroll, then gathered up his pack. Angelika held out a hand for him; the leather of his boots issued only a few cursory creaks as he rose to his feet. The two of them padded painstakingly to the exit, through a maze of sprawled and sleeping bodies.

On a stool outside the doorway, a sentry dozed. His insignia identified him as one of the spares, a man separated from another unit.

They stepped across the threshold and there stood Emil, arms folded.

The sergeant beckoned Angelika closer. 'Leaving?' he asked.

She nodded. Though she gave no outward sign of it, Franziskus could tell she was poised to run.

'Good,' Emil said. With a gesture, he bade them to follow him as he trudged toward the perimeter. There, alert guardsmen patrolled. They snapped to attention as Emil came near; under his breath, he told them to stand down.

'The lieutenant won't be pleased,' Franziskus said.

'I've received no orders to hold you against your will,' replied the sergeant, his expression closed and neutral.

Franziskus, who had witnessed the severity of certain officers in the past, wanted greater assurance that Emil was not exposing himself to punishment. Angelika, however, kept moving and was soon a dozen yards ahead of him. Franziskus waved an awkward farewell to the sergeant, and, when the stoic man did not react, flushed with mortification at the stupidity of the gesture. He dashed to catch up with

Angelika, who moved gracefully down the well-grazed hillside, bouncing from point to point. Franziskus stumbled over rocks and nearly caught his toe in an exposed root, but reached her side nonetheless. When they reached the bottom of the hill, Angelika scanned for a destination, choosing a forest of straight-trunked pines positioned vaguely to the north-west.

Franziskus could not restrain himself. 'You left the lieutenant to his slumbers?'

'He needed the rest.' The words coiled with warning.

They walked to the trees.

'You're welcome to stay with him if you like,' she said, as they stepped into the cooler air of the forest. Its bed of dried brown needles was dotted with dew. 'I figured you'd want me to fetch you before I left.'

'Thank you.'

'Though he is prepared to aid you with your desertion problem. If you go back, and serve with his company as they go about their mad errand, he'll vouch for you. See to it that any warrants against you are dropped.'

'I might do that, if I knew you were safe.'

'I have always been safe.'

He ducked a low branch. 'Is that so?'

Angelika's pace increased. 'What does that mean?'

Franziskus shrugged, though he was behind her and she could not see the gesture. 'Nothing.'

'No, no, go ahead. I know what you're going to say. Say it. You're scandalised. Aren't you?'

'You behave as you desire. What I think is of no relevance.'

'That's more than true, but still you're looking down your nose at me. Aren't you?'

'I wish to protect you, that's all.'

She turned on him. 'I don't need you to be my chastity belt.'

Franziskus stepped back. 'It's just – you are untrusting, Angelika, and in your world, in these circumstances, that is – It is good and necessary. Yet when – when…'

'When what?'

'When you find a man who – ah…'

Hands on hips, she let him squirm.

Franziskus started again. 'When a man seems attractive to you, suddenly you toss aside all risk and doubt and… Who knows what he could have done to you?'

Her knife was in her hand. She twisted it in the air. 'Any man who's ever taken liberties with me has paid a price in blood.'

Franziskus held his hands up. He was mostly certain she'd drawn the dagger for emphasis only.

'You are not my father, Franziskus, and not my priest. I'll take no more of your disapproval.'

'I did not mean to offend you.'

'No, you couldn't help it.'

'I am sorry.' Franziskus plunged onward into the forest, in the direction she'd been heading.

She was at his heels. 'I've disappointed you. You think me some kind of strumpet.'

Heat welled up in Franziskus's face and he sped up, not wanting her to see it. 'I did not use that word.'

She pursued him. 'What word would you use, Franziskus? Harlot? Tart? Something worse?'

'Never any of them.'

'This may startle you, Franziskus, but I am not the first woman who has ever desired a man, and had him, merely for the satisfaction of it.'

'Please, I am sorry. Let's speak no more of this.'

'He struck me as handsome. Compelling. I liked his eyes, and the bones of his face. It has been months since I felt a man's touch–'

'Please, Angelika–'

'–months since I felt a pair of lips against my own. And yesterday I was almost executed. You may not know it from the books you grew up reading, but there's no aphrodisiac like the nearness of death.' She reached him, clamping her hand onto his shoulder. To keep going, he'd have to fight her. 'What of it? What harm does it do you?'

Franziskus turned to face her. He had an answer, but could not give it. Instead he said, 'I find your honesty difficult.'

'No man judges me,' she said.

'I am sorry,' he said, yet again.

Finches trilled in the high branches above them. Franziskus looked up. 'Those are the first birds I've heard in days that weren't screaming for carrion.'

Angelika let the tension fall from her shoulders. She sheathed her knife. 'Must be a high wind in here. Your eyes are wet.'

'Yes. A high wind.'

'You should give some thought to it,' she said. 'Before we go much further. Go back to the lieutenant. He doesn't think you're as good as me–'

'And I'm not.'

'And you're not, but you'll do for what he needs. Go be a soldier, like your family wanted for you. Get your good name back. I am done, Franziskus, with all my wandering. I am out of danger.'

'Everyone's in danger, with Chaos running wild in the heart of the Empire.'

'All the more reason for you to go and fight it, then. We should part now, where it will do you some good. You have been a help to me, Franziskus. Now help yourself.'

'Not until I know you're safe.

'I'll make a vow to you, Franziskus. I will be safe. I'll go find my little farmhouse somewhere, in a corner of the Empire far too boring for any barbarians or Chaos worshippers to bother with. I'll find a place to sell my ring and–'

She patted the secret pocket.

There was nothing there. The ring was gone.

She doubled over. She broke out in a sweat. She swore, using every obscene word in Reikspiel, starting with the worst ones, the compound words, and working her way down to the borderline crudities. She repeated the ripest ones, then dipped into her reserves of Bretonnian and Tilean profanity.

'It's gone.' Angelika wheeled, retracing her steps.

'When was the last time you had it?'

'I check it every – I don't know.'

'Did you check it before you left Jonas?'

'Yes. No. No, I didn't. I – I'd – how could I have been so stupid?' She punched a tree and winced in pain. Franziskus winced with her. 'For what, one day's time, it was out of my mind. First we were captured, then the trial, the fight, then I was unconscious, then with Jonas–' She patted the pocket a third time, a fourth: it was, of course, still empty. 'How could I have been so incredibly stupid?' Her hands went to her temples. 'That's – that's everything. All I've worked for. Five years. In one little object. A hundred times I've risked my life for the gold in that ring. I've been punched, kicked, frozen, stabbed, burnt by Chaos magic, interrogated, imprisoned, terrified…'

Not to mention killed and miraculously brought back to life, thought Franziskus. But she hated to be reminded of that particular incident, and he wouldn't dare mention it now.

'I've lost it,' she muttered. 'I can't believe… I've lost it.' She reversed course, back to the sheep farm. 'Got to retrace my…'

Another question Franziskus dared not ask: could Jonas have it?

'Five years,' Angelika said. 'Five years of my life. My retirement. Everything.'

'A RING?' ASKED Jonas. He stroked his chin thoughtfully, like an actor in a stage play. He stood a few feet from his men as they prepared themselves for muster. They'd emerged from the barn to check packs, inspect belts and scabbards, and rub the road from their boots. Archers counted arrows. Swordsmen examined blades for hints of corrosion. The halflings sat on a blanket to nibble cheese curds and a salad of fragrant mosses, in a dressing of pepper and malt. Emil walked among the men, but also observed the colloquy between his commander and the two scavengers.

'A ruby ring,' said Angelika. She'd already scoured the hayloft.

'If I'd seen it,' said Jonas, 'I'd have noticed it.'

'What about the men?' asked Franziskus.

'I'll have Emil make an announcement. If one of them has found it, he'll turn it over.'

'No,' said Angelika. 'Not yet.' It was too obviously valuable an item; no infantryman halfway in possession of his faculties would voluntarily give it over. An announcement would get them hunting for it in one another's packs, clouding the matter completely. If a soldier had the ring, she'd find it by herself.

'When was the last time you're sure you had it?' Jonas asked.

The question already made her teeth grind together. He did not mean to remind her of her own stupidity, but reminded she was. 'Before I was captured. Before Hochmoor.'

'In the fight with the chieftain – you fell onto him.'

'Yes?'

Jonas squinted as if in recollection. 'Right after that, when the barbarian righted himself. I saw him stoop to pick up some object on the ground. Perhaps I'm imagining it, in retrospect, but I'd swear there was a glint from the sun. In the tumult of battle, I paid no further heed to it – I thought he'd dropped a dagger, perhaps. What if the big Kurgan has your ring?'

Why, thought Franziskus, that would be extraordinarily convenient for you, wouldn't it?

Angelika contemplated the sturdy angles of the lieutenant's handsome, unyielding face. 'You saw the chieftain take my ring.'

Jonas shook his head. 'I cannot swear to that. I know I saw him stoop down. I believe he snatched up some item from the grass – but, bear in mind, I saw it for an instant only. Just as likely, he'd lost his balance, and was only righting himself.'

'But you think you saw a glint.'

Jonas nodded. 'I think I saw it.'

'You think you saw the ring, or a glint?'

'A glint, which might have been a ring.'

Franziskus cleared his throat but she paid him no heed.

'I saw it for barely a moment,' said Jonas. 'If I told you I was sure, I'd be lying.'

'And you think the big Kurgan has it?'

Jonas shrugged. 'I suggest it only as a possibility.'

'You saw a glint in his hand, though? Right after I knocked into him?'

'I only say perhaps I saw it.'

Angelika chewed on her lip. 'Then I'm coming with you.'

'Angelika,' Franziskus exclaimed.

Jonas appeared to be surprised. 'Don't misunderstand me, Angelika. I believe we need you on this mission. But come to save our homeland. Do not do it only to recover your property.'

'Do you want me or not?'

'Yes, but, Angelika... Yes, Filch says the chieftain's headed up to the mountains, too. But that's a big territory. I don't fancy our odds of running into him again.'

'If he's got my ring, I'll find him.'

'But we do not go to seek him. We go to prevent all his kind from invading in a second wave.'

'Our aims are not incompatible.'

'If it comes to a choice, Angelika, you must subordinate your goal to the needs of the whole.'

'If it comes to a choice, you'll avoid telling me what I must and must not do.' She caressed the side of his face, lingering to cup her hands around his ear. The gesture was not entirely affectionate.

Jonas reddened and pulled back. Emil, and some of the men, had seen her do it. He straightened his shoulders and backbone, unfolding himself to his full height. 'One thing you must not do, Angelika, is diminish me in the eyes of my men.'

Angelika cocked her head. 'Fine by me, so long as you don't expect any bowing and scraping. We're partners, Jonas. I am not signing on as one of your men.'

The flush in his cheeks intensified. 'I would never confuse you for such.'

Franziskus felt a sudden and inappropriate sympathy for the lieutenant. More than once, Angelika had flummoxed him into a similar state. This newfound solidarity did not prevent him from boldly hooking his hand into the crook of Angelika's elbow and pulling her aside. Perhaps unable to dumbfound more than one young Stirlander at a time, she followed with minimal resistance. He stopped after a quick march of three dozen yards or so.

'You don't believe his story, do you?' Franziskus said.

'Much is possible, but few things are likely.'

'Which answer is that?'

'Even if we don't believe him, he must think we do.'

'What on earth for?'

'Maybe that war chieftain did take the ring. If he didn't, who did?'

'He did.'

'I'm not going up into those mountains to get close to that barbarian war chieftain. I could happily live the rest of my days without coming within a mile of that monster again, please and thank you. If I'm to get that ring back, Jonas must think we've swallowed his story, bones and all. So we mustn't be seen in anxious conference.' Adopting a casual stride, she meandered after the marching soldiers. She veered slightly, so she and Franziskus could remain out of earshot.

'Acting as if we trust his tale will be difficult. Now that I've had time to mull it, it seems ridiculous.'

'Yet you believed it as he said it.'

'Oddly, yes.'

'It was the skill of the presentation. Making a suggestion we wished to hear, then making it seem all the more credible by backing away from it when I pressed him.'

'And he thinks we'll keep on believing?'

'A liar is his own best audience.'

Jonas looked back to see where she was. She waved at him. Franziskus saw her mouth work itself into a peculiar shape, recognising it only belatedly as her version of a friendly smile.

'I will get that ring back,' she said, out of the side of her falsely grinning mouth.

CHAPTER THIRTEEN

THE GEROLSBRUCH SWORDSMEN marched to the mountains. Emil estimated that they'd reach the mountains in two days. 'Three and a half,' Angelika told Franziskus, under her breath. 'And then only the foothills. Almost a week till we're deep in the mountains proper.'

As they marched, a pattern formed within the column. At its head rode Jonas. In disciplined formation behind him tromped his swordsmen. Behind them, with a notable dip in spirit, the archers trekked. The column then grew increasingly wayward, as the stragglers inducted from other companies, and then the halflings, brought up the rear. Angelika and Franziskus walked with the halflings, out of sympathy and for lack of a likelier rank to trudge in. Emil spent much of his time at the column's head, with his lieutenant, but periodically rode back to herd the strays and archers back into line. The craggy sergeant looked through Angelika and Franziskus as if they were sheets of glass.

Franziskus found himself both offended by Emil's attitude, and apologetic for it. 'We won't be needed till the mountains,' he said to Angelika, after an especially pointed snubbing.

'Good,' said Angelika.

The first morning passed slowly by. Emil's chosen route avoided roads, taking the company through fallow fields and empty pastures. Patches of forested land grew more frequent, but these were kept at bay, too, to deprive the enemy of cover for ambush. The soldiers passed no settlements, and were therefore spared the sight of burnt-out buildings, or the strewn corpses of slaughtered farmers. That first morning, they saw not a single indication of the war raging throughout the Empire. It was as if they'd marched together into a happy memory of the past.

The sun shone every so often through gaps in a cloudy sky, sending down sharp beams of golden light to brighten Stirland's green and rolling ridges. They heard crickets and beetles; they saw no creature larger than a sparrow. Wild flowers bloomed beneath them: regal gentians, trumpeting primroses, and lacy bell-orchids all laid down in meek surrender to the soldiers' treading boots.

Emil rode up beside Jonas and paced him, in silence.

'There is something you wish to say to me,' Jonas observed, in a tone both mild and premeditated.

Emil denied it.

'Come now,' said Jonas.

'Nothing a sergeant ought to say to his lieutenant.'

'That's a womanly tactic, sergeant. Don't make me drag it out of you.'

'It goes against good order, to have the woman with us.'

'She'll prove her worth. You'll see.'

Emil harrumphed.

'This will not be a fight of protocols and formations, Emil.'

'The best officers know how common soldiers think.'

'We'll all have to change our thinking before this is through.'

'I'll say no more, then.'

'No, Emil, go ahead. Out with it.'

'Having her along, it would be unwise even if you hadn't roistered with her.'

'A charming choice of words, sergeant.'

'A footman expects that many privileges denied to him will be claimed by his commanders. But a woman is not a fine brandy or a thicker, drier bunk. Men are men, lieutenant.'

'The soldiers take their cues from you,' Jonas said. 'Show acceptance toward her, and they'll do the same.'

A fly buzzed at Emil's face. He grimaced at it, then swiped it stolidly away.

An hour later they arrived at a fast and narrow stream. Emil nodded to a drum-corporal who tapped out a blistering roll on his drumhead, calling the column to halt.

Angelika drew back, balling up her fists. The drumbeat echoed from ridge to hill and beyond. As the men broke from their formation, she loped up to Jonas. He blinked in apparent annoyance at her approach.

'Better switch to hand signals from now on.'

'What?' asked Jonas.

'The drum. You want every frothing Kurg and goat-headed beastman within ten miles to come lumbering down on us?'

Half a dozen heads turned their way. They belonged to swordsmen, refreshing their canteens in the stream's icy water.

Jonas spoke through shuttered teeth. 'Speak to me more deferentially,' he said.

'I defer to no one. Don't take it personally.' She'd lowered her voice a notch or two.

'The men are watching.'

'I don't care if Sigmar Himself is sitting over there on a silver stool, Jonas. We made quite the opposite arrangement. I'll treat you with the respect due an equal partner. No less, no more.'

Jonas painfully smiled, wrapped his arm around her shoulder, and led her several paces from any of his men. 'Then we must amend our arrangement, or neither of us will achieve our ends.'

'Why do you want me here?'

'To be a good scout.'

'You want me for my knowledge and advice. Maybe none of the enemy heard us this time, but if your man keeps banging that drum, they certainly will.'

'All I ask is that you protect my authority as well as my life.'

'Where we're going, survival depends on silence and stealthy movement.'

'An officer's survival, and that of his men, depends on the preservation of his authority.'

'I suppose that's true, but if I do have something to tell you, I may need to say it quickly, without taking half an hour to shuffle my feet and tug at my fringe.'

'I don't care if you think of me as your superior. I'm merely asking you to pretend.'

Angelika shook her head. 'I don't defer, and I won't lie.'

'Think of it as merely playing a role, Angelika.'

'It's deception. We are partners, and I won't pretend otherwise.'

Jonas walked away from her. 'Matters such as this – minor matters, to drum or not to drum – take them to Emil. Trouble me only when you have something to tell me, and need to say it quickly.'

Angelika stalked back to Franziskus, who knelt over the riverbank, filling clay jugs of water for the halflings, who clustered around him. Evidently they were concerned about falling into the stream, and had cajoled the soft-hearted Stirlander into doing their chores. Each had brought with him a pair of heavy clay jugs, suitable for the watering of a stable's worth of horses. These would prove a hindrance when they reached the mountains, but Angelika had dispensed enough unwanted advice for one rest stop.

As soon as he saw her, Franziskus asked her what was wrong.

'You're right,' she said. 'We're doomed.' She conveyed the general drift of her discussion with the lieutenant.

'I see,' said Franziskus. 'And you did not bring this up with Emil, as he asked?'

'Our deal is not with the sergeant.'

Franziskus heaved the last of the halfling jugs up onto the reedy riverbank. Brushing mud from his trousers, he sought out the sergeant. As he approached, Franziskus felt himself impaled on a lance of the veteran's disfavour. If he had returned from his unit's debacle in the Blackfire, to accept assignment to a new company, Franziskus would still be an officer, the unquestioned superior of a man like this. Now he was an outlaw, a crawling, worthless creature, fully deserving of a sergeant's contempt. His heartbeat sped. Emil made him speak first.

'A question has arisen,' he said.

'Has it?'

'The peal of the drum. For all intents and purposes, we now enter enemy territory. We must presume ourselves to be outmanned, and the enemy to lurk behind every tree and rock.'

'I see. Except when already engaged, orders must be given by hand signal.'

Franziskus nodded.

'This was the subject of discussion just now, between my commander and your... confederate?'

'Ah, yes.' Franziskus fought the urge to adjust his coat collar. He lost. 'I think... In future, I believe it will be best if Angelika conveys advice to me, and I, to you. Do you agree?'

Emil nodded.

'Well, ah – good, then,' replied Franziskus, moving guardedly away. He skirted a pair of swordsmen, one young and tall, the other older and squat, who were engaged in some great discussion. The young one saw Franziskus and called him over.

'You can't see it, Cassel, because you're old,' he said, continuing his argument with the squat one. 'Your heart's curdled. You don't think like a young man, like I do.'

'Pfah!' said Cassel.

'You are young like me,' the tall one told Franziskus. 'You explain to Cassel here how we think. What a young man feels towards a woman.'

'What?' asked Franziskus.

'It's little wonder you confuse others, Rappe,' said Cassel, 'as you are very confused yourself.' He turned to Franziskus. 'Excuse this poor benighted pup here. I have shared with him a fundamental truth, and he wishes to evade it.'

'Truth,' scoffed Rappe.

'Yes, truth. That woman is the natural enemy of man, much more powerful than our poor sex. And that man's only weapon against her is deception.'

'He says I must learn to lie to my girl,' Rappe explained.

'Yes, train yourself now, while she's young, too, and not yet reached the height of her powers.'

'But you have not seen her. She is so beautiful. I don't need to lie to her. With her in my bed, I've no need to prowl anywhere else.'

'You're a man of the world,' Cassel told Franziskus.

'You misjudge my character,' Franziskus replied.

'Yes, tell him,' said Cassel, 'how quickly it will change. I've six women, a child by each, and there's not a one of them who isn't precious respite from the others.'

'Each child is a girl child, isn't that so, Cassel?'

'So what of it, Rappe?'

'You'll be telling me next they're the enemy, too.'

'I dream at night they find each other, form an implacable band, and hound me through the streets,' said Cassel. 'Put up to it by their mothers, I might add. But that is neither here nor there.'

It took Franziskus nearly an hour to extricate himself from the conversation. Minutes later, Emil gathered the men, telling them that formation orders previously communicated by bugle call would now be given with signals. Corporals would be required to remain on constant alert for new orders from the head of the column. This new protocol established, the marchers reconstituted themselves and continued the journey north.

Not long afterwards, a heavy clomping resounded from the eastern horizon, which lay only a half mile or so ahead of the company, on a rocky ridgeline. Emil's hand shot up; down the line, the arms of corporals flagged sharply upwards, repeating his signalled orders. The men ran forward, forming themselves into ranks of ten. Swordsmen crouched down, to allow archers to fire over them. The strays at the rear of the column had to jostle in between the last line of sabres and the first of bow-men; clearly, an error had been made in the relative arrangement of the three forces.

Angelika hit the dirt, lying flat against a gently grading patch of red and violet flowers. Franziskus hesitated, wondering whether he should join the stragglers in forming a final buffer in front of the archers. Angelika grabbed him by the back of the knee and he fell beside her.

'Let the soldiers fight,' Angelika said.

Her comment was not meant to wound, but it did.

Large brown shapes darted between the ridge rocks. They were mountain antelopes, of the breed called the steinbock, the largest known in the World's Edge Mountains. Franziskus counted seven of them. Five were large males, each as high as a horse, their heads topped with sharp, curving horns marked by periodic, gnarled rings. The other two beasts were about two thirds their size, so Franziskus reckoned them to be females. His father used to go with his friends to the mountains to hunt them. A set of their ringed antlers decorated the family dining hall.

It was not usual for these creatures to come down from the mountains. Franziskus could only imagine what dreadful manifestations of Chaos had driven them into unfamiliar territory. They would not long survive here. Even in more prosperous times, such magnificent beasts would be quickly culled by lucky huntsmen.

The soldiers held fast to their formation as the creatures stampeded nearer, assuming that something was chasing the wild beasts, and would soon appear atop the ridge. The archers kept their arrows ready, relaxing only after several minutes had passed, and the antelope were galloping skittishly past them. All but one loped determinedly onwards, but the last steinbock, one of the slim females, halted on the flank of the soldiers' dissolving formation.

'Sigmar's given us a gift of fresh meat!' an archer cried.

'No, wait,' shouted Angelika, but she was too far from the formation.

Bowmen pivoted to launch a half-dozen arrows into the antelope's haunches. The creature staggered at them, then fell neatly on its flanks.

'No,' Angelika yelled again.

A corporal from the archer's ranks, laughing excitedly, separating himself from his fellows to trot over to the slain creature.

Angelika stood and ran, waving her arms and shouting.

The bow-corporal hunched over the thrashing steinbock. A sharp-tipped, keratinous tentacle erupted from the dying animal's flank to plunge between the soldier's legs and up into his body cavity. His throaty grunt of appalled astonishment lasted for a brief instant before falling silent. The corporal's neck distended upwards. Gore spurted from his ears and mouth. The tentacle had pushed its way up through him, and now pressed itself against the roof of his skull. It lifted his dangling feet from the ground. His fellow soldiers stood watching, stock-still, bows held uselessly at their sides.

Stunned inaction was a common reaction to the presence of Chaos.

The steinbock was situated on the column's right flank. Emil rode down its left side, shouting, exhorting the men to fire.

Angelika covered her face with her hand. Franziskus drew his sabre. She reached under his coat to seize him by the belt, to stop him from running at the creature.

The corporal's neck stretched and strained. A second tentacle snaked out from the antelope's carcass, coiling tight around his ankles, snapping them together. The two appendages worked together to snap the soldier's body taut. His arms flailed; he was still alive, struggling helplessly.

'Finish him,' Emil shouted. 'Finish him!'

The archers raised their bows, and, with trembling, wayward arms, loosed a volley of arrows. Contrary to Emil's command, they aimed not for their comrade's writhing body, but at the jigging carcass of the steinbock. A handful of arrows pounded into its ribs and haunches. The rest struck far wide of the mark.

At the junction between neck and torso, the tensile power of the corporal's flesh reached its limit. The head tore bloodily loose, exposing the serpentine tentacle inside. It flopped and writhed, the corporal's head stuck to its end like a puppet. It swung itself at the column of stunned men, who fell back before it. The archers tripped over one another in an effort to escape it. One, his route of escape blocked by the jammed bodies of his comrades, received a glancing blow from the corporal's skull. He fell to his hands and knees and quaked, piteously sobbing.

Sabre in his off-hand and reins in his right, Jonas rode down on the mutated beast. His nervous horse tried to veer but with soothing words and legs tight in the stirrups, the lieutenant kept it steady. As his steed galloped between the steinbock and the slain corporal, Jonas's sabre cut through the main tentacle. The archer's corpse thudded to the ground. The antelope's body shuddered and bucked; Jonas rode his horse back to spear it in the side. He left the weapon inside the beast's quivering trunk. Jonas let his horse carry him a good distance from it, then dismounted. The horse circled and bucked; Emil led his to its side, to help calm it.

What was left of the company's formation shattered. They formed a wide circle around the lifeless bodies of the creature and their comrade.

Angelika approached Jonas. 'Burn the body. Your man, too, just to be safe. The smoke can be noxious; build the pyre downwind.'

Jonas squinted but was otherwise expressionless. 'You were shouting, before the – the *Chaos* thing attacked.'

'Indeed I was.'

'Warning them.'

She nodded, a little.

'You must stay beside me, to give me quick advice.' He wiped something from his eye. 'No matter what the whisperers may say.'

THE AFTERNOON'S MARCH was a dispirited trudge. The clouds parted and the sky grew blindingly bright. As the air warmed, soldiers doffed cloaks and coats, adding them to the weighty bundles on their backs. The soldiers swigged intemperately from their canteens. Few words were spoken. The shock of the Chaos attack resonated in every cough.

Franziskus did not know where to place himself. Angelika walked up front, alongside Jonas's horse. An invitation to join them had not been forthcoming, and he wasn't sure he wanted one, anyway. He found himself among the stragglers. Several of the archers, presumably friends to the slain corporal, had joined their number as well. They shuffled along, dragging their feet, like old men after a long night of over-indulgence. Franziskus assigned himself the task of finding heartening words for them. He failed at it, miserably.

The ground grew rockier as the day drudged on. Eventually they left the long grasses behind to shuttle along a series of stony crests shaped like lolling ocean waves. The company trekked up, then down, then up again. Between the second and third crests, they found an obelisk of polished white quartz tilting from a filled-in crevasse. It was ten feet tall; angular runes, pitted and smoothed by centuries of exposure, ringed only its lower surfaces.

'What is it?' asked Jonas. 'Some Kurgan hex?'

Angelika took a cursory peer at it, just to be sure. 'No, dwarven. And very old. It's just a territory marker. I don't read dwarf script, but you see even older ones in the Blackfire, where their colonies are all long abandoned.'

Jonas ran gloved fingers along the raised runic letters. 'They're not warning us to keep out, are they?'

'As I said, I don't read Dwarf, but my guess is this is one dwarf clan telling another where their lands begin. If you're worried about dwarfs, you shouldn't have come up here. These peaks are rife with them.'

'The dwarfs hate the enemy as much as we do.'

'My understanding is that if they hate something, they hate it much worse than anyone else.'

'I wish we would run across some, to enlist their aid. Or advice, leastways.'

'Maybe they could loan you a scout.'

'Doubtful. Their forces have been drawn north to fight an orcish army that's allied itself with the foe.'

'That may be for the better. Dwarfs can be quick to reach for their weapons if you catch them in a foul mood. Which is how one always catches them.'

'They're our allies in this war.'

'Let's hope they keep that in mind.' Angelika patted the menhir. 'At any rate, if there are dwarfs here, they'll see us before we see them.'

'They'll parley before firing their crossbows at us.' Jonas gestured to Emil, who waved the men onward. They responded sluggishly. From their sighs and grunts, it was clear they'd hoped for a longer stop.

About an hour later, a soft hand tugged at Franziskus's fingers. He looked down to see which halfling it was. Filch held out a small heel of hard white cheese. 'Care for a snack?' he asked.

Franziskus did not, but accepted the nugget of food to be polite. He nibbled cautiously at it. The cheese proved rich and comforting, with a walnut aftertaste. It was, truth be told, the best piece of cheese Franziskus had tasted for as long as he could remember. He gulped it down shamelessly. Filch and the two other halflings, who had ringed around him, smiled proudly.

Filch pointed to the fidgety one. 'This is his cheese. He's a cheesemaker.'

Franziskus tried hard to remember the name, and finally it came to him: Merwin. And the third one, the fellow with the proud carriage, was Bodo. 'That is an extremely fine cheese, Merwin.'

Merwin beamed. 'I don't have provisions for everyone, but seeing as we know you…'

'That's especially kind, given that our acquaintance consists chiefly of your friend Filch here banging me in the head with a rock.'

Filch hung his head. 'The cheese is meant by way of apology.'

'It is such a splendid cheese that any *mea culpa* is unquestionably accepted.' Franziskus proferred a smile.

'Unquestionably,' repeated Filch. 'That's good. I was worried you might bear a grudge. You tall folk are sometimes slow to let go of a grievance. No offence.'

'Our skulls are, compared to yours, regrettably thin and delicate. It is best not to try to stave them in, if you wish to stay in our good graces.'

'It was a lucky shot, I promise you. And also I want you to know that I in no way wished you hanged. Neither did Merwin or Bodo, either.'

'That is reassuring, Filch.'

'Beaten, perhaps. But never hanged.'

'And only slightly beaten, I hope.'

'Oh yes. Only slightly. Would you also like a dash of tawny port?'

Franziskus allowed that he would, and Merwin produced and uncorked a small ceramic jar. He dribbled a tiny serving of fortified brandy into a wooden cup, which he'd brushed clean with his forefinger. He handed it up to Franziskus, but Filch nudged him.

'Human-sized portion, Merwin. Human-sized portion,' he muttered.

Merwin poured again, then passed over the more generous serving. Franziskus let the thick liquor loll about on his tongue; it was potent and sweet.

Filch watched him drink. 'You are experienced, Franziskus, with this sort of business?'

'What do you mean?'

'This business of warfare. And – you know. Chaos.'

Bodo cleared his throat – a deep, disapproving sound. 'What he means to say is, he and Merwin have got cold feet. Now that they saw what they're facing.'

His compatriots fussed at him in protest. Merwin muttered something about having said no such thing. Franziskus gave the cup back. Merwin upended it over his tongue, getting the last few drops out of it before returning it, unwashed, to his pack.

'Well,' Franziskus extemporised, 'I am no witch-hunter. Certainly no bold officer, not like Lieutenant Rassau. But this is not my first encounter with dae-mons and the like. I wish it were.'

'Seeing that,' said Filch, rubbing his stomach, 'it upset my digestion completely.'

'You'll have to harden yourself,' said Bodo, 'if you want to go to war.'

'Have you, Franziskus?' Filch asked. 'Hardened yourself?'

'You can never harden yourself, not completely. Per-haps against orcs, or goblins, or troops from another country. Chaos, though… it never loses its power to knot a man's gut. So if you feel fear, do not think yourselves inadequate. I have heard much talk of Chaos, but from my experience of it, it is pure wrong-ness given solidity and clothed in flesh. It terrifies us, because it is everything that should not be. If you do not feel dread, when you see a thing like we just saw, that is the time to question yourself. Because then you know that madness has taken you completely.'

'I would not like to go mad,' said Filch. 'But even worse would be if the children and old people from my village were forced to meet such horrors. That is why we've come – because the lieutenant's words stirred us, and helped us to see that.'

'Then that is all you must do, if called upon to face a creature like that. Remember why you fight.'

Filch's lips moved, as if he was memorising Franziskus's words for later reference.

'We can fight fiercely, if need be,' declared Bodo. 'Our kind might be small and weak, compared to them Kurgan barbarians. But we have determination, and will not give up.'

'That is my friend Angelika's strength, also.'

They'd allowed the gap between themselves and the last of the human stragglers to widen. Franziskus quickened his stride; the halflings followed suit. Bits of dried brown vegetation crunched beneath their bare and bone-shod feet.

'Filch, who is left to care for your kinfolk, with your two brothers gone?'

'I have no kin, not to speak of. Unless you count Curran's wife, Lily. Which I do not, seeing as she'd as soon hit me with a broom as look at me.'

'All of her people, all the Whiteapples, has always been the same way,' said Merwin. 'Pinched and thin-skinned. Only a fellow as stubborn as Curran could ever have married her. Not to speak ill of the dead.'

'No,' said Bodo. 'Not to speak ill of the dead.'

Merwin could clearly see that he'd upset his friends, but seemed to feel he could dig himself out if only he kept yammering. 'No, not to speak ill at all. Because everyone will be the first to say that good old Curran had a temper on him. For example, him getting all lathered because of your friend Angelika being caught looting the body of Elias Two-Beer. Our neighbour, who he carried on as if they was best friends or some-what. Why, him and Elias hadn't said a kind word to each other in six, seven years. Isn't that the truth, Bodo?'

Bodo held his tongue.

'Curran said that this friend of his had toasted him at his wedding,' Franziskus ventured.

Merwin was undeterred. 'That's just what I'm saying, then, isn't it? Because that was well more than six, seven years past.'

'What does it matter now?' Bodo demanded.

'It's just that people are funny, that's all I'm saying. I find it odd, that's all. I'm not saying a man's not got a right to be odd. Some might say I'm plenty odd, myself.'

'Some might indeed,' Bodo answered.

'Then you see what I mean,' exclaimed Merwin.

Bodo shook his head.

'Perhaps,' said Franziskus, 'if Curran had not spoken to his friend in many years, and then seen him killed, that would be the cause of his passion to have us hanged. Regret, that he had not reconciled with him before it was too late.'

Filch sniffled. Bodo whipped a handkerchief from his vest pocket and placed in his hand. 'You're wise, for a man of your height.'

'If only it did me any good,' Franziskus replied.

THEY MADE CAMP that night on the rock-strewn beach of a cold, round lake. Its shore offered enemies only one approach; sloping hills rose in a horseshoe around the lake from the west, north and east. Alone among the marchers, the halflings took an interest in bathing. They unpacked hand-sized bars of soap and knelt over the shoreline, cleaning their hands and feet. The soldiers gathered from a distance, amused by the high piles of lather the half-men built up on their heads. It gave off a scent of almonds. Merwin offered to share the soap, but only Franziskus availed himself. Though his hair was greasy and lank, he would not risk making a spectacle of himself by washing it in front of the men.

Angelika stood by as Jonas conferred with Emil. She could not tell if she was meant to take part, or wait to be called upon. The men were nervous. Since the steinbock incident, they'd encountered neither friend nor foe. They'd passed a number of farmhouses, each of them burnt, and had called out to any inhabitants still hiding inside. They'd garnered no replies.

The day's heat had given way to a damp chill. Jonas finally consulted her: 'The men will be happier if they can warm themselves. Is it safe to light fires?'

'Might as well. You've nearly six dozen men here. They'll make so much noise snoring and tossing that any enemy scout with half an eardrum could detect them from a mile away. You can't rely on keeping yourselves hid; you'll just have to put up good defences and hope no one comes at you.'

'What about more creatures of the enemy?'

'Who knows what senses they use to find prey? If they come, they come. You'll have to be ready for them.'

Emil went off to lay out a perimeter and assign guard duties. Angelika turned to gaze into the lake's black waters.

'We will of course not be sleeping in any proximity to one another,' Jonas told her.

'I was about to make the same request.'

Only after the words had leapt from her mouth did she remember: she'd hoped to get close to him again, so she could search his possessions for her stolen property.

Angelika tried to conceive a verbal manoeuvre to smoothly move her from her present defensive posture back to Jonas's side. None came to mind. If anything, her mind conceived of a good half dozen select phrases, each of which would inform the lieutenant of her current opinion of him in definitive and exacting detail. The last thing she wanted from him was undying affection, but this kind of high-handedness was intolerable in any man, let alone a recent bed partner. She stalked off, knowing that any further discussion could lead to bloodshed.

IF THERE WERE Chaos creatures or barbarians lurking about the lake, they failed to show themselves. The men woke at dawn and broke camp with wordless efficiency. Angelika stepped across the still bodies of stertorous halflings to rouse Franziskus, placing a gentle boot-tip on his shoulder. He started up and reached out to wake Filch.

She gestured to stop him. 'Why don't you acquaint yourself with some of the men? These halflings won't have the ring.'

Franziskus gazed at her blearily. 'I wasn't looking for it.'

She walked away. 'The sooner we find it, the quicker we get out of here.'

The young Stirlander looked at the busy soldiers, then at the slumbering half-men. They had not asked him if he was a deserter. The Gerolsbruch Swordsmen would.

* * *

FOR THE NEXT two days, Franziskus remained with the halflings. The first day passed without incident, marked only by the eerie lack of all contact with man or beast. Angelika came back from the head of the column several times, to inquire after his success in befriending the soldiers. After a while, she stopped asking.

The entire matter troubled him. Once, Angelika noticed Filch attempting to eavesdrop on them. Franziskus saw that familiar slow fury on her face; it showed itself as a miniscule tightening, an ominous absence of expression. A mental image confronted him, of Angelika's knife at Filch's throat. He thought to tell her that, rock-throwing skills aside, the little man seemed harmless. Then he remembered the fellow's unfortunate name. It hardly inspired trust, did it?

That night they camped in a forest of spruce saplings, situated on a sloping hillside. Their movements stirred up the ash of an old fire, which explained the uniform age of the trees around them. The men woke up grubby and black; some headed for a small stream at the bottom of the slope, to wash themselves. Emil called out to stop them. The soot, he shouted, would dull the shine of their pasty Stirland faces, which would otherwise glare like bobbing lanterns in the gaze of enemy lookouts. Franziskus caught Filch and Merwin edging down to the bank anyway and corralled them with a stern head shake.

'Surely he don't mean us,' Filch said.

'We're not Stirlanders, not exactly,' Merwin agreed. 'Well, we're from Stirland, but we're not human. Precisely speaking.'

'Our faces aren't so pale as yours. We're sunburnt farmers.'

'Nut-brown, I'd say. Nut-brown is what our facial tone is.'

Franziskus shook his head. He felt like the tutor he'd had as a child, always saying no to him and his brothers.

Filch held out begging hands. 'Please. It's a terrible-bad affront to a halfling, to make him go around like a ragamuffin.'

Bodo stomped down to end the argument. 'We're soldiers now. If the sergeant says no washing, then filthy we will be.'

The day was a slow tramp up ever-steeper grades. Earthen ground gave way to naked stone. The horses would go no further. Jonas dismounted to coax his on, but its hooves could not navigate the rock's uneven surface. Emil heaved himself down from his saddle and waddled over to confer with the lieutenant.

Jonas addressed a quiet reproach to Angelika. 'You should've warned us.'

'Of what?'

'To do something about the horses.'

Emil said nothing. He wore the chagrined look of a man who knew he'd made a stupid error.

'Do what about the horses?' Angelika asked.

Jonas was unabashed. 'We should have found a place to put them earlier in the day. Now we'll have to go back and–'

'Find a place to *put* them?' She looked to Emil. He closed his eyes and gritted his molars.

'Yes,' said Jonas. 'A stable or pasture.'

'Do you recall seeing a safe place to leave horses since we entered the borderlands?' The men were watching, so Angelika struggled to muffle her body language.

Emil spoke without moving a muscle. 'If we'd left Hochsmoor on better terms, I would have left them there. After that, I was only thinking to stay away from inhabited places, since that's where the Kurg might be. To be honest, the question of stabling never crossed my mind.'

'And you said nothing, Angelika?'

'What was there to say? I figured you meant to bring them as far as you could, and then...'

'And then what?' Stifling his agitation, Jonas turned his back to the company. 'And then what?' he repeated.

Angelika shrugged. 'Then you... eat them. Don't you?'

Jonas's words hissed through a gate of shuttered, pearly teeth. 'Eat the horses?'

'I assumed you intended a last feast for the men. There's not much forage up here.'

'You expect me to eat Firebrand? Who was given me by my uncle? Who is bred from the stallion my father rode to battle?'

'When you brought him up here, I reckoned you weren't so attached to him.' She noted how the lieutenant's hand had become a fist. It was not, she reasoned, in his interest to strike at her now. 'I'm sorry to learn otherwise. But these horses, Jonas–'

'Lieutenant.'

'These horses, *lieutenant*' – she spat the word out like rotten fruit–' they're dead already. Whether you let them loose here, or walk half a mile back down the slope and do it, they're going to be eaten by someone or something. Wolves, bears, skaven…'

'I can't allow it,' said Jonas. 'I cannot.'

From his posture, it seemed that Emil agreed with her plan, but would not risk a rift with his commander by saying so. Not when he had her to shield him. 'It might be the Kurgs who catch these steeds. You want to feed your enemy?'

'The horses can find grazing, below.'

'If they're lucky, they'll be caught and devoured. If not, they'll starve. If you love that horse, you'll grant it the mercy of a painless death.'

He shook his head. He was out of argument but meant to hold fast anyhow.

'Don't be stubborn.' She immediately wished she hadn't said the word. It was never a helpful one, when trying to dislodge a man from his position. 'You've over seventy mouths to feed,' she continued. 'When the men get hungry – and they will – what do you want them to think, when they remember what you did with the horses?'

'Do it then,' said Jonas, breaking from them to stand near his horse. Emil went among the men, asking who among them possessed the needed skills. Bodo the halfling held up his hand. Back in Hochsmoor, he said, he was the village butcher. Emil marched the bulk of the column on while a few swordsmen stayed to assist the halfling. Jonas stood, stroking Firebrand's muzzle and speaking to it in a low, reassuring tone. Angelika could not bear to watch him; she fetched Franziskus and went ahead with the others.

Twenty minutes later, Jonas joined the others. He passed Angelika by, his eyes blazing. He leapt up to the shelf-like rock that afforded a grander view of the purple peaks ahead. Men found stray branches and laid firewood down in a sizeable depression that would serve as a natural firepit. Soon both carcasses were produced and spitted over a devouring flame. The smoke of cooking horses drew a small party of shy, ill-nourished wolves to the periphery of the camp. Seeing them, Jonas ran to seize a Chelborger's bow. He let an arrow fly at the boldest wolf; it pierced the creature's side and knocked it dead. Its kin yelped away, leaving Jonas to mourn in peace. He ate from the meat of neither horse.

THE FEAST, INCLUDING a suitable time to lie about and digest, stole over four hours of the company's time. Then they moved on, each step a little shorter and more difficult than the last. A chill flowed down from the whitened summits looming over them. Soldiers wheezed and sweated. The tightness in the chest, the laboured breathing – these were familiar symptoms to Angelika and Franziskus. An acuter distress struck Jonas and his men. They mopped at brows; they slipped and tripped and hauled themselves sluggishly onwards. The halflings seemed oddly unimpeded. They bounced like goats on hard-boned feet from one rock to the next. Merwin began a collection of alpine flowers, stuffing them willy-nilly into his sleeves and pockets. Franziskus theorised that their race had to be related to the dwarfs, who were born and bred for mountain travel.

The rocks grew steeper still, forcing the men to grab for handholds as they impelled themselves upwards. As they scrambled, the gradient changed, from twenty degrees, to twenty-five, then nearly to thirty. The rock face extended for at least a mile to the east and west. To the left, it terminated in the steep drop of a canyon, too sheer and deep to act as a pass. It was bounded on the right by a thrusting granite wall, the foot of a peak that extended into the clouds. Straight ahead of them, the slope disappeared abruptly from view, suggesting that it flattened into a plateau.

Angelika listened to the groans of the men as they battled the elevation. Even Franziskus and the halflings had slowed to an exhausted creep. She circuited between boulders to reach Jonas, who had placed himself on point position and was now the furthest up the hill of any man. He had not sought her counsel since the horsemeat feast.

She hadn't disputed his choice of direction. This stretch of mountains was proving to be even less accommodating than those of the Blackfire Pass. Even so, there had to be navigable passageways between the peaks since the Kurgan had found and used them. Neither she nor anyone else in the company possessed a map of the range; if such a thing existed, it was a secret of the dwarfs. They would have to locate its passes and switchbacks by trial and error. For every day of penetrative movement into the mountains, they could easily face two of dead ends, false hopes, and retraced steps. When deciding where to go, they would often reach juncture points where one guess was as good as another. She'd allowed

Jonas to make the first guesses, but now it seemed like it was time to double back and try another way in.

A soldier's foot freed a salvo of rocks and they bounced down the slope, sending the men behind him dodging to evade them. Each impact of rock on rock clattered and echoed. Angelika frowned – the sound could probably be heard for miles. For nearly an hour her sense of hazard had been rising.

The problem was not that the rock face led to nowhere. In fact, it seemed to disappear about a hundred feet ahead of Jonas's position, flattening into a plateau of unknowable size and shape. A flat expanse of gravelly ground would seem like a gift from the gods, if they could reach it. And it could well lead to a switchback or other pass. However, a primary rule of mountain survival was that any spot favourable enough to struggle toward was also sufficiently attractive for some hostile other to occupy.

Angelika imagined a likely layout and pictured the company from the point of view of a person concealed up the plateau. Hiding would be easy, an ambusher could stay out of sight simply by hugging the ground. Worse, a row of boulders perched near the lip of the plateau. Angelika counted at least a dozen of them, each capable of concealing a muscle-bound Kurg from toe to top-knot.

She'd got within twenty-five yards of Jonas when a strangled moan rose from behind her. She turned to see a grey-templed swordsman clutching his chest and gurgling. His right arm shot out from his side, stiff as a rod. His face puffed and froze. He sank backwards, his legs locking straight as the rest of him collapsed. Comrades tripped over rocks to reach his side. A low order hissed from Emil's lips: no one else was to move. He strode to join the man's helpers. They pried off his breastplate and loosened his collar. The fallen man stiffened and twitched. Emil straightened himself about ten minutes later. He shook his head, his tight expression unmistakable: the man was gone.

The cause of death posed no puzzle to Angelika: his heart had given out. It was a common thing in warfare. Maybe one in twenty-five of the corpses she found after a battle hadn't a mark on them – they'd succumbed to burst blood vessels or ruined heart muscles. All the more reason to hunt for an easier route.

Jonas passed her on the way down the slope. 'I suppose you want us to eat him, too,' he muttered.

No, she thought, but you're going to want to drag him along with us, instead of leaving him where he fell, and that's foolishness aplenty.

The lieutenant surprised her. He made his way down through the rocks to confer with one of his swordsmen. The fellow listened impassively, then removed his helmet and wrapped an arm in a phylactery of black fabric. This insignia marked him as a lay officiate of Morr, the death god. Evidently the dead soldier would be interred on the spot. Four of the dead man's comrades carried the body to a comparatively even place, laying him out with the gentle care of parents tucking a child into his bed sheets. The acolyte of Morr performed a muttered ceremony. It was not the complete ritual a full priest would do, but the petty version would suffice. It was more than many dead soldiers got.

The acolyte muttered a blessing, then knelt to ritually close the man's eyes and dust his face with dirt. Each of the original sword company then proceeded past his body to lay a stone over it, until they'd built up a modest, mounded cairn. The Chelborg Archers and assorted stragglers abstained from this duty; apparently they were not yet fully the fallen man's comrades, and therefore unfit to take part in his death rites. Filch, oblivious to this nicety, had a hefty stone in hand and was ready to advance on the burial site. Bodo grabbed him by the collar to stop him embarrassing himself.

When the man lay completely under a blanket of stone, Angelika approached Jonas. She showed him the features of the terrain, reminded him of the noise the company had made already, and pointed at the spots where enemies might be hiding. 'This feels bad to me,' she said. 'We'd best turn around.'

Jonas peered at the rocks along the plateau line. From this more distant vantage they looked smaller, like tiny slate-coloured toadstools. 'No. Sterr died to take this hill,' said Jonas, using the name of the fallen man, which Angelika had not known. 'The men will not let it beat them now.'

'Jonas, our enemy is not a hill.'

'We're to turn around every time you feel bad? We're here to make war. And call me by my rank, Angelika.'

Jonas ordered the company to resume its climb. They commenced their new assault against the rocky incline in tighter order, going up in waves of four and five.

Angelika stood watching them. So what if he disregarded her advice? It made no difference to her whether he fulfilled his orders. Whatever those were – their exact nature seemed vague, even to Jonas. Yes, it was an irksome set of circumstances. And yes, it was beyond contradictory that he'd spent so much effort to inveigle her into this, only to balk at her best advice. And yes, yes, certainly, it was supremely tempting, when confronted with bullheadedness of this magnitude, to argue. To prove herself correct. She was right and he was wrong. That was not the question.

The question was: how to recover the ring? This was the only thing, she reminded herself, she ought to care about. Not the safety of his men. Not the fate of the Empire. Not even the preservation of her self-respect and obvious rightness in the face of overwhelming folly. Arguing with Jonas would not get her ring back. He might think he wanted her to be smart, to be a good scout for him, but his behaviour said otherwise. Deference, that's what he wanted. Loyalty. Assurance that he was as wise and good and strong as this father he kept on about, whether warranted or not. She had to win his trust back, so she could search his pack for the ruby. It was not her task to bludgeon sense into him, or to shine a brilliant light on his inconsistencies. She would cater to his pride, and swallow her own.

If he did have the ruby, though… For every dram of lost dignity, every instant of stolen freedom, she would make him pay. When it was back in her hand, that's when she'd be proven right.

Angelika rushed, clambering through the rocks, to catch up with the others. Now everyone was well ahead of her. Franziskus and the halflings were off to one side. Bodo had determined the ideal series of stepping stones and had jumped his way into the lead, hopping with goatish surety from one boulder to the next. Filch repeated his circuitous yet speedy climb with nearly equal agility. Merwin acquitted himself with less aplomb, stopping on every third rock to regain his balance. Franziskus followed their general path but left the leaping to the experts. Angelika shrugged and headed towards him.

Already, certain of the soldiers flagged. They paused to wheeze and puff. Angelika imagined that they envisioned their friend's collapse, and aimed to pace themselves. Others pressed on, Jonas especially. Whether out of carelessness or a desire to instil spirit in his men, he'd plunged ahead and was now on point. He made up in speed what he lacked in sense, Angelika thought: he was almost thirty yards up the slope already.

Instinct drew her gaze to the plateau's edge. A blur of exposed flesh moved between two of its man-sized rocks.

'No!' she shouted. 'Move it!'

CHAPTER FOURTEEN

THE BOULDERS ROCKED, resisted, loosened, and fell. They crashed down into the stream of climbing men. Three of the massive stones rolled down together. Others came soon after. One landed on a long side in loose gravel, lodging in a crater of its own making. The others rolled violently down into the disordered column of climbing men, who exclaimed in breathless panic. Each time they bounced, the boulders flattened limbs, caved-in rib cages and split helmeted skulls. Panicked soldiers tried to run, but struck their shins on the small rocks around them. They fell, or, worse, flattened themselves deliberately on the unwelcoming ground, making themselves bigger targets for the cascading rocks.

Angelika was seized by the same terrified impulse, but found the willpower to stay stock still. It was the best way to decrease the odds of being hit – just as the person who walks in a rainstorm stays drier than one who dashes through the droplets. Ahead of her, Franziskus and the halflings ducked for cover, falling to their knees and pointing their heads downwards. At first, she thought this to be an echo of the same awful error committed by so many of the soldiers, lower down. Then another boulder, the largest yet, tumbled off the lip, right above their position. It sailed through the air right where Franziskus's blond head had been and it crunched into the slope a yard past him. He'd figured the geometry right: from his position, much higher on the slope, dropping down had been the clever choice.

The same rock now bounced Angelika's way. It hit a sharp granite jut, knocking off a spray of shards. The strike altered the trajectory of its bounce, directing the stone closer to her. It touched down again, but its orbit was unaltered. Angelika postponed all breathing. It sailed through the air. It crunched onto the slope, wildly rolling. Its course was now set.

She looked at the loose stones around her feet. An ill-balanced leap onto any of them could send her unpredictably flying, forward, back, to either side.

If she stayed put, she was almost certain that it would not hit her.

Almost.

She turned sideways, to become a smaller target. She exhaled and held it, rendering her profile infinitesimally smaller.

She felt the air pulled from around her as the big boulder blasted past her. It kept rolling, veering toward the canyon, which eventually swallowed it up.

She turned her attention back to the plateau line; only a pair of dangerously large stones remained there. Outsized figures groaned against them, waging a doomed campaign to sway them from their places. Down on the slope, the surviving Chelborg Archers rallied, setting arrows in their bows. The ambushers scurried and dropped from view. Missiles arced up to the plateau and they caromed off rocks or lodged in grassy clods of earth. The attackers might be pinned down by the Chelborg fusillade, but, so long as they stayed flat, would not be struck by it.

Angelika scanned the slope. Had Jonas survived?

Yes, he had: the lieutenant rose and signaled his men to charge. 'On, men, on,' he cried. 'Avenge your fallen brothers!'

Emil, lived, too. He bolted up to repeat Jonas's gesture. Blood coated the nearest side of his face though it did not seem to be his own. Arrayed around him were broken bodies, some writhing, some still.

The able swordsmen lurched, uncertainly at first, toward the plateau. A helmeted Kurgan popped up immediately to point a bow into the main charge of onrushing men. Though Jonas's archers were positioned behind his close-in fighters, the angle of the slope now worked in their favour: they could fire at the barbarians, certain their missiles would whiz over the heads of their comrades.

A Gerolsbrucher caught a barbarian shaft in the flesh of his off-arm, but kept on clambering. The Kurgan archer slumped, a long, straight Imperial arrow piercing his helmet's left eye-slit. Another rash marauder stood up, bellowing, and was promptly pin-cushioned by the men of Chelborg. The others waited until the swordsmen were nearly upon them. Then they had no choice but to surrender their prone positions, to stand and fight. They surged up as one, with axes aloft.

'Down now, swordsmen. Down now,' Jonas called. 'Let the archers do their work.'

Some obeyed, falling back, allowing the archers behind them to pepper the exposed barbarians. Others seemed leery and instead clambered onto the lip to fight. Barbarian boots kicked them down. Kurgan leapt from the plateau onto the slope, and the swordsmen. There were less than a dozen of them. They fought crazily, downing three Gerolsbruchers before succumbing to the overwhelming numbers of their foes. Angelika was surprised to see Bodo the halfling among the grim-faced bladesmen who hacked them down. The swordsmen kept stabbing and slicing long after all life had ebbed from the ambushers' corpses.

Angelika's knees belatedly shook. She crouched, pressing her hands against them, to hide her nerves. She surveyed the slope: bodies were strewn all along it. Well-accustomed to tallying the dead, she arrived at a quick count. At least twenty men dead or incapacitated. A third of Jonas's men, wiped out in a few moments, by no more than a handful of ambushers.

Franziskus came to her side. Filch and Merwin were with him. Bodo, still up at the plateau line, made no move to rejoin his fellow halflings. Instead, he basked in the grim acceptance of the human soldiers whose comrades' death he'd helped avenge.

'You're unhurt?' Franziskus asked.

She curtly nodded.

'I thought you'd try to duck.'

'So did the rock.' She attempted a smile.

'How did you know to stand still?'

'Haven't you noticed, Franziskus? I'm always right.'
Force of habit brought her closer to the corpses of the
crushed soldiers. She was used to gore and decomposition, but never had she seen so many crushing victims.
Angelika marvelled at the power of the giant stones,
how they could in an instant of impact grind a man
into so much pulverised and unrecognizable flesh. She
ruled out as unduly risky the prospect of a little surrep-
titious looting. This did not stop her, as a mere exercise,
from estimating the value of the dead soldiers' property.

A gold ring stared up at her from the knuckle of a
crushed and bloodied hand. She checked, no one was
watching. Jonas's soldiers worked systematically
through the fallen, starting at the foot of the slope.
Most had gathered around the largest of the boulders:
two men were still trapped beneath it. She saw
Franziskus nearby, seeming stricken, as if he knew
them.

The trapped men were Rappe and Cassel. Cassel was
pinned from the waist down. His chest moved tentatively up and down. All that could be seen of Rappe was
a twitching pair of legs.

From his position, relative to the stone, Angelika
imagined that the stone had crushed an arm, and perhaps his shoulder as well. Their rescuers faced an
unpleasant dilemma: if they attempted to roll the boulder off Cassel, they'd pulverise Rappe, and vice versa.

A few placed palms against its granite surface, but
dared not push. Others stood back, shifting from one

spot to the next, hoping that a solution might be
found in some mere change of angle. Angelika did
not envy them. Soon they'd realise only one could be
saved from severe harm, and would have to choose
between them. She wondered how they'd decide. Was
one more useful than the other? More congenial?

Turning her thoughts back to the dead man at her
feet, Angelika knelt deftly down. She wiped blood
from his ring, to see it better. It was a thick, simple
band, with only a few tiny chips of diamond recessed
into it. Worth half a crown, perhaps. Over the past
five years, she'd taken rings much like this from the
fingers of innumerable dead men. If she failed to find
her ruby, at least a half-decade of the same labour
awaited her. She would not harvest this one, though;
it would be like admitting defeat. She hauled herself
up and stepped away from the body.

She'd never thought it likely that one of the soldiers
had her ring. If anyone here was the guilty party, it
was Jonas himself. However, if there was even the
slightest possibility that her ring was here, on the person of a dead man, she would have to punctiliously
search each and every corpse. So much for getting
back into the lieutenant's good graces.

A delicate negotiation was in order.

She looked for Jonas, expecting to find him directing the effort to free the two trapped men. Instead,
Emil had taken charge, showing the men precisely
where to place their hands, and how to brace themselves. From the way they were arrayed, it seemed that
the decision had been taken to sacrifice Cassel. As the
older man, he had fewer years left to him. Bodo
stretched out on his side, placing stones in small gaps

between rock and earth. The idea, presumably, was to take pressure off the pinned men when the rock moved. Angelika did not think it would help much.

Jonas strode alone over to the canyon's edge and stood staring gloomily down into its shadowy recesses. Angelika permitted him a few minutes of this meditation, then crossed into the periphery of his vision. He beckoned her over.

As she headed to his side, she reminded herself to speak diplomatically, as Franziskus would do. To see what Jonas desired, so she could offer it to him. To hold her tongue when undesirable truths danced on its tip.

'Lieutenant,' she said.

'Please,' he replied. 'Call me Jonas.' He angled himself to steal a quick view of the funeral detail. None of the men were observing him. He lowered his head and pulled at his hair, punishing himself. 'I should have listened to you. Shouldn't I?'

Angelika was not so foolish as to answer in words. His reversal in attitude was too sudden to trust.

'I was worried about what the men would think. To turn back on that hill, after Sterr had died there. What will I tell them now?'

'Misjudgements happen in war.'

An anguished groan cut through the air. Their heads turned: Emil's crew had moved the rock up onto one side, further crushing Cassel's legs. Bodo and others pulled on Rappe, trying to haul him out from under the rock. They tugged and pulled on his hobbled body. Above them, the pushing swordsmen fell back, as the giant boulder resisted their efforts to move it. Rappe's screams intermixed with his friend's.

Jonas paled and clapped a hand over his mouth. When the shrieks waned into sobs, he found his voice again. 'Missteps are for the enemy. So my father always said.'

'He was free of error?'

'He never got twenty of his own men killed. Twenty-four if you count those who're as good as dead.' For an instant it seemed like Jonas would launch himself at her and grab her pleadingly by the shoulders.

Angelika girded herself, but the moment passed. 'So you found out you're–' She stopped herself before completing the thought.

'Not the man I thought I was?'

This Jonas was a damned mind-reader. It was already irksome, to be judged for the things she was impolitic enough to come out and say. To hold her very thoughts against her, too, was unfair in the extreme. 'Let's say your father was the greatest officer to ever sit upon a saddle. Did he get that way by caring what his men thought about him?'

'Those who served under him adored him. Any one of them would have laid down his life for him.'

Angelika thoroughly doubted this, but reminded herself that her job was not to cure the fellow of his delusions. At least, not all at once, by frontal assault. 'And how does an officer win the respect of his men?'

'By keeping them alive.'

'You brought me all the way here because I know these mountains. You'll listen to me next time, won't you?'

He examined the toes of his boots. 'I realise my error, Angelika.'

'Then you'll keep them breathing, as many of them as fortune allows, and the men will feel for you as your father's men did for him. Yes?'

'You won't tell them how you warned me.'

'I have a difficult favour to ask of you, Jonas.'

'You can't tell them.'

'To undermine you is not in my interest. But I wouldn't rest my command on deception if I were you.'

'They cannot know. What is this favour you want?'

'You remember why I'm here...'

His expression was blank.

'To get my ring back. One of your men might have it.'

'How?'

'He might have picked up the ring after that fight in Hochsmoor.'

'The Kurgan chieftain has it.'

'Possibly. Or possibly not. You said you weren't sure.'

'The more I think on it, the surer I get.'

A new round of moans announced a fresh attempt to free the pinned men. Jonas could not bring himself to observe directly, he followed Angelika's reactions instead. She shrank back as the rock was lifted, with half a dozen additional men pushing from below, hindered by loose ground cover and poor leverage. Rappe was now whisked out from under it, but the soldiers lost control of the rock, and it toppled over onto Cassel's chest and face. His arms shook and then went slack. One of the pushing soldiers below yelled out, his hand stuck. He tore it loose, then opened and closed his fingers to be sure they still worked.

The lieutenant still hadn't looked. 'Did they...'

Angelika shook her head. Jonas staggered back. He caught Angelika's slim, cool fingers in a hot, damp hand. She let him take them. In a movement so fast she barely saw it, he pulled her hand to his lips and fiercely kissed her fingers. Then, just as quick he'd released her, pushing himself away. Dislodged pebbles fell into the canyon's depths. Angelika tensed; his boot-heels hit the canyon's edge. He balanced himself forward, forestalling a deadly plunge. 'Only you know how I feel, Angelika,' he said.

She reached into the inside breast pocket of his officer's coat and rooted around until she found a handkerchief. To mop his brow would be too much, so she balled it up and dropped it into his palm. He blotted it onto the sweat that pearled his face.

'It's only war-madness, Jonas. War is accident and disorder, and the deaths of good men, for no good reason. Steel yourself.'

His spine straightened. 'Yes. My father would have done so.'

'I'll help you, if you let me. But you must help me also.'

'Yes, Angelika. Anything.'

'I don't want to see a rift between you and your men. But the dead – you must let me discreetly search them, before they're buried under those rocks.'

He thought for a while, his throat occasionally bobbling. 'Is this blackmail?'

'I'm not threatening to tell them anything.'

'What are you threatening?'

'I thought you were mad when you said you needed me out here, but it turns out you were right. You do need me. And I need that ring back. If you want me to continue along with you, you'll do two things. You'll heed me next time–'

'That much is certain, Angelika.'

'You'll listen to me, and you'll let me search those men.'

Jonas turned a tight circle on his heels – the gesture of an overwhelmed child. He stopped, straightened his shoulders and back, inhaled a deep breath of air, and swept back toward the soldiers.

He signalled to Emil, who called out to the regimental drummer, who rapped out a brief tattoo. Jonas stood on the largest of the boulders, which had landed on its side and presented a conveniently flat surface for him. The soldiers gathered round. Filch bobbed between the legs of taller men for a front-row vantage.

Jonas held his arms out like an actor delivering the prologue at a mystery play. 'My soldiers! My comrades!' He summoned a clear and unwavering voice that betrayed no hint of distress.

The words echoed off the rocks. They'd have made Angelika nervous, if the sounds of the mêlée hadn't already announced their location to every hostile ear for miles around.

'Our brave comrades lay about us, awfully slain,' Jonas continued, his audience rapt. 'The blood of the Empire seeps here, into these harsh and thirsty stones. It has not been spilt in vain. So while we mourn our dead, we also set our jaws in new determination, to avenge them. To persist in our mission, to take the fight to the Kurgan. To slit their every filthy throat. We will be resolute. We will not waver. We are men of Stirland. We will win!'

Some of the men feebly huzzahed.

'We will win!' Jonas repeated.

The huzzahs grew louder.

'We will win!'

Upturned fists punctured the mountain air.

'Yes, the Kurg is a filthy trickster. Could we have known that he would attack us in this cowardly manner? To let the mountain stones do the fighting for him, when he is too weak and pusillanimous to do it himself? No, we could not.

'Too long have we let fear govern our hearts, my men of Stirland. We have convinced ourselves that the barbarians are bigger, braver, more determined than we. What do we see here around us? The sure sign of his desperation. We thought too highly of our stinking foe. He dares not fight us man to man. He hides. He skulks. He cowers. His blackened soul is weak and scorched, damaged forever in his insane worship of the fell gods.

'What you see around you is not defeat – it is evidence of our certain victory to come. Our hearts are the free hearts. Ours are certain, brave, and true. We are resolute. We'll not waver. The gods on our side are the gods of good. The gods of life and virtue. What do their gods offer? Degradation and destruction, even for the twisted scum who bow before them.

'The barbarian hates us. But why? Because he fears us. Our coming here was no folly. Now is when we cease to be defenders, and become attackers. As we bury now our courageous fellows, stop and ponder the inevitability of our triumph. Burn the faces of these men into your memories. Harden yourselves for the trail ahead. Our fight will not be easy. It will not be over soon. But when it is over, it is your boots that will press tightly to the throat of your fallen foes.

'Do I speak truth?'

The soldiers yowled: 'Yes.'

'Do I speak truth?'

'Yes.'

Swordsmen brandished their blades; archers shook their arrows. Bodo held aloft his half-sized sabre. Filch scurried on his outlandish feet, pounding his chest and hooting.

Franziskus had sidled up to Angelika. 'Do you hear that?' she asked him, nearly drowned out by the din. 'We've made no mistakes today.'

'The men need rousing,' Franziskus said. 'He's a skilled officer.'

Angelika made no reply.

'Gerolsbruchers,' Jonas cried. The men of his original company stabbed their swords toward the sky. 'It is you who bravely bore the brunt today. You who were in front. You who charged. You who have suffered the gravest casualties at the distant hands of our frightened, stealthy foe. I am proud to be one of you. Rest assured, this day, both the living and dead among you have wreathed yourselves in glory.'

The soldiers nodded in grunting assent, patting each other on the shoulders. They raised their water canteens to Lieutenant Rassau as if giving him a toast.

'Chelborg Archers,' Jonas called. 'Only a few days have we marched together, but today you proved yourselves every bit the equal of my beloved Gerolsbruchers. Your fusillade held the foe like a vice. From your arrows, he could neither run nor hide. Our great triumph today, we owe to you. In my heart, I consider us to be but one company of warriors, forged together like iron. Today, Chelborgers have become Gerolsbruchers and Gerolsbruchers, Chelborgers. My friends, we are one.'

Now the men of the two companies jostled and elbowed one another in a spirit of boisterous fellowship. An archer offered a swordsman his water skin to drink from and others echoed the gesture.

Jonas stood over them, waiting for their maddened joy to peak. Then he turned, fixing his sights on Angelika and Franziskus, and the stragglers picked up from other units. His delivery thundered with sudden condemnation. 'Yet not all with us today carried their burdens in equal measure. You, without companies. You, our scouts. Were you on that slope with us? Or did you hang back?'

Franziskus's slim frame tightened up with guilt. The stragglers muttered out their consternation. Angelika folded her arms and concealed a smile.

'If you wish to be one with us, you must charge with us. Fight with us.'

'What's he talking about?' complained a stoop-shouldered pikesman. 'I nearly got crushed.'

Angelika shushed him.

The pikesman's dudgeon would not be mollified. 'I came closer to getting killed than he did.'

'As a lesson to you, to make you feel closer to us,' Jonas orated, 'I assign you now to deal with the best of us – those who have courageously died today. It is you who'll prepare their bodies for burial. As you do, gaze upon them, so next time, you can emulate their valour.'

'Pardon me if I don't emulate my way into a grave,' the stooped man muttered.

Jonas pointed to Angelika. 'And you, scout. As you are a woman, I charge you with a womanly duty – to assemble each man's effects, for transport back to his family. To ensure that each slain man is properly shrouded in his cloak, before he's laid to rest.'

Angelika tried to look neither pleased nor displeased by the lieutenant's order. She would indeed subject the possessions of each dead man to an exacting inventory.

ANGELIKA FOUND THE work of preparation peculiarly relaxing. Handling corpses had become second nature to her, and it was refreshing to do it in the light of day, with no fear of discovery, no need to crouch or hide. Jonas had made it easy to search for the ring. As she reckoned, none of the dead men had it. Regret tugged lightly at her each time she made a pile of a man's goods: among the dross there were a few good pieces. A pendant, especially, that had to be worth much more than its owner had known. Its filigree work dated it back five centuries, to the craftsmen of the Altdorf School, whose work was much desired by connoisseurs. She considered having Franziskus write a note to its inheritor, informing the lucky relative of its value. Then she thought, let it go to him who can see its value.

When the sorting was done, she and Franziskus worked together to wrap the bodies. Franziskus, as usual, had some issue or another gnawing at his conscience.

'You were speaking to those two men, earlier,' she said.

'The two who were crushed?'

She nodded.

'Their names were Rappe and Cassel. They had opposite views on women. Not that it matters now.'

'It matters to those who remember them,' she said.

They worked in silence for a while longer.

'I admired Jonas's speech,' he finally said, as he turned the body of a heavy-set, pox-scarred soldier onto its side, so Angelika could fold his cloak over him, 'up to the point where he singled some out for fulsome praise, then pointlessly scapegoated certain others.'

Angelika did not comment.

'It's obvious,' Franziskus said, 'that you worked some arrangement with him, to search the bodies for your ring. But why heap scorn on blameless men?'

'You still expect military life to be fair? No wonder it didn't suit you.'

The comment seemed to sting him, and she regretted it. It was possible to be honest without being nastily blunt, she reminded herself.

'How does that do any good, to set the men apart from one another?'

'Now the stragglers will fight harder, to be accepted into the ranks of the men Jonas esteems. The favoured ones will fight hard to stay that way. And all of them will now measure their worth by Rassau's compass. He may not know the first thing about fighting, but other than that, he's an exemplary officer.'

'He seems quite handy with a sword. I wouldn't want to face him.'

'Neither would I, but that's not what I'm talking about.'

'Then why do we place our lives in his hands?'

'I'm not trusting him with my life. That I'll take care of myself.'

'You do realise that your ring is gone.'

'It's not. I can feel it.'

They finished wrapping their current corpse and moved on to another. All the bodies were arrayed on the plateau, above the slope where they'd died. The stragglers were well into the process of digging a large and shallow grave, spading into a thin layer of coarse-grained sand beneath a field of stones.

'You warned him, didn't you?'

She nodded.

'Yet he said it was a surprise.'

Blood had pooled in the hollow at the base of her new subject's neck. She mopped it with a rag of torn tunic. 'He was surprised, wasn't he?'

'So he lied.'

'That he did, Franziskus, that he did.'

'I thought you esteemed honesty as the highest of virtues.'

'I don't tell anyone else how to behave. Leave that to the preachers.'

'But if his men can't trust him, how can we?'

A long curl of flaxen hair rolled itself down from Franziskus's head and onto the corpse's gore-soaked shirt. Angelika got it out of the way by tucking it behind her companion's ear. 'We can't and shouldn't. You don't know the half of it. But his men – they want to be deceived. They were desperate for those stirring lies. You think they wanted to be told their friends had died in error, and that they're likely to do the same?'

'I think they wish Jonas to be the man he seems.'

'That's a harsh standard for anyone to live up to, isn't it? Besides, all men of power are liars. Their followers depend on it. Demand it.'

'Who speaks harshly now?'

'The trick, Franziskus, is to be neither sheep nor shepherd. A feat very few can manage. Now help me roll him over.'

Franziskus complied, wondering if she'd truly taught the shepherd his lesson, or if their ultimate destination was the wolf's den. He was about to ask her, when he reconsidered. The metaphor was a laboured one.

THE PLATEAU LED to a switchback threading between two sharp peaks. Angelika walked its length for a quarter of a mile as the funeral rites were completed. Franziskus followed after her, and Filch tagged after him. Though perhaps well-suited for use by mountain deer, the trail seemed inauspicious. At its widest point, the flat surface between slopes was barely two and a half feet across. In many spots, there was no flat at all so the men would have to travel on an angle, their boot soles sideways on bare rock. The trail curved out of sight behind the rightward peak. It was impossible to tell where it terminated, and whether it led to a stretch of traversable terrain.

'Not such a bad trail,' said Filch.

'Maybe for you, hoof-foot,' said Angelika.

Franziskus thought she was being a little sharp with him, but Filch, taking her words as a complimentary, beamed and vigorously nodded his head.

'Jonas's men will likely sprain some ankles getting through this.'

When the three of them returned, the company had mustered into formation. Angelika spoke to Franziskus, who approached Emil. Jonas strode up beside them, rubbing his hands together, projecting enthusiasm. A performance, Angelika assumed, for the benefit of his men.

But when he spoke it appeared that his attitude was genuine. 'We've been dealt a terrible setback,' he said to Emil. 'But now that fate has demonstrated her fickleness, we shall worm our way back into her good graces.' He glanced over his shoulder at the mounded rows of graves. 'When we've distanced ourselves from this unlucky place, our fortunes will turn. We'll find our nest of Kurgs and send them packing.' His hand whipped forth to grip and shake Angelika's forearm. 'And we'll find you your lost property, Angelika. I swear it. What did you see, up ahead?'

'I thought we'd established a protocol,' she answered. 'I talk to Franziskus, he talks to Emil?'

'Let us dispense with such nonsense. You were right, Angelika. Right all along. This is no place for protocol. Please, feel free to speak to me directly, when the safety of my men is at stake. You, too, Franziskus. Even you, sir halfling.' He looked down to address Filch and the half-man's face opened up in adoration.

'In that case,' Angelika said, 'you'll need to break that column back down into single file.'

'A lengthening of our lines leaves us vulnerable, does it not?'

'The path's sloped. There isn't room for a double file to move without crashing into each other. The slopes are bare rock, so if anyone comes at us we'll get plenty of warning. Not a spot I'd choose to ambush from, if I were a Kurg.'

Jonas waited for Emil's nod of approval, then mimicked it.

'If it's one long line, sir,' Emil ventured, 'I'd say split the archers between front and back. Our scout, I trust, takes point position?'

Such is the price of increased trust, Angelika thought.

'If she will do it,' Jonas said.

'Yes, I will.'

'And I'll be with her,' volunteered Franziskus.

'No,' said Jonas. 'You and I will take a forward position, but after the first file of archers.'

'It is my custom to accompany Angelika,' Franziskus said.

'I command otherwise, Franziskus. You and I must get to know one another better.'

Filch shot his hand up. 'I'll go along with her.'

'Very well, my sure-footed friend. Angelika will appreciate the company, I am sure.'

Angelika curled her lip.

'Where do you want me?' Emil asked. As usual, Angelika found his mood unreadable.

'Position yourself amid the strays,' Jonas answered. 'I was harsh on them before so you must give them hope that they can prove themselves. Find a trustworthy fellow to promote as their corporal, to lead them.'

Emil nodded, then went out to bellow the soldiers into their new configuration. Jonas, arm around Franziskus, took him aside.

To get Angelika's attention, Filch loudly sniffed. 'This will be a grand adventure, will it not?'

'Grand.'

Angelika waited till the archers came and the line of men seemed to coalesce, then set off without warning. Filch and the archers lurched after her. There were ten archers left in all, which meant five would join them at the head of the procession, and five would take up the rear.

Angelika set a slow and heedful pace into the switchback. Behind her, the archers kept their bows ready.

'Point those things skywards,' she told the nearest bowman, a lean-faced fellow under a windswept mop of thinning hair.

'Skywards?'

'If something comes at us without warning, it'll be some hideous Enemy flyer swooping down on us from the sky. So point your arrows up there, and away from my backside.'

The archer pondered the slate-grey clouds. 'Do such things exist?'

'Don't worry,' Angelika replied. 'I've only seen them once.'

Five bows pointed up. The archers kept an eye on the sky, as if expecting flying Chaos dragons to swoop down at any moment.

Behind the archers, Jonas and Franziskus spoke. They were just out of earshot, a fact Angelika found unaccountably maddening. They ought to be making friends, she told herself, if Jonas was to take him off her hands. That was the entire plan, wasn't it?

'Angelika's concerned for your future,' Jonas told the young deserter.

Franziskus was heartened to hear it, but could not say so. 'While she is in any way under threat, I can give no thought to that.'

'When this mission is done, she'll give up her ghastly career. Then you must think of yourself.'

'When that happens, I will. Somehow I think it will not.'

'You do not believe her when she says she'll give it up?'

'She's broke again. She'll have to start from scratch.'

'But let us say that we find this chieftain, and get the ring back.'

'An unlikely prospect, wouldn't you say?'

'No, Franziskus. Sigmar is on our side, remember?'

'Oh yes. I did forget.'

'Like your friend, Franziskus, I am sure we'll recover that ring.'

'Are you now?'

'Or, if not, I'll see to it she's handsomely rewarded, for her services to the Empire. For her contribution to our coming victory. Ring or not, your need to serve her is coming rapidly to its end. You must begin to think of yourself now.'

'I am perhaps not as selfless as you think.'

'Only an honest man is anxious to claim greed's mantle, Franziskus. I have been thinking. It is a shocking thing, for an officer to desert. A man from society's highest rank. To smooth this out will not be easy.'

'I'm sure you're right.'

'I take it you'd be unprepared to lie your way through? To claim, say, that you were taken prisoner by a Kurgan advance party, and held for all these many months against your will, till you escaped and joined up with Angelika? At which point you immediately returned to Stirland, where I swept you up along with the other stragglers?'

'To lie would only compound my dishonour.'

'Ah,' said Jonas. He slipped on the sloping rock; Franziskus helped to steady him.

'I expected you would say as much. Your concern for honour is admirable.'

'It cheers me to hear you say that.'

'Fortunately there is another way.'

'Oh?'

'A battlefield commission. If I restore your officer status now, and you acquit yourself favourably during this mission, any who would wish to prosecute you will be presented with a *fait accompli*. As a serving officer of the Gerolsbruch Swordsmen, you will be, by definition, a deserter no longer. After the war, our forces will be badly depleted, in dire need of officers. There'll be no hunger to prosecute you. Not if you prove your loyalty now.'

'Don't you already have a second lieutenant?'

'Glauer?' He directed Franziskus's gaze to the fellow; he was picking his nose. 'So far he's proven an undistinguished choice.'

Franziskus averted his eyes, embarrassed for the poor wretch. 'Perhaps he should be given a chance to show you otherwise.'

Jonas clapped him on the back. 'With every refusal you increase my esteem for you. It is gentlemanly indeed that you would decline to displace another man. Even one of middling birth and questionable competence.'

'You flatter me. Jonas.'

A shriek keened from overhead. The archers jolted in anxious unison, pulling back the strings of their bows. A black speck moved through the sky but the crying creature was not a thing of Chaos, just a small hawk. The archers relaxed, slowly easing the tension from their bowstrings, then resumed the difficult hike through the switchback.

Jonas snapped his fingers. 'That's it. The Chelborg Archers. Why didn't I see it before?'

Franziskus waited for him to explain himself but Jonas just punched him delightedly on the shoulder. The sting of pain welled up a feeling of nostalgia in him. The shoulder punch was a staple of the interaction between Franziskus and his brothers. He fought twin urges: one, to smack Jonas back with an equal measure of over-enthusiasm. Two, to surrender his doubts and allow himself to trust Rassau entirely.

'The Chelborg Archers,' Jonas repeated. 'They've been placed under my command, but they are still a unit unto themselves. Thus, they require an officer, to lead them.'

'They are but ten men, now.'

'Nonetheless. The Stirland military code requires me to make a battlefield commission. For that matter, there are the strays. They require greater cohesion, do they not? I can fold them into the Archers. That places sixteen men under your command. A stingy number, perhaps, for a man of your sterling qualities. But they'll surpass the threshold needed to satisfy a court martial, wouldn't you say?'

'If – if you say so, Jonas. I've no experience with such matters.'

'Trust me, Franziskus. Your dilemma could not have a more perfect solution. Do you doubt now that the gods have intervened on our behalf?'

'I am not so much an egotist as to think that the gods take much of an interest in my activities.'

'You underestimate the reach of the divine, Franziskus. Into all our lives they shine their fearsome light, if only we are brave and let it fuel us. They will grant me victory, so I may do my dead father proud. They will lead Angelika to her ring. And you, my friend, shall be cleansed of your dishonour.'

'Your offer is very generous. And your heart is – I trust in the goodness of your heart, Jonas.' Franziskus was surprised to hear himself saying this, but he was, and it was true, as far as it went. He recovered himself, lowering his voice. 'But dual loyalties are difficult, Jonas.'

'I do not know what you mean.'

'If you make me an officer, and then I find myself in a position where I must weigh my duty to you against my vow to protect Angelika…'

'We'll prevail upon her to release you from that vow.'

'She's anxious to do that, I assure you, but my vow was made to the gods.'

'Talk it over with her, at least.'

'I will not disavow her. Not while she is in the slightest danger.'

'You will not need to choose between us, Franziskus. Our goals are not in conflict.'

CHAPTER FIFTEEN

THE SWITCHBACK LED behind the rightward peak and into a steep, heavily forested gorge, the meeting point of two jagged mountains. Centuries of flooding had deposited a layer of loose stones on the valley's narrow floor. It would be easier going, but the dense stands of trees along either side of the ravine would provide abundant opportunities for ambushers to lurk. Angelika beckoned to Jonas for a conference, and laid out the choice for him: to press on despite the risk, or to turn back, reversing a day's arduous travel. Dusk was coming. It brought with it swirls of fog. They rolled in the hollows, obscuring the bottom of the ravine.

Jonas's gaze swept the lurching, scraggly pines above. 'Can we get to the other side of the valley before nightfall?'

Angelika shook her head. It was hard to estimate the length of the ravine, or see what lay beyond it. 'If you ask me–'

'I am asking you, Angelika.'

'Let's camp here for the night. That way anyone who wants to sneak up on us can only do it from two directions, instead of four.'

Jonas nodded his assent and, as the last of the men filed out of the switchback and onto the rocky surface of the ravine, he waved to Emil, who gave the orders for a dig-in. Jonas leaned close to Angelika's ear. 'Speak to Franziskus. I've made him an offer, and if you care at all for him, you'll persuade him to take it.'

Filch offered her cheese. She took it and told him to go away. She sought out Franziskus. He'd found a long stretch of fallen pine log and had sat himself upon it, head in hand and elbow on knee.

'Never have I seen a person so visibly in a quandary,' she said, sitting beside him. She pressed the halfling's rind of cheese, uneaten, into Franziskus's palm. They spent a minute or so debating which of them ought to eat the cheese, which Franziskus knew to be exquisite, before Angelika grew annoyed, ripped it from his hands, chomped it in two, and held the remainder, still moist where her teeth-marks were, in front of his lips. Sulkily he took it from her, turning it over in his hands. He reminded Angelika of a squirrel, deciding whether to devour or bury his latest bit of forage.

He told her about the offer.

'Take it,' she said.

'On one hand, he believes each word he says, as he says it. On the other, he intends to drive a wedge between us.'

'His motives don't matter. Take the commission.'

'I knew that's exactly what you'd say.'

She stood. 'Stop saving me, Franziskus, and start saving your own damn hide.'

She wandered across the bed of rounded, fist-sized granites and quartzes until she reached Jonas. Two of his swordsmen struck a smallish tent for him. Angelika swallowed, despising the necessity of this next gambit. She'd taken Jonas deep into the mountains, but she was no closer to searching his kit and getting back her ring. She stretched, twisting her body into a girlish posture.

'That fog portends a cold night,' she observed.

She got the hungry look she wanted from him. 'You spoke to him?' he asked.

She edged closer. 'Give him some time. He has a heavy load of guilt to wrestle into submission.'

He moved back. 'He can't wait long. It would be best if he performed some great deed of valour after I commission him. The sooner that happens, the likelier it is he'll get his chance.'

Angelika brushed his fingers with the back of her hand. In different circumstances she'd prefer to break them.

Jonas leaned in. He kissed the back of her ear. Despite herself, she shuddered. Why couldn't she prefer the reliable, mousy ones, like Franziskus?

Filch was standing a dozen yards away, cheerfully staring at them.

Jonas pushed away from her. 'I have yearnings, too, Angelika,' he said, under his breath, his lips barely moving. 'But we must restrain ourselves. We must not only have discipline, but be seen to have it.' He headed over to Franziskus's log, presumably to further press his case.

Yearnings. What Angelika yearned for was to shove him off a cliff.

ANGELIKA CHOSE FRANZISKUS'S fallen pine as their sleeping spot. Sentries from the company stationed themselves around the floor of the ravine; Angelika counted eight of them. She wrapped herself in her bedroll and set her back against the log. Franziskus settled in to sleep; by sitting up, she'd claimed first watch. Neither she nor Franziskus trusted the soldiers enough to leave watch duties entirely in their hands. They would swap sleeping hours, two on, two off, until morning, as they did when they were alone. This protocol had been arrived at without discussion. It went without saying, now that they were in the mountains, that they would trust their safety only to themselves.

Filch, with Merwin in tow, skirted his way toward their spot, craning his neck for Franziskus. Angelika scowled at him. They wandered circuitously across the rocks, finally settling in with the stragglers, who'd arranged their bedding out in the open.

The exhausted soldiers fell asleep swiftly. Snores erupted from their unmoving bedrolls. Fog rose up from the valley floor to obscure their bodies from view. The sun had already set; the indigo sky turned black. Angelika scanned the forested slopes until the last light was gone, then waited in darkness, aware only of sound, and temperature, and the hard contact between her bony posterior and the rocks she sat on. There was no wind to rustle the pine branches above, so every noise stood out: the flapping of bat wings overhead. The strangled chirps they used to locate their insect prey. The muffled stirrings of unconscious men. The moist rumbling of her own innards, as they digested the night's meal of biscuit and jerky.

When she'd first embarked on this life, it had been difficult to stay awake like this, in absolute darkness, after a day of enervating travel. Now there was no question that her body would obey her; she would not doze off until Franziskus relieved her. Then she'd fall under immediately, slumbering deeper than a Sigmarite war-priest after a three-day ale binge. She wondered how it would be to sleep in a bed, under a roof, every night of the year. She'd had that kind of life once, but it had been so long ago, she'd forgotten what it was like.

Until then, she'd keep listening for wrong noises in the blackness.

Franziskus took over two hours later, pupating out of his bedroll without her having to wake him. They exchanged shifts twice again.

He shook her awake.

There was pre-dawn light. Her right hand gripped her knife, as it was trained to do.

'What?' she mouthed.

Franziskus pointed to a spot, dense with spruce and low bushes, about halfway up the western slope. A baby spruce wavered and shook, while the trees around it were still.

Someone or something was up there.

Franziskus pointed to the sentries, standing in a bunch on the rocky ravine floor, about twenty yards away. Several were archers; they had arrows already notched and aimed, at the position Franziskus had shown her.

Angelika took off in a crouching sprint toward the archers. Across the way, a sentry poked his head into Jonas's tent.

If those were Kurgan, Angelika thought, they hadn't attacked yet. It would take only a minute for anyone hidden up there to come crashing down on the camp. The archers would only get a few shots off before the mêlée was joined. For maximum effect, the archers should wait for the lurkers to reveal themselves. If they fired and missed, they'd waste an entire fusillade.

Jonas came running, strapping on his sword-belt, nearly getting his scabbard stuck between his legs. Anxious, grunting men poured from their bedrolls.

Idiots, Angelika thought. If they have bows, too, you're running into range. She detoured off into the ravine, to put some trees between herself and a hypothetical line of fire.

Grotesque faces rose up behind the spruces. They called out in an alien tongue.

The archers fired off a volley. An arrow seemed to find its mark; a body fell.

'Stop,' Angelika shouted. 'Dwarfs. It's dwarfs.'

A dozen stocky figures boiled from the trees, like hornets from a broken nest. Each was about four and a half feet tall, wide-shouldered, and bow-legged. Long beards streamed from broad, shovel-flat faces. The tops of their heads were bald, or they wore bowl-shaped helmets that made them look that way. Rings and studs dotted their notched and circular ears. A few wore heavy plate armour, criss-crossed by raised designs and runic letters. Scales and vambraces of hardened leather protected others. A few lofted shields overhead though most went without, preferring instead the reassurance of a long-hafted, double-bladed axe. These, too, were deeply notched and rune-carved.

The dwarfs pelted down the slope in a weirdly graceful, half-tumbling run. Their speed at navigating a treacherous slope put even the halflings to shame. Another quartet of dwarfs rose up behind them, firing crossbows.

The archers stood their ground to fire another round. Jonas and his fellow swordsmen hurried into battle formation, forming a rough wedge against flanking. An archer fell, a bolt penetrating his lower leg. A dwarf rolled down the slope, an arrow stuck in his throat.

'No,' Angelika yelled, first to the humans, then to the dwarfs. 'We're on the same side. We're not enemies.'

Franziskus crouched behind her. 'What do we do?'

She dived behind an ivy-covered rock, then reached back to tug on his arm. He flattened himself behind her. 'It's too late,' she said. 'Too late.'

It was all too common, even for forces of the same nation. In the confusion of warfare, especially in the dark or fog, soldiers on the same side often attacked in error, cutting down allies as if they were foes. Once, down in the Blackfire, she had scoured a battlefield where every combatant had been a member of the same mercenary company, out patrolling against orcs. There'd been no way of telling what fatal miscue had set them to destroying one another.

Franziskus stood. 'Stop, stop. It's a mistake.'

A dwarf crossbow bolt whizzed past his ear. He ducked.

Angelika swore. 'We may not have been enemies a minute ago, but we are now.' The grudge-bearing capacity of the average dwarf was legendary. The prosecution of feuds and vendettas was the central feature of dwarf society. If any of those fallen dwarfs were dead, the wider war, any sense of joint solidarity against the Kurgan horde, now meant nothing. They would exact a blood debt, or die in the attempt.

'Maybe these are Chaos dwarfs?' ventured Franziskus.

'Always the wishful thinker.'

The first of the dwarfs reached the valley floor, sliding down onto his backside and bowling into the line of swordsmen. The back of his hand struck a sharp, upturned stone and his axe flew from it and skidded off. Gerolsbruchers raised their sabres to hack down at his prone, wriggling frame.

Jonas held out his arm to halt them. He leaned over the dwarf, shouting into his face: 'Stand down! We are your friends.' The dwarf reached up, grabbed at Jonas's ears, and tried to pull him down to bite at his nose. Stirland swords pierced him, digging in through gaps in his armour left well exposed by his splayed-out position. He gurgled indignantly as he died.

The archers kept steady as more enraged dwarfs bore down on them. Arrows cut into them, but they thumped onwards. A dwarf axe shattered a Chelborger's bow, then cut through the cuff of his sleeve to slash the arm beneath. The sabres tore up to meet the dwarfs. Their line enveloped the attackers, leaving each of them outnumbered by at least a man, if not two.

As Filch and Merwin dashed for the cover of the trees on the opposite slope, crossbow bolts thunked around their feet. Bodo charged for a dwarf who'd just reached the valley bottom. The dwarf laughed without smiling and grunted out a threat in his native tongue. Bodo ran at him, at the last minute dropping down to sail between the dwarf's bandy legs. The dwarf spun, but not before the halfling butcher had slashed the tendon of his right heel. The dwarf's foot flew out from under him and he landed on his back as Bodo rolled out of the way. The halfling clambered onto his plated chest to stab him in the face and neck. Spitting blood, the dwarf lifted his axe but his strength abandoned him, and the weapon dropped from a claw-like hand.

More dwarfs joined the fray; these had crossbows slung across their backs, and were presumably the last of their unit. One charged at Bodo, whose back was turned to him. Jonas bellowed a warning. The halfling ducked the blow without turning, only to be kicked to the ground. His chin smacked into stony ground, and he lay stunned. The dwarf, who had a red tattoo incised on each temple, readied a death blow.

Jonas tackled him from the side but the thickset dwarf did not budge. The Gerolsbrucher grappled his arms around the dwarf's ample girth and fought to topple him. The dwarf threw him off and paused to decide which foe he most wanted dead. Bodo staggered, dazed. Jonas taunted the dwarf, calling him a fatherless son of a motherless ape. The dwarf hurtled at him, his features twisted with rage. Jonas had time to draw his sabre before the dwarf axe clanged down on it but the force of the strike brought him to one knee.

Franziskus bolted from his position of safety, toward the fight. Angelika grabbed at him, but caught only a handful of fog. 'Don't!' she called. 'Get dwarf blood on your hands, and they'll hunt you forever.' This was an understatement: wronged dwarfs would chase your descendants, to the seventh generation.

As Franziskus ran, he saw that the tattooed dwarf had somehow acquired a solid grip on Jonas's hair. At their feet lay the helmets and weapons of both combatants. The dwarf slammed Jonas's face down onto his armour-plated knee. Jonas rolled and fell, his forehead scraped. His snorting, wheezing opponent stomped him in the throat. Franziskus shouted, to distract him. Startled, the dwarf scrabbled back and stooped to recover his axe. Surprised by his own speed, Franziskus reached his quarry and slashed upwards with his blade. Its swipe parted the dwarf's beard. He tested his chin with gloved fingers; they came up bloody.

He charged at Franziskus, who clouted his back with a glancing blow and then went down. The dwarf butted him above the nose with his exaggerated ridge of a brow. Nimbuses of silvery pain jigged hazily in Franziskus's vision. The dwarf shuddered; Jonas had recovered his feet and stood above him, chopping his neck and skull with the sharp surface of his sabre. The stocky warrior shook in outraged disbelief, half-heartedly attempted to bite off Franziskus's ear, and expired.

Franziskus crawled out from under the stunted hulk of a corpse. The fighting had stopped. Around them were strewn eleven fresh-killed dwarfs. Four more members of the company – an archer, two swords-men, and a stray, lifelessly bled onto the rocks. Jonas struggled for breath. A red stream gushed from his nose. He reached into his jacket for a rag to staunch it.

'Shallya have mercy,' he gasped.

The first yellow rays of dawn haloed the trees on the eastern ridgeline. Angelika moved cautiously into view. 'We'll need more than the mercy goddess if their kinfolk ever find out about this.'

The remark appeared to confuse some of the nearby soldiers, so she acquainted them with the basic facts concerning dwarfs, and their propensity for vengeance.

'This wasn't our fault,' said Jonas.

Angelika moved to the slope, where a dead dwarf lay staring on his back. 'Tell that to their sons and brothers, when they come to even the score.'

'They were supposed to be up north, fighting the orcs.'

'You didn't expect every single able-bodied dwarf to be gone from these mountains, did you?'

'It's their fault for not revealing themselves.'

'They might say the same about you.' She knelt over the body.

'You mean to loot them?' Jonas asked.

Angelika blurted out a horrified laugh. 'By no means.' She addressed the men as a group. 'I don't know how you feel about souvenirs, fellows, but you'd better take not a scrap from any of these dwarfs here. See those runes all over their armour and cloth-ing? Dwarfs mark their possessions well, for precisely this eventuality. You don't want to get caught with dear old Uncle Guthnir's heirloom dagger hanging from your belt.' The words seemed to sink in, but it was hard to tell.

From the dwarf's throat she plucked the fatal arrow and examined its feathering. 'This pattern, with the alternating red and gold fletching – how distinctive is it?'

An archer stepped forward, rubbing the wrenched muscles of his pulling arm. 'That's Chelborg fletching.'

Angelika's shoulders sank. 'Here's what we have to do – and quick, in case this is only part of a patrol, and the rest is headed this way. First, comb the bodies and get these arrows out of them. Every single one. Then we need to make this look like they were killed by Chaos troops. So you'll need to take those axes of theirs and hack those bodies apart like you're the most frenzied crop of drool-spattered barbarians who ever slaughtered a foe. Then we have to get ourselves out of here as fast as our feet will carry us. And never, ever, as long as any of you live, breathe a hint of what we've just done to anyone. Do you all understand?'

'She's right,' Jonas said. The bleeding from his nose had stopped, at least momentarily. 'Get to it.'

Few of the men broke to it, and even they traced stunned, aimless steps around the dwarven dead. 'Get to it,' Jonas shouted, shocking them into action. 'And get our dead onto pallets. We can't leave them here, to be found among the dwarfs.'

The soldiers shuffled like sleepwalkers. They picked up dwarf axes but were reluctant to use them. Angelika wrenched one from a nearby swordsman's hand, stalked over to a dwarf who lay on his back, and hacked at his neck until she broke through the vertebrae and severed it from the body. She closed her eyes, placed her foot on top of it like it was a croquet ball, and sent it rolling.

This action stopped in his tracks any soldier who had been working. 'He said, get to it,' Emil bawled.

Jonas came to her as if wanting to talk, but Angelika hiked up the slope. There were more dead up there, and they'd all have arrows in them. Franziskus came with her. She parted stunted spruces and circuited around spiny gorse bushes, hiking diagonally up the gorge to the spot where the dwarfs had fallen. The ground cover was surprisingly thick; to find them, she'd rely on her sense of distance and feel for terrain.

'I know what he's going to say,' she said.

'What?'

'Before I told him to be honest with his men, and now he's going to rub this in my face and tell me how eager I am to deceive, when need be.'

'And what would you say to him, if he said that?'

'I'd say that certain scenarios nullify all general moral considerations. Chief among these is finding yourself knee-deep in dead dwarfs.'

From below, in counterpoint to their words, played the repeated sound of axes whacking into tissue and bone.

'If we're on the same side,' asked Franziskus. 'Why did they not stand and greet us?'

'They're a distrustful people. I imagine they wanted to be sure we weren't yammering cultists of

Chaos before they offered us stout and sandwiches.'

Angelika reached the approximate point she was looking for. A ledge, about four yards long and six to seven feet wide, stuck out from the ravine wall. Tall pines extended up in front of it, providing cover. A trail led down to it from higher up on the slope. It would have been the perfect place to wait and observe the humans. Angelika clambered up onto it. A dead dwarf lay face-first on the slab. She rolled him and plucked an arrow from his throat.

'Damnably accurate archers Jonas has with him.'

'Perhaps we'll later have cause to cheer that fact.'

To make him an easier bundle to haul down the slope, she bound his ankles with his belt and wrapped him up in his own cloak. 'Was there a second one?'

'I'm not sure.'

There were no other bodies on the shelf. At one point, it offered a natural jumping-off point, to a mound of dirt below. Heavy footprints cratered its surface. To its left was a reasonably surmountable patch of slope; to the left, a collection of rough and peaky boulders. The body of a second dwarf lay flat out on them, as if slumbering in a bed of granite.

Angelika hopped down, asking Franziskus to come and help. He followed, less sure-footedly than her. Together they turned the dwarf onto his back. A blot of crimson stained the rock he'd lain on and a matching wound blemished his forehead. It wasn't an arrow that got him; he'd fallen and bashed in his skull.

The dwarf's lips parted and his left eye slowly opened. He groaned. Feebly, he closed his right hand, as if he hoped to grip his axe-haft. The weapon lay under him, still stuffed into his belt.

'No,' said Angelika. She drew back from him. 'No, no, no, no, no…'

The dwarf gurgled out a stream of red saliva and some barely audible words, which neither Angelika nor Franziskus understood.

'Don't you dare,' Angelika said, her lips barely moving. 'Finish up and die.'

'Human scum,' the dwarf mouthed, switching to Reikspiel.

'What do we do?' asked Franziskus.

Angelika could not move.

'Our fight… your fight,' said the dwarf. 'Without us… Chaos wins…'

'This was not our intent,' Franziskus said. 'We took you for Kurgs.'

This angered the dwarf, and he tried to sit up. He slumped down, the back of his skull hitting his stony pillow. The dwarf tried to remonstrate but was having difficulty speaking.

'It was a blunder of war. But once the first arrow flew, you would not relent.'

'Never…' A fresh spurt of blood gushed from his mouth into his curly grey beard. 'Once attacked, never relent.'

'We can get you to safety,' Franziskus said.

'You must pay,' the dwarf stammered, his voice growing weaker.

'That wound is bad but you may recover. We'll bandage you up. Get you home.'

'I will kill you. My brother will kill you. My son, and the sons of his sons, they will kill you.' He pointed to his brain. 'I enter you in my book of grudges. All of you. You black and yellows, each will pay.'

Franziskus knelt closer. 'Listen. You can't be saying that. I understand that you're angry. That your head throbs, and you're not thinking clearly.'

'For what you've done to us,' said the dwarf, 'you must die. Your fate is as clear as the water of Ulreid's Stream.'

'They will not patch you up, you understand, if you're threatening to kill them.'

'I am Hrund, son of Thorhal, and I will not lie, for any reason.'

'Don't you see I'm trying to help you?'

'I place a grudge on all of you. Patch me or leave me, you all must die.'

Franziskus saw that the dwarf was marshalling a wad of bloody spit to hock in his face, and reared back to avoid it.

Angelika rubbed at the bridge of her nose. She shook her head.

Franziskus pulled her aside. 'We can't just leave him here.'

'No, we can't,' she agreed.

He saw the look on her face and knew what she meant. 'No, Angelika. You can't...'

She moved further off. 'We've got to finish him.'

'The dwarfs are our allies.'

'Not this one. Not now. We can't have him crawling his way back to Zhufbar, or wherever he's from, to enlist his kinfolk in a vendetta. He's seen our faces.'

'He's delirious.'

'Delirious with vengeance. He's not joking, Franziskus. We've got to do it.'

She drew her knife and moved back toward the dwarf.

The dwarf appeared to find a grim amusement in his predicament. 'You'll not give me a fighting chance?'

'If you survive this, and find us again someday, will you give us a fighting chance?'

Hrund, son of Thorhal, laughed up another mouthful of gore. He shook his head.

'You have to admire his honesty,' said Angelika. She edged closer, preparing to stab down at him.

'Angelika…' said Franziskus.

'Very well,' said Angelika. 'I will give you a fighting chance. You're lying on your axe. Stand up, Hrund, and you can die in battle.'

Hrund tried to lift his body up off his weapon. He quivered. Then the tension ebbed from his body, and he collapsed against the rock.

Franziskus's heart soared, believing that the dwarf had expired.

Hrund's chest panted shallowly up and down.

'Curse it,' Franziskus said.

The dwarf chuckled, or wheezed, or perhaps both.

Angelika hefted her dagger.

'You never kill, except in self-defence,' said Franziskus.

'Which this is.'

'He's no threat to you now.'

'If he lives, he will be.'

'In war, soldiers must sometimes kill the wounded. It is something I've never seen you do.'

Angelika shifted the knife uncertainly from hand to hand. 'I've never been implicated in a dwarf-killing before.' She moved toward Hrund.

Franziskus stayed her hand. She was about to argue, until he unsheathed his sabre. He hopped onto the rock beside Hrund and hacked at his neck with an executioner's stroke. The first blow killed him, but Franziskus kept at him until his head was struck from his shoulders. He turned to Angelika and said, 'I am, as always, here to protect you.'

CHAPTER SIXTEEN

ON THE DISTANT horizon, thick folds of naked granite pushed high into a sudden blue sky. Closer by, more than a dozen callow peaks jostled against each other. Centuries of whipping wind had carved their sandy stone into evenly rising mounds. Points adorned each summit, like the tips of meringues. Needled trees and bushes had taken stubborn root in their ever-eroding soil; bare, narrow trails wormed through them. In their folds and crannies, Angelika saw hundreds of hiding places.

Spyglass in hand, Jonas surveyed the expanse. 'Sigmar's blood, do these mountains go on forever?'

'We don't want to go all the way to the Kurgan lands, do we?' said Angelika. She stood at Rassau's side, along with Franziskus and Emil. Filch had somehow attached himself to them. Emil pierced him with a hot-poker glare, and he drifted off, as if hunting for

edible mushrooms. If such things existed here, a
halfling would be the one to find them.

It had been three days since the dwarf-kill, all hard
journeying. The company had seen neither dwarf nor
Kurgan. Nor had Angelika found the opportunity to
safely rifle the lieutenant's personal effects.

Jonas had called the company to a halt after a long
slog over a chalky escarpment. They'd used ropes to
climb it, up one face and down the other, with metal
tent pegs as their pitons. He'd proclaimed it a miracle, a gift from Sigmar, that not one of his men had
fallen. These were stout, square-headed men of Stirland, not nimble mountaineers.

Now they were stopped on the sides of a rocky
sluice, across which a fast trickle of cold, clear water
skittered. It barely possessed the depth to fill a canteen. Silent, dust-caked men bent over it to slap its
contents into their mouths. Those ordered to stand
sentry watched their mates drink, waiting anxiously
to be relieved.

Jonas shoved the spyglass back into his pack and
sighed. 'If honesty is a virtue, I'll be virtuous,' he said.
'I haven't the faintest idea where to head, or what to
count as our destination. We're to go into the mountains and harry any regrouping Kurgs. Well, it's been
days since we've seen any. I reckon this is why I've
brought you along, Angelika. Where do we find
them?'

'Right here,' she said. With the toe of her long, slim
foot, she pointed to a round rock in the middle of the
stream. It stood above the others, out of place. A band
of mud ran across its exposed side. 'See that dirt on it,
there? That's from where it used to be lodged, in the

bottom of the stream. See how it's lying on its side? How the part that's been polished smooth by years in the water is now partly in it, and the rough bit that anchored it has been dislodged?'

Jonas nodded. 'Someone knocked it out of place, while walking across here.'

'And recently,' Angelika said. 'That mud's not entirely dry yet.'

'Could it be more dwarfs?'

'They'd never leave such obvious signs of their passing. Dwarfs can be surprisingly light on their feet, especially up here on their native ground. If they'd been by here, they wouldn't want you to know it.'

'Well, good,' said Jonas. 'None of us are in the mood for more dwarfs.'

The company had yet to shake its melancholy in the wake of the gorge incident. Angelika had expected them to easily shrug off their accidents of war, but instead they'd been dismally determined to reproach themselves.

'If only,' said Jonas, 'we could find some of the accursed enemy scum, and give them a solid trouncing. That's what the men need.'

'Careful what you wish for,' said Angelika.

Jonas bristled. He'd been no less touchy and peevish than any of his men. 'Nothing would please us more than to subject the foe to the full brunt of Sigmar's righteous hammer.'

Angelika gestured to the maze of mounded peaks. 'Take another look in that spyglass, lieutenant. Every shadow you see, every recess in the rock, every hollow – it could have a nice, fine nest of Kurgans in it, massing for the next great march on civilization. You were sent here to patrol? If I were you, this is exactly where I'd start.'

'Then patrol we shall,' said Jonas'. Angelika could not tell if he was irked by her, or by the complexities of the task. 'So advise us, then. The Gerolsbruch Swordsmen are no borderers. The men are trained for open battle in full formation, not patrols.'

Emil cleared his throat. 'I've assigned men patrol duty before, sir.'

'Yes, of course,' said Jonas. 'Break the men down into units. Make a map and mark out quadrants to scour. If there're Kurgs here, we'll flush 'em out.'

The sergeant nodded and went off to fulfil his orders.

'If the Kurgs do stage a second wave assault,' said Angelika, 'and they're anywhere near here at all, I can't imagine them not coming through these hills. They're so much easier than anything to either side.' She pointed out the rougher terrain to east and west. 'Even if we don't stay here, we should lay down some traps. Make them pay a heavy toll to use this route.'

'You know traps?'

'My main interest is in avoiding them. The goblin ones are particularly nasty. But to disarm a trap, you've got to know how to build one.'

'Then I'll send you out with a patrol, to do that. Now if you'll excuse me…' He left, catching up with Emil.

'He's decided this is somehow my fault,' said Angelika.

'Not at all.' Franziskus knelt to fill his canteen. 'You're too much the lone wolf to understand a man like that. He's worried for his men.'

'Always looking for the noble motive, Franziskus.'

'Not to mention, awed by the enormity of his task.'

'It is fairly hopeless.'

'Thank you for offering to build those traps.'

'Why?' Her voice dripped suspicion.

'I am heartened to see you doing your part.'

'Am I?'

'I knew you couldn't resist, when it came to it.'

She threw her hands up and backed away, nearly tripping over a wayward root. 'Oh, no, don't you dare. Don't you think it for an instant. You can go ahead and care about these soldiers and their mission. In fact, for you, I recommend it. But me, I am not forming a scintilla of an attachment. You understand?'

'All I said was–'

'It's about the ring, Franziskus. About the ring, and only the ring.'

As instructed, Emil made a map of the mound range. Each hill he gave a name, each beginning with a different, consecutive letter of the alphabet: there was Mount Apple, Mount Barley, Mount Cabbage, and so on, up to Mount Lemon. The names offered a glimpse into the sergeant's mind: apparently he was mostly thinking of food.

Angelika went up the south face of Mount Eel with three swordsmen and a straggler: broad-faced Madelung, leathery Mattes, bug-eyed Saar, and the moustachioed Pinkert, who hung back from the rest of the group in order to ogle her from a distance. Though thick around the face and shoulders, Madelung could have been Franziskus's slightly younger brother. Mattes was the company drummer.

Saar kept his eyes on his toes and said little; he was not a swordsman, but a handgunner. Pinkert she maintained a close watch on, deciding which of his fingers she'd break if he tried to grope her.

They'd been up the side of Mount Eel for more than three hours before the subject was broached. She'd already shown them how to step lightly onto dried vegetation, to dampen telltale snaps and crunches. She taught them how to hold the branches of spruce trees as they moved through them, so their brushings would alert neither enemy eye nor ear. When Madelung, heaving himself up a slope, dislodged a boulder the size of a bread loaf, she gave them a climbing lesson, teaching them to identify dangerous spots, and to pick a zigzag route around them. Even lecherous Pinkert listened to her with quiet attention. Whenever she taught them something, she could see the mental effort on their faces, as they committed each tiny lesson to memory.

'Now that you know all this, you'll teach the others. Yes?'

They assured her that they would.

Now they stood on a slope covered by a dense copse of leafy bushes. 'First thing before laying a trap,' she said, pointing into the bushes, 'is to check it isn't trapped already, by somebody else. So take out your sabres, and comb your way fastidiously through it, parting the leaves from each bit of trunk. Study the ground cover. If you see anything that raises your hackles, back slowly away.'

The men searched the bushes, as she commanded. When it was plain that there were no traps there, she continued: 'Next thing is to think

like the enemy. Which way will he come from?
Your traps are no good if they're pointing the
wrong way.'

Any enemy troops, they figured, would most
likely be headed downslope, after having come
down Mount Fennel and then up this hill's far side.
Angelika agreed. They'd brought with them a pack
full of sharpened stakes, which they'd hewn from a
pine log found down by the stream. 'From what
I've seen of Kurgs,' she said, angling a stake above
the ground, 'they move none too cautiously. They'll
be waving their axes in the air and rag-tagging their
way down this slope, showing off for their lunatic
gods. So, just like we're setting these stakes to
receive a charge, we can angle them up like so, to
catch 'em in the legs or belly. Their own momentum will drive the stakes in. Don't be miserly with
the stakes; the denser you lay them in, the likelier
you are to impale yourself a Kurg.'

They got to work digging. She showed them to
make the holes deep, so the stakes would provide
resistance when a body hit them. She made them
pack the dirt in tight around them.

'Good thing someone here knows what he or she
is doing,' muttered Mattes, the drumsman.

'Careful,' said Madelung.

'We've all been speaking too careful, if you ask
me,' said Mattes.

'Maybe no one did, though.'

Angelika reposed on a bit of flat ground. Even
though it was more productive to supervise and
teach the men when they went wrong, she hated
sitting still and watching someone else work. 'If

you're worried I'll repeat what you say to the lieutenant, you can rest easy,' she said. 'I'm no tattle-tale.'

'Never mind us,' said Madelung. 'The dwarf incident's got us all uneasy.'

'And the previous fiasco, so many of us killed by so few Kurg,' said Mattes.

Madelung pulled a knifing finger across his throat.

'What?' demanded Mattes, shifting forward, impinging on the younger man. 'You won't be telling me to shut it, would you?'

'Both of you could go ahead and shut it, far as I'm concerned,' said Pinkert. 'Pointless gibber accomplishes nothing. I propose a contest for who can recite the filthiest limerick. The winner gets to sit out while the others work.'

Saar broke his conspicuous silence. 'I was afraid to say it, seeing that Rassau was never my commander till a few days ago. But compared to the officer of my old company, he's got me scared. He don't know what he's doing.'

'So what if he doesn't?' asked Madelung, voice breaking. 'He's the only commander we got, and let's say for a minute he is lacking experience. If we undermine him, it'll only get worse.'

Mattes turned himself around, to face Angelika. 'He listens do you, though, don't he?'

She got up and brushed the dirt off her leggings. 'I'm just the scout.'

'But he does listen to you,' Mattes persisted.

'He asks for my advice and he takes it or he doesn't.'

'But you do know what you're doing.'

All four of the men had rolled up from the digging positions, and knelt around her. 'Tell them,' Madelung said. 'Yes, we've had setbacks, but the lieutenant – that doesn't mean he don't know what he's on about.'

Disliking their supplicating arrangement, Angelika bent her knee alongside them. 'Listen. I've been meaning to ask you something. All of you were in that fight, near the fort, back in Hochmoor, yes?'

'Indeed,' said Madelung.

'I don't suppose any of you happened to see the moment when I crashed down on top of that chieftain.'

They all shook their heads but Saar. 'I saw it. I was, ah, between opponents.' He pulled back from the others as if expecting to be called out as a shirker.

'When the chieftain got up, you didn't see him bend down and pick something off the ground, did you?'

'No,' said Saar.

'And did you see anything come flying out of my pocket?'

'Like what?'

'Like a small object, perhaps.'

'No, I didn't. But if it was small – I was mostly looking out to make sure no marauders was going to smack my head open. I could have missed it. Why?'

Angelika paused for a moment to mull the wisdom of her next gambit. She was impatient to make something happen. Perhaps it was reckless, but the cautious approach was getting her nowhere. Maybe if word got around, the guilty party would smoke himself out. If there was such.

She leaned in conspiratorially. 'I think you're honourable men, and that I can trust you. Right?' Angelika did not put much stake in codes of honour, but perhaps they did.

'We are free soldiers of Stirland,' Madelung proclaimed. 'It goes without saying that we're men of honour.'

'I've lost an item which is precious to me,' Angelika said. 'I won't lie to you. It's a valuable item. A ruby ring. You haven't noticed any of your brothers-in-arms behaving strangely, have you? As if they might be keeping an expensive secret?'

'I can't believe any Gerolsbrucher would descend to thievery,' said Madelung.

The creases on Mattes's face deepened; it might have been an attempt at a smile. 'I've seen more than him, so I believe anything about my fellow man. But I've seen nothing suspicious. I'll tell you if I do.'

'Let's keep this between ourselves,' she said, assuming that the entire camp would know by dawn. 'If any of you help me find it, I'll see that a fair reward reaches your family.'

Mattes chewed on this for a moment. 'We're happy to help, reward or no. Aren't we, boys?' He waited for the others to indicate their vague assent. 'Though I'm sure none of us would turn up our noses at a modest sweetener, would we?'

Pinkert and Saar agreed more vigorously.

Mattes went on: 'But what we need from you, Fraulein Fleischer–'

'Angelika.'

'What we need from you is in the here and now. Maybe the lieutenant will do us fine, like Madelung says.'

'I'm sure he will,' said Angelika.

'I'm not,' replied Mattes. 'I been a Gerolsbrucher longer than anyone, except for the sergeant. I seen commanders come and go. The good, the great, and then the ones that couldn't find their elbows in the middle of their arms. There's an air the good ones give off. Like you'll be safe if only you do exactly as they say. This one, this Rassau, he don't give off that air.'

'He'll figure it out.'

'Oh, I'm hoping so. I'm not one to be spreading discontent and rumours. They can kill a company faster than any foe. But the lieutenant don't know these mountains, nor this kind of mission. And, like I said, he listens to you.'

'What do I, a mere woman, understand of war?'

Mattes snorted. 'That's a good one. Angelika. You have the air. Like you know the lay of a place like this. I don't know what magic you got to work to do it, but you've got to be the one to keep us safe.'

'This is a wilderness infested with bloodthirsty savages. No one is safe.'

'You get my meaning. I heard you talk, back in that halfling town. We all did. You're a truthful woman. Isn't that so?'

He had her there. 'Much to my detriment.'

'Then you answer me this, honestly. Can the lieutenant find his elbow?'

'He's a skilled fighter.'

'That's not what we're asking.'

'Like you say, rumours and discontent can be deadly.'

'You agree to stuff some sense into him. Teach him to lead, like you're teaching us to lay these stakes. And the four of us, we'll do our part. If that ring of yours is here, anywhere in this campsite, no matter who has it, we'll see to it you get it back. Do we have us a deal?'

Angelika stood. 'Yes. You have a deal.'

When they'd finished with the stakes, they tramped over to a narrow crevasse, a few yards across and five or six feet deep. They gathered up logs and branches. After placing more stakes down in the bottom of the fissure, they laid the old foliage across the crevasse. Then they covered it with dirt and rocks. Anyone larger than a rabbit treading onto the camouflaged branches would crash down into the crevasse and onto the stakes.

Angelika watched Mattes and his fellows finish up. She realised that she'd gone and done it again. Promised to protect people. On her honesty, no less.

JONAS OBSERVED ANGELIKA and the soldiers come down from the mound. They were many yards away, too far to hear what they were saying. Something in their body language triggered his sense of caution. Misgivings resurfaced. Perhaps it was unwise to let Angelika deal directly with the men. Beforehand, he'd worried that she'd offend them, that they would hate her, and demand her expulsion from the company. Now that he saw her with the men, saw the easy way she walked, saw their eyes shining at her, a new threat reared its head.

They would like her better than him.

It was a problem his father had told him about. Often, in a company, there would be one fellow who was not an officer, but who was charismatic and held in good esteem by his mates. If the commander was weak, they would look to this shadow leader for their cues. Before following an order, they'd check what he thought best. Under fire, they would waver, between their officer, and this other fellow. That arrangement brought hesitation, discord, and disaster. Dual lines of authority, his father had told him, were not to be tolerated. If you got assigned to a unit, and it had a shadow commander, you had to break him, the quicker the better.

But he could not break Angelika, because he needed her counsel.

It was surely a conundrum. He wanted a Kurg to come crashing from the low reeds, so he could strike him dead with his sword.

He paced and thought. There had to be some way to deepen his hold on the woman. Bind her tight to him.

He searched for Franziskus, finding him, as usual, among the halflings.

'Franziskus,' he said. 'We must talk.'

Franziskus leapt up, returning a bag of nuts to Filch's hand.

The two well-born Stirlanders walked together along the rocky stream.

'You've weighed my offer?'

'I have.'

'If you're to be an officer again, Franziskus, you must be prepared to make decisions quickly and irrevocably.' His eyes followed Angelika, as she stood talking to Mattes and one of the stragglers, a portly fellow Jonas remembered only for his bulging, fishy eyes. He wondered what they were saying to each other. Mattes seemed to be looking at Jonas's tent.

Did Angelika suspect? Was she sending Mattes to search his things? He'd never trusted Mattes. He'd been with the company too long, longer by far than Jonas. He had that attitude of seniority about him as if the time he'd put in gave him the right to judge his betters. The man was too sour to be a shadow commander, but as fomenter of trouble, he bore close watching. And that other one, Herr Protruding Eye. Something not altogether square about him, either.

'Surely you do not seek the fealty of a man who would offer it on an impetuous whim,' Franziskus was saying.

Pretending his attention had never wandered, Jonas latched his arm to Franziskus's shoulder and subjected it to a manly shaking. 'I do want your loyalty, Franziskus. Do I have it?'

'If I was entirely free to give it, I would.'

'You've spoken with your mistress?'

'Another expression you shouldn't use with her. Yes. She wants me to do it.'

'Then do it. Say yes.' He lowered his voice. 'There's a reason for urgency, Franziskus. The men are anxious. I cannot go personally among them and hear what they're saying about me – about the mission. Emil, he is too much the cipher to be of any help. His allegiance is to the company, not to me. I need a right hand, Franziskus. That is what a second-in-command is for.'

'Glauer can't do that?'

'He's as useless as a spigot on a ladder. I'd sack him but the men need no more shocks right now. Anyhow it's better for you if I put you in charge of the Chelborgers. When we get back to Stirland, you could wind up in permanent command of a reconstituted unit. You do wish for that, don't you, Franziskus?'

'I—'

'This is no time for irresolution. I'm offering you salvation. Will you take it or not?' Jonas wiped his brow with the sleeve of his officer's coat. Over his shoulder, he could see that a couple of the stragglers, and that vexingly ubiquitous halfling, Filch, were pretending not to watch them, from several feet down the riverbank.

Jonas marched off toward a line of hunched and sickly trees. 'I fear that I am not instilling the correct impression in the men. Your indisposition to fully commit afflicts me with unease. That is fatal in a leader, Franziskus.'

'Jonas, you're letting the strangeness of the mountains affect you. My first time in such parts, it was the same. We're men of the valley lands. It takes a flat green pasture to put our minds at rest. This place, its implacable peaks, its hostility – it would disturb anyone.'

'This is why I need you, Franziskus. At first I thought it was Angelika, but now, I see it is you who understands. And possesses the sense of responsibility I require. Must I ask you yet a third time?'

'You're skipping breaths. The air is thinner here. Take the time to fill your lungs with air, and immediately, you'll feel better. I was the same way, at first. You can't let the men see you like this.'

'No, I can't.'

'This fear is natural, but you can master it, Jonas. Just breathe.'

'Yes.'

Jonas calmed himself. 'I am sorry.'

'Don't be.' Franziskus thought he heard something. Edging slowly, so Jonas would not detect his alarm, he saw a yellowed, weedy bush rattling in the wind.

'It is humiliating to you, to see me panic in such a base and childish manner.'

'I did the same, Jonas, I did the same. I hid my fear, from Angelika, who seemed so cold and masterful. I felt ashamed, but I should not have. Only a madman comes here and feels no fright.'

'How can you want to join with me now?'

'I will,' Franziskus blurted. 'I will help you, I swear it. Too much hangs on this. We must defeat the Kurgan. You will recover from this moment. I promise you.'

Jonas dashed behind a tree and doubled over, sure he was about to throw up his meagre morning meal. Nothing came. Eventually he straightened.

Franziskus, to his credit, kept his distance, and leaned against a tree trunk as if they were engaged merely in casual conversation. 'I can't count the number of times I nearly did that, my first few months in the mountains,' he said.

Jonas examined a tremulous hand. 'You must teach me to conceal these awful shakes.'

'It is mostly a matter of practice.'

'I've no time for that. I must lead these men now.' He moved closer to Franziskus. 'At least now I have a confessor. That will help. You have a helping instinct, Franziskus. There is no trait more admirable.'

Though intended as a compliment, the comment set Franziskus's nose to twitching. Would he always be the helper? Perhaps it was time to become the primary actor in his own life.

'Have I offended you, Franziskus?'

'No, no. What would make you say that?'

Jonas fixed his gaze up to the ribbon of rock covering the south-eastern horizon. 'And Angelika. You can tell me honestly. How does she regard me?'

Franziskus found this new mood difficult to read. 'She wants her ring back.'

'Yes, yes, that I know. But aside from the ring. How does she see me?'

Franziskus felt suddenly cold.

Jonas saw him draw back. 'Don't misunderstand me, Franziskus. It's clear you feel… like a brother to her. A protective brother. If she has said anything to you in confidence, I would never…'

'She would not speak to me of such matters.'

The bush was wavering again. The actions of winds were sometimes hard to discern, but it seemed to Franziskus that the dry fronds shook more heavily in one spot than in any other, and that they did so against the general direction of the breeze.

'Again I am ashamed,' Jonas announced.

Franziskus moved toward the bush. 'How so?'

'Suddenly I see that your feelings for her are not those of a brother.'

'We needn't speak of this.'

'No, no, my friend, it goes without saying that you have the earlier claim on her. I shall remove myself from all contention.'

'You're not in contention.' Franziskus braced himself, as if ready to give Jonas a good shove. He swallowed his anger and lowered his voice. 'Jonas. She thinks you have her ring. Do you?'

'No,' said Jonas. 'By no means. How can you think that of me?'

'You were concerned for the men, and their safety. So you took the ring when the two of you were… together, and you concocted the story of the Kurgan chieftain picking up the ring. To secure her services. For the greater good.'

'This is how the both of you see me?'

'If you did it, it was for a noble reason. I'll not blame you.'

'You think me a thief. A common pilferer.'

'I'll do as I've said, and serve you as loyally as I've served Angelika. If you give her the ring back and let her go on her way.'

'I don't have it, Franziskus.'

'It means her entire life. Her freedom.'

'I've said I don't have it. How can you persist in accusing me?'

'I'm merely asking you if you have it.'

'I do not, I swear it.'

'Then I will believe you, Jonas. Because you are a worthy man, more so than I, and would never seek to win a man's fidelity by dishonest means.'

'I would never do that. I am not capable of such baseness.'

'Then the issue is closed.'

'Tell Angelika. Tell her I did not do it.'

'Do not set yourself on winning her admiration, Jonas. I've saved her life on several occasions and, depending on her mood, rate only grudging toler-ance.'

'I think you're wrong on that point, Franziskus.'

'Truly?'

'As for myself, I'll do what is necessary to recover her trust.'

Franziskus shrugged.

'More importantly, I am glad to have gained a valuable officer, Second Lieutenant – what is your last name, Franziskus?'

Franziskus's attention turned back to the wavering bush. 'Pardon?'

'Your last name. You've been unwilling to tender it. I can't commission you without one.'

Franziskus drew his sabre and charged at the bush. A tattooed Kurgan bolted out from it. Franziskus ran at him, interposing his sword between his legs. The Kurgan toppled, landing face-first in the gravelly soil. Franziskus braced himself, holding until the intruder could stand and arm himself. Were their positions reversed, the barbarian would give him no quarter, but Franziskus was better than that, and still believed in a fair fight.

'Thank Sigmar,' shouted Jonas. He'd circled around the bush to rush at the fallen barbarian. The Kurgan leapt gracefully into a crouch and reached for his knife. Jonas kicked it gleefully from his hand. He launched a second kick at the marauder's throat. The Kurgan fell to his knees, gasping.

'Surrender,' cried Franziskus, 'and you'll not be harmed!'

The Kurgan stared at him, uncomprehending. Of course, Franziskus thought – they do not speak our tongue.

Jonas's sabre lacerated the barbarian's face and neck. When the Kurgan dropped to cover them, Jonas slashed and speared his back. Franziskus stepped back, appalled, as Jonas struck the scout, continuing long after he'd gone limp. Finally Jonas stopped, his chest heaving, his face wild and proud. He knelt and grabbed the Kurg by the hair; he was dead all right.

'Aha,' Jonas exclaimed. 'Where there's a scout, there's a force. No more running. No more fear. I have prayed to the gods for redemption. Now that chance is ours, Franziskus, for you and me both. Now is when we, the Gerolsbruch Swordsmen, hunt and slay our cruel foe.'

CHAPTER SEVENTEEN

'THERE'S KURG ABOUT,' Jonas said, his soldiers gathered close around him. 'Our job is simple – get them before they get us.'

Franziskus was heartened to see that the lieutenant had thrown off the waywardness he'd shown during their little talk, just a few minutes earlier. He'd reigned in his gestures and tamed his fearsome expression.

'No longer will we sit and be acted upon by others,' continued Jonas. 'Now it is we who'll act upon these mountains, and the scum who hide here.'

The soldiers inspected one another's faces for the signs either of encouragement or disquiet. Franziskus saw a collective decision settle on them: they would be brave. They would again believe in their leader. A few, though, like Mattes, the drumsman, withheld their enthusiasm, until they could measure Angelika's response.

'We'll break into our earlier patrol squads,' said the lieutenant. 'Even numbered squadrons will head to the hills, to seek out the foe. Each squad takes the hill he already mapped. Odd numbered squads stay here. Establish a perimeter. Keep in tight and brace for assault. They could pour down on us at any moment. There could be ten of them, or a hundred times ten.

'Maintain that patrol scheme until the sun says three o'clock. Then come back down and swap off with the other squads.

'This is not a stand-up war. There is no dishonour in attack by surprise, or a fight against inferior numbers. If the enemy outnumbers you, fall back without shame. Find a hiding spot, or retreat to camp. If Kurg boil down to overwhelm the camp, do what they would do – melt into the hills. Come back to kill them later, when they are unprepared. Pick them off one by one. Stay with your squad. Be prepared to act on your own. If we're scattered, we'll regroup later. Be stealthy. And fast, and clever. Obey your squadron leader as if he is Sigmar Himself. Do these things and you will win. You will slay them, my Gerolsbruchers, my Chelborgers. Now let us fly.'

The men jittered from the crowd, swarming around each other to find their squads. Men clapped each other on the shoulder. Their hands curled into eager, shaking fists.

Jonas took Franziskus by the arm and hunched to speak into his ear: 'We'll make the announcement afterwards. After the men have a few kills under their belts, and there's a mood of celebration in the camp.'

'There is no transaction so worthy that good timing will not enhance it,' said Franziskus.

'Try to kill a barbarian or two while you're out there. Your elevation will go smoother once you've proved yourself.'

Trepidation fluttered in Franziskus's breast.

Jonas marched off, to find his own squad.

Angelika came toward Franziskus. Her squad, Mattes and the rest, stood at a remove, waiting for her. 'Stay behind,' she said.

'What?' asked Franziskus.

'Stay behind. The camp will only be half full. And Jonas has them worked up into a panic. They'll be staring at the hills for swarming Kurgan. You can stand lookout while I go through Jonas's things.'

'You must go with your squad.'

'I don't have a squad. I'm a scout, not a warrior.'

Franziskus edged away from her. 'And I'm about to be a lieutenant again, in the Stirland army.'

'Good for you, but did you have to pick this minute to do it?'

'Angelika, Jonas needs our help.'

'He needs more than we can give.'

'He's brave but unsteady. You need to tutor him, like you did me.'

'Anything you learned out here, you picked up on your own.'

'Surely you don't believe that.'

'There's no teacher more surly and impatient than me.'

'That I agree with.' Franziskus dropped to near inaudibility. 'He's afraid, Angelika.'

'Fear's the first step toward common sense.'

'He has the makings of a good leader. A heroic one, even. We must do our part, and nudge him toward his destiny.'

Angelika stared at his undefended tent. 'I'm staying here.'

'I beg you. If he took the ring, he did it only to secure your aid. Give it to him, and you'll get it back.'

'What a beautiful world you live in, Franziskus.'

'I'm not asking you to strangle a child or burn down a nunnery. I'm asking you to do good.'

'Eloquent words – lieutenant.' She said it like it was an insult.

Angelika tried to break from him, but, as the men bunched up into their squads, there was nowhere she could stand that was not conspicuous.

'It was a lieutenant I should have been, all along,' said Franziskus. He stomped off to join his squad.

Angelika moved toward Mattes and the others. They knew about the ring. They wouldn't object if she stayed behind to find it, then caught up with them. Not if she worded it in the right way.

Jonas intercepted her. 'No, Mattes will lead that squad. You're coming with me.'

She shrugged. 'It's all the same to me.' Inwardly, she was cursing. 'But shouldn't you, as commander, stay behind?'

Jonas's brow wrinkled up. 'On what account?'

'You're the leader. The men can't afford to lose you.' She wasn't exactly sure what good it would do, to have him remaining in camp, but it would be better than tramping off into the hills with him. The lieutenant was unpredictable, and Angelika could think of no trait she valued less in an ally.

'Fraulein Fleischer, I can never tell when you're jesting with me.'

'Think of the blow to morale, if you were to fall beneath a Kurgan axe.'

'What kind of army would this be, if its noble leaders eschewed personal combat? No officer ever won a spot in the chronicles by hanging back to let others fight for him. Now let us go. There's Kurgan in need of killing.'

Jonas had picked his squad personally. Angelika did not want to know about them, so she would suffer no unwanted consternation if their lives were threatened. She couldn't say this, though, so Jonas introduced them. Caven stood tall and broody beneath a heavy brow and thick sheaves of black, feathery hair. Egerer was a hungry assemblage of protruding bones. Hertwig perpetually petted a long, forking goatee and regarded his surroundings with a beady stare. The fourth man, Kollek, wore a knotted gold ring on each finger of his left hand, and an even larger silver one on each of the right.

Angelika estimated their value at just under a hundred crowns, making him the one she'd most want to find dead on an abandoned battlefield. All four of the men were Gerolsbruchers of long-standing. From the pride in Jonas's voice as he announced their names, Angelika gathered that these were among the company's best soldiers. He meant to have a glorious encounter with the foe, and had brought with him the right men to accomplish that.

Mount Gander was Jonas's hill – the rockiest, and closest to the distant mountains. Its rough shelves of pitted rock and thick patches of pine forest would make a good hiding place for lurking enemies. When the introductions were done, they hiked its way,

passing other, less imposing hills. To reach its foot
would take half an hour of hard treading, and during
that time Jonas allowed the men to calm their nerves
with jokes and banter. They discussed the soldier's
perennial topic, food. The skeletal Egerer got onto a
naming jag, listing the name of every soup he could
think of. His fellows attempted to steer him to a
different subject, but could not help adding to
Egerer's roll call of broths, as they thought of obvious
items they'd so far omitted.

Angelika hung back, surveying the slopes of the
hills as they walked between them. They could just as
well be attacked on their way to the hill as on it. The
movement of a black shape up on the slope to her left
stopped her momentarily before she realised it was
only the shadow of spruce branches, jostled by a gust-
ing breeze.

Jonas spoke. 'You think I took your ring.'

She'd detected him, coasting up behind her, into
her blind spot. 'What makes you say that?'

'Franziskus says so.'

'The two of you have formed a pact, I hear. That is
good.'

'He needs looking after, as you said. He'll need a
future, when you get that ring back.'

'Your confidence is most encouraging.'

'I did not steal your ring. I'm surer than ever that
the big Kurgan has it.'

'Let's hope he's up on Mount Gander, then, so you
can kill him for me.'

'Oh, I'll kill him. If you're certain of nothing else, be
certain of that.'

Angelika did not reply to this.

'I require your allegiance as well as his.'

'Good thing I'm looking for a lost ring, then.'

'Not just in your deeds, but in your heart, as well.'

'Don't use that word.'

'Which word?'

'The one that starts with *H*.'

He chuckled ruefully.

She slowed down, letting the men go ahead. 'You truly want my allegiance, Jonas? Learn to be honest with your men. That's heroic – to blunder, and admit to it, and then do better.'

'An officer must maintain his authority.'

'If you have to call on your authority, you've already lost it. Once your men start to suspect your honesty, they won't believe you even when you tell the truth. They don't want a man they can worship. They want a man they can trust.'

'I've not thought of it that way before.'

'You're right to battle the barbarians, yes?'

'They'd burn the whole world. There's no cause more righteous.'

'Then you don't have to lie for it.'

An arrow appeared in the side of Caven's neck. He dropped down onto the trail, dead.

Kollek clutched his throat. It, too, was pierced by an arrow. It was crudely fletched with thick tufts of dark feathering – the work of the Kurgan.

Egerer and Hertwig had Kollek under each arm before he could fall. They dragged him down to a meagre depression by the side of the trail and pushed themselves into it. Hertwig could not go fully prone, the angle of the arrow prevented it. A third arrow landed in the dirt before them.

The shots came from a slope to their left. Angelika ran toward it, pressing her back to its side. Jonas did the same. They watched as more arrows sailed down to the depression where the three men lay. Kollek shuddered as he was hit again, this time in the calf of his right leg.

None of Jonas's men were archers; they could not return fire.

Angelika gauged trajectories: the arrows came from a band of bushes covering a wall of sheer rock, about six feet high. Above this modest cliff hung a stretch of sloping hillside, surfaced in a thick coating of dry soil, dotted by the occasional hand-sized stone. The bushes were thick enough that she could not see the barbarians behind them. That was good: it meant they might not be able to see her, either. So far all of the arrow shots had been made at the soldiers, who'd been a good dozen yards ahead of her and Jonas. If they were lucky, they hadn't been seen.

Jonas seemed ready to bolt toward the soldiers, to shield them with his body. She pointed to the slope overlooking the rock wall. 'Have you got a throwing knife?'

'I'm not good with it.'

'Then you won't mind lending it to me.' Angelika had only two daggers; those leaves enshrouded at least three archers.

Jonas wore his knife strapped to the back of his cuirass. She unsheathed it and tucked it into her belt. 'I'm going up there. Kill them from a safe remove. Stay down here. If it looks like they're going to spot me, distract them.'

Grabbing onto a jutting tree-root, Angelika hauled herself up onto the slope. She started by moving further away from the hidden archers, using the curve of the hill to conceal herself. She inched along slowly, so the dried grasses would not crunch beneath her feet. Only after she'd clambered to a point higher than their position did she creep back toward them.

After a moment's pause, the snipers resumed firing. Below, a soldier groaned. Angelika could not be sure, but it sounded like Caven. She checked to see that Jonas was still in place but he'd moved out slightly from the hillside. If the archers looked his way, they'd be able to draw a bead on him. She wished she could shout to him, urge him back to safety, but of course that would only expose the both of them. His foolishness gave her a new appreciation for Franziskus; he'd never be so rash. Unless those in need of rescue were children or ducklings.

She reached the bare slope over the snipers' roost. From there she would have to step even more cautiously, any dislodged stone could easily roll down onto the archers, alerting them to her presence. The slightest trickle of dirt would betray her. Angelika planted a testing foot into the dirt. The soil was firm and sun-caked, sufficiently deep to brace her as she eased along the slope.

Another scream. She couldn't tell which soldier had been hit.

The curve of the hill hid her original position from her, just as it did the snipers. There was no way of knowing if Jonas had stayed safely put.

She concentrated on her own slow progress down the slope. The cliff was angled unforgivingly. To get a clear sightline, she'd have to reach a point practically on top of them. She'd hurl two knives, then leap down with Jonas's blade – it wasn't properly balanced for throwing – to slit any remaining throats. If there were more than three or four of them, she'd be in trouble. The ledge didn't look like it would hold many more than that, so her plan was risky, but not insane.

Angelika had about a yard to go before reaching her mark. An ovoid stone stuck out from the dry soil near her toe. It was loosely anchored. To stop it from falling, she crouched to press it down.

Then she saw it: she'd put herself in an even better position than she'd imagined. All the way down the slope, she'd been at pains to prevent a rubble cascade. Now that she was this close, though, it would be just the thing. The entire scenario played out in her mind's eye with splendid precision.

She'd kick a few rocks down. The barbarian archers would pop their heads up to see what was up, giving her a clear shot at them. If the archers moved back to take aim at her, they'd topple from their ledge. They'd have a tough time climbing up onto the slope. While they struggled, she'd have all the aiming time she needed.

Angelika could scarcely believe her luck. All the angles were completely in her favour – she had a superb chance of taking them all, with almost no risk to herself. Seldom had she found herself in such an ideal position. She took her knife from her boot, transferred it to her left hand, and hauled back her foot, ready to dislodge a large and convenient chunk of quartz-laden stone.

Thrashing sounds came from down below and the tops of the bushes shook. She heard Jonas's voice, and the angry grunts of surprised barbarians.

He'd charged their perch from the bottom of the hill. It was a terrible spot to fight from – they had the higher ground. Jonas would have to struggle up onto their ledge, through the bushes, as they fought him off. It would take the Chaos troops a few seconds to drop their bows and haul out the hand weapons, and then he'd be at their mercy. The blasted fool was about to get himself killed.

There was little she could do about it, without exposing herself to the same danger. Now that they were under direct attack, a few falling rocks would do little to get the Kurgan's attention. Jonas's impetuosity had ruined her perfect opportunity.

She'd stay safely on her perch and let him do it. He was a good fighter. He could take them.

There were three of them, at the very least. And they enjoyed nearly every tactical advantage over him.

She edged closer to the ledge to take a peek down at the mêlée. Jonas was indeed in trouble. His head poked up through the bushes; his off-hand desperately held a woody trunk of hedge. There were four Kurgan, not three. One had his boot planted solidly on Jonas's sword-arm; the commander's sabre lay flat on the ledge, his fingers still clamped around its hilt. A second Kurgan, axe in hand, jostled for the proper angle, preparing to saw at the lieutenant's other arm.

Angelika hurled a dagger into the back of the axeman's neck. He fell back into the two men behind him. The three of them resolved into a protesting tangle of limbs. The fourth barbarian, who held Jonas's sword-arm, committed the fatal error of looking back. This presented Angelika with her favourite target; her second throwing knife squelched deep in his eye socket.

Angelika hoped that Jonas would have the elementary sense to let go, dropping down away from the ledge. Then the remaining Chaos troops would have to jump down through the bushes to pursue him, allowing her to remain safely on the slope above.

Jonas did the opposite, capitalising on the confusion to haul himself further up onto the ledge. The two unharmed Kurgan freed themselves of their injured comrade, tossing him aside to crash through the foliage and out of sight. Given little room to swing long blades, they instead drew their hunting knives, nine inches long and improbably serrated. Jonas batted his sword at them, hitting the bushes, filling the air with fragments of shredded leaf. His shorter blade, the one he'd need to win this fight, was in Angelika's hand.

The bigger Kurg lunged at him, ducking under his sword to butt him in the face. Jonas's feet wobbled drunkenly under him. The Kurg sheathed his dagger and got behind Rassau. Immobilising the lieutenant's arms with his own, he wrenched him over, so his mate could stab him. Jonas kicked out; the knife-wielding Kurg slashed at his legs.

Angelika pulled in a deep, involuntary breath and leapt down onto the Kurg with the knife. Both of her hands were wrapped around the hilt of Jonas's dagger; her momentum drove it deep into the shoulder of the shrieking Kurg. Angelika hoped he'd lose his footing, so she could land on top of him, but he remained upright. She bounced off him, sticking one hand out behind her to brace herself against the ledge as she fell backwards. Pain jabbed through her wrist as it caught the brunt of her weight.

Seeing that the Kurgan she'd hit had dropped his knife, she let herself drop to the floor of the ledge, then rolled to snatch it up. The Kurgan, a dagger lodged in his beefy, naked shoulder, tried to stomp her, but missed. Angelika curled up onto her knees, got partway between his legs, then pushed her back up against his left leg, shoving him off-balance. He toppled backwards, his head hitting the bushes on the way down. They broke his fall, preventing him from breaking his skull on the rocky ledge.

She spun; the big Kurgan still had Jonas in a sturdy grapple-hold. He bulled forward to smash Rassau's body into the cliff wall. Jonas stuck out a leg, to blunt the impact, but still winced in agony. Angelika sank into a crouch, the Kurgan knife in her hand, readying herself for a good opportunity. She couldn't get at the barbarian while he had Jonas as his shield. The ledge was too small for her to get around him.

The Kurg puffed with the effort of keeping the well-muscled Jonas suspended; he tightened his grip on his captive but let his feet touch the ledge. Jonas slumped down, then pushed off, and the two of them disappeared through the rough, thumping onto the slope below.

Angelika felt sour breath on the back of her neck and ducked just in time to miss a blow aimed at her jaw. Her Kurgan had risen again and was ready to fight her unarmed. He was three inches taller and fifty pounds heavier than she; his torso a riot of defined and writhing muscle. Across his face crawled a pair of open-mouthed snake tattoos, their reptilian bodies intersecting on the bridge of his nose. A long tail of dark hair swayed from his top-knot as he swung his blocky fists at her. With each move he made, droplets of blood from the wound on his shoulder flecked from it. The dagger still protruded from the wound, apparently doing nothing to slow his rage.

He feinted a blow at Angelika's gut; she whirled under it to cut a superficial wound into his forearm. With bruising force, he elbowed her into the rock wall. He caught her weapon-arm with his knee and ground it into the wall. Her hand opened and the knife dribbled from it. The Kurgan grabbed her by the fabric of her tunic, intending to throw her into the bushes. She jumped up onto him, pincering his waist with her deceptively spindly legs. Angelika climbed him like a cliff, grabbing onto the dagger in his back. She wrenched on it and the serpents on his face constricted in pain.

She felt the tension drain all at once from him and, before she could slip aside, his slack, but weighty body was tumbling on top of her. Angelika hit the ledge first, landing painfully on her back. An instant later came the leaden form of the unconscious Kurgan, pushing the wind from her lungs. She lay helplessly pinned for several long minutes, as her exhausted body refused her instructions to it. On the other side of the hedge, axe clanged against sabre, as Jonas's fight against his barbarian banged on.

Don't lose this fight, Angelika thought. And if you do get yourself killed, at least hold him until I can shake this off.

It was impossible to tell, from the sounds of the duel, who was winning. She counted out the seconds in exhalations and sword blows. Angelika tried again to move the Kurgan off her. She lifted his still-breathing bulk three or four inches up over her torso before succumbing to the weight, letting him fall back down on her. Though he was out like a doused campfire, his eyes still stared open, directly into hers. His stink put her, seasoned corpse robber that she was, on the verge of retching.

She would need to summon all of her concentration to get this Chaos-loving lummox off her. She pictured the life that would be hers, when she got her ring back. The little farmhouse. The fireplace. Beside a well-stuffed chair, an unassuming side table. Sitting on that, a cup of lovely brandy.

From a few feet away, on the other side of the bushes, an unmistakeable sound burbled out – the distinctive, disappointed last breath of a dying man.

One or other of the combatants was no more.

Angelika pushed up against the heavy Kurgan. The victor, whichever he was, crashed and fumbled through the bushes. The Kurgan was lifted from her.

Jonas held out his hand for her; she took it, pulling herself to her feet.

'I had a perfect vantage,' she said. 'I could have got some of them, maybe all of them, without their getting near me.'

'I could not stand idle while they killed my men.'

Shrugging, she recovered her nearest dagger, from the neck of a slain marauder. She used it to finish the one who'd fallen on top of her, drawing a red line across his throat. After watching to be sure he was done, she yanked Jonas's dagger from her victim's shoulder. She handed it back to him and then found her own second knife.

He turned around and pushed his way through the foliage and down onto the slope. She went after him.

They walked over to the bodies. Caven, Hertwig and Kollek were all dead. Egerer had an arrow sticking through his left hand. Another had grazed his leg, on the same side, leaving a long but superficial cut on his upper thigh.

Jonas stood regarding the three dead soldiers.

Egerer came up beside him and quietly said, 'we'll have to leave 'em here, sir.'

'So far we've given every fallen man his proper rites,' replied Jonas.

'The three of us can't drag them back to camp, not if there are other snipers about,' said Angelika. 'We'd be easy targets, each of us lugging a dead man.'

'Is there a spot to bury them here?' Jonas asked.

'Sir,' said Egerer, 'they'd understand. We're in enemy lands. If it was me, I'd only like to be laid out under a blanket. Sooner let the vultures get me than think one of my comrades got himself killed securing my carcass.'

Jonas nodded. Angelika limped over to the men's packs, withdrawing their field blankets. As she'd done earlier, she examined their possessions, gathering up coins and jewels and wrapping them in three handkerchiefs to send back to the dead men's families. Kollek's bag of rings jingled richly as she handed them over to Egerer's care. None of them had her ring.

The three of them travelled in watchful silence. Any frank words Angelika had for Jonas would have to wait until they could speak in private. They couldn't distance themselves from Egerer, as they had from the four soldiers together. It would be good to let him stew in his sorrows for a while before working on him any more.

As she considered the matter further, her attitude toward him softened. True, the scrap might have gone better if he'd done as she'd told him. If it were Franziskus lying in a ditch getting shot at, and she was the one told to sit tight, would she have done it? No, not for a moment. And although she'd been battered, nearly killed as a matter of fact, she'd suffered no permanent damage, had she?

The project was not to get him to follow her orders, she reminded herself. It was to make a better leader of him. In truth, then, there was nothing more to say. Men had died, and that was a difficult thing, but his poor judgement, if you could even call it that, was not to blame. He had no cause to be ashamed and, fortune be praised, nothing to lie about.

By DUSK, TO Angelika's mild surprise, all patrols had returned safely to the base camp at the stony stream. She learned this from Mattes, who stood facing away from her, as if taking no heed of her presence.

'Sounds like yours was the unlucky patrol,' he informed her.

'Naturally.'

'Fengler's patrol spotted a few Kurg off in the distance, on another hill. They hunkered down, to follow them later. But by the time they got up to track them, they'd melted away.'

'Was their patrol spotted?'

'They think not. But the head on Fengler's shoulders is made of solid bone, and the men he had with him aren't much brighter. I'd wager even odds the Kurgs seen them.'

'And went off to fetch reinforcements.'

The creases deepened in Mattes's sun-ruined skin. 'If that's so, we're all gathered neatly together for a cosy little massacre. We got to get ourselves out of this camp formation.'

'You raise this with the lieutenant?'

He coughed up a sceptical laugh. 'I'm only a drumsman, Angelika.' His tongue tripped briefly at the mention of her name.

'Call me Fleischer if you like that better. What about the sergeant? Did you raise it with him?'

He shook his head. 'Question the commander, to Sergeant Emil Raab? I wouldn't like to do that.'

'You soldiers need somebody trustworthy who can get word up the command chain when you can see they're about to wet their own trouser legs.'

Mattes scratched inside his ear. 'That's why we keep women out of the military. You'd try to apply common sense to it.'

Angelika sighed. 'I agree it's best to split into small groups. Jonas has, however, taken all the advice he wants to hear from me for a good while. He needs a second voice, to talk into his other ear.' She heard crackling and spun around. 'I don't believe it.'

Under Jonas's supervision, a number of the stragglers bent down over a large campfire. They'd struck alight a pile of dry weeds, and now piled chunks of pine log around it.

'That'll bring them down on us.' She marched over to Jonas.

Midway through, she took hold of herself, slowing her advance, suppressing her sense of outraged logic. When she reached him, she said, with all the insouciance she could muster, 'Bit of a risk, isn't it?'

Jonas smiled. 'No, no, watch this.' He leaned in for a conspiratorial whisper. 'The men need cheering up. Some warmth in their bones that'll turn them around.' He snapped his fingers, and the stragglers ran up, ferrying over lengths of canvas and an armful of tall, thin poles. They stuck the poles into the ground, and lashed the canvas to them with lengths of tent cord. Jonas proudly regarded their construction efforts. 'This way we can have a fire, but not be seen by observers.'

'We're surrounded by hills,' said Angelika.

'Yes, but any enemy would have to be nearly on top of us already to see our flame. Wouldn't they?'

Angelika watched as the men piled up a veritable bonfire. 'A fire that size? A sharp-eyed scout could see it as far away as that ridgeline.'

'No, I think this time you're incorrect, Angelika.'

'I thought we resolved all this. This is why you brought me here. Because I know lines of sight.'

'I am grateful for the admonishment, but must balance it against other concerns. Such as the morale of the men.'

The men slowed their work, clumsily concealing their eavesdropping. Jonas snapped his fingers at them and they redoubled their speed.

Angelika knew it was useless; the soldiers had already been ordered to act. If he pulled down the blind and doused the fire, he'd be reversing himself, and in a way that all the men could see. She'd have an easier time convincing a fish to play the flute. 'This one night only, then,' she said.

Jonas withheld his acknowledgement. The sky darkened and more of the men gathered around the fire, as it leapt up above the limits of Jonas's blinds. At first the men talked little, transfixed by the leaping flames. The names of Caven, Hertwig and Kollek were not spoken aloud, but were heard just the same. Angelika listened past the sounds of the talking men, for noises outside the blind. Though there were watchmen posted all around, there was no pair of ears Angelika trusted better than her own.

Still, she heard the tone of their words, and Jonas was correct in one respect – the men were badly frightened. Perhaps their poor morale was a worse threat to them than a Kurgan incursion. People who survived in the mountains were cautious, but not fearful. A panicked man could find a hundred ways to die.

Angelika took a new look at Jonas. The lieutenant hunched forward on a log, seated with a straggler on one side and Filch the halfling on the other. He was studying each of his men in turn, and appeared to be honestly concerned for their welfare. This was more than Angelika could say for herself. It was possible, she had to admit, that he was right and she was wrong. The campfire might be worth the risk.

Saar was talking, a haunted expression behind his buggy eyes. 'Me, I'd sooner fight an inhuman foe. If only we were up to the north-east, fighting Grimgor's orcs. You look a greenskin in the face, and you see nothin' in his tiny crimson eyes but hate and malice, well, then that's just the way they is. They's inhuman, ain't they? But to stare back into a face on the battle-field, and to understand it's the face of a man, a man like yourself – but to see ten times the hate, ten times the malice gleaming in eyes exactly the same as yours – that's what I call terrorising.'

Jonas had been growing increasingly restive throughout Saar's monologue. 'Surely you do not mean to say that a Gerolsbruch Swordsman is terri-fied.'

'I didn't mean to say that directly. I mean…' Saar gulped. 'Not if you say I don't, sir. Though I wasn't a Gerolsbrucher till a few days back.'

A nervous silence descended. Jonas cleared his throat. 'You may speak freely – what is your name again?'

'Saar, sir.'

'Saar, I did not mean to speak as your commander, to enforce my views on you. If I disagree with you, it is merely as a fellow soldier. We may all speak frankly here.'

'I've said all I meant to, sir.'

'No, no. Please, continue. If we are to fight this foe, I would hear all theories on him. If fear stalks us, we must dispel it.'

Saar loosened his collar. His fellow stragglers scowled at him. 'Well, ah. In all honesty I've forgot what I've been saying.'

'You were comparing the orc to the Kurgan.'

'Ah, yes. I said, that's what I, ah, don't like about the Kurgan in particular, sir. To know that he's the same as me, save for his unquenchable madness. Because

276 Robin D Laws

orcs are stupid. They're brutes, sure, and strong, and fast, but dumb as a post. You can fool orcs with the exact same trick a dozen times and they never learn. Whereas a man, even a man drunk on hate, he's a clever creature. He'll outfox you in a dozen ways. He's determined. You put an obstacle in his path, he'll show the determination and the ingenuity to over-come it. Brute force alone is frightening, yes, but pair that up with the human mind, and you've got the worst enemy you could possibly face.'

Jonas rose from his spot on the log. 'I did not want to tell the tale of our exploits on patrol this morning. An officer does not engage in unseemly boasting. And it is sad to remind ourselves that three more of us have bravely fallen upon this hostile mountain soil. But, Saar, I must stand and speak, to disabuse you of your false estimation of our foe. The Kurg is numerous. The Kurg is savage. Yet clever he is not. In fact, a Kurg is stu-pider than an orc. An orc is bred to savagery. It is in his bones. It is what animates him.

'Yet man is innately good, and is born blessed by the gods. When he swears fealty to that force we cannot name, the Kurgan goes against man's nature. He is warped and twisted by this act of insane worship. When you go out to fight him, Saar, know that his mind is muddled by madness. What we have over him is mental clarity.

'Let me tell you what happened. We were on the trail when the arrows hurtled down on us. They had taken refuge on a rocky ledge, covered with a thick hedge of foliage. Yes, we were ambushed – but it does not take any great acuity of mind to find a cowardly place to fire from. Kollek, Hertwig and Caven fell dead on the spot.'

A sense of dread, verging on nausea, coursed through Angelika, pounding in a double rhythm with her pulse. He was at it again. She searched the rapt faces of the soldiers – where was Egerer, who'd survived the day with them? She coughed, hoping to warn Jonas off.

But he forged on, avoiding her gaze. 'Egerer crawled away into a mere hollow on the ground, flattening himself down there. Arrows landed all around him. He was wounded.'

Egerer, Angelika realised, was absent – assigned to sentry duty. Jonas couldn't have planned this, could he?

'Angelika and I outsmarted them immediately,' he was saying. 'She ran up the side of the slope, to pounce from above. Whereas I did what they thought no civilised man was capable of – I rushed at them, the courage of my virtuous faith suffusing the very muscles of my heart. I did not curl up in fear. I made myself a moving target.'

Angelika coughed a second time, also in vain. It would be too obvious if she did it a third time, so she resigned herself as Jonas dug himself deeper.

'Shocked by my valour, they drew back, and I crashed through the bushes at them, swinging my sabre above my head. Leaves and Kurgan blood flew everywhere. There were eight of them, cowering there, perched on that tiny ledge. Eight! If that isn't stupid, what is? In instants, three had fallen beneath the furious strokes of my blade. Others fled, cowed by my daring and certitude. When you face them, you must do the same. Be bold. Make them fear you.'

Angelika could not remember the last time she'd heard anything half as idiotic as this. It was true that barbarians were superstitious and far from subtle, but they never fled from a head-on charge. Among the Kurgan there was no greater sin than cowardice. Any Kurg who ran from an Imperial warrior, especially a single, foolhardy charger, could expect to be killed by his war-leader.

'Angelika dropped from the sandy slope above, landing on those who ran.' Now he turned to her. 'Our scout has been hiding her true skills from us. As she slashed them, she showed herself the equal of any Kislevite warrior queen.' He regarded her as if he expected her to be pleased by this nonsensical flattery.

Her fist trembled with rage; a thick warm hand appeared on it, squeezing it steady. It belonged to Mattes, who'd at some point sat himself beside her. 'Not now,' he said, under his breath.

'So show courage, my friends, and the Kurgan will reveal his true colours – those of a wretched slave and bully. What do you say to that, Herr Saar?'

The mood among the soldiers was different now than it had been after Jonas's previous orations. They gazed off into the inky distance, or down at their boots. Men straightened their collars, or adjusted the scabbards of their swords.

The man next to Saar elbowed him. He started; his tongue shot out to dampen his thick and nerve-dried lips. 'I say, you, er, you and Fraulein Angelika showed, er, cleverness indeed.'

For, as was clear to all but its author, Jonas's tale had not been one of ingenuity, as he had promised

The tactic it appeared to recommend was one of sheer idiot daring.

Jonas shifted his weight, then moved next to Franziskus, who sat opposite Angelika, mirroring her morose demeanour. She'd already told him of the Kurg encounter, so he knew as well as she did how far Jonas had diverged from the truth. Jonas treated him to a comradely thump on the back. Franziskus dredged up a flustered smile.

'I've a decision to announce,' said Jonas. 'In celebration of our small but significant victory today. You may not know that Franziskus here holds the rank of lieutenant in the Stirland army. It was a fact he kept humbly secret from me for too long. It transpires that he and Angelika are agents of our beloved elector count, long dispatched on a mission to the Blackfire. Remind me, Franziskus, what the nature of your mission was.'

Franziskus found his voice with difficulty. 'Ah. It was – I do not believe I am at liberty to specify, lieutenant.'

'But you can say that it was a secret mission of great importance. To protect the Empire.'

'The protection of the Empire is foremost in my mind, lieutenant.'

Jonas turned to address the men. 'Given our need for leadership, Franziskus has kindly consented to help us. Beginning tomorrow, he will take command of the Chelborg Archers.'

The archers traded doubtful glances.

Jonas pulled Franziskus up to his feet. 'Franziskus has impressed me greatly in the past few days. You archers, you will soon appreciate his qualities as well, and be grateful for his leadership.'

He waited. Franziskus saw that he was meant to contribute some words of his own. He thought for a moment, then addressed the archers, most of whom sat together, apart from the other men.

'Excuse my lack of preparation,' he began. 'I do not share Lieutenant Rassau's eloquence. I knew that he would make this offer, but not that he would make it now.'

He seemed so trapped and helpless that Angelika could not bear to watch.

'Chelborg Archers,' Franziskus resumed. 'Though I did not think I would again find myself a leader of men, I now embrace the role, as I hope you will embrace me in it. Our straits are far from easy. But our homeland depends on us. Though we are few, though we are far from home, we must not only survive but prosper here. For each of us, we must slay a hundred foes. It is a daunting task. But together we shall do it. With, as the lieutenant says, hearts filled with the certainty of our righteousness. Above all, I pray for Sigmar's guidance.'

He moved his head up and down to indicate that his speech had come to an end. A few of the men began to clap but when no one else joined them, they stopped. Franziskus went to the archers and shook the hands of each in turn.

It was Pinkert who broke the unfortunate silence. 'I know a lengthy poem,' he said. 'About Sigmar's battle against the daemons of Nebligrücken. Perhaps now would be a good time to recite it.'

No one disagreed, so Pinkert launched in. The poem was in an archaic form of Reikspiel, and Angelika was too impatient to follow it. She left the campfire, sweeping through the blind's canvas folds. The sky was so dark and starless that it was hard to see where it ended and the surrounding mountains began.

Jonas had followed her. He tried to grab her by the elbow but she was too fast, whirling around to face him.

'You seem displeased,' he said.

'What did I tell you?'

Little light escaped from the blind, but she could still see his hardening expression. 'The word is counsel. You counsel me. You do not tell me to *do* anything.'

This had not been his attitude after the three men had been killed, which had been closer to whimpering. But Angelika knew better than to say so.

'I painted you at least as brave as I. Surely you can't expect me to place you at the centre of the tale.'

'I expected you to stop lying to your men.'

'That?' He seemed puzzled. 'That was hardly – Yes, yes, that promise still stands. I would never deceive the men on a matter of consequence.'

'What was that, then?'

'Mere campfire talk – a restorative for weary spirits.'

'And what happens to that when they ask Egerer for his version, and mark you out as a braggart and a tale-spinner?' She headed away from him, toward her bunk.

'Egerer is loyal. He won't impugn me.'

She shook her head. Egerer already doubted him.

'And you,' he called, 'are loyal too – so watch what you say.' He whirled back toward the blinds, bumping into a soldier emerging behind him.

It was Mattes. 'Begging your pardon, sir,' he said.

Jonas jettisoned his anger in favour of a superior officer's jaunty condescension. 'A simple bump, my good fellow. No harm done.'

Mattes waited until he was out of sight behind the canvas wall. 'I did as you asked,' he told Angelika.

'As I asked?'

'While he was in there, telling his stories, I was in his tent, going through his pack.'

'And?'

'If he's got your ring, he isn't leaving it about in his tent.'

'Naturally. If he has it, it'll be on his person, won't it?'

'You see the faces of the men in there?'

'Yes,' said Angelika.

'They're more and more frightened of what clot-headed excursion comes next.'

'Restive, are they?'

'If you told me you hadn't noticed, Angelika, you'd be lying. Wouldn't you?'

She answered the question by saying nothing.

'Don't want the men getting too edgy, do we?'

'Is that my concern?'

'It won't be so easy, necessarily, to get your ruby back, if the good lieutenant is out on the trail and happens accidentally to get, let's say, an arrow betwixt his shoulder blades. Would it?'

'Now, Mattes, you're over-egging the pudding.'

CHAPTER EIGHTEEN

ANGELIKA AND FRANZISKUS were filling their canteens at the stream the next morning when Mattes came to fetch them, worry written on his face. 'Angelika,' he said. 'Lieutenant. He wants you both quick.'

'What is it?' asked Angelika, taking a drink from her water skin, then filling it to the top.

'Some hare-brained scheme–' He caught himself short.

It took Angelika a moment to understand. 'Don't mind Franziskus,' she said. 'What you can say to me, you can say to him.'

The drumsman did not seem especially reassured.

'Franziskus, this is Mattes,' she said. 'He's agreed to help us out. To see if the ring is anywhere to be found. In exchange, I've... made a... commitment to take an interest in the men and their welfare. Do what I can to instill in Jonas a scintilla of horse sense.'

'Congratulations on your commission, sir,' Mattes said to Franziskus.

'Speak freely, Mattes. What's said in confidence will remain so. And lead on, if we are wanted quickly.'

They strode north, toward the nearest of the mounded hills. Jonas and Emil stood waiting at its foot.

'You were saying, Mattes?' Angelika prompted.

'I don't know what it is, Angelika. Just that I've seen him like that before. And it's never good.'

Jonas was a distant, hopping figure, spare energy erupting from his rangy limbs. He clapped his fist into an open palm, casting frequent looks up to the stony rock layer bounding the mound valley's western edge.

'I'll leave you to it,' said Mattes, peeling off. 'But remember what we talked about, last night.'

Franziskus stopped. 'What did that mean?'

Angelika marched on. 'He's concerned that the men have little faith in their leader. That a stray arrow might unintentionally find its way into the lieutenant's neckbone. Good thing then, that you're in charge of the archers, isn't it?'

'I did not like lying to the men about my past.'

'I could tell,' said Angelika. 'I hope no one else could.'

'He put me on the spot. How could I gainsay him?'

'You couldn't. Don't blame yourself.'

Jonas waved at them.

'He's watching,' said Angelika. 'Seem happy.' She waved back at the lieutenant, her mouth fixed into an insincere smile.

Franziskus did the same. 'Don't seem too friendly, though. He'll know you're up to something.'

'Franziskus, it's a bad time to tell you this, now that you've yoked yourself to his destiny, but it's clear to me now that Jonas is a hopeless cause.'

'Good thing, then, that you've decided to help the men after all.'

'It's bad enough you get me into these situations without your gloating about it every time.'

They were too close to continue their conversation, and so went quiet. When they arrived, Jonas clasped Franziskus's arm for a hearty shake. 'Your first day as an officer again, hah?' He did not know how to greet Angelika, looming near her for a moment with his jaws slackly apart. She folded her arms.

'Well then.' He pointed to the rock layer. 'This morning at dawn I awoke full of new determination. I could not contain myself and so went out for a bit of a ramble on my own. And as I did so, I saw figures up on the ridge there. A mile away, you understand, but I saw them.'

'You're sure they were Kurgs and not dwarfs again?'

'Definitely not dwarfs. Had to have been Kurgs.'

Emil broke in. 'If you'll excuse my interrupting, sir, that's what I was saying. All the more reason to break camp.'

Jonas shrugged indulgently. 'The sergeant here proposes that we dissolve the company. Break up into patrol units and each go our own way, for the duration.'

'With respect, I believe that is the course of action implied by our orders, sir.'

'By no means, Sergeant Raab. I'll not be separated from the men.'

'Sir, we were instructed to harry the foe. Though Commander Vogt didn't say so straight out, I think that makes it clear. We're to avoid direct engagement and pick off as many as we can, opportunistically. It's a stealth mission, sir. One we can't perform with all forty-four of us clumped together.'

'You'd have me leave them to their own devices out here in the teeth of hell? Unthinkable.'

'Yes,' said Angelika. 'What is a lieutenant without a company of men to follow him? Merely an over-dressed corporal.'

'I did not bring you here,' said Jonas, 'to remedy a sarcasm shortage. Franziskus, you explain to her.'

'Explain what, lieutenant?'

He pointed again. After some determined squint-ing, they could see what he was indicating: a tiny black rectangle carved out of the rock, very near to the top of the formation. Its shape was too regular and geometrical to be a natural formation.

'A sangar,' said Angelika.

'Is that what you call them?'

'A dwarven lookout, hewn into the mountainside. You see them in the Blackfire, too. Though there they're usually half crumbled.'

'What's it's capacity, do you reckon?'

'It'll be scaled to dwarf height, but they can extend quite a way into a rock face.'

'How many men can it hold?'

'Hard to guess. Six? A dozen, two dozen. Three?'

'I'm betting it will hold all of us. A tight squeeze, perhaps.'

Mattes had been right – he was hatching a hare-brained scheme.

'But you saw Kurgs up there?'

'Oh, yes, it will be defended. But once it is ours, it will allay both my concerns, and those of the sergeant here. We'll have a secure base from which to send out our harriers. No more clustering exposed on the valley floor. And we'll still be a company, unified and strong. Isn't that right, Franziskus?'

Angelika answered instead. 'You do see the contradiction in attempting to capture an impregnable fortress, don't you?'

Franziskus tensed. 'What Angelika means to say is–'

'I didn't make you an officer to tell me what Angelika thinks. Your job is to explain what I think.'

'Jonas, we know you're a tough leader,' he said. 'That's why we feel at liberty to express the odd contrary opinion – you can hear it without crumpling. We'd never question you in front of the men, but here, you wish to hear all counsel before you decide. Yes?'

'That goes without saying.'

'Then let us think this through. Angelika, perhaps you'd tell us what it is that makes the sangar a difficult target. Leaving out the wit.'

'Dwarfs never pick poor spots to install their defences. When this was in use, you can bet they had a ballista or even cannons in there. The Kurgs won't have that, but there's no easy approach to the sangar from this side of the ridge. Below it there's sheer cliff for a good hundred feet. The climb will be tough to impossible.'

'Could you make it?' Jonas asked her.

'I'd have to get closer, to see. But we know the Kurgs have primitive bows, and can fire down at any climbers.'

'How do the Kurgs get in, then?'

'From above – first of all, you saw one on top, so that means they've sentries posted. There's likely a bolthole entrance, so its defenders don't have to rappel down the cliff to the opening.'

'That's the point of weakness, then. We'll get up on the flatted rock above it, storm the entrance, burst in, and overwhelm the defenders. Push them out of their own hole, onto the rocks below.'

'But sir,' said Emil. 'What good will it do us? What good is it doing the Kurg, really? Without cannons or ballista, it's got no strategic value that I can see.'

'The men need a victory, Emil. What do you say, Angelika?'

'Honestly? I can't think of a greater act of folly.'

'Splendid. Beforehand, the defining triumphs of military history have always been derided as acts of supreme folly. Afterwards, they are remembered as masterstrokes of verve and boldness. Franziskus, what say you?'

'You, Jonas, are our leader.'

As FRANZISKUS RETURNED to the camp, he veered to follow Emil, leaving the others behind. Emil stiffened.

'I am hoping we can work well together, sergeant,' said Franziskus. The note he meant to strike was conciliatory. His nervousness spoiled the attempt; instead he sounded crisp and forbidding.

Emil spoke without inflection. 'To fulfil an officer's commands is a sergeant's duty.'

'And I would not doubt that you'll do that duty, Emil.'

'It is best if you addressed me as Sergeant Raab.'

'Please hear me out. You've made your opinion of me plain.'

'I've said virtually nothing to you, sir.'

'But with gesture and glance, you've heaped me with contempt.'

'If you say I did, sir, then I must have.'

Franziskus stopped walking. 'Emil, listen to me. You must be asking what I will do, now that our fortunes are reversed. A spiteful man would take petty revenge. Make your life a misery. So I must assure you I've no intention of mistreating you.'

'A doubting man, placed in such a position, would be relieved to hear it.'

'That you would hold a deserter in low regard – that is right and proper.'

'Yes. I could not have known you were on a secret mission, and merely posing as a coward.'

Franziskus sighed. 'Let's neither of us pretend you truly believe Jonas's story.'

'He's our superior, lieutenant. He says it, so it's true.'

'You've devoted your entire life to this company, haven't you, sergeant? Officers come and go, but you remain. You are the Gerolsbruch Swordsmen.'

'I would never lay that claim.'

'That, too, is part of your devotion. So I will say it. And I'm an officer, so it's true.'

'Very well, sir.'

'You've served under steadier leaders than Jonas.'

'A sergeant does not speak ill of his commander.'

'You and I, we must help him find his feet.'

'A sergeant does not betray his betters with unwelcome aid.'

'You take the vows of rank very seriously.'

'A man is lucky if he is blessed with clear rules to measure himself by.'

'It would be a deplorable thing indeed, Emil, if you were forced to choose between loyalty to your company, and loyalty to your commander.'

'It will not happen, sir.'

'No?'

'They are one and the same, sir. By definition. One and the same.'

FRANZISKUS FOUND HIS archers lingering by the remains of the bonfire, cinders at their feet. He counted nine men. 'Is this everyone?' he asked.

The unit's corporal stepped up, snapping neatly to attention. He boasted a thick, dark head of hair and burnished, coppery skin. Franziskus was reminded of a pear: the corporal's jaw was much wider and rounder than the crown of his head. 'All but one, sir,' he said.

'Fetch the other. We're going on a bit of a scout.'

'Yes, lieutenant.'

Franziskus asked the men for their names. The corporal was Lehn. Hoven, the tallest and stockiest of the men, impressed himself on Franziskus's memory because his nose was copiously running. Periodically the man blotted it on his sleeve.

The sky began to leak, too, sprinkling an intermittent rain on the camp. At the present moment, Franziskus could not help thinking of the Chelborg

Archers as the sorriest bunch of men ever to take up arms together. The prospect of a scouting mission had done nothing to relieve their despondency.

'Get yourselves assembled; we'll set out in five minutes,' Franziskus said. He had never commanded a unit before, not even a small one. In his old company, he'd merely been a conduit for the transmission of orders from the first lieutenant to the sergeants and corporals. He worked to recall how an officer should speak and hold himself. He owed it to these men to imbue them with a sense of surety, even if he did not feel it himself.

'Yes, sir, lieutenant...' Corporal Lehn trailed off.

He was waiting for Franziskus to say or do something. Franziskus wondered what it could be. He tried to keep his features blank, so the men couldn't see him searching his mind for the desired response. He felt sorry for his men; as it was, their lives were in the hands of an impulsive truth-bender. Now they were saddled with a green and useless second officer.

'Sir,' said Lehn, 'we have not been told your last name. If we are to address you properly, we must know it.'

'Yes, yes, quite so,' said Franziskus. What name should he give them? 'Ah, Weibe. That would make me Lieutenant Weibe.' A patently idiotic choice, he immediately thought. Lieutenant White. Why not Lieutenant Deserter, while he was at it? Lieutenant Fugitive. That had a pleasant ring to it.

With the tenth man gathered and the men's packs slung on their backs, they joined the other components of the scouting mission: Angelika, a quartet of swordsmen, the halflings (chosen for their deft-footedness) and, to the astonishment of none, Jonas himself.

Angelika peered at the rock ridge, searching for the most likely point of entry. She chose a spot where the ridge had crumbled into a criss-crossing patchwork of natural terraces. By weaving to and fro along them, it seemed likely that they could pick their way up it with relative ease. Angelika pointed the way.

Jonas accompanied her at the head of the procession; two swordsmen with them, the other pair bringing up the rear. Filch the halfling buzzed up to Franziskus, but Bodo pulled him away, whispering, 'He's an officer now. He mustn't be bothered.'

The archers spread themselves out in two lines, ready to fire at any marauders from the left or right. Franziskus stood between them. As the zigzagging uphill march eked on, the unit cohered into a single, disordered file. The party inched along bare, drizzle-slicked stone.

Franziskus heard Hoven whisper to the corporal. 'Where do you think he's leading us now?'

Lehn elbowed him in the ribs and cast a significant glance back at Franziskus. 'There's ears about,' he hissed.

'Indeed there are!' Franziskus barked.

The two men started as if doused by a bucket of icy water.

'You're weary, you're frightened, and you're in danger. Welcome to the life of a soldier,' he exclaimed, taken aback by his own fervour. 'The only way out of this misery, back to the safety of your homes, is to kill the foe, and to keep killing him till we've won. And that's just what we're on our way to do. Understood?'

The archers shrank from him.

'Understood, Hoven?

'Yessir, Lieutenant Weibe.'

'The next man I hear griping gets a lashing when we get back,' he threatened – convincingly, he hoped. The prospect of such a punishment, necessary as it might be, sickened him.

Hoven slipped on the wet rock; a man behind him propped him up. The archers' speed increased, and soon they'd caught up to the rest of the party.

As they neared the top of the flatted ridge, half a mile roughly south of the sangar, the slope grew shallower. Clouds, small and diffuse, slipped across the ridge's opposite edge and nosed along its surface. For a moment, the party stood in bright sunlight, while clouds scoured the rocky surface to their left and right.

'What a sight,' said Filch.

'Gawp quieter,' Bodo commanded.

'Never thought I'd see anything like this,' Filch said, less emphatically. A low rumble, like thunder, but continuous, filled their ears.

'What's that sound?'

At the column's head, Angelika sniffed the air. 'Waterfall, somewhere. Distant but big.' She stopped, but not because of the sound. She'd sniffed a trace of an ominous and familiar smell.

'There's death nearby,' she told Jonas.

'What?'

'I smell death. Better turn around.'

'We're not returning empty-handed.'

'Then wait here while I get a closer look.' Angelika headed off further south, away from their destination.

'Catch up with us,' commanded Jonas. 'If it's off that way, it's of no consequence to us.'

Jonas led the group along the rock ribbon. Aside from the occasional patch of scrub weeds, holding with perverse determination to thin mats of soil, the ridge itself offered no cover. The drifting clouds, however, created a shifting zone of lowered visibility. Rassau beckoned his followers into their enveloping fog.

ANGELIKA TRACED A provident route along the width of the plain of rock, the smell growing stronger with every step. It was the high stench of bodily decomposition. The back of her throat closed and acrid tears bulleted from her eyes. With practiced technique, she fought the gagging sensation. She called to mind other, fresher odours: lilacs, brandy, fresh-scythed wheat. Reminding herself that she'd encountered it dozens of times before, she subdued the natural urge to flee in the face of death.

Two or three hundred feet along, she came to a crevasse in the rock. It began in the middle of the ridge and ran all the way to its far side. Clouds of humming, feasting flies billowed up from it. These included the familiar metallic blue bottle flies Angelika knew from the battlefields of the Blackfire, intermingled with a variety she had not encountered before. These larger, brown-jacketed carrion flies flew sluggishly, bumping stupidly into one other. Occasionally one of these bigger insects would leap onto another, engaging in frenzied congress with it or ripping off a wing or mandible.

Angelika stepped into the cloud, prepared for the carrion flies to bite at her. They left her alone. Peering down into the crevasse, she saw why: they had plenty of easier meat to sup on. The fissure was six feet across at its widest point, and extended down into the rock for nearly a dozen yards. It was stacked nearly to the top with corpses, of both dwarfs and barbarians. They were heaped in layers, with the freshest dead on top. These, a few dwarfs and twice as many Chaos troops, crawled with flies, their complexions greyed.

In Angelika's expert estimation, taking into account the cooling winds that coursed across the ridge face, these would have been slain less than thirty-six hours ago. Beneath them another layer of mingled corpses writhed with maggots, and were in a few places stripped bare to the bone; these would be three to four days dead. Yet another stratum of cadavers lay beneath it, reduced almost entirely to skeletons.

Though it brought the reek even closer to her nostrils, Angelika dropped straight away to the ridge. Trouble had to be near. There was only one reason to hide corpses after a battle, and that was to conceal one's presence from the enemy. It was not the sort of thing dwarfs would do, not in territory they saw as their own. They'd haul their enemies into a pyre and burn them immediately. So the corpse-hole had to be the work of the Chaos troops. Each layer recorded a clash with a dwarf patrol. Even though they'd lost two men for each one they'd slain, they had nonetheless won all three engagements.

There were Kurgan nearby, probably a good number of them. And not only in the sangar – the dead piled here far outstripped its capacity. Chances were good they'd spotted Jonas's men on the ridge. Yet they had not attacked. Why?

They were waiting.

Waiting for what?

For the right moment.

Which would be...?

When Jonas reached the sangar.

Why would that be the perfect moment?

Because then they'd surround him. And he and Franziskus and the halflings and others would become the fourth layer of corpses to fill the fissure.

She crawled along the ridge to the precipice. Right below her, the cliff dropped suddenly. Less than a hundred feet to her left, though, the ridge formed a rough but lowly graded natural ramp, leading easily down to a second valley floor, much like their own. In the far distance, she saw the waterfall they'd heard earlier: a crashing font of white water, falling nearly two hundred feet from a horseshoe-shaped ridge into a deep, pooling lake.

A multitude of half-naked figures calmly moved about its pebbled shore. This new valley sheltered a Kurgan war camp. The waterfall's clamour muffled whatever sounds its inhabitants made.

Angelika counted a hundred tents, calculating five to seven men per tent. This was no remnant force, it was an entire army. One with the patience and guile to bivouac here, escaping their notice the whole time. For this many warriors to remain so quiet and inactive was a feat of restraint even Imperial soldiers would be hard pressed to duplicate. That these marauders were capable of it was chilling. A disciplined barbarian was supposed to be an oxymoron, a contradiction in terms. Yet here they were.

Lashed to the tops of tall trees Angelika saw crude platforms, manned by barbarian sentries. Anyone moving along the flatted ridge could easily be seen from them. War horns dangled from the watch-posts.

Angelika turned back towards Jonas's position. For the moment, clouds hid them from view. As soon as the air cleared, those alarms would sound.

If they came for Jonas, they'd find the rest of the company, too. There was only one way out of this. She had to stop him before he attacked the sangar.

JONAS LED THE men deeper into the cloud.

Its fog surrounded them and Franziskus could not tell who stood to the left or right of him. He saw the blurry shapes of bows in their arms, and so they had to be the Chelborgers – his men.

'Why in hell's name did he bring archers here?' one voice muttered.

'We won't be able to hit an inch in front of our faces in this soup,' another affirmed.

'Stupid idiot will get us all murdered.'

'Officers are present,' Franziskus warned. The men shut up.

The cloud blew away.

Jonas stood face to face with a sallow-cheeked Kurgan.

Jonas jumped back.

The Kurgan jumped back then reached for his axe. Jonas swung his sabre. It bit deep into the barbarian's sinewy neck. Blood fluxed from the wound. Jonas screamed and charged for the sangar. Bodo, Franziskus, and the swordsmen followed. The archers dropped to their knees, ready for any targets that might appear. Filch ran sideways. Merwin hit the ground, covering his head with interlaced hands.

Barbarians emerged from the sangar entrance, a hole in the rock ringed by yard-high rune-carved menhirs. With Franziskus and Bodo close behind him, Jonas ran at them, sword swung above his head. Their blades whacked into the axes and clubs of their foes.

Kurgan sentry-horns wailed from the opposite valley. Neither attackers nor defenders much heard them, above the din.

Jonas's blade cut through the axe-hand of a bare-headed marauder. A brother-in-arms, who might have been the other's twin, swept into Franziskus, meeting his heavy blade with the haft of a spiked hammer.

WHEN THE SENTRY horns groaned, Angelika made a quick decision and changed direction. Jonas and Franziskus would have to look out for themselves. They had at least a chance to hear the horns. The same could not be said for the remainder of the company, sitting unawares in Jonas's camp by the stream. There were more soldiers down in the valley than by the sangar. She could not warn both, so she would warn those most in need of it. She beetled to the zigzagging rock formation leading back to camp, skittering along it, jumping chancily from one terrace to the next.

A CLOUD FLOATED toward the sangar. The archers aimed at it, as if it were the vanguard of an opposing force. Filch stooped from spot to spot, gathering up a store of fist-sized rocks. Each swordsman had a Kurgan to fight. Bodo ran behind the uneven barbarian line, busying his knife at them, searching for tendons to slit. Jonas's foe ducked his wild swings, laughing and waggling out his tongue. Franziskus's adversary hammered him into a defensive posture, flurrying blows into his sabre, bending it out of shape.

The cloud blew off, flying over the mound valley. The archers wauled in dismay as a new line of Kurgans surged at them from the other side of the ridge. They fired. A few foes fell, tripping others, but most kept on, unruffled by their volley.

Franziskus's hammerer executed a gleeful shimmy at the arrival of his mates. Franziskus seized the moment to slash him, carving a steak's worth of thigh muscle off the bone. The hammer-man sank and Franziskus wheeled to face the new wave of foes. 'Fighting retreat,' he shouted. 'Fighting retreat!' It was Jonas who should have been shouting those orders, but to blazes with it. Franziskus was an officer now and it was the only way. The archers jumped from their kneeling positions, loosing an unaimed round at the oncoming Kurgan. None of their arrows won places in the flesh of their foes.

A seven-foot Kurgan came like a battering ram at the archers as they jogged tentatively backwards along the ridge. He raised a caber-like cudgel to dash out Hoven's brains. A stone sailed neatly through the air to thump into the centre of his wide, indented forehead. He growled, raised his weapon in search of his new tormentor, fell over backwards, and expired, a red trickle running from his ear.

'Keep 'em comin',' Filch shouted to Merwin, whom he'd parked beside his cairn of throwing rocks. Merwin handed him another stone. He pitched it expertly into the jaw of a weedy, hirsute barbarian.

'Grab 'em up,' he yelled, as the rest of the squad fled. More barbarians dashed up over the opposite slope and onto the ribbon of stone. Clouds followed after them.

A marauder moaned as Bodo hamstrung him. He turned and, ruined leg and all, seized the halfman by the neck and groin, dashing him into a dwarf marker. Jonas saw this and pelted his way. The Kurgan tossed Bodo into the sangar hole and the last Jonas saw of him were the soles of his callused feet.

'Bodo,' he shouted. Clouds surrounded him. An axe shot from the mist, clouting him in the shoulder. Stunned, he tripped sideways. A punch caught him in the ribs. He spun around. A third unblinking orb, tattooed between a Kurgan's brows, stared into him. He flung his sabre out and felt the gratifying squish of contact as it cut into his enemy's gut. Then another marauder was on him, and another.

Pain shivered through his head. His sight blurred, and he couldn't hear anything. He swung his sword and kept swinging; sometimes he hit something. A body crashed into him, knocking him down, pinning his sword-arm. With his free fist he smashed viciously into the man's skull. Then he realised the enemy was dead, or at least unconscious, and rolled him off.

FRANZISKUS AND HIS archers ran from cloud to cloud along the ridge. Franziskus cried for them to stop:

they'd run too far, bypassing the stepped path leading back to their camp.

JONAS STOOD, DAZED, his vision blurred. The battle-
din had ended, but he could not tell if that meant his
enemy had gone, or only that his hearing was not
right. Feeling something amiss beneath his feet, he
realised he'd stepped onto the cliff's edge. Instinct
told him to leap, but the swift move sent him slip-
ping on the rock's damp surface. His legs flailed; he
bounced down, hitting his chin on the stony
precipice. He clung to the rock, forcing all the
strength he could summon into the muscles of his
chest and arms. Reaching out blindly, he grabbed
onto something. At first he thought it was a root or
branch, then, as he got a better grip on it, he realised
he'd wrapped his fingers around a man's belt. He'd
saved himself by holding fast to the barbarian he'd
just slain.

Booted feet came his way: they belonged to one of
his own soldiers, in black and yellow leggings.

'Help me,' he moaned. He pushed his neck back to
see who it was. It was Egerer. Good, old gaunt-faced
Egerer, all vinegar and gristle and impossible to kill as
always.

Jonas reached a hand up, the free one that wasn't
pressed desperately into the rough-edged belt of a
dead barbarian. 'Give me a hand there, Egerer.'

Egerer loomed over him, mouth drawn into a thin,
withholding line.

'Egerer!'

Egerer placed gnarled, pensive hands on his sharpened hips. 'I ought to let you dangle.'

'What?' Jonas cried.

'Puffing yourself up with foolish lies. What kind of commander needs to do that, except a useless one?' Then he bent down and thrust out his hand.

Trembling, limbs like damp cloth, Jonas struggled off the cliff's edge and to his knees.

Egerer aimed a disgusted look at him and walked into a swift-swung axe. A rubber-limbed barbarian sheared his throat open, then kicked him to the ground. Egerer clutched his throat with one hand and reached up at his slayer with the other. He grappled it around the Kurgan's leg and bent his knee, bringing him down. The barbarian struggled to disengage; they sprawled on the edge of the precipice. Jonas ducked down to kick at the enemy, but it was too late. With a last reserve of energy, Egerer rolled himself off the cliff, taking the marauder with him. Jonas staggered to the edge and saw their shattered bodies tangled in the trees dozens of yards below.

He found his sabre on the rock and picked it up. Clouds brushed by him. His head throbbed. He saw the sangar entrance and considered a dash at it. There was some small chance Bodo was yet alive inside it. He inched toward his goal, but his aching body rebelled.

New war horns sounded from the valley opposite. Fresh adrenaline jolted in his veins. He bumbled to the other side of the cliff, and saw what Angelika had seen: the waterfall and the Kurgan camp.

Another column of barbarians, clanking weapons into their shields and chest-guards, had mounted the slope and was headed his way.

He staggered to its head. Egerer was right. Why did he tell all those stories anyway? He ought to die – but gloriously, redemptively. He would stand and ward off an entire marauder platoon.

'Jonas,' a voice hissed, to his right.

He scanned the ridge, and saw no one.

'Over here.'

A red cloth fluttered up from the surface of the rock. Jonas shook his muzzy head and the scene came into focus. There was a fissure in the rock, and someone down inside it. He shuddered toward it. A horrible stench repelled him, like he'd struck a wall.

'Quick.'

He placed the voice as Franziskus's. He ran toward the crevasse. Flies assailed him; one zipped into his mouth. Sickened, he swallowed it. He reached the fissure and Franziskus and one of the halflings pulled him down into it.

He landed on a dwarf corpse, its cold skin slippery with gore. Desperate hands pulled him down further into the charnel stink. Along with Franziskus, both halflings had hidden themselves here, and the archers, and two of the swordsmen.

They waited, listening, as the boots of the barbarians thudded by.

Though he had his tiny hand clamped over his mouth Merwin vomited, overcome by the reek and the horror. The others felt ready to do the same, but overcame their rising nausea.

Finally it sounded as if the overrunning army had cleared the ridge.

'Oh sweet Sigmar,' gasped Jonas.

'Indeed,' said Franziskus.

'In this, our hour of wretchedness, oh divine champion of wrath,' continued Jonas, 'preserve us, please.'

ANGELIKA RAN, LUNGS burning, to the camp by the rocky stream. The soldiers had already heard the distorted, echoing bleat of Kurgan war horns, and had gathered themselves into a square, set to receive a charge. Emil waited, sword in hand, in the front line. Alongside him stood the unit's stragglers, whose specialties were more useful in a defensive formation: the gunners, a couple of pikemen.

Angelika hadn't the breath to speak. She waved her arms, signalling them to flee.

Emil stayed steadfast, and the battle square held its place.

'Run,' Angelika gasped. She'd reached them, but marched lightly in place, to ward off the cramps and dizziness of a sudden stop.

Emil shook his head.

'Don't be daft. There's a legion of them, and all they're all coming – now.'

'You are not a soldier and need not stand with us,' Emil said.

'Run, I tell you. There's a hundred places to hide in these hills – you found them on patrol. Go to them now, and hide. Now.'

Roughly half of the soldiers, including all of the stragglers bunched up around Emil, heeded her advice and sprinted from the square, jostling past the men who stood their ground. 'Jonas sent me,' she shouted. 'Hide yourselves, he says.'

At this even Emil broke formation, his stocky legs banging gracelessly under him. Angelika beckoned to him; he had not been out on patrol and would not know where to hide. She steered him with her to Mount Eel as an excellent redoubt waited for them there.

The war horn's ululation deepened. Angelika glanced momentarily back to see the first of the Chaos legion appearing on the rocky rise. At this remove, they seemed no larger than swarming ants. To their eyes, the Gerolsbruchers would appear similarly minute. The marauders would see them flee, but, Angelika fervently hoped, were too far off to accurately follow their specific movements and track them to their manifold destinations in the hills.

To safely navigate those crumbling rock terraces would take them precious time. She altered her own route to Mount Eel, taking her and Emil behind another of the sharp-topped mounds, where they could not be seen from the granite ribbon. If they were smart, the other squads of retreating men would do the same.

Pinkert was already a few paces ahead of her. Mattes and Saar ran behind. She slackened slightly to let them catch up. Always keeping a hillside between themselves and the Kurgan invasion route, they crept to the base of Mount Eel. The multitudinous crunch of barbarian boots on complaining rock reverberated from around the stream bed. The wind carried to Angelika and the others a refrain of disappointed grunts and howls. Horns bleated uncertainly. The marauders had found no force to slaughter.

They shinnied up the dry and dusty hillside to the spot where Angelika had installed her pit trap. She meticulously dismantled the disguising canopy of

306 *Robin D Laws*

logs and soil, then slid with even greater attentiveness into the crevasse, avoiding the spikes she'd installed inside its mouth. Once she'd found her footing, she grabbed each sharpened stake in turn and heaved it from its resting spot. After stacking them in a pile, she beckoned her three companions to come down. When they were in, she had Mattes and Saar boost her back up again. She replaced the false thatch of logs and debris, leaving a space to wedge herself through. The last logs she returned from the inside, her feet on the shoulders of the men. When it was in place, sealing off the last shaft of daylight, they lowered her to face Sergeant Raab.

'Jonas ordered this retreat?' he asked.

'I lied,' said Angelika. 'For some reason I decided you'd all be better off alive.'

'Good thinking,' said Saar.

Emil scowled.

'I'm trying to conceive of a polite way to ask this,' said Angelika.

'Don't trouble yourself,' said Emil. It was impossible to sit in the tiny space of the crevasse. He leaned against its crooked earthen wall, letting his weight go slack against it.

'What in the name of Sigmar's beard were you doing there, waiting for the enemy army to overrun your position?'

'There is a book of protocol,' Mattes volunteered. 'When there is no officer present to issue commands, the sergeant is required to choose the established response best fitting the pertaining facts. Though you might say the book refers only to standard engagements.'

'I did not know the enemy's strength,' Emil growled. 'Had I imagined an entire legion, obviously I'd have called for a retreat.'

'We've been right on their doorstep for days,' said Angelika, more to herself than the others. 'They only came at us when we climbed practically into their noses.'

'That's more discipline than you'd expect of the Kurg.'

'They're holding for something,' said Angelika. 'Or someone.'

CHAPTER NINETEEN

IN THE CORPSE-FILLED fissure, Merwin the halfling shifted his weight. Beneath him, a maggot-ridden body squished and resettled making him squirm in revulsion. Filch reached out a hand to him, pressing it reassuringly down on his friend's forearm.

Icy tears rolled down Merwin's face. The archers scowled their disapproval at him. In a case like this, a fellow was supposed to hide his fear, out of consideration for his comrades. It was plain to Franziskus that the halfling could sense their hostility, and that it worsened his distress. He wished he could speak to them, to order them to knock it off, but the Kurgan were still up on the ridge. Their scraping footfalls could be heard on its surface, and not too far away, either.

Low words were coughed in the Kurgan's booming language. From their mere tone, Franziskus could not

figure what was said. Instructions issued? Simple soldiers' banter? If the latter, what might that consist of,
precisely? Would they speak of home, complain
about their commanders, bemoan the petty discom-
forts of the trail, as human warriors would?
Franziskus could not imagine it. Surely they joked
only about blood and murder, or babbled of their
mad devotion for Chaos.

Franziskus rubbed his chapped hands quietly
together and attempted to project the air of calm self-
control that was an officer's greatest gift to his men.
Whatever effect he rallied was countered by Jonas.
Rassau, inert as a post, stared at an invisible point a
few inches in front of his face.

He'd succumbed to shock. Franziskus knew the
symptoms well as he'd fallen prey to them himself on
a similar occasion. These were not the first hours
Franziskus had ever spent in a corpse pile; he'd been
stuck in one on the day he first met Angelika. Grop-
ing for a cheery thought, he decided that this present
dilemma was not so bad, in comparison to that previous circumstance. Then, there'd been dead men not
only below him, but on top as well.

The throaty barbarian voices came closer, combined with grunts of effort.

Corpses cascaded down from above. Franziskus
braced himself as the gored and naked torso of a tattooed barbarian sluiced down onto his neck and
shoulders. Other slain men followed, the remains of
several Gerolsbruchers included. Somewhere from
among the party Franziskus heard a muffled weeping.

The voices receded a little, as if the enemy troops
had moved away from the mouth of the crevasse.

Apparently, even Chaos barbarians shrank from the stink of death.

'Lieutenant,' murmured Jonas.

It took Franziskus a moment to realise that Jonas meant him. 'Yes?' he said, equally hushed.

'How long must we stay here?'

'You decide, sir.'

'But how long?'

'I've been in worse spots.'

'How many of them up there?'

'We daren't look.'

'Let's guess, then.'

'They wouldn't have thrown more bodies down if they knew we were here.'

'From the sounds of it – how many?'

'Let's just wait.'

'How many?' Jonas repeated. A harshness crept into his whisper.

Afraid Jonas could be heard, Franziskus merely gestured: a resigned and baffled shrug.

Filch obligingly cocked his ear, then held up all the fingers of his right hand, plus the forefinger of his left.

'Are you certain?' asked Jonas.

Filch stuck both his thumbs up.

Franziskus was not so sure. As far as he knew, the halfling ear was not noted for any special acuity. Perhaps this was a unique talent of Filch's, much like his preternatural skill at rock-throwing.

'Follow me,' Jonas intoned.

None of the fresh bodies had landed on him so he boosted himself up by climbing onto the shoulder of the archer next to him. He launched himself clumsily from the crevasse, faltered, recovered his balance, and hauled his sabre from his scabbard. Bellowing an unintelligible war-cry, he blundered at the marauders left to guard the ridgeline. Jonas was well into his charge before he saw that Filch had underestimated their numbers by half. Worse, no one else had yet emerged from the crevasse: Franziskus and the others still grappled their way through the layer of dead men.

Jonas forgot them, choreographing the series of feints and slashes that would allow him to survive until his allies caught up. He dived at the nearest barbarian, slicing muscle from his ribs. He ducked down, rose up, thudded into the dying man, and used him as a shield while the axe-blows of three of his fellows darted his way. Two dug into their comrade's back while the third went wide. Jonas threw the man at his attackers; two fell back. One slipped in the spilled viscera of his compatriot and fell backwards off the precipice.

Meanwhile, Jonas had scourged the axe-hand of one Kurgan and stabbed through the breastbone of another. A Kurgan rushed at him from each of four directions; he spun his blade around, holding them at bay. Arrows whizzed into their necks and shoulders. At Franziskus's urging, the Chelborg Archers had braced themselves with feet against one edge of the crevasse and backs to the opposite wall. From this graceless position, they could fire their missiles right away, without completing the difficult clamber from their hiding place.

A Kurgan on the mêlée's periphery reached down for his war horn. Jonas bulled his way through his closest opponents to sabre it from him. He smashed the pommel of his sword into the sentry's lips and teeth. The barbarian went down.

Jonas had now manoeuvred himself so that all of the Kurgan were between him and his archers; a new volley blacked the air. Heaving, growling barbarians either ducked or collapsed. Franziskus made it out of the crevasse, followed by Filch. The halfling dashed past the Stirlander and neatly plucked a dagger from his belt. He dived onto the back of a thrashing marauder and plunged a dozen speedy cuts into the back of his head.

Distracted by the arrows rushing at them, the Kurgan were now easier prey for Jonas's blade and he scythed them like wheat. He laughed frenziedly as he slew the last two standing barbarians. Franziskus ran to the archers and helped them up out of the crevasse. As they freed themselves from it, they pivoted to help their comrades. Merwin shinnied out and ran to Filch, whose stabbing arm still worked ceaselessly on the carcass of his foe, and pulled him off. Filch's numbed expression combined fury and dismay.

'Go, before there are more,' Franziskus ordered his archers. They required no further exhortation, and ran full out back to the slope leading to their valley. Thick halfling feet rumbled after them.

Jonas whirled, grinning like a wolf, as if daring invisible opponents to teem at him.

'Jonas,' Franziskus shouted.

The lieutenant jolted, as if from walking sleep, sheathed his sabre, and followed his fleeing party back down the slope.

IN THEIR OWN hiding spot, sliced into the side of Mount Eel, Mattes and the sergeant argued.

'You must,' Mattes demanded.

'To even ask it of me is mutiny,' Emil replied.

'Quiet, both of you,' said Angelika. Her eyes were closed and her arms were folded. She'd decided to attempt a nap, to recover strength she might need later, and had nearly nodded off. Then the debate had started.

'He's incapable!' said Mattes.

'You know that's insubordination.'

'You think he's a good leader?'

'It is not for me, and especially not for you, to judge.'

'Anyone with half a lick of sense can see it. The men trust you, but they don't trust him.'

'Soldiers need not trust. They need merely obey.'

'They will both trust and obey you, Emil.'

Emil clouted him sharply on the mouth. Nothing in his bearing had heralded the arrival of the blow. Mattes touched his bleeding lip.

'That's my answer to that,' said Emil.

'But–'

'No matter how you put the question, I'll have the same answer for you. So, if you enjoy having teeth to fill your gums, I say shut it.'

THE CLEAR WATER of the pebble stream washed against Ortak Nalgar's blood-blackened boots. Chest out, hands hard at his side, the Chaos chieftain strode among his men, deciding which of them he would fatally punish. A force of nearly two hundred wove around him, in the midst of an empty valley, with no foe to slay.

When he spoke, his voice reverberated through the steel chambers of his antlered helmet. His breath collected damply on the inside of his mouth-guard. 'Who,' he demanded, 'was the fool who sounded the horn of war?'

The marauders snarled and cawed. They shoved and grappled, pushing a lightly armoured man to the fore. They punched at his kidneys until he doubled over, then kicked him flat. He was seized by the back of the neck and turned around, so that his face touched the earth where the chieftain's feet were planted.

'Speak your name,' Ortak Nalgar demanded. He waved off the other marauders, leaving the man to grovel unencumbered.

'I am Zaba Gor,' the shamed man spat, 'of the Sanxal tribe. I answer to my chieftain, who is Tharken Urtza. And to Vardek Crom, who defeated my chieftain in single combat. As you were defeated by him.'

Ortak Nalgar ordered him to stand, and he did so, a defiant leer slashed across his face. The bravado was admirable, that of a true Kurgan war-maker.

'Yes,' said Ortak Nalgar, 'I, like your chieftain, am now, by right of conquest, commanded by Vardek Crom. And he has commanded me to command you to exercise the thing the *mutaa* of the Soft Lands call discipline. Do you know what this thing is, Zaba Gor of the Sanxal tribe?'

'I spit on it,' said Zaba Gor. 'It is not our way.'

Ortak Nalgar reached to his waist and unbuckled a set of vicious-looking fighting claws. Zaba Gor quailed when he saw them: heartpuncher claws.

'Answer me, this, then, Zaba Gor of the Sanxal tribe. How, despite our superior courage, the relentlessness of our blood-hunger, and our utter submission to Chaos Undivided, have the fat suckling pigs of the

Soft Lands, for so many years, eluded ultimate destruction at our deserving hands?' Slowly, Ortak Nalgar slipped the fighting claws onto his right hand.

'They have not died, because Zaba Gor has not yet had the chance to kill them.'

'You are wrong, Zaba Gor. After Vardek Crom defeated me, after he brought his swift axe down upon my helm, and sank me to my knees, and I was forced to make the four supplications to him, he held out his vast hand to me and he pulled me up. And then he told me his secret. He would use the Soft Ones' weapon against them. The weapon they've used to eternally thwart us,' said Ortak Nalgar, 'is this thing called discipline.

'They think. They wait. They act in concert. Thus do plump, cowardly foes defeat us time and again. What Vardek Crom has taught me, I now teach you. We will think. We will wait. We will act together. To do this, we must follow orders. Even from chieftains who are not of our tribe. Tell me, Zaba Gor, how did you fail to obey the commands of Vardek Crom?'

Zaba Gor did not answer but steeled himself to receive the inevitable blow.

Ortak Nalgar did not yet strike it, but flexed the talons of his heartpuncher claws. 'I will explain, then. You sounded the war horn when you were instructed to keep silent.'

'I saw the foe.'

'A few men. Hardly worth the charge. Yet if there are Soft Ones, or accursed dwarfs, anywhere near, they'll have heard the horn. They'll know where we muster. We did not want them to know this.' The thumb was the final digit to receive its claw. 'We are concealing our presence, Zaba Gor. Waiting. Do you understand?'

Emboldened by his imminent death, Zaba Gor straightened his spine. 'It is *mutaa*, to wait, and hide, and sneak.'

'It is not *mutaa* if it brings victory.'

'What victory? Waiting? Waiting is not victory.'

'Your chieftain of chieftains says it will bring victory, and so it will.'

'Chaos does not wait. Chaos strikes.'

'Chaos has waited three thousand years and now it will win. So says Vardek Crom.'

'I have not heard Vardek Crom say this. I have only heard you say it.'

Ortak Nalgar jolted his open hand into Zaba Gor's breastbone, piercing his heart in four places. He held his hand there and shook it.

Zaba Gor tried to spit at his killer, but could manage only a meagre dribble of drool, which ran down his chin. 'He who thinks like a Soft One will die like a Soft One,' he choked. 'Then we will be free again.'

Ortak Nalgar threw him to the ground. Zaba Gor's last choking words were words of challenge. If others were ready to pick them up, Ortak Nalgar would have to fight and kill them. Several of the men seethed breathy hate at him, but when he presented them his helmeted face, they hung their heads in submission. None would dare strike at him. While he commanded them, they would obey the edicts of Vardek Crom, no matter how peculiar they seemed.

'Where is the tracker?' he demanded.

One man stepped forward nervously. 'Many were here, glorious one.'

'How many?'

'Two warbands' worth, maybe three.' The tracker tried not to look at the red ends of the heartpuncher claws.

'Where have they gone?'

'Into the hills, great one.'

'They must be caught and slain. We cannot let them return home to warn of our gathering here.' Ortak Nalgar marched toward the terraced cliff that would lead him back to their waterfall encampment. 'Point to where the Soft Ones hide.'

'I don't know, fearsome one. Our other tracker died crossing the mountains.'

Ortak Nalgar twisted the tracker's neck until it snapped and threw him aside.

'Do we have another tracker?'

The barbarian horde answered with silence.

'Unleash the hound.'

'IT'S HIM,' EXCLAIMED Jonas. Only after the first word was uttered did he remember his predicament, after that he calmed his tone. He and the remnants of his assault force crouched behind a cresting line of boulders near the bottom of the slope. It, and a patch of scraggly mountain briars, concealed their presence from the two hundred or so Kurgan marauders milling in their abandoned encampment by the stony stream. Rassau couldn't help counting the size of his squadron: there was himself, one swordsman, ten archers, two halflings, and, at his right hand, Franziskus. Thirteen to one odds. And one of those on the other side was the Chaos chieftain, who had to count as an entire patrol of men, all by himself.

'What can we do?' he asked Franziskus, who replied with a gesture of silence.

The soldiers took worried note of this reversal of command.

Together they watched as Ortak Nalgar eviscerated the chest of his henchman with his taloned hand. An archer whistled softly, and was rewarded by a pointed elbowing from the man next to him.

'They don't seem so pleased to follow him,' Jonas mouthed.

I know the sentiment, thought Fengler, who had gone up to the ribbon as one of four swordsmen, and was now the sole survivor.

'They obey out of fear, and nought else,' said Franziskus.

Jonas's face took on a resolute cast.

The barbarians broke from their parley, heading back toward the slope, and the Imperial troops' hiding place. Jonas's soldiers pushed themselves closer to the earth. The Kurgans moved in a roiling, half-ordered mass. None of the Stirlanders had ever seen their Kurgan foes in a casual and sportive state. Some picked up rocks to sail them pointlessly into the distance. Others grunted out the rough melodies of their clan war chants.

One small group struck up a sort of game. They would spit into the necks of the men ranked in front of them. Then, when a victim of the copious gobbing turned around with raised fist ready, they would each point at one another and savagely laugh. One annoyed recipient swung back a leg to kick a participant unerringly in the groin. As the Kurg doubled over, his friends erupted in sadistic amusement.

The chieftain, who now passed within a hundred feet of the Stirlanders, raised his axe and bellowed. Stifling their guffaws, the marauders marched sullenly on.

All but a few dozen of the barbarians had passed by the Imperials' hiding spot, when a low-slung, dark-browed Kurgan separated from the pack to make straight for the briar stand.

CHAPTER TWENTY

THE KURG SLIPPED behind the briars, blocking himself from the view of his fellows. Pulling at his rancid loincloth, he squatted to relieve himself.

Halflings and archers wrenched and gagged. Franziskus slipped his sabre from its holster and crept out from the rocks. He scudded up into the blind spot of the preoccupied barbarian. When the marauder completed his crude ablutions, and was tugging at his breeches, Franziskus slammed his weapon's heavy hand-guard into his temple. The Kurgan rose indignantly from his crouch, then pitched face-first into the briar. Franziskus waited until the rest of the barbarians were well up the slope, then hauled the limp-limbed Chaos minion from the thorny bushes. Filch skittered up to supply a pair of leathery thongs, with which they tightly bound his arms and ankles.

'Clever work, Franziskus,' said Jonas. 'We'll extract from him knowledge of the chieftain's scheme.'

'Seems to me like they're assembling the largest force they can, at which point they'll attack Stirland again, all together,' said Franziskus.

'Yes, but it will be good to know it for a fact.' The last of the Chaos troops had disappeared over the ridge, presumably to rejoin their camp. Jonas cast a lost look after them. 'What now, then? Where have our men gone?'

'Angelika was assigned that mound, yes?' Franziskus pointed to Mount Eel, a quarter of a mile to the north.

'You would know better than I.'

'She was,' said Filch.

'She'll have gone there, to hide.'

'But last we saw of her, she was up on the ridge, with us. She could be anywhere. They could have slain her, or captured her.'

Franziskus idly examined his hands for signs of uncleanliness. 'How else did your men know to hide? No, she'll have somehow realised, before we did, that hundreds of Kurgs were about to rush down here, and warned them. I admit that I merely guess, but if we go to Mount Eel, I wager that's where she'll be.'

'You admire her greatly,' observed Jonas.

For this Franziskus supplied no answer.

Jonas nodded to him, and he ordered four of the archers to lift up the slumbering carcass of the careless Kurgan.

HALF AN HOUR later they reached the foot of Mount Eel.

The prisoner stirred as the archers put him down, so Fengler stooped to apply a fastidious chokehold, and he passed out again.

Jonas peered up. 'I see nothing.'

'She said something about laying in a pit trap,' said Franziskus. 'Wait here.' They watched as he footed it nimbly up the mound, scrutinised its terrain, then zeroed in on a place of interest. The ground moved and like cicadas wriggling from the earth, figures emerged from it. Franziskus and Angelika marched down, alongside Saar, Mattes, Pinkert and the sergeant.

'Where are the others?' Jonas asked him.

Raab explained; all was as Franziskus had assumed.

'What about Egerer?' Emil asked Jonas. 'The others…?'

'Gone,' was all Jonas needed to say. He cleared his throat. 'How then do we gather ourselves?'

'The sergeant kept a good survey map,' volunteered Angelika. 'He had the men mark on it the traps they laid. From looking at it, it's fairly clear which ones could be used as hiding spots. I'll take it and go and collect up the patrols. Meanwhile, you head to that tunnel, there.' She pointed to the rock wall, at the foot of the ridge.

'Tunnel?' said Jonas.

'See that dark spot, there? It looks like just a shadow, but I'm certain it's the entrance to a dwarf tunnel. Disused, we'd better hope. Blocked off, probably, but I'm hoping there's enough of it left to shelter us all. We can't camp in the open any more, that's for certain.'

Jonas peered at the dark shape Angelika had shown him. 'I can barely see it.'

'That's what I like about it. Go on ahead, I'll send the others to you as I come across them.'

They wended between hills to Angelika's dark blot in the ridge wall. When they were within five hundred yards of it, they could see she'd been right. An artificial cave had been hammered into the rock there. Its opening was artfully blended into the granite's ruts and corrugations, so it looked from a distance like a mere patch of shade. Once inside, they saw evidence of exacting dwarf workmanship. Near the threshold there was a groove, where a portcullis once fell. The remains of its chain and pulley mechanism sat a few yards away.

Emil kicked at it in disappointment; a functioning iron gate would have been a great boon. Franziskus moved back into the tunnel, stopping when the layer of cobwebs grew too thick to penetrate. Behind them, in the darkness, he was pretty certain he saw an unbreachable section of collapsed rock, impeding further movement. If he knew his dwarf archaeology, it had been sealed on purpose, hundreds of years ago. He sighed in relief. The incident in the gorge had sapped his appetite for further dwarf encounters.

Over the next few hours, patrol teams drifted in. The seasoned warriors settled themselves down for an immediate nap. Little was said.

Franziskus felt sorry for Jonas, the target of furtive and reproachful glances. Rassau paced the truncated passageway, oblivious to the unease his movements bred. Franziskus could tell he was rehearsing a speech – composing, rejecting, revising, and rejecting again his opening lines.

He took a risk and sidled up to his commander.

'You mean to address the men?' he asked, too low for others to hear.

'Hope leeches away from us like blood from a wound. I must staunch the flow.'

Franziskus knew not to say anything, instead deploying his best doubtful face. Months on the trail with Angelika had honed it to keen perfection.

'You think not?' asked Jonas.

'After a certain point, words do more harm than good.'

'Yes,' agreed Jonas. 'Something more concrete, perhaps.'

Angelika arrived, bringing with her the men from the furthest hill. The sky outside was indigo, surrendering to starry black.

'A fire?' Jonas asked her.

'Very small, as far to the back as we can get.'

She set herself the task of clearing the cobwebs, so they could hide deeper in. Filch's busy fingers made a tiny fire.

Jonas slapped the Kurgan awake and dragged him to the blockage. He kicked the marauder in the throat and drew a short knife from his belt. 'You will confess,' he commanded. 'You will tell us all of your filthy master's plans.'

The Kurgan yelped defiantly in the harsh language of the Wastes. With eager fists, the soldiers gathered around him.

Angelika withdrew without comment to the mouth of the tunnel.

Franziskus came moments after, ashen. 'Can't we stop them?'

'The sound of screaming's an awful giveaway, but you think they'll listen?'

The howls from the back of the passage grew in wretchedness. 'I told him already what that chieftain likely intends,' said Franziskus.

'The plan is not mysterious, no.'

'And unless he speaks Reikspiel, he couldn't tell us anything, even if he wanted to.'

'Also true.'

A shriek tore the air, then was abruptly smothered.

'Even when something might come of it, a man of good conscience despises torture. But this...' he persisted.

'They're angry, Franziskus. Not to mention petrified.'

'Does that make it right?'

'No, just inevitable.'

Twenty minutes later, Jonas approached them, his hands thick with blood. Beneath it, his knuckles were cut. His blows had exacted a greater toll on the Kurgan, whom his men dragged out to dump past the tunnel's edge. 'Take that a good way off,' he told the men. Franziskus saw in the soldiers a crazed and fervent complicity. Jonas had won them back, without words – though he suspected it would wear off, as strong drink always did.

'He kept repeating two words, over and over,' said Jonas. 'Ortak Nalgar, I think it was. Ortak Nalgar. Either of you know any Kurgan?'

Angelika shrugged.

'Maybe we heard those words before,' said Franziskus, 'when we spied on them. I think the one the chieftain killed kept using them, too.'

'They sound familiar now that you say it.'

'I could be wrong, but from the intonation, I think it was maybe a term of address. The chieftain's name.'

'So the chieftain is called Ortak Nalgar?'

'Merely a surmise,' said Franziskus.

'Ortak Nalgar,' said Jonas, testing the name, rolling it about. 'Ortak Nalgar.'

'If true, a sublimely useful piece of intelligence,' said Angelika. 'Now if we want to write him a letter, we know the proper salutation.'

Franziskus hawked phlegm around his throat. 'What else did you learn, Jonas?'

'It was hard to tell with only his beastly language to yammer in,' said Jonas, 'but I'd say that chieftain is waiting to amass a single great force, and take it sweeping down on Stirland.'

THEY BURIED THEIR captive in a depthless grave less than a hundred yards from the tunnel mouth. It was dug fast, the barbarian dumped carelessly in. Before spading loose dirt over him, his diggers spat on his corpse. It was more burial than the Gerolsbruchers who'd died on the ridge had been given. Angelika stood grumpily by, anticipating the thrum of Kurgan war horns. When the men were done, she hushed them, herding them back into the safety of the dwarven passageway, as a goose would shoo her goslings.

She was the last one back in. Jonas approached her, a question on his lips. Angelika braced herself for some new idiocy.

'We should clear the blockage,' he said.

She turned her face away, so the soldiers couldn't see it. 'Whatever for?'

'Perhaps it leads somewhere,' he said. 'It could go all the way through this ridge, allowing us ingress into the enemy camp.'

'I don't think that's where we wish to be, lieutenant.'

'Mmm,' said Jonas.

'Besides, where would we stack the rocks? We'd expose ourselves every time we haul one out.'

'We've got to do something.'

'Let's dream up a halfway intelligent scheme, and do that instead.'

Jonas seated himself at the tunnel threshold. His fingers tapped out an arrhythmic beat against his knee. After a few moments of fidgeting, he uncurled the map of the valley's hill mounds, which he'd liberated from Emil. That he studied for a quarter of an hour. Then he pushed up to his feet and paced the tunnel. Finally he struck his pose, the one he adopted in preface to a bout of thrilling oratory.

Angelika pressed her fingernails into her palms.

Jonas aimed his words at the two halflings, who'd desolately propped themselves on a whitish bundle. Angelika couldn't tell what it was, until she realised they'd taken the old cobwebs and rolled them together, industriously compacting them into a pillow of singular unpleasantness.

'You were separated from us when your friend Bodo met his end?' Jonas confirmed.

'It was like you was swallowed by the clouds,' said Filch.

'Then I've committed a gross omission. Let me tell you of his heroism, that we might all take inspiration in this moment of dread. Bodo and I staggered together through the clouds, with Egerer, and the other swordsmen who did not return with us. Suddenly we passed into a clear spot, and there before us were half a dozen of the largest, most fearsome barbarians you would ever care to look upon.

'I've done my best to seem brave, so's to stand as an example to the rest of you. Now though, I don't mind saying that any fighting man is scared, and it's no shame to say so. The only shame is in letting the fear rule you, instead of taking it and making a flame in your heart, to push you to further glory.

'Well, I might have thought that at the time, but my body would not obey me, as these six mighty men came at me with their flailing axes cutting the miserly air up on that ridge. But Bodo – Bodo, though he was half my size, though he was not a trained man of arms, but a simple butcher – his body had the courage mine, for that instant, lacked. And he impelled himself onward, bowling into them, taking the disadvantage of his size and using it against them.

'He ran through the legs of the lead Kurg, forcing him to turn, and then the others swung, and before any of them knew it, they were hacking and cutting away at one another's flesh, as Bodo, from behind and below them, added his short sword to the carnage. Bang! One of them goes down! Bom! And then another! All of it flashes before us in an instant, and four of them are lying dead on the top of that ridge.

'I tell you, there was no moment in all my career as a fighting man that I felt prouder of a comrade. And it was his example that restored my own nerve. And after that, I don't mind saying, my sabre rang its tune against them, and took a toll of its own.

'It was then that good dauntless Bodo was slain, as more of them poured on, and one took him from the front and another from the side. Yet even as he died, he tripped one of his murderers, and the men fell before him, and as the last blood leaked from his side, he took the edge of his blade and swiped it against the throat of he who'd impaled him.

'Together Egerer, myself and the others, we wiped out every Kurg who'd so much as breathed on that great and tiny martyr, your friend Bodo. He died a hero, Filch and Merwin. Know that. Know it, and take the tidings home to Hochsmoor, that he might be celebrated in the hallowed place that birthed him.'

Angelika observed the men as they resisted Jonas's eloquence, shifting guardedly, searching each other for indications of belief. Then they'd given in, their postures folding toward him. Now more than a few sniffled or wiped at their eyes, a condition which could not be fully explained by the glacial draft now mounting an incursion into the tunnel.

It was not the mere unreality of Jonas's speeches that caused him trouble, Angelika reflected. The truth wouldn't seem so bad, if it weren't for the touching beauty of his lies.

THAT NIGHT, BETWEEN the hours of three and four, a monstrous baying tolled through the hills outside the tunnel entrance. Angelika was awake already; Franziskus jarred instantly from his slumbers. Jonas leapt to the mouth of the passage. Stars faintly twinkled in the dark and blanketing sky; all before them was blackness. The soft skin of Angelika's neck crawled. They detected a wrong and distant odour.

'Chaos,' she said.

The baying, reminiscent of both a hound and a wolf, yet containing other elements entirely, chilled and burned them.

'That's why they didn't leave marauders to patrol for us,' Angelika said. 'They've got something else to do the job for them.'

'How do we fight it?' asked Jonas.

'Pray we don't have to, that's how.'

'Douse that fire,' he hissed, down the passage.

They listened for another iteration of the sound. None came.

'Is that a good sign?' Jonas asked.

'With that force we cannot... With the enemy–' Angelika ceased her euphemising. 'With Chaos,' she said, 'any sign is ominous.'

'What do we do?' Jonas repeated.

'Nothing,' said Angelika. 'For the moment, at least, we're trapped.'

CHAPTER TWENTY-ONE

THE RAVENOUS GROWLS of the unseen monster kept the tunnel's inhabitants sleepless until dawn. Then the jarring presence of Chaos receded, leaving the Gerolsbruch Swordsmen pale and shivering.

Angelika poured water from her canteen onto her palms and clapped it onto her face. Her head seemed light, yet insupportable. Propped against the tunnel wall, she tried in vain to steal some sleep. Instead a restless energy filled her.

She stepped over the sleeping forms of Jonas and Franziskus; the former snored with his head buttressed on the latter's fine-boned shoulder. Behind them, deeper into the tunnel's gloom, exhaustion had taken the other soldiers. She would walk out a bit, and stand sentry. Her guess was that they were in immediate danger only when the Chaos feeling was on them. But surely there would be lookouts posted on the ridge by now – in the sangar if nowhere else. If they went too far out into the hills, at least in any numbers, they'd be seen. The war horns would trumpet, calling down any combination of Kurgs and daemons.

What should they do now? There were now thirty-eight in their party, measured against an entire army a mere ridgeline away, its strength growing daily. Even the only half-sensical option, escape, appeared daunting at best. Yet Jonas would still want to stay, and attempt some gambit against them. She and Franziskus could slip away, she was confident of that. Perhaps it was time to bow to fate's cruelty, and accept that her ring was gone. That would abandon the Gerolsbruchers to Jonas's whims, and therefore to nearly certain doom. She had promised to help. And an idiotic promise was a promise nonetheless.

There was Mattes's plan: arrange a convenient demise for Jonas, take over the company, and lead them out of the mountains and back to Stirland, somehow. Now that Franziskus was second-in-command, she could exercise her control through him. No military niceties need be flouted.

No. Even if Rassau were the worst kind of villain, she couldn't do it. Angelika had promised herself never to engage in murder. An inconvenient promise was a promise nonetheless. And a promise to oneself was a promise most of all.

A twig snapped behind her. It was Mattes and Saar. Their depleted packs hung flatly across their backs.

'Departing?' asked Angelika. It was a rhetorical question.

'Too bad we never found your ring,' said the leather-faced drumsman.

Merwin appeared in the tunnel mouth, regarding them apprehensively. He wavered, then slunk out to join them.

'You'll want to keep on the other side of the hills, away from the ridge,' she told Mattes. 'Remember there're watchmen up on that sangar.'

'Aye, Angelika,' he said. 'You made a pledge to me, to help me and the men. I'm releasing you from it, now. Time we all shifted for ourselves, and you, too. Futile to do otherwise.'

'Go quick, then,' said Angelika, and they did. Mattes took the lead and they travelled in a running crouch, disappearing around the other side of Mount Lemon.

Jonas emerged from the tunnel, stretching and yawning. His exertions pulled up his tunic, exposing his hardened midriff. 'Did I hear voices?'

'From inside the tunnel?'

Jonas scowled and fumbled for his sabre. 'You're an appalling liar, Angelika.'

You're the authority, Angelika thought, as Rassau careened past her, his weapon half out of its scabbard.

'Who was it? Which way did they go?' The wind ruffled his sleep-tousled hair.

'You'll be spotted,' she called.

'If damned deserters can risk it, so can I.' Jonas spotted the route they must have taken, circling around Mount Lemon. Angelika followed hard after him. She stole a peek at the black shape of the sangar indented up in the rock wall, a quarter of a mile up. There was no telling if they'd been seen.

Together they cleared the hill. The trail between mounds was empty. Jonas, confused, turned a circuit. Angelika saw where they were: the three deserters had heard him and were scuttling up the hillside. She cast her gaze to the opposite hill, so Jonas would not track it. But he spotted them on his own and was then huffing up the slope, sabre now fully exposed.

'Don't you do it,' Angelika warned.

He charged on heedlessly, herding Mattes, Saar and Merwin around the hill's rounded circumference.

Saar cried out, clutching his ankle. Mattes stopped when he realised any further flight would place him in the sangar's sightline. He sturdied his feet on uneven ground and pulled loose his own sabre. Saar's thick fingers groped for the holster of his handgun. Merwin gulped and swerved up for the hill's pointed peak.

Angelika had seen Jonas fight; even in concert, the three escapees were no match for him. Once again, fate had situated her so that the only choice available to her was the stupid one. She ran up the hill after Rassau.

Jonas halved the distance between himself and the deserting men. Saar pulled out his tinder, to light the wick of his matchlock, then abandoned the useless effort. He dropped the rare and expensive weapon and it rolled down the hill. When Jonas reached him, Saar held out a palm in pleading surrender, his other hand massaging his twisted ankle. Rassau raised his sabre, ready to lop off Saar's head. 'No man shall desert from my company,' Jonas shouted.

Angelika tackled him from behind, driving her sharp, slim shoulder into the backs of his knees. He teetered backwards, rolling over her. She swept to the side, snatching her knife from the cuff of her boot. Jonas landed on his back, the wrist of his weapon-hand striking a stone. Angelika dived onto him, pinning the wrist with her knee. Her dagger's tip hovered over his right eye.

'I told you you didn't want to do that,' she said.

'Get off me, woman.'

'You make that demand from an exceptionally poor bargaining position.' She sensed that Mattes and Merwin had gathered close around her. Though Mattes had his sword out, ready to back her up, and Merwin clutched an admirably pointy boulder the size of his hand, she would have preferred they not encroach. Even in his current posture, lying flat out facing down the slope, blood rushing to his head, a combatant of Rassau's deadliness was not to be underestimated.

'I am still the commander of this company and those men are deserters. If you leave off me this instant, I promise to chalk up this crime against my person as an act of womanly rashness.'

Angelika's dagger darted closer to his eye, as if drawn by a magnet.

Jonas shut up.

'You speak of promises,' Saar suddenly babbled, 'but your word isn't worth a handful of spit. My life may not be much, but I've grown fond of it and I'm done entrusting it to you.'

'That's a problem, then,' said Angelika. She adjusted her weight, momentarily placing most of it on Jonas's wrist, eliciting a groan. 'Because we're all going to have to make promises to one another if we're to extricate ourselves from this.'

'I just want us to go home,' said Saar.

'Well I suspect that Jonas here won't agree to taking the whole company back, will he?'

'You'll be sorry you ever pressured me at knife-point.'

'No one likes hearing this, but it's for your own good, Jonas. Now answer the question.'

'The Gerolsbruch Swordsmen will remain here and perform their duties.'

'There we go. The unit will remain. But you, Saar, and Mattes and Merwin would like to go anyway, yes?'

'Yes,' said Mattes.

'In that case,' said Angelika, 'I've formed such a bond of attachment to the lot of you that I'm prepared to do an extraordinary thing. I will lie for you. Jonas, tell us why desertion is never permitted.'

The lieutenant began with an exasperated sigh. 'If one is allowed to desert, all will do the same.'

'Then we will compromise. Jonas and I will return to camp. Mattes, did you tell anyone else of your intention to scarper off?'

'I begged Pinkert and Madelung to accompany us, but they would not come.'

'Inconvenient. Well then. The five of us will return to camp. The three of you did not intend to desert. You heard rustling and thought it might be game. I unthinkingly let you go off in pursuit of it.'

'Let me up,' Jonas said.

'You think me a mooncalf? Not till we've agreed on a serviceable lie.' As Angelika constructed her proposal, she used her contact with Jonas to subtly frisk him for her ring. With the sides of her thighs and her free arm, she brushed against him in any place that contained a pocket, or might conceal a hiding place. 'The three of you went off. Jonas woke and realised the dangers you'd put yourselves in, exposing yourself to barbarian sentries. So he and I came out to collect you. *Voila*: there has been no desertion.

'You, Mattes, will assure Madelung and Pinkert and whoever else thinks otherwise. Later, after a seemly interval, Jonas will send the three of you out for another forage. You won't come back. The Kurgs will have taken you. The company shall mourn your sad demises. Jonas preserves good discipline, and the three of you get to leave. What say you?'

Jonas had grown increasingly flushed; his head had taken on the colouration of a beetroot. 'A fatal flaw blemishes your scheme. As I said not long ago, Angelika, you are an atrocious liar.'

'The four of you will do all the lying. I'll simply keep my mouth clamped.' She finished her search. She was now certain that her ring was nowhere on him. Either he'd secreted it somewhere nearby, in a hole or cranny, or it, and five years of clammy, fearful labour, were truly and irrevocably lost.

'I don't know if I can trust them,' Jonas said.

Saar goggled. 'It is we who can't trust you. Once we believed you, but you've proven yourself false with us, time and again.'

Angelika grimaced. 'I've come up with a perfectly decent, bloodless way out of this. If you won't join in, Saar, I can step off Jonas's chest with conscience clear, and let you resume as before.'

'We agree then,' Saar replied.

'You there. Halfling,' Angelika said.

340 Robin D Laws

'I don't think I ever should have left. I snuck away without my friend Filch, who got me into this. That doesn't make me such a boon companion, does it now?'

'Is that a yes or a no?'

'Yes, I'll take part in this white lie of yours. For a white lie it plainly is, seeing as it's for the benefit of all and sundry.' He let his rock fall into the dirt. 'This wouldn't have done me so much good. It's Filch who's a dab hand with the thrown rocks. Me, I likely would have dropped it on my–'

'Thank you, Merwin. And now you, Mattes. Will you swear in?'

'I have one more condition.'

'What is that?' She felt Jonas reposition himself under her. A little test. She jabbed her knees tighter into his ribs. He bared his teeth, then relaxed.

Mattes bent down to peer into his commander's ruddy face. 'There's a second lie required here. Jonas, you got to start doing what Angelika here tells you. No more ignoring her advice. You can pretend to be the commander, and strut and posture as you please. But before giving any orders that might cost the men their lives, you must get her say-so.'

'I'm no commander,' said Angelika.

'And you don't have to act as one. But you've got to be it, in secret. You're the one knows what she's doing out here.'

Jonas sneered. 'And this vow remains in force till you make your unmanly exodus?'

'If you swear it, I'll stay.'

'How magnanimous.'

'Not a bit of it. I'll have to see you keep your word, won't I?'

The lieutenant's muscles knotted. His breathing sped. Angelika thought it possible that he might begin to weep. Finally he said, 'Then get off me, for I agree to it.'

'To all the terms?' Angelika asked.

'All that you have said,' he replied.

She leapt free of him. For a long moment, he remained still. Finally he sat up, hanging his head between his knees.

'You must all agree to lie about this as well: that you've seen me betrayed, and brought so low.'

THE SKY WENT blank that afternoon, dropping first slushy rain, then pelting, icy snow. Swordsmen peered mournfully from the tunnel at the whitening hills. Franziskus came to see and his archers gathered around him.

'This can't be happening,' said one.

'That's the mountains for you,' said Franziskus.

'Is it enemy magic?' he shivered.

Angelika strode up to investigate. 'No, just ordinary snow,' she said. 'If it was Chaos, it'd be the colour of blood or bile, and it would bubble the surface of the skin, or whisper crazy thoughts into your ear, or somesuch.'

'How long will it last?'

'Could be a few hours. Could be weeks.'

'That bodes ill.'

The soldier was right; they were nearly out of food. Now if they sent a party out to forage, their tracks could easily be read in the snow. The Chaos chieftain would need no baying creature to locate them. 'That's true,' said Angelika.

'I am glad,' the archer said, 'that you did not tell me it heralded a glorious victory, or would light our path and strengthen our spirits.' He pressed his back against the frigid tunnel wall, wrapping his cloak around himself. 'I weary of false hope.'

'It is bad, but we'll find some true hope yet,' Franziskus said

He went with Angelika back into the tunnel, to the blockage, where Jonas had been sitting since the party's miserly noonday meal. Near his feet a low fire lapped at twigs and branches.

'Excuse us, will you, Emil?' Jonas requested. The rest of the company had given him a respectful berth.

The older man stood, subjecting his commander to a circumspect reckoning. 'If you say so, lieutenant.'

Jonas watched him go. 'Is that snow out there?'

'Yes,' said Angelika, seating herself across from him.

'I'm sorry. It's a poor time for you to take command, isn't it?'

'To lead a troop of soldiers is the last thing I want. I agreed to Mattes's deal for one reason alone. To get the lot of you back in this tunnel without any throat-cutting.'

'So you're a party to my untruths then, hah?'

'Seems to be contagious.'

'I thought the soldiers were tired of lies.'

'Even Mattes expects you to present a good front. So belay your cursed moping and eventually you can win them back. Unless you've told some other absurd fairy story that'll come back to bite you.'

'Unless, unless…'

Angelika's chest tightened. 'There isn't, is there?'

'What?'

'If there's some other lie that will later catch us by surprise…'

'No, I swear it.'

'Then lash yourself together, Jonas.'

'There's a part of me worth salvaging, is there?'

She waited for a moment. 'Yes. Yes, Jonas, I tell you that there is.'

'But we're trapped, aren't we? A day's worth of food, if that. Now the creeping cold. Tonight I expect the baying of that ghastly hound to draw closer. Do you think it has six eyes, or merely a set of grasping tentacles? Mattes has set you an insurmountable task, to get us out of this.'

'To blazes with Mattes,' said Angelika. 'I don't pretend to be a military officer.'

'Then delegate to Franziskus, as I have been made to devolve power to you. What can we do, good Franziskus Weibe?'

'Angelika's right that we can't give up.'

His bitter laugh rattled. 'But what to do?'

'We wait?'

'For what? For that chieftain to lead his army back to Stirland, burning what's left of it to the ground? Slaying our families, razing our towns? Then we stagger back, starved, and find only pestilence and famine? Yes, that is a fine plan. It is good that my responsibility for it is only decorative.'

'Something will break our way,' said Franziskus. 'When it does, we'll be ready.'

Jonas cackled. 'Oh yes. I am sure that will work. Shall I announce it, with fanfare and foofarah?'

'You can tell the men to pack themselves close together, for warmth,' said Angelika. 'A bigger fire's tempting, but too great a risk. The lower the temperature, the more visible the smoke plume. Also it will melt the snow around the entrance. Have them gather snow in their canteens. It's not far below freezing now, but if it gets much colder, they'll have to keep the water close to their bodies, to stop it turning to ice. And it goes without saying that whatever food they have left, they should eat in the tiniest of nibbles.'

'Tiny nibbles. Yes, I shall proclaim that, and in a stirring voice.'

Revolted, Franziskus turned from him. 'If you cared for the men as much as for their opinion of you, you'd be capable of encouraging them now.'

'And Angelika,' Jonas continued, 'when you set out from the Blackfire, with your ring in your pocket, did you imagine you'd spend your retirement in a freezing cave, counting the hours till Kurgans came to violate you?'

'You have it, don't you?'

He flung the back of his helmeted head against the wall behind him. 'Yes indeed, why hide that now? Naturally, I have the ring. I took it from you on that night.'

Angelika thought about knifing him. His sabre was several feet away. 'Care to hand it over, then?'

He reached into a pocket. 'By Sigmar's cumbrous hammer, why not? I thought I was such a clever boots. Luring along an indispensable minion. Had I but suspected how double-edged an underling's indispensability can be.' His face convulsed in bafflement. He turned the pocket inside out. He checked his pack, and the inside of his purse. Jonas's mouth fell silently open.

'You've lost it,' said Angelika.

'I must have,' he said, at length.

Her hand clutched tight, as if it held her knife. 'You had it, and you lost it.'

'You'll not believe this, Angelika, but – but my remorse is genuine. I meant for you to get it back. Never did I intend any of this–'

'I don't give a fig for your remorse. Where were you when you lost it?'

Emil drifted into view. 'Is all in order, sir?'

'Yes, yes, Emil. Please let us talk in peace.'

The sergeant faded back.

'I did not trifle with you, Angelika. It was not meant to happen as it has. Please believe me.'

'You took it from me that night, in the hayloft?'

Franziskus's fair skin flushed with crimson. He got up to leave but Angelika tugged his sleeve, to keep him there.

She repeated her question. 'That is when you took it, yes?'

Jonas resembled a sheepish child. 'When else?'

'And where were you when you last knew you had it?'

'I don't know.'

She coiled to launch herself at him.

Franziskus glanced with deliberate portent to the men. She was not so certain they wouldn't cheer her, but eased herself anyhow.

'Think,' she demanded.

'I am thinking but it's impossible to know, isn't it?'

'You didn't keep checking it, to be sure you still had it?'

'I forgot about it.'

'When I had it, I could not stop testing my pocket, to be sure it was there.'

'It mattered more to you than it does to me.'

'Do you know what that ring was worth?'

He shrugged. 'Merely money, I imagine.'

'Did you have it up on the ridge?'

'I can't say. You can't go looking for it now.'

'Did you have it at any time here in the valley?'

'Perhaps.'

'Can you say for sure you had it in the dwarven gorge?'

'If I could only be certain, I would surely say so.'

'The rock slope, where the boulders were rolled on us. Did you check it then?'

'Let me think. It can't be the case that I never ever looked once. Can it?'

'Do you know, or don't you?'

He lit like a chimney fire. 'It must be. He has it!'

'Who?'

'The chieftain.'

'What?'

'The chieftain. I must have lost it near the camp. That is most likely, yes? We spent more time there than anywhere else. And yes, yes, now that I contemplate it, I did, I did take it out and look at it on the night when – on the night when I made Franziskus here a lieutenant. I remember now. I was thinking, thinking that it was an irony. Yes? That an act of dishonesty on my part, could lead to such a righteous result, as this fine fellow here regaining his honour.

My theft was his redemption. Is that not so, Franziskus?'

'Redemption is neither yours to grant, nor mine to claim.'

Jonas faltered for a moment then his confession recovered its tumbling momentum. 'At any rate, then. Yes, yes, whether it was a true thought, or more of my pervading lunacy, it remains that I did take the ring from this pocket and hold it up to peer into the red translucency of its ruby. And I thought, how lovely, yet how like blood. Therein were all the contradictions of our precarious existence.'

'Any more philosophy and I'll forget I'm not a murderess.'

'Oh Angelika. You are as strange and precious as your lost gem.' He reached out to trace the tip of his finger along her face. It took all of her restraint not to catch it between her sharp incisors and try to gnaw it off.

'But lost it is not. Or rather, we know where it is. For when Franziskus and I spied on the enemy army as it combed our camp, we saw this chieftain bend down and pick up something glinting from the ground. Did we not, Franziskus?'

'I saw him stab through a soldier's heart with his fighting claws.'

'Yes, yes.' Jonas was impatient. 'But we saw that other thing happen, too.'

'That's your story?' Angelika asked.

'Yes, yes, I saw it, the chieftain has it. We need only slay him, and then you'll get it back.'

'You absolutely expect us to believe that, don't you?'

'It had to have happened.'

She laid her own hand aside his face, letting her nails gouge in. 'I thought you a liar, but you are much worse than that. Truth and falsehood – you haven't a glimmer of the difference between them.'

He slipped sulkily free of her touch. 'How much more prostration do you require of me?'

'That's the exact tale you spun before, Rassau. That the chieftain stooped to pluck it up.'

'But this time it happened. Yes, yes, it's the story of the boy who cried wolf. But it happened. Franziskus can tell you.'

'It didn't, Jonas.'

'It did, it did, it did.' Fever gleamed in his pupils. 'The chieftain has it. Together we'll slay him, and you'll see. How could it be otherwise?'

Angelika patted his bobbing head. Wearing false, bored stares, she and Franziskus strode past Emil, along the length of the tunnel, and out into the open. They moved up to the ridge wall, leaning there, so as not to be seen from above.

'To state the obvious, he's gone mad,' said Franziskus.

'I suspect it's temporary.'

'Something's snapped him. Angelika, what did you do to him, out there?'

'Just a wee knife to the throat. Nothing a man shouldn't be able to handle.'

'You've untethered him completely.'

'His moorings were uncertain long before I sawed at them.'

They noticed that the wind had warmed. Fog swelled from the snow as it melted into slush. Soon its wisps enveloped the lower reaches of the surrounding hills.

Angelika stepped into the thick, obscuring mist. 'You take care of them,' she said. 'Get as many of them home as you can, Lieutenant Weibe.'

'Angelika!' He couldn't see her. 'Where are you going?'

'Where do you think?' said the fog. 'To get my ring back.'

CHAPTER TWENTY-TWO

ANGELIKA HAD NEVER been in a thicker haze. She could barely see her feet as they imprinted themselves in the sodden earth. Though she thought she could navigate through the hills by feel and memory, she soon grew completely disoriented. She'd travel for a few yards along a trail, only to wind up on a slope heading where – east, west? Toward the camp? Into the arms of the Kurgan, and their baying hound?

She forced herself to stop, until the fog dispersed a little. If fate favoured her, it would burn off slowly, leaving remnants to hide her from barbarian sentries. Angelika occupied her mind by evaluating the sanity of her present course.

Jonas's new account of the ring's whereabouts was deranged in both detail and intent. Nonetheless, it contained a gossamer filament of reason. Jonas had been in the camp by the stream longer than he'd been anywhere else. The first, most logical place to look for it was at the spot where he'd pitched his tent. Angelika understood that the chances of her finding it there were slim. She did not like to think what she would find herself doing if she didn't. Would she really retrace the expedition's entire journey, combing through dirt and grasses the entire way, in a vast mountain range packed to the crannies with slavering barbarian warriors?

She had to admit to herself that she just might.

Five years of her life was worth a few months of fruitless searching, just in case. But first she would check the camp.

The fog loosened its grip and the hills revealed themselves around her like mute giants coming quietly from slumber. Now that she could see where she was going, she made a hasty meander to the site. Angelika headed straight to Jonas's spot and knelt to minutely examine the rocks and dirt. Now the grey sky impeded her work; if there'd been sunlight, either the gem or its fine gold setting might flash up at her.

A pained growl rumbled out. It came from the east – the direction of the Kurgan horde. She sprang up, dagger in hand. It couldn't be too far away. She heard a slapping sound, of a flat object slowly pressing into the slushy ground. Then again. Again. A wall of fog slipped toward her; within it resolved an abbreviated, shambling silhouette.

The fog wall disgorged its contents: Bodo the halfling staggered blindly onward, attracted by the sound of her searching. He'd escaped and returned to camp.

Angelika's breath halted.

Bodo was alive but sadistically mutilated. One eyelid had been sewn shut; the other, its white replaced by red, sewn open. His ears had been cut off, and his head patchily shaven. Something horrible had happened to his toes. He moaned in agony, revealing raw sockets where his teeth should have been. His tormentors had left him with only his trousers; his naked torso exposed a dozen deep and raking wounds.

He fell at her feet, murmuring miserably.

She stooped to take him into her arms. He was small but muscular, and as heavy as she expected. Fear impelled her on and filled her limbs with surprising strength. The Chaos forces had let him go for a purpose. They wanted Bodo to find his comrades. Maybe they sought only to demoralise the Stirlanders, by sending them a sample of their handiwork. More likely, they would track him, perhaps with that monster hound of theirs.

Bodo would never have found the hideout on his own. By taking Bodo back there, she'd be endangering everyone.

She stopped, between a pair of scraggy hills. She listened for Kurgan boots, or the snuffling of a lupine Chaos beast.

They had no means of treating his wounds. In all likelihood, he would die, and soon.

She should not take him back. Rather, she should show him genuine mercy, and pull the keen edge of her dagger across his throat.

To do it would require an honesty too bitter even for her. She lurched further along the trail.

* * *

BODO'S MOANS INCREASED in pitch as Angelika drew closer to the tunnel mouth. The slush had completely melted, pooling into shallow puddles. The halfling's weight in her arms left her little chance to detour around them. Cold water seeped in through a new-found break in the stitching between sole and boot.

Filch scrambled from the tunnel opening, with Merwin hard after him, crying Bodo's name. Worried about sentries, Angelika waved him back. Undeterred, his friends ran to her side. She gave in to exhaustion, lowering Bodo's body into their arms. They bore him like a stretcher toward the tunnel – Filch carrying his arms, Merwin, his flat-footed legs. Soldiers spilled carelessly out, forming a cordon around him.

'Get inside,' Angelika called. Freed of the burden of Bodo's body, she wove and lost her balance. Franziskus appeared beside her, to keep her from falling. 'Tell them to get inside,' she said to him.

'Archers,' Franziskus shouted. 'Back in the tunnel.'

His men tore themselves away, but stopped a few inches inside the tunnel. Impeded by well-wishers ringing around them, Filch and Merwin stopped, low-ering Bodo to the soppy earth. 'Those beasts,' Merwin bawled. 'Savages. Loathsome, torturing pigs.'

The soldiers muttered their outrage. A swordsman whose name Angelika had never learned tended the halfling, cleaning his wounds with the pooling water he'd been laid in. Behind him, another unfurled the company's final length of clean bandage.

Jonas levelled his shoulders and firmed his jaw. 'He shall be avenged, I swear it.'

Mattes lunged at him, shoving him back, away from Bodo. 'You lied again.'

Jonas, taken off guard, slid in the mud. Speedily finding his balance, he pulled his sabre from its sheath. A serpent's grin crawled across his face. 'You wish to challenge me, Mattes?'

Mattes left his weapon in its scabbard and ran at Jonas, fists milling the air before him. Saar and Madelung grappled him, holding him back. He aimed a wad of spittle at his commander, but it fell lazily to the ground, far short of its goal. His face purpled in helpless fury. 'You're five times the swordsman I am, Jonas Rassau, but still I'll fight you.'

Emil interposed himself between Jonas and the struggling men. 'Leave this to me, sir,' he said.

Drizzle spattered down on them.

Jonas stayed ready to receive a charge. 'I will not, sergeant. Stand aside.'

'Discipline's a matter for the sergeant, sir.' He placed his nose within an inch of Mattes's. 'Saar. Madelung. Let this man go. If he must have at some-one, let him poke at me.'

Mattes's restrainers slipped hesitantly aside. The leathery drumsman thrust out his chin, offering Emil a target, if he wanted it. 'You'll defend this fable-teller? He clutched at all our hearts with his story of Bodo's heroic demise.' He directed an aside down at the semi-conscious halfling. 'Did you know that you were dead, good fellow? Though it looks like you were instead left behind and tormented by the Kurgs, we know it can't be so, because our com-mander says otherwise.'

'You've been trouble all along, Mattes,' Emil said, 'but now you've taken it too far and I can't let it go.'

'You saying he's not a liar? That any of us can trust a word he utters?'

'I'll smack that lip of yours open if you don't button it now,' Emil replied.

A swordsman with a long mournful face moved to Mattes's shoulder. 'Then when you're done, sergeant, you can smack mine, too. This one's no leader, and you know he isn't.'

'A lieutenant's a lieutenant and a soldier's only a soldier, and that's all you need to know.'

'Stand aside, Emil,' said Jonas, 'I'll finish them both.'

Emil's cheek twitched. 'Sir it would be best if–'

Madelung planted his feet beside Mattes's. 'He'll have to deal with me, too, then.'

'So it's open mutiny, is it?' Jonas traced a circle with the tip of his heavy sword. 'How many more of you wish to accompany these three to Hell?'

'Sir…' said Emil.

'Any lies told,' shouted Jonas, 'were for your benefit. Yes, our condition is hard. But we fight for freedom, against barbarians. How do you expect to win this battle if you do not believe in it? Are you too weak and cowardly to see that?'

Pushing the flat of his blade against Emil's arm, he impelled his sergeant out of the way. He raised his sabre over Mattes's head. The men beside him faded off. Mattes, glowering his defiance, stretched out his neck to facilitate the blow. Jonas wavered.

Then Angelika saw his fingers tighten around his sword hilt; he was ready to do it.

Jonas screeched, dropped his sabre, and bent down, rubbing the fingers of his weapon hand. The pommel of Angelika's dagger had hit its mark. She strode up to retrieve her knife from the muck.

'That,' she said to Jonas, 'was for your benefit. Now the rest of you, get in that cave, where you can bash each other's brains till your hearts' content, before–'

An unearthly yelping vibrated off the rocks and among the hills.

The Chaos reek returned.

Bodo stirred and thrashed, as if caught in a nightmare: 'No! You should have left me.'

Angelika uttered her favourite curse word and dashed for the tunnel maw. 'Inside,' she yelled. The archers retreated further into the passageway, making room for their comrades as they panicked across its threshold. 'Franziskus. Where are you?' she called. He was right beside her.

Spasmed by fear, the humans had forgotten the halflings. Merwin and Filch knelt beside Bodo's palpitating frame.

Mattes and Saar had been crammed side-by-side by the reckless press of men. They swapped glances, reached silent accord, and sprinted out to lift up Bodo between them. They returned, Filch and Merwin in their wake.

'Take him all the way back,' Angelika commanded.

Then the creature made itself apparent, squirming on distended, padded paws around the side of Mount Lemon. Angelika had heard a great lot of nonsense talk about Chaos and never knew which of the stories to believe. She'd heard the Kurgan took innocent beasts, like mountain lions and oxen, and deformed them with their dark sorcery. Supposedly, over the generations, they bred monstrousness into these

animals, as one would breed fleetness into a racing
dog or keenness of eye into a hunting falcon.

The thing they now beheld showed that the stories
were true: at one time it, or an ancestor, had been a
mastiff or other strong-jawed hound. Now it was a
bloated, elongated thing moving sluggishly forward
on four leprous limbs, bowed by the jiggling mass of
its pink and naked torso. Wide, misshapen ears flared
from the top of its boxy skull. They turned on stalks
of fibrous muscle, detecting the gasps and shattered
breaths of the men all around her. Long strands of
viscous slobber dangled from its great, encasing jaw.
Slow as a ruddering sea vessel, its gargantuan head
turned their way. Tiny black orbs glistened and
blinked at them, suspended in sockets of pale pus. A
nubbled carpet of tongue rolled out of its mouth,
panting eagerly up and down. With glacial inevitability, the creature plodded at them.

'Archers,' commanded Franziskus.

The Chelborgers formed a rank around the tunnel
mouth.

Behind them, Saar fumbled with his tinder, to light
the wick of his matchlock pistol.

'Fire!' Franziskus called to his archers. A volley shot
crisply out to meet the Chaos hound. Arrows
bounced from its rubbery flesh. One stuck briefly in
the creature's tongue. He slurped it into his mouth,
and when the jaw gated open, it was gone. The beast
continued, unimpeded.

'Ready,' yelled Franziskus.

Behind him, a swordsman unabashedly wept. The
men arrayed near him shook him to his senses, so
that he only whimpered.

'Aim,' said Franziskus. 'Fire!'

The creature stomped close, blocking the day's hazy light. All of the arrows found their target, but the hound was unfazed. It shook its head in momentary annoyance and padded nearer.

'Back. Back to the back,' Angelika called.

The soldiers packed themselves back into the dwarf corridor, so tight it was a labour to breathe. Angelika meant to stay in front, for a purpose she hadn't yet arrived at. Instead the hands of the men grabbed her and pulled her into the middle of their tight-packed ranks. Young Madelung, she noted, had stuck himself in the front.

The creature tested its head into the tunnel opening. Steaming drool dropped and sizzled beneath it. It opened its mouth to bark at them exposing dozens of strange insectoid parasites hanging from the tissue of its gums. The hound pressed itself across the threshold, then stopped. The width of its shoulders had halted it. It growled its displeasure, tried to free itself, and wedged itself more thoroughly into the doorway. It whined pitifully, as if expecting one of its prospective meals to step up and free it.

'It's stuck,' exclaimed Filch.

'It can't get us.' chimed Merwin.

The hound shoved itself further into the tunnel, its bones wetly groaning with the effort. No one breathed.

'Get stuck again, get stuck again,' Filch begged.

'Come on, doggie, get stuck. Get stuck,' said Merwin.

'By Sigmar's beard, will no one quiet those blooming halflings?' a soldier asked.

Deeper into the tunnel the creature slithered. Half-uttered prayers whispered through the passage.

'Valour, men, valour,' Jonas urged.

It oozed within sword's-reach of the front rank.

'Stab it. Now!' ordered Jonas.

Madelung made a step up to spear it in the eye with his sabre. The hound dropped his mouth down over him. The fresh-faced warrior died without a scream, his bones crunching between the hound's broad, crushing teeth. Sabres hacked down at the wattles of loose flesh wreathing its jaw but the creature continued chewing contentedly on Madelung's body, crimson infusing its ropy slobber.

The soldiers gasped, appalled, and shrank closer into one another.

The hound retreated, forcing its constricted hulk of a torso backwards. Loose skin wrinkled and pulled against the tunnel wall. It pointed its head upwards, exposing its venous throat, positioning Madelung's well-masticated remains to slide down its gullet.

'Attack now,' Jonas yelled.

A pair of swordsmen marshalled their courage and speared their swords out at the creature's neck. It reared on them, fragments of meat spilling from its mouth. Before they could reach it, it bulled its head down. A vast paw came squashing down on an attacker, pinning him to the floor. The hound rolled its weight down onto the immobilising foot. Cracking noises issued from the swordsman's body as his bones were reduced to paste.

'In the name of all the gods,' said Jonas, 'I will find the man who sent this horror against us, and I will strike him dead.'

Ducking its head down, the beast caught the ankle of its latest victim between its jaws, then achingly withdrew from the tunnel. It bounded to the slope of a hill overlooking the tunnel entrance and sat there, methodically tearing its prey apart, devouring him piece by piece.

The soldiers eased apart. Angelika and Jonas squeezed to the tunnel opening.

'What now?' he asked her.

'We run.'

'Where to?'

'Good point.'

'Well then?'

'I guess we have to kill it.'

As she said this, a swordsman pushed out from behind her, forcing her sideways. He tripped free of his jostling comrades and out of the tunnel mouth. Drunk with panic, he sprinted off to the left. He hugged the rock wall for a dozen feet or so, then scurried for the fractured trail between two hill mounds. The hound's snout quivered skywards then it roused its ungainly body and thumped after the fleeing soldier. It propelled itself like a catapult on its muscular haunches, landing on its target with all of its several tons of weight. The swordsman's spine cracked like the report of a blunderbuss.

A sickened flinch rippled through the trapped tunnel inhabitants.

'I have to think,' Angelika muttered. 'Got to be a way.'

Seeing that the hound was occupied with the dismemberment of his latest catch, another swordsman, a double-chinned fellow who had kept his black-and-yellows surprisingly clean through all the hardships of the journey, chose his moment to bolt from the front rank. He darted to the right; the unearthly mastiff wheeled and galloped at him, flinging great shovelfuls of mud behind his mammoth back paws. The swordsman might have made it a few yards further, but slowed to commit the classic blunder of the terrified: he turned to see how close his pursuer had come. The beast pounced, snapping him into its gate-like mouth, then shaking him to death.

It flipped the double-chinned swordsman's slack-limbed corpse up above its head, playing with it.

'Who here,' Angelika asked, 'was in the squad that booby-trapped that hill, there?'

Filch squeezed in beside her and raised his hand. 'Me, Fraulein Angelika.'

'Any pit traps up there?'

'Like you instructed, ma'am.'

'With stakes?'

'Without them, a pit trap's pointless.'

'I'm going to pretend you didn't say that, at a time like this. Show me the spot.'

He jabbed out a compassing finger, to little avail. 'It's hard to see. We hid it well.'

'Then congratulations, halfling, you're coming with us.'

'And by the way, after we both survive,' he said, 'there's something I've got to show you.'

'It can't eat more than one of us at a time,' said Angelika. 'Franziskus, you come with me. We'll run to the right of it. Jonas, you make like you're escaping in the opposite direction. Take someone with you.'

'I'll go,' said Emil.

'No,' said Angelika, 'I need you here to lead the men.'

'Me, then,' said Mattes.

'Good. You and Jonas, then. Filch, you feeling fast?'

'Fleet and hearty, milady.'

'Whichever pair of us it decides to follow, you've got to run and join. They run interference for you while you lead it up the hill and into the pit. The pit will contain him, yes?'

'His toothy end, at least,' said Filch.

The great mastiff plied the soldier's head free of his body and snouted it around until it got lodged between two boulders. It tried to retrieve its plaything, applying a slapping forepaw to the task.

Angelika shuddered. She'd never been gladder of an empty stomach. 'The second pair then comes at it from the flank and helps us herd it. But don't get too close. We don't want it to change direction and chase you instead.'

'And then?' asked Mattes.

'Then we steer it into the pit, get it stuck, and kill it while it's helpless. Meanwhile, Emil, if at any moment it seems like there's a clear break, take it, and get the men out of here. Watch for missiles from above, though.'

'Or Kurgs out there before us, in the hills.'

Angelika nodded. The beast likely came with handlers, though it seemed the type of pet from which even its masters kept a cautious distance.

The Chaos hound grew bored with its latest plaything and nosed its bulk back toward the tunnel. It licked its floppy chops in anticipation.

'Now,' cried Angelika. She and Franziskus ran to the right; Jonas and Mattes scooted left. The dog's head stupidly roamed from the first pair of runners to the second. One foreleg suspended in front of it, it feinted first to Angelika, then to Jonas, then paused in confused hesitation.

'Follow us, you brainless mutt,' called Angelika.

'Face my slashing sword,' taunted Jonas, his blade already drawn.

Their shouts served only to cement the monster's indecision. It snarled its yellowed, gore-flecked teeth at both in turn.

Emil readied the company for flight.

From the precipice above, throaty Kurgan jeers urged the beast on.

Emil signalled the men to stand down. A swordsman behind him suppressed sobs of frustration.

Filch sailed a rock at the beast, bonking it squarely on the crown of its skull. It shook and stamped the ground as a bull would do, then flung itself at him. He ran to Franziskus and Angelika, and further up the hill. It surged behind them, corrupt breath heating their skin.

'This way,' Filch called. Angelika saw the spot where the trap had been laid. If she fell back a few paces, she could induce the beast to follow her. She charted a route from stone to ledge to flat, plotting her way up the slope. If she hit every footfall just right, this ludicrous plan of hers would, in fact, work.

Behind her, the beast yowled. No longer feeling or smelling its breath on her neck, she glanced back: it reared up on its haunches, facing down-slope, batting its paws at Jonas. He'd cut a lengthy but superficial tear into the hide of the dog's flank.

The idiot. He'd ruined it all. Done precisely what she'd warned him against.

'I said, face my slashing sword, misbegotten hound of hell!' he cried.

The beast thumped down on its forepaws and snapped at him. Ably, he dodged its clamping jaws. He hit the thing a glancing blow with his sabre, to no apparent effect.

'Jonas,' yelled Angelika, 'get him up here.'

Instead Jonas hacked at the monster's front legs. It reared again. He attempted to roll under it, presumably to jab up into its underbelly, but the creature bumped him with its shoulder, sending him sprawling. Mattes, grimacing in unsurprised disgust, came in from its other side, feinting his sabre in the monster's face. It shrieked at him, leaving Jonas time to recover his footing. Jonas jigged back; the creature snapped at him, leaving stripes of froth to drip down his breastplate.

'Angelika.' It was Filch, he'd skipped up above her on the hill. His toes held a prehensile grip on a gently overhanging shelf of rock. 'Crouch down,' he shouted, waving for her to turn around.

She doubtfully complied, anchoring her hands as best she could against the moistened earth. Filch leapt from the rock and onto her back. She rolled up and sent him flying on his way, to land on the creature. Loose folds of hide served as his handholds as he inched his way up its squirming back and onto its neck. Jonas wobbled, dumbfounded, as the halfling stirruped his legs around the beast's head. It lurched and screamed, but could not buck him off.

Filch gathered up the mastiff's jiggling wattles and pulled them tight, using them as reins. The monster pitifully barked and crashed along the hillside, struggling to dislodge him. The halfling steered him up the slope in an unpredictable zig-zag. Angelika dived out of the way as his behemoth of a head flew by. Reaching his destination, Filch jumped uncontrollably off the creature's crown. A dull, smothered impact followed, shaking the mound, dislodging miniature mudslides.

The hound's back legs cycled haplessly in the air: its head had been swallowed by the pitfall. Judging from its doleful whine, it seemed a good bet that at least one of the trap's impaling stakes had badly pierced it.

Filch lay on the hillside with little more dignity; his upended body resembled a bundle of discarded laundry. He slumped down.

Angelika and Franziskus cautiously approached the floundering beast from opposite sides, steering clear of its wheeling back legs. She saw little point in stabbing it with her dagger; the hide was too thick for such a short blade to do the necessary damage.

Franziskus readied his sabre to butcher it, but then Jonas ran in. He slid his sabre between the beast's ribs and its torso accepted the weapon all the way to its hilt. He withdrew the sword, moved it up a rib, and plunged it in again, pushing with his shoulder to overcome resistance. After five such terrible strikes, the hellhound ceased its convulsions and died.

At the bottom of the hill waited a quartet of axe-brandishing Kurgans, their postures expressing varying quantities of awe and outrage. Jonas clanged his sabre-hilt to his streaky cuirass and charged down at them. Mattes ran in from the side to engage the barbarian closest to him, who was also the smallest. The two of them stepped warily around one another.

As his three companions readied themselves to move in, Jonas arrived, swimming among them, diligently hewing their limbs and torsos. Within a minute all three were dead, and the fourth, left facing Mattes, had Jonas's sabre plunged into his back. He glanced down to see its exit point, just below his sternum. His dying hiss was less than defiant. Jonas kicked him off his blade, and he crumbled to the grass.

Swordsmen and archers gushed from the tunnel mouth, holding their weapons aloft in tribute. Emil shouted them into orderly ranks, for a proper march out of the valley.

A rain of stones, none smaller than an anvil, spilled from the ridgeline. They fell onto the exposed ranks of Gerolsbruchers. Their impacts threw men to the ground. The formation broke as the men escaped back to the shelter of the tunnel. Some succumbed to panic wholeheartedly; others stayed to drag felled comrades. Primitive arrows sang around them, though the few that found their targets did scant harm: the distance from ridge to valley floor exhausted the range of the barbarian bows.

Jonas braced himself for a run through the hail of boulders. Angelika wanted to hold until all the rocks were spent. Logically speaking, they'd only have so many of them to drop. But then she let him go, and followed after him besides. Franziskus and Mattes

Robin D Laws

obeyed her cue. Filch piped up beside her, puffed with exhilaration.

'Wasn't that impressive?' he asked. 'How I landed on the beast, and steered it?'

'Yes,' replied Angelika, preferring to save her air for running.

'Who'd have thought?' Filch continued. 'Before this began, I'd never seriously picked up a stone to throw. Yet it turns out I'm a splendid rock-tosser. And now also it seems I'm a first-class leaper on, and tamer of, beasts.'

To be precise, Angelika thought, it was not so much a taming as a slaughtering, but now they neared the zone of dropped boulders. They bounded through, passing the bodies of three men who'd sustained fatal stonings: two swordsmen and an archer.

Including those killed by the monster, the entire incident had claimed the lives of seven men.

A smallish chunk of granite, no bigger than a croquet ball, bounced between Angelika's legs as she pelted for the tunnel. This was as close as she, or any of the other monster-hunters, came to injury.

Inside the tunnel, the momentary exuberance of imminent escape had reversed itself. The men pitched against the smooth-hewn walls, wordless and bereft. Everyone understood: the Chaos troops knew where they were, and would be down soon to finish them off.

Merwin drifted numbly to greet Filch. 'Bodo,' he said. 'Bodo is dead.'

The two halflings miserably embraced. A shame, thought Angelika, that Filch hadn't been given a few more minutes to savour his new status as splendid rock-tosser, first-class leaper, and tamer of beasts.

Emil stood at the tunnel mouth, gazing intently into the surrounding hills. He gesticulated to Jonas, who waved him off, gulping from his water flask.

'You go,' he said to Angelika. 'You're in charge here, now, aren't you?'

Angelika sped to Emil's side. He glowered at both his commander and at her. Angelika twitched uncomfortably.

'I am an officer,' said Franziskus. 'Tell it to me.'

Emil pointed to a black bobbing shape on the crest of a nearby hill. 'They're already here.'

The barbarians were attempting to conceal themselves, but, unaccustomed to stealth, they fared miserably. In a quarter of an hour, Angelika counted at least a dozen separate marauders. For each whose helmet or elbow peeked up, there had to be two or three others, at the very least, who'd successfully hidden themselves.

'What are they waiting for?' asked Emil.

'Deferred violence is hardly a barbarian watchword,' said Angelika. 'But somehow this lot have learned the art of patience. Next thing you know, they'll be dining on scones and dancing the gavotte.'

'It's that terrifying chieftain of theirs,' said Franziskus, 'keeping them to the master plan, against their natures. But why wait to attack us?'

'Maybe they overestimate our numbers?' suggested Emil.

'There's an army of them on the other side of this ridge,' said Franziskus. 'Perhaps it is because they saw us slay their monster, and think we have great champions among us.'

Angelika crossed her arms. 'No, you were right before, Franziskus.'

'I was?'

'Their chieftain wants his restive hordes to wait quietly. So he's given them some toys to play with. So long as we're nicely trapped here, they're going to draw this out as long as they can.'

'We must escape, then,' said Franziskus.

'That valley will be crawling with them. We'll be fighting an entire army.'

'We are already,' said Emil. 'If we stay here, they'll pick us off one at a time. If we go out and fight them, a few of us might break through their lines and make it to safety.'

'You're right,' said Angelika. 'Given a choice between the nearly and completely hopeless, one has to go with the former.'

'You've got a cheerful way with words,' said Emil.

'An all-out assault on enemy lines exceeds my expertise,' she said. 'That's a matter for military minds.'

'What about you?' Emil asked Franziskus. 'Can you create a battle plan?'

'I was a junior officer. I entered one engagement, and, by good fortune alone, was its sole survivor. Without Angelika, I wouldn't even have been that.'

'But did you attend a college of war?'

'I did, but confess to little mastery of the subject. It's up to you, Emil.'

'I've seen many a battle from the filth and the muck. I transmit orders; I don't conceive of them.'

'You underestimate yourself.'

'No,' said Emil. 'I'm a sergeant, no less, no more.'

They looked back to Jonas. To the dismay of Filch and Merwin, he'd dragged Bodo's body into his lap, where he cradled it like a child. His men regarded him with appalled pity, but he took no notice of anyone except the tortured halfling.

'Then you've left yourself no option,' said Angelika, 'but to snap him back to his senses.'

Emil scratched his bald spot and eased his way towards his lieutenant.

'And good luck to you,' she said, so only Franziskus could hear.

'How can they trust him?' Franziskus asked.

'He's the best swordsman here, by far,' she said. 'We need him in fighting spirit.'

'He wouldn't do as you required, just now.'

'Even when he's ignoring the strategy he can still sickle his way through four Kurgs a minute.'

'Point taken.'

'Who knows? Maybe, if he makes the plan, he'll go so far as to follow it.'

Emil stopped, reconsidering, and returned to Angelika and Franziskus. 'I know what must be done. You go to him, woman, and say what ought to be said.'

'What do you have in mind?'

'Indulge me, fraulein.' A new, though no less stoic, demeanour had settled on him. Angelika wondered what it meant.

She knelt beside Jonas and talked quietly. 'If there was ever a time for a man to get ahold of himself, Jonas, that time is now.'

'I should have done as you said, I know it.' He spoke without emotion, as if noting a change in the weather or a good place to stop and feed the horses. 'All I could think was, if I could slay the beast, you would all forgive me.'

'If it's escaped your notice, we've a new battle on our hands. You can flagellate yourself over the previous one when you write your war memoirs.'

'Who would read such a chronicle of defeat and folly?' He saw Emil, hanging back. 'Ah,' he said, 'I see. You send in the woman, to prick my guilt, and then you step in. With your hard-bitten sergeant's wisdom. Let me guess. You intended to invoke the deeds of my father, to stir me from this tarry despair.'

Emil's expression fell.

'No, Emil? Have I not accurately sussed your intent?'

'She's right, sir. You must compose yourself.'

Pasty soldiers blanched and fretted. They pointed their faces at anything but the squabble between lieutenant and sergeant.

'Yes, I must, mustn't I?' Jonas allowed himself a despairing chuckle. 'You, Emil, who served under my father, must burn with a special shame. To watch me as I so utterly besmirch his legacy.'

'If your father were here to see you, Jonas, my boy, you would not see him hang his head in shame.'

'No?'

'No.' Emil stood, gripping his leather gloves onto the sides of his commander's breastplate and hauling him to his feet. 'You'd see the backswing of his boot as it whirled towards your rump. He would say what I say: pull yourself together.'

A shark's grin opened across Jonas's face. He butted the older man, hitting the bridge of his nose. Emil tottered back, stunned. A fast trickle of blood dropped from his nostrils. He blinked and caught himself in mid-gesture, staying his hand from the hilt of his dagger.

'And what would my father say to that? I should have done that to him, Emil, you know, on my sixteenth birthday. Oh, what a different man I would have been. When you pass from this world, good sergeant, and encounter him in the afterlife, please pass the gesture along to him.'

Jonas swerved down the passageway, addressing his troops. 'You are weary of my speeches, are you not, my fine Gerolsbruchers? Alas, I am at my best, you see, when I am either tub-thumping or killing. At other tasks, you've judged me and found me wanting. So I beg you, let me do what I am skilled at.

'Before we go on to examine the reasons, let us agree that I am a failure, as a man and, above all, as a leader. You won't deny that, will you? That I've led you into deepest nowhere, got half of you killed, and am about to do the same to the rest of you? Come now. This is hardly controversial. Surely I am the last of us to come to this conclusion. Yes?'

He rounded on Mattes, the lone man who dared look directly at him.

'You will not answer?'

The drumsman held his tongue.

Jonas swept the tunnel with upraised arms. 'You'll not say what is on all your minds? No, no, it is only natural that you would not. For I am the orator, and you my audience. The high sheen of my eloquence renders you mute. Indeed, indeed. But please pay this humble minstrel minimal homage, and look at me, at least.'

Reluctant as corpses, the men stiffened to attention, facing front.

'Yes, yes, both submissive and reproachful,' Jonas laughed. 'Forget my own claims of eloquence. You say it all without a word.'

Merwin snuck his last port jug from his pack.

Though he sat far to Jonas's side, the lieutenant spotted him, stomped his way, snatched it from his grasp, and swigged its dregs. He wiped his mouth with a broad, theatrical flourish. 'It is the truth you sought from me, was it not? Is not truth the standard borne by your great heroine here?' He snarled at Angelika. 'Truth, truth, truth. Well, here is truth. We're surrounded in this cold hole. There's twenty companies of the enemy out there. Ten and twenty, perhaps. Before I die, I can kill more of them than can any of you. But still I'll die. As will you. We're dead already, and merely lack the sense to fall.

'We're denied even the defiance of a spectacular demise. Without chroniclers to remember us, we'll leave nothing to this world but our bones and robes. No example for others. From no poets' lips will our names spill. You know what, Mattes?'

'What?'

'As a child, the stanzas of the epic poets were my mother's milk. Yet now I've seen real war, I know they're lies from first verse to last. The woman's right. The world's a ball of blood and dung, and men but crawling maggots on it. So let's take heart: what do worms suffer when their tormentors tear them apart? Let us then wriggle senselessly to our demise.'

Angelika drew her dagger. 'Wriggle all you want, Jonas. But I'm no worm, and I'm getting out of here alive. Who here is with me?'

Jonas chortled. 'Oh. So now it's you who makes the empty speeches. A splendid reversal.'

'A reversal indeed. You've traded one lunacy for its opposite.' Angelika checked Franziskus's position. Along with Mattes, he had crept to the tunnel mouth, to watch the massing Kurgs.

'If I've lost my footing,' said Jonas, 'it's you who's pulled the rug. From the first you sought to undermine me.'

'I guess you shouldn't have stolen from me, then.'

A blush profaned his face. 'Oh, yes. That's the truest truth of all. I pursued you. More than that. I swindled you into coming. Had I only known how you'd spell my doom. Your sharp tongue, your unforgiving gaze.' He turned his accusatory finger from her to his men. Filch seemed ready to peep out an argument but Jonas stared him down. 'And you have fallen under her spell. None of you have defended me.'

Merwin stood up. 'Stop it. Can't you see we need you both?'

'We're all far beyond need, my poor doomed halfling.'

Merwin stamped his foot. 'No. Some of us can survive this, at least. So let's all try.'

Angelika risked a step toward Jonas. 'He's right. You've always measured yourself by what the men think of you. Yes, you've disappointed them. Just now, you've terrified us all. Are you telling me you're incapable of redeeming yourself?'

'There's no good in me to redeem. You've shown us that.'

'More nonsense. Grab that sword, let that brandy calm you, and together we'll find a way out of this.'

Jonas paced a worried circle. He sighed and dropped his shoulders, as if relenting.

'None of us is dead,' said Angelika, 'till Kurgan axes halve our brains.'

'One of us is surely dead.' Jonas unsheathed his sword and rushed to slash her. She ducked and the sword bashed against the wall. Soldiers scattered to the ends of the tunnel, leaving them room to duel. Angelika drew her blade. She knew when she started that he'd either give in or try to murder her. Preparation was not consolation: he was a far better killer than she was. This was not her first bout against a superior opponent, bent on her demise. Usually she survived by ducking their blows, wearing them out, and finally pouncing when her would-be slayer made an exploitable mistake. Here, the narrow space left her little room for evasion.

'Stop it,' Emil demanded.

The soldiers jeered Jonas.

Merwin scuffled up to wrap his arms around Jonas's leg. Rassau slashed down at him. Merwin drew back, a red groove incised into his forearm.

'Everyone stay back,' said Angelika. 'I'll handle him.' She likely couldn't, but she didn't want them trading their lives for hers.

As Jonas swooped in at her, she readied her blade for throwing. She feinted with it; he interrupted his strike to dodge a non-existent toss.

Franziskus stopped short after dashing down into the tunnel. He was behind her, and she would not make way for him. 'Get back,' she yelled. 'Keep a look-out for the Kurg.'

'That's just it,' he yelled, as Jonas hacked at Angelika. She slid down the wall, kicking out at her foe, trying vainly to trip him. 'Jonas,' Franziskus shouted. 'They're coming. The marauders are attacking.'

'Liar,' Jonas barked.

'No, it's true,' countered Franziskus.

'It is,' confirmed Mattes, at the tunnel mouth.

Jonas turned ever so slightly toward the tunnel entrance. Angelika essayed a kick at his groin, but made contact only with his thigh. 'All of you are liars,' he bellowed.

Including Emil, there were thirty soldiers in the tunnel. Two-thirds were stuck at its back, behind Jonas. Less than a dozen stood in the front. 'What do we do?' an archer cried.

'Go and shoot at them,' Franziskus commanded. 'Hold them off.'

'Should we go outside, to shoot in a rank?'

Franziskus did not know.

'No,' Angelika called, grappling Jonas's sword-arm. 'They outnumber us. Don't give them any extra targets.' Jonas loomed over her, bending her down, as she held him off. She suddenly released her grip, sweeping under him, letting his own force knock him into the wall. The crown of his head banged firmly into it. He staggered back, shaking off the impact.

At the tunnel mouth, arrows whizzed from their bows into an unruly rank of charging marauders.

Filch was sprawled by the rubble pile at the tunnel's end. He looked at the back of Jonas's head.

Then at the rocks arrayed around him. Most were too big for his stubby hand.

Jonas surprised Angelika with an off-hand punch. It tagged her jaw and sent her reeling. He stepped back to ready his sabre for an overhanded wallop.

In the far corner of the rubble stack, Filch spotted the perfect stone. Already imagining its trajectory as it sailed towards Jonas's cranium, he reached over to yank it loose.

The tunnel shook. The balking groans of ancient machinery, forced suddenly to life, rumbled from beneath the floor. Angelika's eyes widened. Jonas glanced back to see.

Stray hunks of granite tumbled from the rubble stack as it slowly receded down into a cavity below the floor. By moving a key stone, Filch had triggered the trap door mechanism providing an entry into the old dwarf complex.

The stack sat on a platform. Aside from a few loose stones laid in for the purpose of disguise, the entire heap was a single mass, fused together. It was, in effect, a secret door, ingeniously concealed.

A passageway lay revealed, beyond it.

CHAPTER TWENTY-THREE

How LIKE THE dwarfs, Angelika would later think, to design an entrance that appeared to be a permanent blockage. A simple wall would have inspired no end of searching, for secret pull-chains and hidden levers. Instead she and the others had been sitting like a conclave of cretins on the very brink of an escape route. Yes, how like the dwarfs. Those furtive, stunted, tight-fisted, dirty-bearded, unforgiving sons of curs.

But for the moment she was concerned only with her opponent's momentary distraction, and the pommel of her dagger as it shot toward his temple. Jonas grunted in pain but did not fall. However, the soldiers pressed along the wall marked their commander's lapse of attention, too, and boosted up to wrestle him to the floor. They thumped him on the back of the neck; they kicked at his ribs and between his legs. Glauer, his second lieutenant, stooped to grab his hair and dash his face soundly into the floor.

'They're nearly upon us,' shrieked an archer, at the tunnel's rim.

The rubble stack completed its leaden, shaking descent down into the floor. There was a stretch of flat stone tile; it nestled into place, flush with the opening, leaving a flat expanse of corridor. The passageway continued on for at least a hundred yards, darkness obscuring its ultimate destination. Closer by was an open doorway leading to a set of stone stairs, heading up.

'Go,' Angelika shouted.

'Which way?' Merwin asked.

Good question, Angelika thought. From its direction, the ground-level passageway could only come out in one spot: on the ridge's other side, right in the middle of the enemy encampment. The route upwards would lead into the ridge itself, and could terminate anywhere or nowhere. Angelika had always shown the good sense to keep out of dwarf complexes, abandoned or otherwise, and could not be sure exactly what lay within.

She was prepared to stake her life, however, on the probability that its crawlways at some point led up into the sangar at the top of the ridge. Given no better choice, they could fight their way up into it, and from there clamber onto the rock ribbon. Still chancy, but there would be fewer enemies up there than were on either side of them now.

'The stairs,' she ordered. 'The staircase!'

She waited for the nearby soldiers to scatter into it. Filch and Merwin waited for her. 'Go, go,' she shooed them on.

With the exception of Glauer, who lingered to deliver a few extra kicks, Jonas's assailants deserted him for the staircase. Angelika waved on swordsmen and archers as they rushed down from the head of the passage.

'Enough,' she told Glauer. He wiggled his mutton-chops unrepentantly and moved on.

In the tunnel mouth, a bottleneck of men battled. Among them was Franziskus, who'd stepped in with his sabre to relieve his archers. He kept his sabre flying, two Gerolsbruchers arrayed beside him. They fought defensively, feinting and parrying. Every time they dodged a blow, the pressing marauders drove them deeper into the passage.

The last of their comrades cleared the hidden entry and drummed up the curving stone steps. Angelika went to Jonas's side. He groaned at her, eyes half-lidded. She strained to drag him past the trap door, then crouched by its mechanism. A steel peg no thicker than a child's finger jutted from it. Angelika tried to depress it. It wouldn't go in.

The barbarians pressed Franziskus and the swordsmen further back. The three of them were all that stood between the Kurgs and Angelika. She smacked the peg with the butt of her knife. Pain vibrated up through the bones of her forearm: the button hadn't budged.

The sabre to Franziskus's left skidded into the wall; barbarians attempted to force their way past him. Franziskus swung his blade into a big Kurg's eyes and nose. The marauder wailed and fell to his knees, hands locked onto his mutilated face. His intended prey regained his balance, gripped his hefty sword by hilt and tip, and used it to smash the blinded Kurgan down. The marauder's fellows climbed awkwardly over him, giving Franziskus and the sabre ample opportunity to carve their thighs and loins. The recipients of these injuries collapsed, forming a temporary barrier of bucking, wounded bodies.

Angelika spotted the stone Filch had withdrawn from the pile, triggering the device. She reached for it and slammed it into place. Metallic clicks rang in sequence as gears turned beneath her feet. The floor she stood on juddered and rose.

'Franziskus,' she cried. 'Time to go.'

He whacked a Kurgan soundly in the side of the head and glanced briefly at her. He nodded as he saw the floor ascend below her. It jerked up incrementally; if it maintained its current speed, it would take over two minutes to seal completely shut.

'You'll have to let some through,' Angelika shouted. She wanted to throw a knife, but that would leave her only one.

'You two go,' Franziskus told his mates. They fled eagerly, skidding across the polished floor slab as it inched its way up. Franziskus stood alone as he held off a rank of three barbarians, scores of replacements waiting behind them.

His best-positioned opponent arced an axe down at him. Franziskus slipped. A rock sailed from behind Angelika to crunch into the Kurgan's fingers. Franziskus pivoted and capered toward her. Filch stood proudly beside her.

'I thought you'd gone,' she said.

'I was here all along,' he replied. Merwin, she saw, hung in the doorway leading to the steps. 'You should look down more often,' he continued, as he, Angelika and Franziskus ran to the stairs, Kurgs pursuing behind them.

Jonas tottered into a bleary stance. He stepped in to meet the Kurgans, cleaving them as they came, painting the grey walls with their slick, red blood. They bowled into him, forcing him back. He sank under the weight of the men he'd killed. Barbarian footsteps resounded around him; he slackened his limbs as if dead. A scrawny pair stayed to poke and prod at him. When the noise of darting boots crescendoed, he resurrected himself, rolling out from under his blanketing corpse. He grabbed the closest man's ankle and ripped it out from under him. The marauder ululated his dismay on his way to the hard floor. He landed on the back of his head, vermilion fluid pooling from his impacted skull.

Jonas snatched a horn-handled dagger from the dead man's hip and plunged it into the other's thigh. The barbarian drew back, astonished to see that the knife had buried itself in the main artery of his leg. Throatily giggling, Jonas wrenched it out. Pressurised gore geysered from the wound. The Kurg went pallid and dropped.

Rassau sorted through the pile of dead, freeing his sabre. He collected a serrated short sword and a quintet of crudely forged daggers. Intoxicated by his kills, he cursed the empty stairway. 'I could go and save you all,' he cried. 'But I won't. You would only blame me for it. Wouldn't you? Wouldn't you?' He bent his way down the corridor, to the other side of the ridge, where a Chaos army would greet him, with axe and hammer.

* * *

LIGHT GREW SCARCER as Angelika and Franziskus followed the halflings and swordsmen up the stairs.
The gloom intensified as they climbed. Filch and
Merwin skated easily up the steps, which were engineered for dwarf legs, but the humans slipped and
overstepped. Judging from the thwarted barbarian
grunts reverberating behind him, the Chaos troops
were suffering the same frustration. Their retarded
advance came as a pleasant surprise to Angelika.

'Hmm,' said Filch, 'looks like the barbarians of
the steppes are unaccustomed to them. Steps, that
is.'

Angelika winced. 'Say anything like that again
and it won't be the Kurgs who kill you.'

They found the top of the stairs. In the darkness,
it was difficult to measure the extent or nature of
the chamber they stood in. The remainder of the
company bunched behind them. From the way it
magnified their choked breaths, the room was
likely to be cavernous and boxy. Sparks flashed
from the cluster of men; it was Saar, working to
light a torch with the flint-striker for his
matchlock.

Their flickers lit up a pile of round balls stacked
against a wall: shot for dwarf cannon. This place
had been an armoury – still an active one, for all
Angelika knew.

'You think there's a cannon in here?' asked
Franziskus.

'We don't need one. Ferry those over.'

The soldiers formed a line and passed the heavy
balls hand to hand, with Mattes last in line.

Kurgan war-cries clamoured below.

'Drop it,' Angelika commanded.

Mattes loosed the ball; it bounced down the steps. They counted each hard thump, until angry shouts of pain and grievance boomed up the stairwell at them.

'Drop another,' called Angelika.

Mattes was passed a second ball; this, too, traversed a banging route down the stairs to impede the enemy throng.

Saar got the torch going. In its first luminescence, Angelika beheld large, draping tapestries hanging from balconies ringing the room. Fierce dwarf faces, stylised and murderous, gazed out at their foes – the woven artwork depicted a series of martial scenes.

Mattes dropped a third cannonball. It jounced as resonantly as before, but aroused less fury from the marauders, who now came into view. They broke across the room to engage the outnumbered soldiers. Saar's torch fell to the floor, burning a fringe of tapestry. Popping flames ate rapidly through it, bathing the battle in a hot yellow glow.

THE TUNNEL ENDED in a flat piece of rock wall. From its well-worked surface, Jonas figured that it had to be a secret door, less clever and elaborate than the one Filch and Angelika had found. He placed his ear to the wall. Scratchy Kurgan voices muttered restlessly on the other side. Only these few inches of trick granite panel separated him from his final glory. There had to be a way to open it.

The throbbing of his skull strained his thinking. This was the interior part, the side where you already knew it was a door. He felt the wall's inner surface, painting a track of crimson smears across it. There – there was a

seam down the middle. The trigger on the other side
would be well hidden, but here there was no such need
to conceal it. So where was it? Was it a handle? A lever?
Obvious, obvious, it would have to be –

Obvious. There it was, a small ring of green-pati-
nated bronze, camouflaged only by a streak of
mossy-coloured granite. It was not hidden at all. It was
merely lower than he'd been looking – at dwarf height.

Jonas yanked on the ring.

Articulated brass stakes, hinged in the middle, shot
out from recesses in the wall, breaking it in the middle,
pushing the two halves open.

Jonas stepped through into the daylight. He was in
the midst of the Kurgan encampment. Less than a
dozen yards away from him loitered a party of barbarians, shifting restlessly and croaking complaints at one
another. A boar sizzled on a nearby spit, its fire stoked
by a trio of gigantic marauders, improbably clad in
sweating jet-black armour. Off to his left, a grubby boy,
no more than eleven years old, tended the festering
back wound of a white-bearded marauder, systematically spearing maggots from it with the tip of a long
iron needle.

None moved to molest him; instead, they stared at
him, with his fine coating of blood and his mad
expression, as if he were a grisly apparition treading
into this world from the realm of ghosts. Sabre in one
hand and knife in the other, he beamed and spread
wide his arms. 'I have come to kill you,' he announced.
'Each and every one.'

Now the barbarians drew their weapons, though
cautiously. Only the mightiest of champions, or even
an enemy god, would dare meet their army alone.

'Ortak Nalgar,' he bawled. 'Ortak Nalgar. I will fight Ortak Nalgar!'

The Chaos troops exchanged dumbfounded glances. Their leader's name was all they could make out amid his softlander babblings. Was he an agent of their chieftain? A spy against the Imperials? Such things were impossible not long ago, but under these strange new laws of war, was not anything possible?

'Ortak Nalgar,' Jonas shouted. 'Ortak Nalgar.'

Ortak Nalgar stepped out from behind a bearhide tent.

'Is he an ally?' asked his shieldbearer, a scuttling creature called Goragir.

'No,' said Ortak Nalgar. 'He is not an ally.'

CHAPTER TWENTY-FOUR

JONAS, NOT COMPREHENDING the conversation of his foe, started taunting his enemies. 'Ortak Nalgar,' he bellowed.

Common marauders, sub-chiefs and clan heads formed a hubbub around Ortak Nalgar. They kept their distance from the rabid softlander.

'I know this one,' said the chieftain. 'He fought me before, and lived.' Slowly he drew his multi-bladed sword from the sheath on his back. 'This time he will die.'

Jonas ceased his gesticulating and braced himself for Nalgar's onslaught.

'You may come and watch,' said Ortak Nalgar to his followers, 'but he is mine to slay.'

He clattered at Jonas, gravel spraying behind him. He ploughed his greatsword down on Jonas's upraised sabre. The force of the strike trembled Rassau back across the uneven ground. Jonas parried a second grunting hit, then a third. A barbarian mob gathered to shout out homicidal encouragements to their general.

Jonas parried blow after blow. The chieftain fought with a relentless power, never giving him the chance for even a perfunctory attack. Jonas was forced back towards the rock wall. Nalgar's hardest, best-aimed thrusts were always wide and sweeping.

Rassau inched back towards the doorway. He let himself falter and seem uncertain. He lured the chieftain on toward the dwarf corridor, where there'd be less room for that scything weapon of his.

A yard from the entryway, Nalgar hesitated, as if suspecting a trap. Jonas wished there was one. He landed his first hit, against Nalgar's weapon-hand. Roaring, the chieftain elbowed in, smashing Jonas with a rattling body blow. Jonas let the momentum carry him into the corridor. Nalgar followed.

Jonas lightened his step, bucking and weaving. He would fight as he'd seen Angelika do. Hers was a woman's style, designed to wear out a bigger, stronger foe. Once inside the tunnel, Nalgar's assurance seemed to ever-so-slightly slacken. Jonas had no lethal surprises to unveil, but the chieftain thought otherwise, and that was something.

As Nalgar drove him farther into the dwarf complex, a glimmer of sanity returned to him. Behind this greatest of enemies a host of others jostled for the best view. His doom was certain. As he fought, he detached his mind to envision himself from a distance, becoming like a figure in a dream. Regret suffused him. His decisions had been foolish – clouded by the sin of vanity and its twin, the fear of failure. The men were right to distrust him.

The insight came all too late, but at least it had come. He would not be granted a second chance, but if by some miracle it happened, he would do it all differently, transform into a wiser leader and better man.

Ortak Nalgar was toying with him now. He reached the staircase and was forced onto it. Behind him, he heard the clang of clashing weapons and felt the heat of a consuming blaze.

THE TAPESTRY BLAZE lit the corners of the dwarf armoury. Dark smoke poured up to the chamber's high ceiling. Stone walls radiated the fire's heat, intensifying it, aiming it at the contending men. Scorching sweat doused the brows of Stirlander and barbarian alike.

Swordsmen pushed up around the stairwell mouth, to bottle up their foes, forming a protective ring around the archers and halflings. Stragglers with hand weapons ranked themselves beside the Gerolsbruchers. The Stirland line slashed and prodded at the marauders, and, for the first moments of the engagement, gave them pause. Soon the barbarians switched tacks: rather than fight the black-and-yellows blade against blade, they shouldered their way into their line, shoving them back into the chamber. They widened the lines, making room for more of them to engage the defenders.

Emil and Mattes found themselves fighting side-by-side. 'Loyalist and malcontent go to the wall together, hah?' the drumsman shouted.

The sergeant's reply was a curt upthrust of his sabre, lacerating the throat of his hairy-backed opponent. 'Shut up and fight,' he added.

Mattes grinned, and, not to be outshone, stabbed deep into his attacker's belly.

The marauders fought with crazed abandon, and Kurgan bodies were the first to hit the floor. When one died, another steamed over him to usurp his place. Together the sergeant and drummer were confined against the armoury's western wall, which was stacked with the disassembled parts of cannon. Long, forged firing tubes, inlaid with dwarf runes, comprised one pile. Their wheeled oak carriages loomed in a neat tower beside them. At their ankles stout barrels squatted.

The two men glanced at them and knew right away: gunpowder.

Across the room, flames licked onto a second tapestry.

They shared a profane exclamation, then went back to hacking at the Kurg.

To ANGELIKA, THE fire revealed an oak door across the room from the stairwell, and a catwalk fifteen feet above the armoury floor. This balcony level wrapped around the entire room, and was bounded by a solid stone wall incised with murder holes. It was from this impenetrable railing that the burning tapestries hung. Angelika couldn't see an entry point for the catwalk, but some kind of access to it had to lie behind the far door. She shouted to gather the archers to her side. If they could get onto the upper walkway, they could fire down into the enemy ranks. On the floor, they were useless.

She tested the door. Locked. The mechanism was small yet blocky, in the dwarven manner. 'Filch,' she yelled.

The halfling floundered into view, his hair singed, pointing to the spot he'd emerged from, behind the tapestry. 'Merwin's back there,' he cried.

'What?'

'The fear's got him. He thinks it's safe there. It's not.'

'I'll go coax him out,' Angelika shouted. She pointed to the lock. 'I don't suppose, with a name like Filch, you're an experienced lockpick?'

Filch beheld it gravely. 'Depends on how you mean it,' he said. 'Do years of mere practice count?' He stepped up and reached into a vest pocket for a set of delicate lockpicks. The tip of his tongue poking from the side of his mouth, he got to work on it, as the archers ringed him. 'My whole life I've yearned for such a moment.'

Angelika moved beneath the catwalk, behind the encroaching fire. Merwin's gaze was glassy, his posture rigid. Angelika slapped him.

He sputtered a spray of saliva. 'What? How dare–'

Angelika hauled him by the collar. 'Go mad on your own time, halfling. We've an escape to rig.' She ducked aside as a volley of arrows zoomed from the bulging semi-circle of archers to pelt a trio of barbarians breaking across the floor. They clutched their throats and sank as the swordsmen closed ranks to stop others from following.

Angelika reached Filch with Merwin. 'How goes it?'

'This lock is much like one I acquired from a peddler, to practise–'

A weird percussive chant bellowed from the lungs of the Kurgan horde. Something new had entered the room, from the stairwell. Marauder and Stirlander parted to make room. Jonas stepped backwards, his sabre desperately countering a rippling sequence of strikes from the pronged and spiky sword of Ortak Nalgar.

* * *

'THAT IDIOT,' CRIED Mattes. Behind the chieftain, he saw a new column of Enemy forces, most of them still grouped on the stairwell. Their exotic, flanged helmets and heavy armour identified them as high-ranking warriors. They had not yet seen fit to join the fray, but that was no source of cheer. The hardened opponents already ranked against the beleaguered Stirlanders were tough, but these newcomers would comprise the top of the heap. All the army's leaders, their status won by right of combat. Against this force, there would be no survival. Jonas had found the forest's fiercest wolves and led them to their prey.

Mattes shouted in Emil's ear and dropped his sabre. 'Cover me,' he shouted, stooping to grab a powder barrel. He slipped free of the battle; Emil followed, pursued by barbarians, wildly swinging his blade to deter their nail-filled cudgels.

Mattes pell-melled across the floor to the tapestry. The cutting flame had portioned it into dangling strips. Keeping the powder cradled out under his left arm, he reached up and yanked free a great length of burning cloth.

He wrapped it around himself like a cloak and ran toward the stairs.

Emil saw what he meant to do, but was too occupied with his pair of opponents to persuade him otherwise.

'Make way. Make way,' Mattes cried. The Gerolsbrucher line parted for him. Flames leapt from the tapestry to his tunic. In instinctive fear of them, the barbarian line shrank back, too. Mattes's skin seared as he ripped the lid from the barrel and leapt toward the stairwell packed with Kurgan war leaders. In mid-air, he touched his scarf of flame into the reservoir of black powder.

The barrel exploded. It blew Mattes to bits. It tore through Ortak Nalgar's subordinates, separating limbs from torsos, pulping organs, demolishing bone. The roof above the stairwell buckled and collapsed. Those not slain by the concussion were pulverised by blocks of tumbling stone.

The explosion threw debris across the armoury floor, killing three Kurgan and a pair of Stirlanders. The battle line dissolved into a general mêlée.

Emil felled one of his Kurgans, but the barbarian grabbed him on the way down, exposing the back of the sergeant's neck to his partner's club. Its rusty spikes jabbed deep into him, and he fell to the tiles, writhing.

Franziskus, his scalp rent by flying debris, staggered through the room in search of a new target. He found the Kurg angling for a coup de grace against the sergeant, and crippled him with a bowling slash to the legs.

JONAS AND ORTAK NALGAR circled in the centre of the room. He'd knocked the chieftain's helmet off; the barbarian had torn a jagged hole in his breastplate. The chieftain's face bore the typical marks of Kurgan physiognomy: it was a round burl of bone, its cheekbones wide, its nose upturned and flattish. Yet somehow he was reminded of his own face, or perhaps that of his father. Or, at least, the hard, unfeeling visage he wished he had.

'I was born to kill you,' Jonas said to him.

Ortak Nalgar did not comprehend the speech of the soft lands, but guessed at the meaning. 'You are nothing to me,' he said.

Jonas didn't understand him, either.

FILCH FINISHED MONKEYING with the lock and stepped back to fling the doors open. Angelika slipped through into a vertical shaft leading straight up. Staple-shaped metal rungs ran the length of the narrow, piping passageway. She jumped onto them and shinnied up to the height of the balcony level. There she found an exit onto the catwalk.

Angelika shouted to the archers to follow her, but heard no response. The noise of the fight, she reckoned, had drowned her out. She rushed down the ladder to alert the archers to her find. As her feet hit the floor, she saw the real source of the delay. The fight between Jonas and the chieftain had moved into new territory. Ortak Nalgar threw Jonas into the wall beside the door. Jonas leaned against it, bleeding and panting, his sabre nearly dropping from his tired fingers. She edged out through the doorway and palmed a dagger.

'No,' said Merwin, held rapt by the fight between Jonas and the barbarian chief. An involuntary step brought him closer to it.

The movement caught Ortak Nalgar's attention. A gauntleted hand left his greatsword and wrapped around a long iron dart, casually flinging it into the halfling's chest.

Filch howled in protest and belted at Nalgar. Franziskus, who'd wandered across the floor to help against the chieftain, encircled Filch in his arms and pulled him up off the ground. The chieftain took up a second dart, to aim at Filch.

Jonas widened his mouth to scream, but only a choking noise issued from it. With renewed vigour he clouted Nalgar's head, cutting into his ear. Then he fled through the doorway, luring the chieftain away from the others. He hustled up the rungs, into the shaft. Nalgar followed.

Angelika's sense of direction told her where the tube ended – it led to the sangar, of course. Jonas would have more than the chieftain on his hands when he got to the top. 'Don't follow me all the way,' she instructed the archers. 'Turn onto the catwalk about fifteen feet on.'

She climbed onto the rungs.

Above her, Ortak Nalgar prodded skyward with his blade, while Jonas flung his feet out to miss it. When he could, he aimed a kick at Nalgar's gashed head. He dropped a wad of spit into the chieftain's eye. As Angelika climbed, red driblets spattered her; they could have come from either man. Below, she heard the archers mount the catwalk.

The graceless, attenuated fight continued all the way to the end of the shaft. It terminated in a wooden trap door, which bore a thick wooden handle. The planks creaked, bowed by weight on its upper side.

Jonas braced himself and ripped it open. A Kurgan, who'd been standing on the trap, fell partway through. The Kurg frothed belligerently at him, but Jonas held fast, grappling up the man's body, using him as a climbing aid. He slithered up into the sangar, then kicked his unwilling accomplice down onto Ortak Nalgar.

Nalgar cursed all the holy gods as his stinking underling landed on him. The impact wrenched his sword-arm from its socket. He wrapped his other hand around the man's chin and twisted until his neck was broken. Then he pushed himself tight against the rungs and let him fall. Angelika did the same, and the slain barbarian brushed rudely past her on his way to splat against the ground.

The sangar's inhabitants greeted Jonas's arrival with stunned surprise; he clouted one with his sword on his way through it. Turning to receive Ortak Nalgar, he edged to the stone steps leading to the sangar's exit point, leading to the flat-topped ridge between the two valleys.

Nalgar cleared the trap door as Jonas backed out onto the ridge. Nalgar followed him. A lithe young barbarian absconded, leaving two others to defend the sangar against further intrusion.

Angelika hauled herself into the sangar. The Kurgs launched themselves at her. The first took a dagger in his bare and knobby chest. She stepped aside for the second, tripping him into the shaft opening. His head pinged along the metal rungs on his way down.

She retrieved her dagger from the heaving breast-bone of the mortally wounded Kurg and slipped up the small flight of steps to the ridge. The last of the sangar guards had positioned himself on its brink, giving her his back to watch the duel between the softlander and his warlord. Angelika threw her knife into the space between his shoulders. It slumped him to the surface of the ridge.

Jonas rocked on his heels, panting.

Ortak Nalgar's arm hung slackly at his side; his fingers dangled an inch or so lower than they should have been. He grabbed his forearm and replaced it in its socket. Agony billowed across his filthy face, revealing his clenched and mouldering teeth. He kinked his neck and held his sword.

He charged at Jonas.

They clashed. The chieftain thumped into Rassau, pushing him onto his back. Jonas's sabre flew from his hand. The combatants rolled and grappled along the ridge line. Their flailings brought them steadily closer to the precipice, on the side of the ridge overlooking the Chaos encampment.

Jonas levered his legs to pitch Ortak Nalgar off him. Nalgar rolled to the side and jutted his thumbs into the lieutenant's windpipe. Jonas choked and gurgled. Nalgar banged Rassau's head against the stone. He cursed out a Kurgan imprecation.

Exactingly judging the ever-changing location of the chieftain's blind spot, Angelika traced a geometrically precise route along the rock. At the height of his distraction, she slipped up behind him, straddling Jonas's lurching legs. Calmly she took hold of the chieftain's slimy hair and yanked it back to expose his neck. With her free hand, she coolly gashed his throat. He swatted her with a reflexively threshing arm; she smoothly untangled herself from him.

He rose, hand clamped over his fast-leaking wound.

Jonas got up, grasping for his sword and leaning on it like it was a cane. He shuffled up, slapped the staunching hand from the chieftain's neck, and laid into him with a decapitating blow. Ortak Nalgar's severed head bounced along the ridge and came to a stop, face up, where it wore an expression of indignant disbelief.

Jonas teetered to the precipice above the enemy camp. He held the head up for its gathered army to behold. Ortak Nalgar, the fearsome one, the chieftain only Vardek Crom could defeat, the overbearing general who kept them to the chafing and foreign rules of discipline, was vanquished, and could impose on them no more.

CHAPTER TWENTY-FIVE

CONFUSION BUZZED FROM the valley floor. The face-plates of countless antlered helmets pointed mutely to the ridge top. The ant-like thousands of the Chaos legion were momentarily stilled.

Angelika held her breath; this would not last for long.

Jonas panted great, ragged gasps into his emptied lungs.

She grabbed him by the collar and hauled him into the sangar. Recovering his wits, he threw himself through the open trap door and into the shaft that led to the armoury. From the sounds of it, the clash inside the dwarf chambers had ended, too. Jonas sighed in relief: the voices he heard were not in Kurgan, but in Reikspiel. It was his men who had won the fight.

Angelika lowered herself into the tube below the sangar, bringing with her a long-handled barbarian axe. She jammed it down into the staple-shaped ladder rungs, bracing it against the trap door leading from the lookout above. It would not hold for long, but it would warn them when the Kurgs came to exact their revenge.

BUT THE KURGS did not come. Hungry days passed inside the armoury. Twice on the first day, once on the third day, and again on a fourth, banging noises resonated down the shaft. The trap had been reinforced by then with plates of barbarian armour, flattened and fixed into place with nails scavenged from the dwarf cannon carriages. Angelika did not think it would withstand a determined attempt to breach it, but each time the marauders assaulted it in a merely desultory manner.

The company subsisted on what little scraps of food they'd had on them when the Chaos hound attacked. On the bodies of the barbarians they'd slain, they found skins of water and the odd morsel of horrid, desiccated meat. They stacked the corpses on the catwalk. The cool air of the underground complex retarded their decomposition, so that it was the fourth day before they began to stink.

All in all, the Stirlanders had killed two and a half dozen Kurg, not counting the numberless war leaders claimed by the staircase collapse. Against these were weighed five Gerolsbruchers, two Chelborgers and two of the stragglers. Among the slain was Second Lieutenant Glauer. One swordsman lay badly wounded, as did Merwin, who passed in and out of wakefulness, sweating and tossing his head. Filch sat by his side, clasping his hand, crying frequent and shameless tears.

Emil, a thick swaddling bandage around his punctured neck, spent much of his time gazing at the demolished staircase, where Mattes was interred.

Periodically Jonas would stand, as if to embark on yet another speech. Each time the resentful glares of his men halted him before he uttered so much as a preamble. When there was a question to ask, they approached Emil, Franziskus, or Angelika.

Jonas withdrew into a sulky gloom, sitting and sleeping beside the cannon barrels.

The archers said to Franziskus: 'You'll come with us, back to Stirland?'

Franziskus had not decided. Now that Angelika's ring was definitively lost, she would surely return to her old ways. If so, he'd have to go with her. His first loyalty was to Angelika.

On the fifth day the last of their water was gone. Angelika ventured up to the sangar, removed their improvised barrier, and saw that the valley was deserted. The Chaos horde had dispersed.

'Time to go,' she told Emil.

'Where have the Kurgs gone?'

She shrugged. 'We killed not only their leader, but most of their officers, too. I bet they thrashed off in a dozen directions, or even fell to fighting each other.' Later, they would learn that she was right. A segment of the horde had swept on to attack the Empire, but they did so as isolated bands of raiders, not as the disciplined army of Vardek Crom. Their victims numbered only in the thousands. The combined Gerolsbruch Swordsmen and Chelborg Archers had not won the war alone, but when the war was ended, few companies could claim a greater victory.

Led by Angelika, the men exited up the shaft. The wounded were bundled and ferried with all the ginger care their comrades could summon.

Shortly after the company had assembled on the ridge, Merwin coughed, mumbled his mother's name, and expired. Filch knelt beside him, weeping.

A wind whipped up, softly moaning across the empty valley.

'Very well, then,' said Jonas. 'The halfling's name will be well remembered when our time here is chronicled. Yet now we must move on.'

'Lieutenant...' said Emil.

It was a warning, but Jonas ignored it. His chest expanded, and he readied himself for another speech. 'I realise that certain actions have cost me the reliance you once gave so freely. As I fought the Enemy chief, I thought this revelation had been granted to me too late, but now I see I've been granted the chance to win you back. Has my judgement occasionally been in error? Yes. Error is war's handmaiden. Is it a good result, that we comprise a third of the force that left for these dark mountains? No, surely not. But we knew the mission was daunting when we departed.

'Plainly we must count it a divine gift that so many of us have, in truth, survived. Should we have instead retreated to our homes, and let the Kurgan swarm over and burn them? No, none of us would say that.

'Thus, upon our return home, when we turn our exploits into a tale for the edification of the common man, we must endeavour to speak only of that which mattered here. We must burnish away any flaws that would obscure our glory. And although we must thank Angelika and Franziskus for stepping into the breach when I was robbed of my rightful senses, now I must reassert good order, and insist on the obedience you owe me as ranking officer of–'

Filch pitched a rock at him.

It bounced off Jonas's forehead. Shocked, he touched his fingers to the rising red bump the missile left behind.

Filch stood, another rock in hand. 'Liar,' he cried. 'Mattes is not here to say it, so I will say it for him – liar!'

'You're a brave little fellow and you just now lost your friend, but don't press your luck with me, half-man.'

'Liar,' Filch repeated.

'What warning did I just give you?'

Tears drenched the halfling's cheeks. 'Deceiver. Even when what you say is right, your mouth is so full of lies the truth is smothered.'

'Silence.'

Filch tore an object from his pocket and showed it to the men, who'd subtly clustered together. 'You want proof? I don't think you need it, but here it is. I slipped this from his pocket, before–'

'Thief,' accused Jonas.

'I overheard certain things, and wanted to return it to its owner. And Angelika, I started to tell you once, but that was in the middle of the fight, and after that – after that–' He faltered, then seemed sheepish. 'After that, I admit I forgot about it for a while. But here it is.'

Between his stubby fingers he displayed Angelika's ruby ring.

'I thought your name would prove significant,' she said. 'But how could you forget–'

'I'll tell it from the beginning,' began Filch. He reached out to hand Angelika the ring.

'Don't listen to him,' Jonas shouted. He dived for Angelika, pushing her down, and tackled the halfling. Seizing the arm that held the ring, Jonas bent it back behind Filch's back. An awful snapping marked the breaking of the bone. Filch shrilled in pain.

Angelika was up already, her knife out. She faced Jonas, shepherding him back towards the precipice. His tangle with Filch had disarranged the scabbard of his sabre, wrenching it around his waist and between his legs.

He held the ring, as if to toss it over his shoulder, down the cliff. 'Don't take another step, Angelika.'

'Give me the ring.'

Jonas popped it into his mouth, smiled and swallowed.

Angelika yowled a strangled curse and leapt on him. He punched her in the face and knocked her over. She tried to rise but sank back down. He got ready to give her a kicking. 'This is what happens,' he paused, 'to the disloyal.' Dissatisfied by his positioning, he backed up to take a run at her.

Ortak Nalgar's head, pecked fleshless by crows, still rested on the edge of the precipice.

Jonas tripped over it. He lurched onto the precipice's edge, his heels suspended over empty air. Windmilling his arms, he fought desperately for balance.

The rock Filch was clutching dropped from his fingers and Emil knelt to take it from him.

The sergeant cocked his head, resigning himself, and overhanded the stone into Jonas's chest.

It was more the surprise than the force of it that balanced Lieutenant Rassau off the cliff. He fell abruptly from view, his body smashing against an outcrop fifty feet down, lodging itself between two folds of vertical rock.

Led by Emil, his men peered down at him. 'That was contrary to regulations,' he said, 'and if you want to report it when we get back, you'll be complying fully with the laws of military justice.'

'Terrible how he tripped and fell like that,' said Saar.

'Yes, terrible,' the men agreed.

'Ironic how it was the skull of the foe he'd killed what did him in.' They patted Emil on the shoulder.

'A hell of a warrior,' said Emil, and turned away. 'A dung-awful commander, but a hell of a warrior.' He tore up a length of cloth as a sling for Filch's arm.

Angelika recommended that they head down to the stream to replenish their water skins. 'We'll be down soon,' she said.

THE SOLDIERS DEPARTED, leaving her and Franziskus on the lip of the precipice.

'Will you be staying as their lieutenant?' she asked him.

'I can't.'

'Why not?'

Crows were already investigating Jonas's crumpled body.

'I'm very sorry,' said Franziskus.

'About what?'

'That you'll have to return to the trail. Seeing as there's no way to recover your ring from the lieutenant, now.'

She showed him her knife. 'What are you talking about?' she said, and dangled herself off the edge, beginning the hard climb down to the vessel containing her property.

ABOUT THE AUTHOR

Robin D Laws is an acclaimed designer of games, perhaps best known for the roleplaying games *Feng Shui*, *Dying Earth* and *Rune*. He has also worked on computer and collectible card games and is currently a columnist for *Dragon* magazine. Just recently, Robin began working as a writer for Marvel Comics, including an *Iron Man* story arc and the upcoming miniseries *Hulk: Nightmerica*. *Liar's Peak* is Robin's fifth fantasy novel.

Honour of the Grave

Robin D Laws

On the grim battlefields of the Old
World, corpse looter Angelika Fleischer
gets entangled in a deadly plot involving
two mysterious brothers and a threat to
her very existence!

www.blacklibrary.com

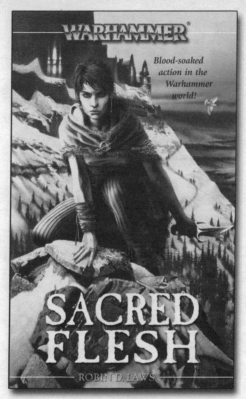

Sacred Flesh

Robin D Laws

Out in the wilderness, Angelika finds herself babysitting a group of religious
missionaries on their way to meet a holy
miracle-maker. But is everything really
that simple?

www.blacklibrary.com

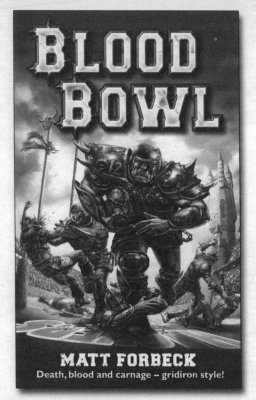

READ TILL YOU BLEED

DO YOU HAVE THEM ALL?

WWW.BLACKLIBRARY.COM